Glycerine

Selah Leah

NEWMAN SPRINGS PUBLISHING
320 Broad Street
Red Bank, NJ 07701

First originally published by Newman Springs Publishing 2024

ISBN 979-8-89308-329-3 (Paperback)
ISBN 979-8-89308-330-9 (Digital)

Printed in the United States of America

In memory of Mother Dear, your gift lives on.

CHAPTER 1

With each traumatic event I survived, another part of my livelihood felt as if it was a band-aid being ripped off. Instead of letting it naturally fall off in its timeframe and letting it scab over, I would take it off much too soon. The scar hadn't stopped bleeding.

What was meant to heal the last wound instead ended up as salt that added to the sting of pain. Trying to fill a void within myself turned into numerous amounts of heavy burdens that piled on top of the other. I never learned to carry my own in a way that got rid of the heaviness.

Even when I thought I had resolved an internal issue, it turned out that healing had as many layers as an onion. One trauma wound equals a whole onion. I can't begin to say how many onions I need to peel away at. I'm not sure how far I have truly gotten with each one either. I just know that it is time to start peeling again before the smell becomes unbearable to manage. My unpredictable emotions and very often triggers over the littlest things have started to show for it and take a toll on my well-being. I feel like a ticking time bomb waiting to go off.

The truth that really sank in with how lost I have become is when I realized I had been pretending that I'm okay when I haven't been anywhere near it for a long time. Sure, I got good at coping and found enough good to keep me hanging on, but survival in comparison to

1

living isn't something I feel I should settle for anymore. I want to soar above the clouds and have freedom from this prison that my mind developed, which has been caused by all the trauma that I went through and am still going through.

I want to climb mountains and breathe in the freshness of the air. I need to find the person who believes in magic again. The person who saw so much more for herself. The ugly truth behind the wall I have built up from everyone is that this toxic environment that I am manipulated into isn't allowing me to do more than daydream my life away.

I'm trapped in a web of torture, and every day the spider wraps me up and tries sucking the liveliness from me. I never let it define who I am, but an overwhelming darkness does surround my soul. Things never harden my heart to the point that I quit entirely believing that it will get better, but I would be lying if I said it didn't become first nature to think negatively. I especially have a hard time believing that people have pure intentions; I don't think highly of myself either.

I still can't help but feel that it is possible that the spider is wrong about me being a meaningless fly. What I saw had always been a caterpillar trapped in a protective cocoon that somehow kept the spider from truly ruining my process of what I'm growing as but remaining stuck, nonetheless. Still, it never stops the spider from trying to sink their fangs into me, draining the ideas that were truly beneficial for my well-being. Venom injected into you daily really does cost you so much more than just heartache. It weakens your ability to see that you deserve more, causing you to continue letting them hurt you in a way you can't be the same as you were before. That you cannot ever grow.

Nothing is certain in this life as far as I see things except the slight hint of hope that I somehow hold onto.

There had been many times I thought I had wanted to die, and a few of those moments I had been close to meeting death itself, but I suppose that wasn't meant for me. I'm not sure I have a real clue what it is that life has in store, but everything in me feels that there is much more than any of this. Even if I couldn't believe I deserved more, it has become a fact that I don't want to keep suffering like I have.

Some other part of me is stuck in the web, nonetheless. The same hope that stays believing in a better tomorrow convinces me that it could be better where I am currently somehow. Deep down the truth held on tightly that it isn't going to be possible and that a specific lie like this would be the very thing that stops me from growth in life and very much within myself.

The good in us always wants to believe that there is good in everyone. The reality behind an ugly truth is that ugliness in people is a very real and cruel thing. The heartbreak that hurts more than most is not all hearts beat a beautiful melody. We can love deeply, but we forget to understand that a lot of others can't be held to that standard. We break our own hearts believing otherwise.

People are who they show you, and oftentimes love blinds what you thought you could fix in others. At the very least, it will cause you to ignore what you never should have and leave you aching for a false reality that you created. Addicted to something that never existed.

It sounds rather insane, but I find it more tragic that people go out of their way to use and abuse those same people who were willing to give you everything when they required so little in return. What real harm came from being a good person? If everyone became genuine, we'd have a lot of problems resolved to the point that a worldly peace has a real chance to become our existence.

Nighttime had a different effect than daytime. The sun welcomes a new day to do things differently than yesterday, a good reminder that you have another chance to make greatness happen. You get an extra day to inspire loved ones and to spread kindness to a stranger in desperate need to see good exist.

The night had a comfortability that seemed to be made for myself. A realization of the impact you make and the reflection of who you are or who you would prefer to be. However, there are times the night offers a darker truth that a busy day often blocks out.

It's a step back from everything around you except the thoughts that constantly race through your mind. This is where the real struggle comes from. You either are being consumed by the negative, which turns you bitter in certain ways and leaves you constantly feeling overwhelmed by the heaviness that holds you back from growth.

Then there is the other option, which is like a puzzle you try to piece together, figuring out every aspect of your life and searching for the missing pieces of yourself that make a completion of something wonderful. Both are highly difficult, but only one is worth living through.

I often catch myself in a battle between both of those. I had lived my whole life in survival mode, trying to rewire my mind to make a breakthrough from a challenge I wasn't prepared to do. Many nights I felt defeated with more questions and less answers that made me believe I'd never find a solution.

As if I had been staring off into the distance as I stood at the edge of a cliff. I would only need to make one step to fall and fight for the rest of my life not to drown. Even the best swimmers can't swim forever. There is still the possibility to swim back to shore and climb back up the hill; either way you go, you're making it harder on yourself than it needs to be. I can't say I'm innocent from making matters worse than needed. I hate how my triggers control my reactions.

It is the decision to turn around and head forward into the unknown that terrifies us all and oftentimes causes us to either stay stuck or take the wrong move. Truly a tragic thing that fear usually has a way of stopping us from the greatest joys in life. It is in those moments of finally facing those fears that we recognize what kind of unique strength it takes to conquer what most never overcome or even set out to do. The exhaustion that comes with that can take a toll, but somewhere down the line of fighting for better, better is to come. It has to, or what is the point of trying?

It's really hard to keep that mindset when your mind shifts to negativity so easily due to being unhealed. Added hardships that, more often than not, get thrown your way, causing you to have to make a different move. I'm very much a believer that everything happens for a reason. It also involves the choices we make. A clouded mind often takes away a clear solution, which causes us not to make the most practical move. This can lead to a dangerous cycle of self-sabotaging for a better future.

When it's out of your control and it is unexpected, I have found myself in a panic and reacting worse than I should. I later on realize that the outcome that happened was for the best, given the current situation I'm in. Sometimes what we believe to be good for us really would have just held us in a spot in life that wasn't meant for us. It's the difference between a want and a need. What we want at the time takes away the purpose of a need that leads to our overall betterment.

I still have to wonder if it will ever become easier. I don't expect easy but something less chaotic. I suppose it is more of a problem of when I am going to learn how not to let things bother me so much and to be better *about embracing what I have in the moment. This all comes back to shifting my mindset and rewiring my brain to be more in control over my thoughts so I can make wiser choices.*

I needed to be better about holding myself accountable for what I can control and knowing I'm doing my best to get through the rest of it. I need to be my strongest reminder that the best parts of life take more time than the hardships ever will. The wisest of people usually become built from a lifetime of painful lessons and mistakes that transform them from a survivor into a warrior.

CHAPTER 2

It's the sickening feeling of betrayal in the pit of your stomach. It's the lies being told as you see the truth unfold in front of you. It's you wanting to break everything around you because once again you feel your heart shatter. It's you wanting to scream, but nothing leaves your mouth. It's the agonizing memories that come rushing back, reminding you that you've been here before. It's your eyes burning with rage, but tears do not fall. It's the panic attack that starts to begin as you disconnect from reality, making your body shake as you do everything to hold back from losing your composure.

What a tragedy it is when you're a hopeless romantic and continue to believe someone will change because they whispered sweet nothings you've been begging for. A helplessly defeated feeling takes over you when they continuously add damage from mistakes they hadn't fixed before. My heart is so scarred up and hurt that I'm not sure how it's capable of still loving the same person, or anyone at all.

It's almost torturous to be built differently than most people. When you feel deeply in a closed-off world, everyone just wants to take but not give anything in return. It's worse when they pretend to care the way you do. They break down that wall to gain any bit of trust you have just for you to build it back thicker and higher than before. Feeding them a high they get from chaos you know they live for while you once again are left drained, confused, and unlovable.

People are labeled crazy for reacting poorly to disrespect but look the other way when someone pushes them to the point of freaking out. We're expected to settle for something that isn't forever while they play the game of pretend that they will become better for you. In a fake world with fake people, being genuine makes it nearly impossible to not end up heartbroken and questioning your worth. The truth with their lies causes you to question your sanity as confusion really sets in.

I'm sure writing this is bizarre, especially when I plan to share it with the world someday, but I'm wise enough to know that I can't be the only one fed up with the wrong kinds of people. I can't be the only one who feels like they're gasping for air every time they choke back words that have so much meaning. I can't be the only one who means well no matter what they are put through. I can't be the only one who believes in a better life after a lifetime of trauma. I can't be the only one wishing to disappear while begging myself to hang on a little longer.

I feel alone, but I know I'm not. Sometimes what we feel and what we know to be true do not align; they clash together to make a beautiful and unpredictable disaster. I'm not going to pretend that makes any sense, but I do believe it has every bit of truth to it. Hear me out on this.

We wouldn't know happiness without sadness. We wouldn't know the difference between anger and laughter if the feelings felt the same. We wouldn't cling to the beauty of life without knowing what a disaster looks like. We wouldn't embrace the good; we would always disregard it as ordinary. We would stay away from the chaos unless the addiction for it followed. We *would be shaped by anything, and no one could be defined as beautiful or ugly. I'm not talking about looks.*

We all have a character, and the rare ones are soulful. They are the ones that inspire you to be good yourself. They light your life even if only for a little while. They create new places that give you some of your favorite memories. They paint pictures of mountaintops with a background of the most magical colors. They create music that relates to thoughts you can't express and make you move when you ache to get out of bed. They speak words of wisdom and advice that make you realize what you deep down already knew, or they even make you discover what you hadn't yet. They write stories of fairy tales that give you an escape that plays into your imagination, stories that remind you that your life isn't over just because you're in the hardest chapter you'll ever have to live through; they write about people who change the world. I refuse to believe that all this art is made by people who are anything except extraordinary.

I shut the notebook. It felt easy, knowing no one had read it yet, but the thought of ever having another read that deeply into my mind made me panicky. I can't shake the feeling that I have to somehow share a story that involves vulnerability I usually keep to myself. Writing has been a part of me since my mother introduced me to the powers of her own words.

It started with journaling at a very young age, in the preteen years, I believe. But it was when I read her writing and the emotional depth it held that something lit inside of me to do the same. Like a flame starting a fire, it changed the course of my life—one of the biggest milestones within myself that was awakened and discovered deeply within.

I've been hesitant to share that personal part of me since her passing. When she was alive, a part of me felt inspired to share with the world, to someday share the vulnerable side of me because it can light beauty inside of someone. They wouldn't have found that talent within without being exposed to that beautiful part of themselves.

It was when she died that I felt I lost a piece of my heart and the innocence the cycle of life has. Once death greets you in a personal manner, there's a part of you that cannot recover from that. Either you let it kill you in such an agonizing way and stay in that dark, lonely ache of despair or you rebirth into a whole new person.

Either way, it's going to be a trauma from which you cannot be the same. I truly do not believe every soul can suffer such a devastating event and come out better than before. There are only certain ones who decide they're going to be the difference. I do not believe most will survive through it simply because giving up is easier.

I would have never thought I would be that person who would still somehow continue trying, but there has been so much that has happened in my life that would have made others give up with no return. I can't say why any of it hasn't killed me yet, but I very much sit with broken pieces that I have no idea how to fix.

The truth behind the severity of her death isn't just because of who she was or her relation to me. It was how and it was not fully knowing what happened. Without a doubt, she meant much more than most could compare to, and her loss would have broken me regardless. Add an unexpected, unanswered death with an unresolved fight we had that day, and you are not only given something shattering to your world but everything you knew about death had another level of misery most cannot grasp. What you knew as painful now became only a hint of the misery you are strangled with.

Maybe I needed to write about death and how there is no possible way to have things be as they were with yourself. Not that it could prepare anyone. You can warn someone before, but until the experience happens to them, they have no real idea. You can let others feel related to, or at the very least have another see a bit of the reason for them not handling it in a way your mind believes you would. It could spread compassion and understanding. I like to believe it can for the people who want it to.

It's the ache that someone's not coming back. It's trying to grasp that reality is without what you've always known. It's trying to rebuild what destroyed a part of you that you cannot fully heal from but only cope with the fact that this is the reality now. I'm not entirely convinced that everyone understands that, though.

Then again, maybe some do heal, or they claim to be, to bear things easier. I can't speak for others who have experienced something similarly tragic. Someone else can go through the same thing and have a very different lesson they learned from it, different feelings that are just as heavy. They could feel something I could never and vice versa. No one is the same, even when they pretend to be. Maybe they truly did figure out how to heal the wounds while still admitting that they do miss them. If they did, I hope to someday be that kind of person.

I opened the notebook back up. Thoughts were one thing to write, but I preferred painting a picture from a story much closer to home than anyone realized and making people feel things they bury deeply. Coating it with imagination that seems like another fictional story but is actually another way of me telling my story.

I want the emotions everyone buries so deeply inside to rise to the surface, giving them no choice but to face every emotion that comes with what I write, especially the emotions that feel like they are going to kill you when in fact it will just cause you to have a breakthrough. I needed to know that my words had that much effect when everything I pondered on came from deep within me. I want to help others even if I can't help myself.

It's the warriors who are tired but never defeated. The warriors overlooked and talked down to. The warriors that have fought the hardest battles and won every war. Warriors that have lost more than they ever gained. Warriors that conquer evil in ways that don't exist to others because the warriors had already fought the demons for them.

It's the battles against our own demons that are the most complicated part of living. We can go through everything meant to destroy us, but it is the power we give it to control us that defines how we handle the situation. If we let it eat us alive, we will find pieces of ourselves lost from every demon who decided they wanted a part in making us into less than who we are. If we decide to fight the demons off us, we will find ourselves bleeding, bruised, possibly broken somewhere, and gasping for air as they try to suck the life from us. The difference in the two situations has everything to do with our outcome. We won't feel defeated forever if we build strength in a way that can't keep us down.

I can't say I'm at a spot of total peace, but there are moments. When those moments come, they feed me hope that creates a hunger for more. It's the reason I continue to fight myself, and I believe that is how hope has never truly died within. No, I'm not so sure that I'll ever stop battling demons; I'm not sure it'll ever be easier than it is. I just try to believe that there are options worth surviving through so I can live for moments of happiness. At one point, I numbed out that possibility existing because all I was doing was surviving. I'm not sure how I got through those times, but I found out it doesn't storm forever in the same way.

A rainbow does come, and the clouds turn white. The sky a light blue and the rays from the sun warm your skin, reminding you that life has beauty to it too. You'll look back and wonder how you got through what now seems like a soul-crushing nightmare. You'll possibly feel shameful for how you reacted to some of it. Just remember, you did what you had to; none of us should judge the other for what we thought we needed to do to feel better.

Depending on the severity of survival mode, you've probably been bitter. After so much trauma, being surrounded by toxic people and behaviors, you become fed up and filled with rage. I can't tell you when it happened for me or when it stopped, but it did. I remember the mindset I had, the misery I carried, and the vengeance I desperately wanted to return. I hated life, and the only thing that caused me to stay alive in that timeframe of my life was getting even. Little did I know, I was only hurting myself even more.

Deep down my soul is good, but I had let the pain define me in every way, and I had let others have so much control over me. This made it seem like I was a terrible person. Sometimes I wonder if I am just because at one point, that's what I was capable of. I wouldn't say I've forgiven myself the way I should, but I also realized it doesn't do any good to beat yourself up over mistakes, especially when you learned and changed what you needed to.

No one is given a perfect guide on how to live your life. There are times we're thrown into a pit of fire and expected to escape without burns, and when we react poorly to the agony, we feel guilty, but you shouldn't let the past haunt you and stop you from living a better life. You didn't deserve being put there; don't be the reason you stay stuck there. Don't beat yourself up for not getting everything right when you've not been treated fairly.

If you're alive, it's for a reason. Use the rest of the time to make a difference. Be the inspiration that you needed when you felt lost and misunderstood. Be the adult that you needed as a child and as a teenager. Spread love. Stand strong. Believe in yourself.

CHAPTER 3

I lifted my head from rereading what I had written in the notebook and looked outside the window, then went back to writing, looking up after every paragraph I finished.

The sun had a different glow to it today, brighter than it has been in a while. No doubt, it was warmer than most people preferred, but I love the heat. I love how the outside looks alive; it made me feel hopeful that I would feel that lively again.

The desk used to sit next to the bed, in front of a wall, but I couldn't write that way. I can't handle being reminded of how trapped I am. It's bad enough to have walls built inside of me that keep everyone out, but I have to protect myself in some way from totally crumbling into pieces of despair.

I needed a different change of perspective to help me fight for more than where life is currently. I want to take any bit of inspiration that I am offered because a little bit of beauty is better than all the ugly I constantly face.

I don't always feel that way; sometimes the negative is eating me alive. I somehow always find a way to come back to reality. Better comes to those who survive and fight through it. It's just not anything close to easy. Life is difficult and complicated, and so is everything we feel, at least for those who feel deeply.

I believe that is why a lot of people suppress their emotions. They're made to feel wrong when there is no right or wrong way to feel things. It is the action behind that feeling that makes the difference in what's harmful and what's healthy. Without a doubt, there is always a reasoning behind it. There's a reason for everything we do, even if we don't understand why at the time. The reasoning stands, but it cannot always be justified.

I want to know what freedom tastes like. All my life, I've never felt safe enough to know that there's a space where I can let my guard fully down. I've felt trapped in a vicious cycle of never-ending emotions and thoughts. This started because my life has never really been mine to control, which led to multiple seasons of my life spiraling out of control from the lack of critical thinking. Impulsive decisions due to some type of panic going on inside have led me to make many poor choices.

I grew up constantly moving around after a certain age and never stopped until I had no choice but to be stuck here. I grew up trying to protect those who needed someone when I was someone who needed protection too. I ended up right where I tried to run from, not knowing how to protect myself. I've been irrational many times trying to break free. I've escaped but have found myself being forced to come back; other times, I chose to and regretted it.

I let the pencil drop from my hand and watched it roll a little on the notebook. I stretched my back; I have a bad habit of slouching when I write and sitting without good support. I could go for a bath filled with bubbles and a candle lit to ease the slight ache slouching causes.

I've heard adults discuss bubble baths as being a childish thing, but I find myself really enjoying them and not understanding why more don't. Another thing I never understood is why things are labeled for a specific gender or what is age-appropriate either. To some extent, there are occasions that make sense to separate adult and children's activities. Overall, I believe most are separating something that doesn't need to be separated into an age group or a certain gender. People should enjoy what they like in peace. Adults still need to take the role of being the responsible one, of course.

Then again, the same adults who disagree with this idea are usually the ones who prefer to gossip about people rather than discuss ideas or things they love. They prefer to focus on others rather than themselves and the difference they could possibly make in the world. Kindness and acceptance go much further.

I put my notebook and pencil in the long, skinny drawer that was above my legs. The right side of the desk had two square sliding drawers, while the left side had one tall door that opened outward. The color is a rustic white. My favorite part is how sturdy it was built; I'm not sure about which type of wood it was made with, but if I had to guess, it would be oak by the solid structure and design.

I stood up from the chair and headed toward the bathroom. Next to the bathroom was a small closet where towels are kept; next to that door was a big walk-in closet. That door is the closest to the other window. There were only two windows, but they were massive compared to what I had grown up with. The bright side to them being the size that they were is the amount of natural light that came in.

I grabbed a towel and decided I would pick out clothes afterward. In the moment, it felt like a lot of work to decide what to wear when I felt drained. All I wanted was to relax in whatever way I could. Not that it would stop my mind from having racing thoughts, but my body would at least feel better.

I entered the bathroom. I sometimes still have to process how nice everything is, especially this. The shower was separate from the tub, which could easily fit four people. The toilet had its own area next to the shower, which stood on my left side. On my right side, the tub sat against the wall in a corner away from the door opening. Across from the tub, a counter sat. The side closest to the door has a sink, while the other half, closest to the wall, blended into a beautiful vanity area. The mirrors were separate; the vanity one had lighting around its frame to make every detail more noticeable. This helped perfect makeup.

No matter the amount of makeup I wore, I never felt pretty enough. I've been called beautiful by quite a few others, but I never see it for myself. It doesn't help that I've also been bullied for my nose at a few different schools I went to and by remarks made by others who have visited the castle. I've even been told my nose is the reason I can't be pretty. I wish things that are said didn't get to me, but words really do hurt and tend to stick with me. The only pattern I've noticed is, it's always females and males if they're trying to be in favor of those females.

My hair is brunette with natural golden highlights. It's not thick and is straight, but it's healthy and usually has a shine to it. The length is to the top of my breast, but the goal is for it to grow a little past my breast. Unfortunately, it grows slowly.

My cheekbones sit high, but my cheeks aren't sunk in, so they aren't super noticeable but noticeable enough if you're paying attention. My bottom lip is bigger than my top lip. It's my nose I hate the most. The bone part is my mother's, so that didn't bother me, but where the cartilage is, it bulges a bit.

Thankfully, my face has grown, so my nose isn't horribly big in comparison. Not as much, anyway. From the side, it's a bit long, though. I suppose this is why the remarks have been made. Still, does it hurt to just keep quiet when it comes to thoughts that aren't uplifting? Why are we so focused on looks?

It's not like they last. This is why building good character traits should be our main focus. I'm not saying you'll be perfect, but I've met some ugly attractive people. Then again, I'm someone who can't focus on another's looks without being observant of who the person is internally. I don't believe most are like that.

My eyes, on the other hand, I'm grateful for. I'm not a fan of the darkened bags underneath. They're very noticeable when I'm not feeling well or haven't gotten much sleep—embarrassingly noticeable if I've been crying. The shape is my mother's, and the color is one that's been passed down from my grandpa on my mother's side. I take the most pride in the fact that the dark blue will shine with the sun, but the gray will always make itself known. I'm not someone who welcomes eye contact, so not too many get to see them for their beauty.

I can become tan, but the paleness will always overrule if I'm not getting sun, making it seem like I've barely seen any sunlight at all. I used to only burn, so I suppose I'll count my blessings that I don't anymore.

I'm five feet and six inches with my lower half built bigger, my breasts smaller, and my stomach curved in on the sides while the stomach is close to flat but not quite there. Keep in mind, I'm not built in a petite way, and my shoulders are built broader. So depending on the shirts I wear, they make me look bigger.

I turned the knob to the tub and put in extra body wash. It always gave off a nice smell that fed my dopamine, which seemed to be starved a lot of the time. I grabbed the big candle I hadn't used yet and lit it. I then turned off the light but waited to strip my clothes off. It didn't take much for me to be cold. I would often be in a hoodie or jacket of some sort, especially since I had started being held here.

The castle grew cold easily, and my guess is because of the stones with which the castle had been built. The inside looked nothing like what you would expect from a castle but more like a modern-day fancy mansion. The hallways did have history to them that I always found fascinating. Every room I have been in had a much different look and sometimes a different feel to it. Some of it was so off-putting that it made me and, from what I could tell, everyone who entered, uncomfortable. I don't think those rooms ever got used for that reason.

The tub finally filled up to the level I usually stop it at. I took my clothes off, throwing them into a pile, and slowly sat in it. My skin usually has a cooler touch to it, so a slight shock from the change in temperature happened as my body adjusted to the warmth. Like an ice cube melting from heat. My mind went into a state of relief as a way of telling me I could relax into myself without any stress or interruptions.

Being here, I never had to worry about food being a problem, where I was sleeping, clean clothes, or anything a lot of people had to worry about. But where I am now made me feel so much worse mentally. I didn't have a choice to be here. Call me a privileged prisoner if you will.

I still couldn't process how I got here. How much had changed in the timeframe. How I let myself fall into this soul-sucking trap. None of the basics in life meant as much to me as freedom does, especially after it's been taken away. I couldn't breathe without being watched when I got a chance to leave the room. I was told how to be when it's everything opposite of who I am.

Life has always been difficult. Even before I was born, my life was planned out for me in a way that wasn't for my favor. My mom didn't agree with that, thankfully, so she ran off when time got closer. We jumped from place to place, pretending this was finally going to be our forever home together. We always struggled in some way, trying to settle in.

There were times I had to struggle alone while she would be gone for days at a time. That started when I was about ten years old, which is around the same time we ran off. You learn to not be particular about food when you're not left with much and have no idea how to make anything except cereal—that is, if there was milk. It was easy to forgive her when your innocence hadn't left yet, and at that point, I was glad she came back at all.

The struggle she put me through didn't compare to the sacrifice and love she gave. There were many more good times than bad. I cling to those moments when remembering her. The older I got, the more I understood how difficult her situation had been. At fourteen years old, you barely understand how to take care of yourself; add a baby to that, and there's no way you don't make some trauma-based decisions. Many adults do that twice her age.

If I had understood what I do now, I would have been easier on her during my teen years. I knew she was an amazing mom and person, but I had grown a lot of anger over the years for the random disappearances and the lack of basic needs that needed to be met. I had moments of being too harsh on her with the things I would say.

Then again, I had validation for what I felt as well. Her reasoning for what she thought was best didn't make it any less harmful to me. Sometimes no matter what is done, no one can get out of pain in a difficult situation that neither should have been put through in the first place.

I still struggle not to hate myself for how I handled those times, especially on her last day. I would have chosen to at least say I love you back if I had known that would have been our last words spoken. I would have cherished one more hug. I would have tried to save her. Unfortunately, what's done cannot be undone and, if you let it, it'll eat you alive.

CHAPTER 4

They consider an eighteen-year-old an adult, but that's ridiculous. There's so much about that age that makes you not ready to figure everything out about yourself, about life. Half of us don't even get a chance to decide for ourselves what we would like to do. Add severe trauma to that mix, and it sets you back years compared to the standards that are already set so high. Expectations you have for yourself are usually harsher.

At eighteen, I had gone through losing the most important person in my life. I had no idea who I was. I was still surviving to make it through the day while contemplating if I should just remove myself from the world. The war in my mind made the battles from life so much harder to handle. Unbearable, really.

I removed the plug to watch as the water drained. I can't handle going down this spiral of thoughts without needing to write or to drink. I've wasted years trying to drown myself and realized it doesn't work. Alcohol led to terrible choices and made me someone I wasn't. Writing releases some of the darkest parts of me while allowing me to stay honest with what I feel and who I am.

I've come to terms with the fact that writing is meant for me. Without it, I lose focus on my truest self. I start to feel lost, and my mind becomes overloaded with thoughts, ideas, and stories—overwhelmed to the point of wanting to shut down and fall back into the hole I worked so hard to climb out of. I promised myself I'd never end up there again. No matter what I feel or what happens. I knew I had to be alive; I wasn't meant to throw away my life even though I have no clue what I can possibly do to do good for the world.

Still, it doesn't stop the pain from hurting the way it does. I'm not sure I'll ever get past things that shook my world. Maybe I can't. Maybe when it's that hard of a hit, that hard of a loss, you learn in whatever way you can to cope with it until it becomes a healthy habit that helps you grow into the change instead of damaging your well-being. Maybe the layers of healing never end. Maybe that's why growth never ends until we do. Maybe that's why being stuck causes us to become bitter.

I wrapped myself in a towel and walked into the closet. I grabbed black sweatpants and a tank top, then grabbed my dark blue hoodie that had the strings removed and slipped on my black slippers that felt like wool on the inside.

I studied my desk as I walked out of the closet and approached it. The sun shining on it made me more drawn to what it stood for. Like a phoenix, I began to feel ready to let the words burn me into ashes, to rise out of them and be born again. Each rebirth has a greater importance than the last. My soul becomes more whole as I discover the truth behind my power—at least the power of my words.

I approached the desk and sat in the chair. I slid out the middle drawer and opened the notebook; I didn't have to take a moment before my hand had the pencil scribbling away. More emotions than thoughts were put toward the words.

I am on the run with no direction on where I should go. My mom had always directed my feet on the next steps to take, and without warning, that was ripped from my grasp. Not in the way most mothers guide because there had been times I only had myself. It was when I would collapse that she was there to remind me who I am. She was there to love me when I couldn't stand myself. I became dependent on her to tune out my self-esteem issues. I depended on her love to know I deserved to be loved. I depended on her for things that couldn't be done physically. I had no idea that I was worth anything outside of her and what she saw.

Within a moment's time and without warning, everything about life crashed around me. The emotions exploding inside of me sent a tidal wave of reckless behavior with no sense of care about the damage I was doing. My insides are being eaten alive by the guilt of a haunted nightmare that I can't wake up from.

At any moment, I have been self-destructing without meaning to, then falling apart with the intent to get back up but not knowing how to. Fighting to breathe and fill this ache with anything that could numb out the agonizing remembrance of everything that has happened. To forget in the moment that an existence like hers existed, to somehow let go that she was here and is now gone.

That's how you know you had someone irreplaceable. Someone who shined like the sun when the world became dark. Someone whose smile lit the room with genuine acceptance. Someone who hugged you with all the warmth and care they had to offer. Someone who could speak life into a tired soul. Someone you admired because the growth you witnessed sparked inspiration in you to believe that miracles are real. Someone strong enough to carry the burdens of others while she herself wasn't sure what to do with hers. Someone who fought to give you everything when she barely had anything. Someone who leaves behind a lifetime of memories and wisdom that isn't comprehensible without a certain type of intellect. Someone who gave you all their love when she herself did not learn to properly love who she was.

I could feel that ache begin to empty my inside. An endless pain that cycles back around like a record player. Years didn't stop the pain from happening, and it hadn't stopped me from missing her. Missing her felt harder as time passed. What could be done, though? Nothing. Not unless I decided to end my life. I wanted to, but something always stopped me. I had to stay here, even though I can't explain what it is that's keeping me. Life doesn't stop at twenty-four, right?

I needed to figure out a way to start somewhere new. Away from here. Somewhere I won't be forced to be tied down to something I never asked for. Something I never wanted. Being told that there's no choice, when you're being demanded, in how you should live your life. That your purpose is to serve them causes you to act more rebellious toward the situation and people. Anger will form in ways that make it seem as if you are hateful. For a time, you are.

I looked up and out the window. It seemed cruel that I get to see where I craved to be but never get a chance to feel. I stood up; I could feel panic rising. I need to get out, but there is no way of that. There's no way of knowing anything right now except that I would be doing something that caused a sickening feeling in the pit of my stomach. It was something so dreadful that it felt like it would kill some part of my soul that I'd never find again.

After everything I had gone through, I couldn't imagine this being it for me. I was not going to accept chains from duplicated words of "I do" while everyone watched as they whispered about the little imperfections that gave character to such a day. A day that was meant to be harmonious but for me would be devastating. I couldn't imagine letting a piece of paper determine what my forever looked like, not when this didn't feel right. I sat back at the desk and continued writing but more aggressively than last time.

Suffocation forms by unwanted hands. I did not ask for this. It is in my very core that I cannot be bound to you. These chains you locked me away with are causing me to bruise as I fight to escape. Bleeding as the cuts deepen, screaming from the rapid pace of thoughts reminding me that I'm nowhere near okay. Barely able to move as I drown in my desperation to break through to the other side. Do you understand the damage that has already been done? I don't believe you care.

Your hunger for control is fed as I starve for freedom. You trying to manipulate my sanity causes my need for peace to be greater. I've begged you to change and when you couldn't, I pleaded for you to let me go. Now I'm left wondering how it is I can run when I feel I can hardly crawl. You asked me to prove my worth to be with you while you decided to beat me down and twist my words until I couldn't trust myself anymore.

You smirked as tears of agony and defeat ran off my face and onto my feet. The same feet that you stepped on one too many times and pretended to wonder why they broke. You had the nerve to call me crazy as you watched me lose my mind from lying as the truth was laid out in front of us. You pushed every nerve I had until I cracked and reacted poorly to the disrespect, claiming that this is why I'm not stable.

Watch me crumble as you take the pieces that are left and finish them off. You're trying to suck my soul dry so when there's nothing left you can display me on a shelf and prove a point that I wasn't anything more than what you wanted everyone to see. You took something full of life and decided that the shine was too bright for your dullness so with every chance you had you decided to sand instead of polish.

Even with sanding, something can be made bright and smooth again. The imperfections of a broken mind do not make the heart less genuine. It never takes away the value of a beautiful soul. I'll pick up what you left me with and give myself what you weren't willing to.

CHAPTER 5

The chains around my wrists tightened with a grip that caused them to bleed; on my neck, a rope of subjection caused suffocation. I could not bear to stay stuck anymore. I needed to escape today. If I do not leave, I won't survive.

A knock at the door startled me. As I turned around, Venon came through the door. Every time I looked at him, the anger rose like lava in a volcano; it didn't take much for me to erupt in an outburst. I looked away to better contain myself from an explosion.

"I wasn't sure if you would be up yet." He shut the door in a gentler manner than usual. "We need to talk."

I glanced at him. He was standing not far from me, with his arms crossed and a serious look spread on his face. I nodded my head and looked away, expecting something to come from his mouth that would set me off.

"I know you don't want to marry me because of what I did. I know what I did was wrong, but I want you to forgive me so we can move on."

Heat started to rise to my face. The urge to lash out began to rise to the surface, exposing how little patience I had left for him, practically demanding something I doubt he would do himself if the roles were reversed. I didn't want to give him the satisfaction of that reaction anymore, but I often failed at keeping my composure toward him. Not a single soul triggers me the way he does.

"We both know if I had done what you had, that—"

"You have done that." He interrupted with a harsh tone. "We've both done wrong."

He stepped toward me until he was on his knees next to me and spoke in a softer voice. "I've been doing everything I can to prove I won't do it again. I want us to be happy together. I thought you wanted that too."

He then grabbed my hands and started kissing them. With his mouth slightly away from my hands, he whispered, "I love you so much. Please, baby. Let it go."

I yanked my hands away and shot up from my chair. "You haven't proven anything. I've barely seen you! You can't just put someone through years of trauma and expect them to let it go when you keep showing you won't change!" I paced back and forth. My mind was racing, and I felt like my heart might thud out of my chest.

I paused with heavier breathing before responding. "You're a charmer, Venon. I know you too well by now to know you're going to do it again. I don't want to marry you anymore, but I have no choice. I never did. Do you know how much it hurts when you don't get to say what you want in life, let alone with whom?" Tears rolled down my cheeks.

He sat up and leaned against the window ledge, taking a moment before saying anything in response. "You need to get out of the room. Let's go for a walk." He held out his arms as he slowly stepped toward me and had this look that always made me want to never see him again while wanting to run into his chest and collapse. It made me want to believe his lies could someday be the truth.

The confliction of loving someone you shouldn't made it so difficult to remember what is right to do and not what feels good in the moment. Like a drug, you know it's only a temporary fix to something that would later make you feel worse.

I do my best to resist, but most of the time, I fail at it. This time, every minute spent around him, I reminded myself I knew giving in would cause me to stay, dooming myself to what would eventually kill some part of me I had a chance of never recovering from. I'm not willing to let him destroy me.

I could hear him exhale a deep breath. From my peripheral vision, I saw him put his arms down. His hands were halfway in his pockets with his thumbs poking out. I couldn't explain why that was attractive, but I fully turned away from being able to see any part of him to lessen the distraction I already had a difficult time fighting.

"I could really use a walk. Some fresh air in general." I tried to show as little emotion as I could. It always made me feel uneasy knowing he got satisfaction from me lashing out or exposing any sort of negative emotion, really. That he still had control over me to get that kind of reaction.

He walked to the door and unlocked it. I followed at a short distance behind him. The hallway, no matter the time of year, had a chill to it. The stone walls that were left were what made the castle still considered a castle. If Venon could have his way without upsetting others whom he considered valuable, he would have torn the place down and completely rebuilt it to make it all modernized. I thought the originality gave the place a lot more character and beauty.

Neither of us talked. It seemed pointless to bother trying to communicate when it only led to a fight. I didn't want to converse either. I was always left feeling defeated and unheard, while he seemed to thrive from the chaos. I gave up trying to make whatever it is we had work. I was not ever sure when he would bring something up or how either. Today seemed unusual.

We ended up on ground level where the main lounge area, kitchen, and dining room existed. On the other side of the stairs, which were unnoticeable unless you were paying close enough attention, was a narrow stone hallway with doors that I assumed hold secrets. Something about the whole thing stood out, mainly because they had locks the other doors didn't have. Locks that needed special keys with original doors.

The stairs led into an area that gave a choice to walk into the dining room or the lounge area, but the flooring by the stairs matched the lounge. The kitchen could be walked into from either of those rooms through an open area. We walked toward the dining room. The long, dark, and narrow table sat with the same shade of dark wooden chairs. Memories started to fill my head of moments we had together. Good ones we hadn't had in a long time.

"Would you like some food before we go outside?" His tone spoke with a gentleness I hadn't heard out of him since we first met.

"No." I turned my head from looking at the table and toward him. My eyes moved slowly to look at his, waiting to be convinced to eat with him, but he didn't say anything. He walked over to the glass doors and opened them.

I stepped into the opening where the sun's rays beamed onto my skin. The warmth traveled through my body, sending a shock of recharge that gave a sensation only the sun can do. A wave of fresh air filled my lungs, and as I exhaled, I felt the tension of being cooped up release a bit.

Even though an oversized stone wall blocked out the rest of the world's beauty, the garden contained its own fair share of elegance. Rows of different types of colorful flowers covered the ground. The only scene of green was a trail that made a path to walk around the whole area. Lined with the wall were bushes that somehow always stayed a vibrant red all year long. There were a few trees in random spots that also kept the same vibrant red leaves. The bark on the trunks of the trees had a more gray than brown color.

I stepped out of the castle. The grass felt soft on my feet. Venon followed behind as I walked farther from the castle. Usually, his presence disturbed me enough to cause tension, but something about nature always relaxes me. Nothing in the world feels wrong being outside, especially when the sun decides to shine the brightest.

I could never quiet my mind, but something made it travel in a positive manner when I could walk around things that felt right. Nature always feels right. It has this peaceful presence that I haven't discovered anywhere else. A unique beauty that makes everything seem freeing.

"Have you decided which dress you're going to wear?" I turned to look back at him. His expression had annoyance on it. I've realized every time I began to be any bit of happy or content, he seemed bothered.

"I have. None of them are fitting for me, though," I responded.

"I made sure to get the right size." His tone had a bit of a snap to it.

I looked away and back toward the garden. "That's not what I meant. They just aren't—"

"They are a great fit for you. Besides, those are the styles I want to see you in," he interrupted.

I could feel myself becoming frustrated. Everything always had to lead back to what he wanted. If it wasn't what he decided on, it wasn't alright to him. I swear he had more concern being with me for some twisted benefit that gave him an inner power than to become something a real couple was meant to be. It seemed he wanted to do everything against anything I wanted, with no compromising whatsoever. The worst part about this is that I didn't have a final say. I could argue all day long, and in the end, I'd still lose. Who wants to marry someone who treats them like a prisoner?

I decided to change the subject. "I haven't been able to practice my powers in a while."

"Yes, well, I'm not sure you have a need for more training. You aren't going to use your powers, so I think you are better off not wasting a trainer's time." I could sense him tense up. It was more noticeable when he put his hands behind his back and straightened his posture. He almost sounded threatened that I would bother bringing it up.

Before I had a chance to say more, the head guard came out. Venon's eyes followed mine and looked back. "Perfect timing, General. What is it you have for me?"

He nodded his head. "I've come to inform you that King David and Princess Rezna of Egyptstra have come with an unexpected arrival."

Venon's expression showed he was surprised but pleased. He never failed to be happy when Rezna was involved. "That is unexpected. Inform them I will gladly be with them shortly."

The general nodded his head and turned around to go inside. Venon stared at the door for a moment, then turned around toward me. His face had gone from smiling to hardening as he looked at me. It never failed to crush my heart knowing he loved her in a way he'd never love me, almost as if I was disgusting compared to her.

"I'd really like to stay out here." I spoke. His expression said he didn't trust that. "I assure you there's nowhere I can escape from, let alone anywhere to go. This also gives you time with Rezna without me around."

Venon didn't say anything at first, then sighed. "Alright." He turned around to go inside, but before he did, he stopped, slightly turning his head. "You will never compare to her."

He finished walking inside as a guard took place and stood there watching me. The words circled around my mind until I felt dizzy. Tears began to form; my breathing became heavy. As I looked down, a tear fell, hitting the grass. The grass. My head shot up, and I turned around to see the garden.

How I wish the walls would dissolve. I'd run away until my legs gave out and collapse. Until I ran out of breath and I'm nowhere near here. Maybe then I could be at peace. I want nothing more than that.

As nice as this moment was, I knew it would come to an end. I knew I would have to go back in and pretend to be okay in front of people who drain me, making me feel so out of place and irritated. People who believe small talk equals an intellectual conversation. It'll take everything in me to focus on what was being said.

The moment I didn't keep up, I would be asked something I didn't care enough to listen to and then treated as if I was stupid because they believed I lacked the comprehension. The reality was, they bore me to death, and my time was better served living in my own world.

Not to mention I'd have to pretend I didn't notice Venon's hardcore flirting with Rezna while she mockingly soaked it in and displayed her spite toward me yet played it off as if she looked at me as a friend. It was embarrassing, to say the least, and made no sense to me. I've never done anything as repulsing toward them but especially to her. Foolish me, at one point, believed we were friends.

I continued to walk around the rows of flowers, being careful not to step on one. The world is cruel enough; I didn't want to add to the reason beauty is dying. I got closer to the wall until I could touch the bushes, my fingers sliding along the leaves. These were the moments that gave me the slightest bit of hope that one day things won't be so bad. I can't be living in a nightmare forever.

As I inched closer to the edge of the wall, farthest from the castle, I noticed a small golden ball of light right underneath the leaves on the bushes. At first, I thought it came from my overactive imagination, but as I reached it and stood in front of it, looking down at it, it became brighter and grew bigger.

I watched it grow to the size where I could fit in it if I were to crawl. This wasn't anything I'd seen before. It was a ball of gold-colored light that moved in a slow motion of waves that twinkled with sparkles.

Its presence felt magical, and for whatever reason, I felt drawn to it. Like a magnetic pull, I couldn't help but reach out and move my hand to touch what seemed unreal. As my fingertips touched the glow, a sensation traveled through my body and sent chills up my spine. Destiny was calling me.

I couldn't explain how I knew, but I knew. I had to go through it without knowing the outcome, without knowing what came next. I had to reach into this and trust that this would lead me to so much more. This would lead me to a better life. This would take me to what I'd been longing for, the peace I desired.

I bent down and, without looking or hesitating, went through it.

CHAPTER 6

I didn't know where I was, and I didn't know who was standing in front of me. We were alone, surrounded by nature. Beams of the sun's rays poked through where the trees didn't give shade. Everything felt still and calm. Wherever we were, we were far away from any sort of society, deep in the woods.

After looking around at the beautifully full forest, I looked at the stranger. He had been staring at me with an expression that showed disbelief. He seemed stunned in place. I was sure anyone would be if a random person appeared out of nowhere.

He was tall and slender but well-built. His skin was light but not washed out. His hair a dark shade of brown grew in thick, with sides that were thinner than the top part of his hair. A bit of a messy look, which suited him very well. His nose fit his face perfectly. His cheekbones sat slightly higher than most, and while his jawline wasn't super defined, it was not undefined either. His lips weren't filled out, but they fit his face. They seemed soft but not in a feminine way. His eyes were a light green that showed quite a bit of gray.

I've never been struck by anyone's appearance before. This made him that much more attractive to me. However, aside from his attractive look that seemed exceptional to my wandering eyes, his presence made me feel drawn to him. Like the magnetic pull I felt from the golden ball of light, I wanted to reach out and touch him. I craved to be near him in a way that felt almost painful to resist. I was not sure how this could be possible, but I felt something much more powerful than love.

Scarier than that, I felt something deep within awakening a part of me that I didn't realize I needed brought to life. The other part of my soul finally learned how to dance to a rhythm that never sounded so sweet until now, calling me to a forever home that I didn't know I'd been searching for.

"I've seen you before." His voice wasn't what I thought it would be, but it sounded comforting, nonetheless. "In my dreams." I tried to think of a response, but I just kept looking around and then back at him. I didn't know what was more bizarre—my insane attraction and feelings toward him or him seeing me in his dreams. I suppose both weren't typical.

"Where did you come from?" He shifted his body to cross his arms together as he asked the question.

"The question is how," I whispered. I felt like I could hardly speak as shock still took over from everything that has happened and the feeling of not knowing if I could have comfort to speak without being judged.

"Sorry." I blinked a couple of times and took a deep breath in and then exhaled. "I came from the ruler's castle."

His brows furrowed together as he looked me up and down, and he responded, "And you appeared here so suddenly. Interesting."

His eyes met mine as he said the last word, and I felt my whole body wanted to melt into a puddle while feeling struck by lightning. We stood there just staring for a moment. I have never in my life met someone's eyes this way. I'm not someone who lets another stare into mine, but I found myself getting lost in his eyes. As I forced myself to look away, I felt like a tree that was split from the lightning I felt.

I looked around nervously as I talked, doing everything to avoid eye contact at this point. "I went into this ball of light, as strange as that sounds." I figured he'd laugh at that, but to my surprise, his eyebrows lifted, and he seemed even more interested.

"A glow, you mean?" My expression must've answered for him. "That's extremely rare. Almost nonexistent. Legend has it that if it appears to you and you're able to travel in it, then you're on a journey toward your destiny."

I could feel my eyes widen, remembering what it was I felt before I stuck my hand in it. "How is it you know this?" I asked.

He gave a smile and a look that would have brought me to my knees if I weren't steady in my stance. "You'll come to find I know lots of things, love."

I did everything I could to keep the focus on the conversation and not his charismatic tone and the insane attraction I felt toward him. The sarcastic side of me would have asked why he would be a part of my destiny, but I didn't want to seem I had interest in flirting. As tempting as it was, I really wanted to understand what was happening, what was possibly to come.

"Tell me what you know then. I'd like to learn as much as I can."

"I'm not sure I'll have the answers you're looking for, but I'd be more than glad to help you in whatever services I can give, especially since you're clearly of a greater importance." For some weird reason, I believed he meant what he said.

Usually, I didn't trust a man's motives, but he seemed genuine. I couldn't explain why he seemed so trustworthy, but it bothered me. Everything about him struck me in a way I didn't have enough words for.

He continued to speak. "I don't have any sort of detail outside of the glow being a part of an important path to take, but I do know someone who does. She's a highly gifted individual. Actually, I was on my way to seek some answers myself until you"—he looked me up and down again with a facial expression that made me want to melt again, his eyes so soft and calming—"until you appeared. I'm not sure if I have less or more questions at this point, but I do believe it would do you some good to meet her."

"Who is she? Is she a healer too?" I felt almost monotonous asking, but I had to try and seem more collected than I feel.

"Her name's Sasha. She's a telepath." The confusion on my face gave away that I have no idea what a telepath is, let alone who Sasha is. "I suppose you don't know anything about a telepath, do you?" His smirk reappeared.

I gulped before answering. I had that feeling there was going to be an overwhelming amount of information I receive. "I've only ever known of healers and drainers. I'm not sure I even know enough information about both of those. I've been kept locked away from the world, especially within the last few years."

His expression showed curiosity, but he played it smooth. "That's more common than you'd think. Shall we walk as I do my best to not overwhelm you? I promise any questions you have I'll answer without judgment. Nothing's dumb when it comes to learning."

I felt a wave of shock come over me. He was considerate of my feelings, but not just that; how could he possibly know what went through my mind a moment ago? I wasn't complaining because it felt nice to be a little understood without explaining, but it seemed all the stranger coming from a total stranger. I couldn't explain why he didn't feel like one, though. Had I known him before and forgotten? That wasn't typical for me. I was horrible with names, but I never forget a face. I surely wouldn't have forgotten his.

"Indeed, ignorance comes from those who decide they know all." I shyly smiled. He looked at me with a playful smile, then toward the direction I guessed he was heading before we met.

"Indeed. Now tell me, what is it you know of drainers and healers? We'll start with the obvious." He seemed eager to discuss this topic, which felt nice. Anything other than small talk.

"Well, I'm a healer. We heal things. Depending on our level of strength, we can heal others who are dying, or it's as simple as only healing a withered flower. We give life, which in turn drains us. Which is why we must be careful how much we give. Drainers, on the other hand, are opposite. They can suck the life right out of you if they are capable, or they can only dehydrate a weed. This ironically gives them more liveliness to continue being the horrible beings they are."

I felt my eyes widen and glanced at him. Surprisingly, his expression didn't change. He only waited for me to continue talking, but I felt a bit guilty to continue talking. Thankfully, he didn't seem fazed or offended, so maybe he was a healer and understood where I was coming from.

"We can be pretty terrible, can't we?"

Never mind. The guilt took over, which wasn't usual. I usually took pleasure in having chances to call them out for all the chaos they'd caused, especially in my life. He hadn't hurt me, though, nor did he seem like he wanted to, but then again, I could very well be wrong.

I noticed him look at me and then stop. I couldn't help but stop with him and sheepishly look around. "Don't feel bad," he stated, then continued walking.

I followed alongside him. "I agree with you. I used to be a typical drainer until I realized our gifts aren't meant to define us as people. More so for the world to be balanced. Our character is who we decide to be. It's a choice to be good or bad. Unfortunately, society has programmed everyone to think how you're born is what defines you. That you can't just be you without it having to have some sort of sense by small-mindedness."

I felt slightly ignorant. I had always felt that way with people defining what a female or male should like instead of just letting them enjoy what they wanted without it defining what gender they are, but I never thought to put the same perspective toward drainers and healers.

"Don't get me wrong," he continued. "I do believe as a drainer, we have less of a conscience than a healer does. It's much easier to lean toward the bad. Being a healer, you'll lean toward the good. That's not always good either."

I looked at him. He then looked at me. He seemed to know what I thought without speaking. Somehow, I knew I didn't have to speak much for him to know. "Not everything deserves a positive reaction. If someone decides they are going to try and hurt you, you shouldn't want to be taken advantage of. You should want to fight back. Healers tend to give until they cannot, while drainers will take everything you have."

Like a light bulb, it dawned on me what he meant. "This is why both exist. We're meant to balance the world together, as you said before. Instead, we're divided because drainers let the powers define them, while healers have done the same." I looked at him, and as he turned his head to look at me, I turned my head forward again. "You're not the typical drainer," I said softly.

"No, I'm not. This took years of growth, so don't be fooled into thinking I have a pretty past." His expression said he wished he hadn't said that, then he changed the direction of the conversation. "I have a feeling you're not the typical healer. Maybe once upon a time you were, but you've been through things that changed the level of boundaries you have toward others."

I had no idea what to say. In one sense, he was correct; in the other, I'd done things a typical healer wouldn't dare do to someone. Still, he seemed to know me better than most who'd known me for years. This made me feel incredibly comfortable yet alarmed. How was any of this possible? Should I really be trusting him?

My past with drainers screams no, especially with men, but everything in my soul said otherwise. My intuition had never been wrong about someone, even when I ignored it. However, this seemed more powerful than that. This felt on another level I had never experienced and one I felt I could never again with anyone else.

I knew him. In a way, I'd never known someone. It was that, or my imagination had finally run so far off the grid that I'd lost my mind completely. This was very possible. One could only go through so much before it broke them entirely.

My mind came back to the telepath and wondering what that was—who Sasha was. "You've given me a perspective I needed. Thank you. Which brings me to the next subject to discuss."

"Yes, telepaths." His smirk faded as quickly as it came. "They aren't at all as common. Matter of fact, they're dying out. We can thank my kind for that." I let him continue without asking the story behind that. I had a feeling there would be plenty of time to figure out everything until it fit together like a puzzle. "They can't read your mind directly, not that it's been recorded at least. They get glimpses of the past, present, and/or future of someone."

"In what way? Like what will happen? Is it when they want to see it, or does it come randomly?" I stopped myself from asking more questions. They would be endless if I asked every single thing that came to mind.

"From my understanding, it's random, and it's almost like when a memory pops in your head. Except you see it play out while the reality around you is nonexistent in the moment." He seemed not to be in the moment entirely himself.

"Something troubling you?" I wanted to know more, but I couldn't help but feel bothered that he became off, especially so suddenly.

He seemed caught off guard by my question. "What makes you ask that?"

I took a moment to figure out how to respond. "I'm not sure how to explain it. I can just sense the change in you."

He stopped in his tracks and stared at me. I turned toward him, but I didn't stare back. I wanted to look at him, but I couldn't. I've never been good at eye contact, but something about staring at him made me feel something deeper than the ocean's bottom. A vulnerability I swore off to others. I can't imagine eye contact being anything other than an intense explosion of emotions I'd never be able to let go of. I already had a glimpse of that earlier.

He took steps toward me until we stood a few inches from each other. This usually would have made my heart race and cause me to be tremendously nervous, but I only felt an urge to step closer. I wanted to so badly, reach out, and touch him.

"Look at me." His whisper sent chills up my back.

His voice was smooth as freshly sanded wood that had been glossed over. He wasn't saying it in a demanding tone, but more so with signals of a plea. I slowly looked up, but I couldn't gather myself to look him in the eyes.

"I'm not good with eye contact. It makes me uncomfortable." I finally spoke. My head dropped, and I started messing with my fingers. A bit of shame came over me.

"I can tell. What is the reason behind it?" he asked with a patience and kindness in his voice I'd never experienced from a man.

Something about the tone made me want to be vulnerable. I couldn't imagine him willingly being okay if he saw all the worst sides of me. More than likely, he wouldn't be convinced of me being a total healer. It's not possible to be anything else, though. Is it?

I took a deep breath in, then exhaled out of my nose. "The eyes are a very personal thing. I'd hate for someone to look into mine and see something ugly."

He gently grabbed my chin and lifted my head. Usually, I would have pulled back and bounced at least a foot away, but the magnetic pull started to become unbearable to fight. Just the touch from his fingers made my whole body weak and crave him for so much more. I went ahead and gave in.

Our eyes met. I could feel my heart stop, and everything around me numb out. Both of his eyes were soft and mesmerizing. I've never in my life felt so strongly for someone, and everything in me lost control of my senses. I grabbed the side of his neck with my hand and pulled him in for a kiss. Both of my hands were on his face as my body sank into his.

I felt something way more powerful than an explosion. An electric surge traveled through my body and into the deepest parts of my soul, awakening a part of me that had been waiting to be brought to life. I couldn't explain this other than I know anything before him had been completely and utterly wrong for my well-being. His touch fed a hunger inside of me I didn't realize had been starved until I tasted the sweetness of his lips on mine. So much of what I craved had been missing, and it now became filled by the simple touches of a long-lost love, making this the definition of an eternal entwining.

CHAPTER 7

I pulled my head back. I couldn't imagine what he was thinking.

"I…" I looked away as I spoke and realized we had traveled to another place, totally different. "Do you know where we are?" I looked back at him, and his stare hadn't moved. His mind had gone somewhere totally different, and his eyes said they had been entranced. My experience had been like nothing else with anyone else; did he experience something similar?

He finally shifted his look, and his eyebrows furrowed together. "We're closer. Much closer." He then looked back at me. "Who are you?" he asked in bewilderment and something else I couldn't quite explain.

"I'm Ann. Who are you?" I supposed this should have come first. Leave it to me to do things out of order.

"Ann." He said it as if it had become his new favorite name, followed with a smile dancing in his eyes. "I'm Mavryk. Spelled M-A-V-R-Y-K." Being a visual person, I had to picture it in my mind to grasp what that looked like.

"I've always wanted a unique name. The spelling makes it that much more fascinating," I responded.

"My mother had a knack for differently spelled names," he responded as he adjusted his body a bit differently. "What are you? I know you possess healing, but there's much more than that to you. I could feel it when you kissed me." He slightly smirked as he said it.

I looked away before I lost control and before I started to laugh. I was sure he'd find me weird then. I couldn't explain it myself either. I felt overjoyed and giggly, ready to burst into this goofy, childlike person I hadn't felt in years.

"I'm just your average healer. Until today, I've never experienced something like this. With the glow, I mean." His expression showed a bit of concern and confusion. "Something troubling you?" I could sense his feelings more than I could read his facial expressions.

He took a moment before responding. "You only felt something with the glow?"

I waited to see if he would say more, but he wanted me to respond.

"I definitely felt something since being around you. I just—"

Before I knew it, his lips had locked on mine, with his hands on my face, and the magic traveled through my body again. Every inch of me was filled with an electric charge, feeding something deep within me that had been caged and locked up.

I pulled away again. I felt alive and wired, ready to conquer the world. I was not the type to open up out of fear of being misunderstood or rejected in some form or manner, but something came over me to speak what it was I had really been thinking.

"There's something going on. I have no idea what all of this means. Moments ago, I was locked away in the castle, being made to stay stuck somewhere that was slowly killing me. The next moment, I'm entering a magical portal to you, which you say is called a glow and leads a person to their destiny. I'm not sure what to believe or what to even think, but I do know what I'm feeling is not of this world. I know when we kiss, it is nothing I thought existed, and I have definitely never traveled somewhere else while doing so. I never knew you could travel in a blink of an eye. Being around you alone has made me feel something I could have never imagined. Whatever it is I feel, it is not something I have enough words to define." I stopped and realized I had said far more than I wanted. I waited for him to mock me, give me a look that said I'd lost my mind, but his voice spoke with a calmness that gave no hint of judgment.

"We're here." His eyes were looking behind me. I looked away and around. We were somewhere else again. I turned to see what he had been looking at—a small but cozy-looking cottage. Enough room for two people.

The yard had soft-looking grass. Farthest from us lay a vegetable garden and trees in random spots that held fruit. Surrounding the area was the forest we came from, I assumed, anyway. Sunshine beamed down but not too brightly. The forest gave enough covering to keep the sun from totally shining down in this area.

"Do you mean we're at the telepaths' place?" I finally asked.

"Yes. Sasha and Steven live here." He looked at me and spoke in a gentle voice. "You are a very beautiful soul, Ann. I hope one day you decide to see it for yourself." Then he walked to the cottage.

I've never heard so few words be spoken so sweetly and captivatingly. Out of all the things anyone has ever said, that had been by far my favorite compliment.

As amazing and fairy tale–like as this all had been, I needed to snap back into reality and follow behind him.

Besides this romance mystery going on, there had been so much else that left me confused and anxious. Why and how did the glow appear? Is it true that it has something to do with a destiny aligned for me? I didn't even want to think about what would happen to me if I ended up in Venon's control again. Was I even free from him at this point? He was the ruler. It was not possible to hide forever. That had already been proven.

As we reached the cottage, a man walked out of the door. He looked so familiar, but I couldn't remember why. He had a broad build to him. His hair was a shade lighter than the dirty blond I had. His freckles were light but noticeable. His eyes were shaped with a bit of a slant to them, naturally seeming mischievous. His skin tone wasn't fair but not tan either. It looked like it kept a bit of the color the sun gives him, just not much of it.

"My brother. We've been expecting you!" He threw up his arms, and Mavryk did the same, both smiling from ear to ear. They must be close.

They did a swift, tight hug, and then he spoke. "How the heck are you? It's been months, man, you know your company is always wanted here."

Mavryk looked down from him but had a smile, nonetheless. "Believe me, Steven, I know. I've had important business to take care of. Something happened just today, though. Something I've never encountered. I had been heading this way when suddenly—" He looked at me. "I still can't believe what has happened." Mavryk then proceeded to explain what I had said to him about the glow, the traveling while we kissed. He even went ahead and explained in detail the feelings he had gotten the moment I arrived and how he felt something very similar to what I felt while we kissed.

I wanted to feel relieved because then this would mean he felt the same as I had, but he kept it simple, which made me think that maybe his unusual feeling was different than mine. We both experienced something you don't hear about, but perhaps this meant I gained undeniable feelings for him while his only had to do with what had happened and not with me.

Steven's face showed a lot of surprise. "Sasha's going to have to answer for all of that. In all my time, I'm not sure she's even come across something like this. Boy, this is one for the books!" They both laughed a little, then Steven opened the door. "You both come on in." As he looked at me, his smile turned into a mouth that dropped open with eyes that grew big. "Ann. My gosh. You're alive."

I felt myself freeze in place. I knew I recognized him, but why couldn't I remember him the way he remembered me? "I'm sorry, I don't remember you. I mean, I do. I just can't recall how." I wish how I spoke in my head and on paper came out as smoothly in person. Unfortunately, I would never say things out loud without a bit of awkwardness and more than likely stumble on a few words.

"We thought they killed you, Ann." He reached out and hugged me, squeezing me tight. He then pulled back with his hands on my shoulders. "How did you survive?" His voice was lower but no less serious.

"I'm confused. Survive what?" As soon as I said the sentence, it clicked. He's talking about the night my mother died.

I gulped and looked around, trying to remember how that day happened. I did a lot of blocking it out every chance I could. "I just—" I could feel my breathing become heavier and panic rise inside. "I don't know. I don't understand what happened."

His grip relaxed, and then he let go. "I'm sorry, Ann. That wasn't fair to ask." His voice conveyed how sorry he was. "Let's get you inside."

I felt my eyes move fast to look at him. He said those exact words years ago with the same tone, feeling so bad for me. I hadn't eaten for three days, and my mom had been gone for almost a whole month. He and his mother not only fed me but also let me stay for a few weeks while they comforted me over what had happened. I had gone from wondering when I'd die to laughing tears of joy, feeling grateful to have had a night that lightened the grieving and a couple of weeks to get back on my feet. The night they found me in particular stopped me from killing myself.

Tears filled my eyes. "Steven. I remember." I was the one reaching out and squeezing him this time.

I pulled away and realized Mavryk didn't have a clue what had been going on. "His mom and my mom were close friends." I spoke. "He and his mom fed me, clothed me, and gave me a place to stay for a couple of weeks not long after my mother died."

He looked taken aback. "I see. How long ago was this?"

"Six years ago," Steven answered.

"Ann, how old were you?" Mavryk looked concerned.

"I was eighteen." I could feel the questions causing me to shut down, wanting to run away and say nothing else.

I didn't have to look at Mavryk to know he was upset for me. I could feel him wanting to ask more, but he didn't. He spared my emotions by changing the subject. "I suppose we should continue going inside." I looked at him and hoped he could see the gratitude on my face for not pushing me to talk.

As we walked inside, I smelled candles. I was not familiar with the smell, but the fragrance had a smooth and sweet combo, relaxing the tension that had built up. The place was even cozier-looking than the outside had shown.

As small as it was, it really wasn't crammed. The living room had a couch right by the door we entered and a painting above it. Across the living room stood two doors. One looked like the bathroom; I was guessing the other was a closet. On the right side, there was another door to a room where I could see the headboard of the bed, which seemed to beam a lot of natural light. To the left was a kitchen with a little dining area that had a round table and four chairs. The kitchen was separated from the living room by a counter that had an opening between cabinets and a passageway to look into the living room. The cabinets and passageway did not enter the dining area. The color scheme was dark and light brown all around the place. Not a common look, but it strangely went together. The carpet was dark brown, while the hard flooring was an almost beige color. The carpet stopped at the bathroom entrance and at the edge of the dining area.

"Who is this you brought with you, Mavryk?" Startled, I turned my head toward the bedroom where the unfamiliar female voice came from. A dark-skinned woman stood by the opening. Her hair had tight black curls that went a little past her shoulders. Her eyes were fierce and darker than her hair color but glossed beautifully. Her lips were full. Her figure wasn't at all big, but the curves really showed. She was one of the most beautiful women I've ever seen.

"Sasha. The girl I need." Mavryk smirked and seemed relieved to see her.

"Woman. I am no girl. We've discussed this." She definitely has power behind her voice. "But yes, I knew you would need me. I saw you heading this way a couple of days ago. However, I did not expect you to bring someone else. A woman at that." She raised her eyebrows and gave a look that said she was being funny in a serious manner. It made me smile.

"My name is Ann. I apologize for intruding on your home." I figured to speak up before she took it some kind of way that I didn't say something.

She smiled. "You are not intruding. I find it odd I did not see you in my vision. It is not something that occurs to me, ever."

"Is it possible that a glow can cause that?" As Mavryk spoke the word *glow*, her head whipped toward him, and her look became very serious. "As I was heading here, a light appeared right in front of me. Ann came through it in a matter of seconds. We weren't anywhere near here. We at least had a day left until arriving. We kissed twice,

46

and each time traveled closer. The second time, we landed right in your yard."

Sasha looked at Steven with a facial expression that said she couldn't believe what her ears had just heard.

Steven broke into a laugh. "Man! That's one heck of a kiss!" Mavryk laughed with him, but Sasha's expression didn't change. My giggle quickly faded. I couldn't help but feel concerned that she seemed so shocked by that. In all fairness, I still couldn't wrap my head around any of it either.

"Ann," Sasha came next to me and studied my appearance, "did you see anyone summon this glow?"

"No. No one was outside with me. I had no idea something like that even existed. It appeared at a small distance from where I stood. I noticed it, but more than that, I felt it the closer I got. Like a magnetic force field pulling me in."

"Glows do not appear for anyone. Not unless there is a greater purpose involved." Sasha walked into the kitchen looking for something. "I cannot see anything with you. This is not common either. There's always something that I'm shown involving a person, but I cannot see anything to do with you."

"You can't see anything? What do you mean you can't see anything? That's never happened before." Steven's voice expressed surprise. "You mean to tell me that there's nothing you're seeing. Not anything?"

Sasha stopped what she was doing and looked at Steven. "I can see the history of you two through you. I can see what it is Mavryk thinks of her. What he saw when she appeared. She is not in the form of herself as she stands. I am seeing her as a light. She shines with a pearl color. Not golden like the glow." She went back to looking.

"What does this mean for her?" Mavryk asked. He seemed more curious than concerned, almost fascinated.

"I do not know. I can only assume it means she's going to have to conquer a lot of hardships and make many sacrifices to pursue her destiny."

CHAPTER 8

Time seems to be speeding up, the change going on around me and within me, which makes it hard to grasp all that's happened. The morning started off with heartache and pain, a longing to be furthest away from what I knew didn't belong to me. My soul had been withering away and pleading to somehow be set free.

Before long, I'm certain the fire would have went out and left me in ashes of agony, forever tortured and tormented not only by my surroundings but also the demons that danced with my deepest fears and darkest insecurities.

A light, a glow, showing only a slight hint of existence. The part of me that always demands to look the other way couldn't fight off the feeling to walk toward the unknown. Uncertainty wasn't what I felt deep down though, no, there had been a calling about it.

A strong, powerful, and unreal sense that shook me to my core that I had to not only seek out but also to reach for in that moment. I did not feel there was another way to escape from the misery. It felt scarier knowing I'd be stuck than to risk taking this chance without any clue on what sat on the other side besides change. What did I have to lose?

The travel, I cannot recall, but the arrival awakened the part of me I never knew had been missing. Within the hours that everything has happened in, I've felt something old shed off while a newness is trying to *come through. Something within myself grew, as did connecting with someone else in a way others would tell you is delusional.*

However, what awakens the soul is the kind of love that makes you face your fears and battle your worst insecurities within. A fiery passion burning so bright that the sun itself becomes stunned. The touch of their skin electrifying your blood as it travels through the veins and into the heart. You'll know why it never stopped beating once you've discovered that. You'll know why no one else felt right.

You're naturally wholesome in their presence, and with every moment together, you're recharged. As your lips press together, you discover the match made by something higher. Sparks of magic fly around the two of you as the souls entwine back together after a long separation. A glorious calling to finally be home and conquer what the two of you are meant to do.

It's the two of you together, facing the wars that are happening and the ones that are to come. It's not the two of you at war with each other.

I put the pencil down and reread what I wrote.

Before I could rip it out and tuck it away in my pocket, Sasha spoke. "There was a strange sense of needing to find those. It didn't make any sense until now." She had been standing by the bathroom door as she talked, then walked over and sat across from me.

"I'm sorry. I should have asked. I usually use my own, but I didn't have a chance to grab anything before I went through the glow." I didn't know how to explain that writing feels like it's a part of me without sounding weird either.

"There's no need to apologize. I'm glad there was a purpose for it. I would have been driving myself crazy until I could make sense of it." She looked at the paper with interest, then at me. "Mind if I read it?"

"Sure. I mean, yeah, that's fine." I handed her the paper. "It's nothing that good. More so something really good for me."

I was not used to someone having interest in what I wrote. It felt nice, but on the other hand, it made me nervous that I would be criticized in a harsh way. Hardly anyone had read anything I'd written. The few that have always said something positive, but I've had enough people belittle and criticize me enough to make me question how good I really am.

Ironically, the ones who hadn't read anything I wrote pretty well told me to be more realistic and use my time more wisely. Little did they know the words written spoke more freely than I ever could. Writing felt like a part of me that I needed. Without it, I felt like an empty canvas, taking away my form of art.

She set the paper down and looked at me. "This is beautiful. You write with your heart, and I can feel that." She adjusted herself to face me more directly. "I can't tell you where you're going or what your purpose is, but if you ever get the chance, take yourself somewhere with this. Your writing can be used to inspire in a way you never imagined."

I felt my eyes water. No one had ever told me that before. "Thank you." I gave a shy smile. "I usually prefer not to share, but I'm glad I did. I'm glad you enjoyed it."

She smiled back with kindness in her eyes. "It was my pleasure to read. I plan to make a feast of a breakfast in the morning. Would the two of you care to stay and join us? If I have the ingredients, I can make special requests. Mavryk always asks for waffles." She playfully rolled her eyes and waved her hand.

"I'll keep that in mind. That's if I ever get the chance to make him any. But yes, I'd love that, and I'll assume he would too," I responded.

Her brows furrowed together. "Why wouldn't you have the chance?"

I adjusted myself a bit to try and relax the tension that question caused me. "I meant—" I looked around, trying to gather my thoughts.

I tend to do that the more serious a conversation gets. "I don't know what any of this means with us. I know what I felt, what I feel, but who's to say he feels any of it too. I doubt he'll want to be around that long."

"Honey, are you serious?" Did she know something I didn't? Her facial expression changed when she realized I wasn't joking. "When the glow appears in front of someone, it is for a greater purpose. It led him to you. I wouldn't think that's a coincidence. Besides"—she leaned back some, exposing an amused smile—"I see the way he looks at you. No man would ever look at a woman that way without being in love."

"Maybe he's still shocked by all of this. I did appear out of nowhere. I'd give some type of look myself," I responded rather quickly.

She shrugged her shoulders. "I've known him for a very long time. There's something about the way he looks at you that is different. I'm sure that you can agree there is something there that can make you believe it's possible he feels the same." She looked at the paper, then at me. She then stood up and yawned. "I'm not sure how you're not tired. It's close to one."

"I tend to be the restless type," I responded.

"Have you always been like that?" she asked.

I shook my head and tried to give a smile. She gave a sympathetic smile back and held her arms out. "It's been lovely chatting. Can I get a hug?" She made a dancing motion with her shoulders as she extended her arms out. We both laughed.

I stood up and hugged her. The moment our bodies locked, I felt a jolt shock my body. We both jumped back, and her face showed sheer terror. Tears rolled off her face as quickly as they swelled in her eyes. She stood there for a bit, sucked into her mind. I wanted to say something, but nothing seemed right to say. She didn't say anything for a while.

"Ann. Oh my gosh." She sounded almost breathless. "Your mother. She was—" Sasha sat back down in the chair, holding her chest as if she felt heartburn.

"Killed. I know." The word felt like poison as I let it leave my mouth. "Wait, does this mean you saw something?" I tried to remain focused and lock away my emotions.

She couldn't stop crying and took a while before responding. "How have you survived?" Her voice had a slight shake to it. "Your life. How did you manage?" She must've seen the details of that night.

"The night was har—"

"No, Ann. Not just the night. Your life." I didn't know how to answer that, not when there were times I tried to end mine. "When we hugged, your life played out in my head. Most of it sped through, but there were moments that slowed, and I saw you. As a little girl, as a teen. Recently. You've been through too much for one person to endure."

I could feel the flight mode starting to take over me. I did what I could to block it all out. For years, I drank until I woke up, not remembering most of the night, hoping that would take me. Hoping something tragic would happen to cause my death. Every time I tried, something wild would happen that caused it not to go through.

"You saw my dad?" I finally asked.

She looked at me as if she felt terribly ill. "He's the reason the ruler possesses power over you."

I felt ringing in my ears. My heart dropped and shattered into pieces all over again. "What do you mean?"

She grabbed my hand. "I know why your mom ran away. The real reason." I wanted to pull my hand away and pull back.

"I already know why Mother left. It's because they were going to take me to groom me in the way they wanted me to be once I started bleeding," I said sharply.

Not to mention, Father belittled and yelled at us more often than not, especially at Mother. The scars were still there for her when she died. He seemed to have hated us. Nobody really realized the pain he caused that left us both so bruised and wounded on the inside.

"Is that all she told you?" she asked gently.

I looked at her, confused, and then looked away, my eyes beginning to stare at the ground. "What is it that I don't know?" I asked a bit bitterly.

"She left because your father was going to give you over to the ruler at the time. Lucus."

"Venon's father?" I asked, saying as little as possible to get all the information without having a lash-out that would break into a meltdown.

She nodded yes. She looked away as she spoke with a quiet, sorrowful voice. "Your father was a capturious—"

"Capturious?" I asked, confused. "I thought he was a guard. What's a capturious?"

"That's what your mother thought too. Your father lied about many things." She took a deep breath in, then continued and let go of my hand. "A capturious is someone who captures escapers." She looked at me, and I was guessing she could tell I didn't know what those were either. "Escapers are the ones who help healers get to Coastra. They're the real heroes."

"Coastra?" I sat back and put my hands on the side of my head, ready to pull my hair out. "I'm sorry for all the questions. I just don't understand any of this. As much as I've gone through, there is still so much I was sheltered from."

"You don't need to apologize for everything. You're not doing anything wrong." Something clicked as she said that. I always felt wrong for asking and not knowing. I felt wrong for anything I did that wasn't perfected. I've felt wrong most of my life because people have made me feel wrong about myself. They ridiculed everything I did and never praised me for my rights. Those were nit-picked too.

"Coastra is a place. We can discuss the parts of the world afterward if you'd like," she mentioned.

It was more of a statement than a question. For whatever reason, she knew I needed to know all of this. I had a feeling the world I know is very much about to become what I knew. She adjusted herself to relax a bit, and I did the same. I wanted to make sure I'd save any questions for the end instead of interrupting.

"Your father, being the capturious that he was, grew close to Lucus. The closer you are to the ruler, the more you and your family are involved. Freedom doesn't exist even for those that are close."

"I know that all too well." She made a face, agreeing, then continued.

"Your father really swept your mother off her feet. He promised her a very different life than the one he could give. Shortly after that, you were conceived. It wasn't known at first what you were born as."

"My father made a very big deal about me not being a boy. From what I was told, I wasn't wanted at all unless I, at the very least, could be born that. I suppose being a healer made that even worse." The sad thing is, at one point, I would have given anything to be what he wanted me to be, just for him not to look at me with disgust.

She didn't know how to respond to that and continued where she left off. "You displayed incredible strength, but no one, except your mother, knew to the extent. As time went on, they labeled you as a healer. Not just any healer. The only healer born on your birthday. The rest are drainers. I'm sure you can imagine the commotion this caused."

I gulped. What were the odds of that? Why did my mother never mention any of this? How in the world was I supposed to take any of this?

"The ruler saw that as an opportunity to keep the bloodline strong and wanted you for his son. Your father agreed since it gave him a higher position, and your parents could see you as often as they wanted this way. The decision made between your father and the ruler decided they wait until your next birthday to give you away, it didn't matter if you bled. When he told your mother, she snapped. They fought. Your mother won, almost killing him. That was when she grabbed you and ran off."

My stomach became sickened. "I was only eleven when we left." I could feel tears swell in my eyes. "He never did love me, did he?"

She looked at me with a look that said she wished my outcome had been different. "We cannot change who people are, unfortunately. We can only accept that how they hurt us is not a reflection of our worth. It does not mean we are not deserving of their love. You are more than deserving of that." She grabbed my hand with both of hers. "I know nothing I say will take your pain away. I know

54

you wish things would have been different. I'm sorry they weren't." I couldn't hold back anymore—I broke down.

Suddenly, Mavryk kneeled beside me and gently wrapped his arms around me. The words he spoke not only shocked me, but his touch somehow began to calm my nerves from completely breaking down.

"I don't know where you'll go from here, what you are meant to do, Ann, or how I can help, but I do know that whatever happens, you will show him and everyone who wronged you why they should have treated you better. You will show everyone that cruelty from others doesn't have to kill kindness, and you will show everyone what true strength is. You will be the difference the world needs, and I will help you succeed in that."

CHAPTER 9

I rubbed my fingers through my hair. The last time I spoke to my father, he went on a quest, which I knew wasn't usual for a guard. He didn't mention what kind either. He never wanted to talk about anything to do with his job, or much of anything for that matter. Now it made a lot of sense why he never did.

This was about a year ago. When they found me and brought me to the castle three years ago, he was the one to verify who I am. He never stood up for me against Venon. Instead, he would join in on the belittling behind my back. Not that I was surprised; I just kept hanging onto hope that he would eventually change. There were moments he'd agree that what Venon was doing was wrong, but he seemed to push it to the side in the same sense and act as if he couldn't do anything to help.

Sasha mentioned the escapers being the good ones. That made a capturious not good, in fact, no better. He could have chosen to do better. However, I'm not surprised he would be involved with something like that. If it benefits him in some way, he doesn't hesitate to do it.

I still don't quite understand what an escaper and a capturious are, though. This is probably because I can't quite wrap my head around there being a place like Coastra, a safe place for healers. I'd have to ask for more details when she woke up, if she even wanted to talk anymore. She seemed pretty shaken up after the vision she had. I can't blame her. If more people saw how it all played out, they would wonder how I'm still bothering to stay alive. At least that's what I've been questioning.

After the discussion of my father, Sasha had gone to sleep. Mavryk stayed up a little while longer as we discussed some of his past. He had heard everything between me and Sasha. It amazes me how similar our lives have been, especially with our fathers. His was a lot more physical than mine had been, but the pain of his father's emotional neglect held onto him about as much as mine.

When he went back to lay down, I wanted to join, but I knew I would just toss and turn. As exhausted as I am, I knew what would await me if I dared to sleep. Until you experience nightmares, you can't imagine what it's like to wish your mind would let you be, hardly ever getting a break from the constant thoughts and tortures.

It was much worse when a flashback happened. Someone would say something, do something in a certain way, that would cause me to spiral into my thoughts so badly that it ended up in a panic and sometimes a reaction that you wished you had never shown. People don't understand that their action has a much harsher effect when I feel something similar and connect it with my past.

In the moment of a panic, you can't explain anything either. Not without totally losing yourself from trying to get out what it is that's going on. You can't speak like you want because the thoughts crash together so intensely your mind can't begin to keep up with the paralyzing sense that you're falling apart again. The pressure from even trying to talk while in a panic sends me spiraling so badly I end up losing my control to keep levelheaded.

It doesn't matter if someone keeps provoking me or not, I always feel shame afterward. I hate that certain people can get underneath my skin so badly that it has such a negative effect on my well-being, one that I feel wouldn't be me if I could understand what it is that's happening.

However, people who purposely bring out the worst in you and seem to enjoy it are a different type of twisted individuals. It took me a while to realize these types of people have their own disorders that are a lot less likely to be fixed than people who are triggered. They attack until you're as low as they are, even then they want you beneath them. To feed their hunger of needing to be satisfied is to sacrifice your sanity. Once they destroy you, they leave you to die and move on as if they never did a thing wrong. They'll drain you so dry as you walk around lost and shattered while they try to steal the last piece you hang onto to keep going.

The sad thing is, you love these people. You forgave them as they stabbed your back. You justified their ill intentions, thinking your kindness might give them a change of heart. You want to save them from staying in such a dark place. You were willing to sit there and battle their demons with them while having your own, hoping it would break them free. Instead, they watched as their demons corrupted yours worse than ever before, leaving you to pick up all your own pieces.

How much of yourself can you give before there's nothing left of you? Are you truly okay with giving up everything for people who would watch you burn alive? I was. I was willing to wait forever just to know I was finally accepted, that I am enough. I didn't even require love back.

However, I'm no longer accepting unacceptable behavior. I'm done caving into the delusional thought that these people will be better, that they care enough to stop harming another for their benefit. They are as they show themselves to be. Let that show you how they really feel. Some people only know how to strive on controlling others in some form of way that makes the other feel less than.

I grabbed the last piece of paper on the table and decided I would write a letter. In another world, in another way, if I had the chance, I would give it to each person who has done this to anyone. At this point, I will be content for now, knowing I finally stood up for myself and others in a way where they can't shut us up.

You trapped me inside a cubicle of hatred that I couldn't stop drowning in. The pressure of its weight sinking me to the bottom. You watched me beg not to be stuck. I fought to stay above the surface, but I couldn't breathe. When the breathing stopped, you'd give me just enough air to stay alive.

There came a point in life I only felt my fingertips touch the air from above. I screamed but nothing left except the bubbles that were filled with my fear. You ignored my plea to be saved and watched me become silent.

If I fought hard enough to come close to the top, you pushed me down harder, making it impossible to ever catch my breath. You can't say you didn't want me to sink because who I truly am angers you.

When I finally found a way to break the glass and let the water pour out, you convinced me to be chained in place in a much more confined space.

Every day that passed, those four walls consuming me filled with harsher words from most of those who should have looked out for my best interest, not their own.

The walls closed in so tightly that I became suffocated. All over the walls were reminders of a past that constantly haunts me, and the chains reminded me of being stuck. They remind me that I cannot survive because of how weak others convinced me to be. When I finally broke the walls to escape and freed myself from the chains, I ran away.

However, too little, too late. Words that you and others smashed into my head caused a major head injury. The blood that spilled out spelled out the same things you decided were fitting to describe me.

How selfish I am, as you would say, for setting myself free from the torture of misery that kept being thrown my way. Acting as if the trail of lies that you carried actually meant something. Giving me breadcrumbs when I had enough to only knock me down harder each time I came back. I thought I could trust you.

Now I hear myself scream that I'm worthless. My life being meaningless. Now I'm trying to learn how to breathe properly without feeling like the air is choking me with the anger you projected onto me. Now I'm *fighting for dear life to feel okay. I'm figuring out who I am without your opinion affecting my ability to see what it is I deserve.*

Maybe now you'll see that the love I tried giving you should have never been pushed away. Maybe now in the empty silence ringing through by my absence, it will fill your ears with loud whispers and ugly regrets that you finally pushed me away. For good. The truth of it all came out. Your actions have shown me exactly how you feel.

I'm not sure I'll ever understand why you resented me so much that loving me became foreign to you, but I do know, with time, I will find peace from this while you still wage war with yourself. You will see it was not me who was against you. That you are wrong about me and should have never turned your back on me like you had.

I'll always love you despite everything regardless. I'll wonder if time finally softened your heart a bit. Even though you meant to harm me time and time again, I still do not wish harm on you. I hope you never make another feel the way you have made me feel.

Here is my final goodbye to you.

I put the pencil down and reread what I wrote. The pain spilled into every word, yet I feel myself set free a bit. I no longer feel the obligation that had held me trapped in place with people who meant nothing good for me. This isn't just about letting them go; it's about letting everything I've let define me go. This is a step toward walking into my confidence to do what is right and empowering. This is me realizing my worth. If only this feeling could stay with me and not disappear so quickly.

I felt myself yawn. There are only a couple of hours left before the sun comes up, but a few hours are better than none. I'm pretty used to not getting much sleep either. Almost like normal amounts for most are oversleeping to me.

I stood up and watched Mavryk sleep on the pull-out couch. He offered for me to sleep there while he slept on the floor, but I hated the idea of him doing that, especially knowing he'd be on it much longer than I would be. I wonder if he knew what holding me earlier meant. That him caring enough to get out of bed said a lot when I've cried many nights alone, trying to hold myself together.

Almost everything he said seemed to weaken my heart a bit. It wasn't what he said that did it; it was the way he said it. He meant every word, and I could feel that. I wonder if he knew how much it meant that he encouraged me to write because he knew it helped me. He has no real idea of the impact he has on me already.

As quietly as I could, I lay next to him and put my body under the blanket. I can't imagine him staying around once he realizes I'm not a typical healer. I'm not always good, loveable, or easy. Frustration happens more often than not, and I'm filled with tons of insecurities and doubts. Then again, we aren't technically anything, so the level of obligation he might feel to handle me at my worst is none at all.

Sasha says he feels what I do, but I can't imagine that being possible, not when I feel something this deep and unearthly. Even if he did, I can't believe he'd still love me after realizing I'm filled with multiple insecurities and so many doubts. That I'm broken and not sure how I'm going to get to a place of true healing.

I turned away from him and closed my eyes. A few tears escaped. Healers are supposed to be full of positivity and calmness. I feel the opposite of that more often than not. Maybe that's the price that comes with being around chaos and toxicity your whole life.

The only thing I can say that didn't leave, most of the time, is the childlike hope that it can't hurt like this forever. That on the other side of all this suffering comes a turnaround point where I no longer live in the haunting thoughts and the feeling that I don't matter enough. That I'd be better off not living anymore.

A bit of shuffling on the bed came from Mavryk. "Ann, are you awake?" Mavryk whispered.

"Yes," I managed to say back without sounding like I was choking back tears.

"Can I hold you? You don't have to turn around. You're welcome to tell me no too. I don't want you to feel like you have to do anything you don't want to."

Before I could think to respond, I turned around and buried myself into his chest. He lay on his back and wrapped his arms around me. I popped my leg onto his.

I wasn't sure how, but I felt wholesome and safe. The warmth of his body caused my mind to be still and in the moment. Everything about this felt wonderful and completely right. It didn't take long for me to realize how exhausted I truly was and drifted into sleep.

CHAPTER 10

I wasn't sure where I was or how I got here, but it was filled with an overwhelming darkness of despair. I had been defeated by something that left me with the familiar ache of hopelessness, that I wouldn't make it to tomorrow. I could feel myself fade into the nothingness that surrounded me. My heart was shutting out possibilities that true love exists, that I was loved at all. I was swallowed in my own sorrow.

From a distance, someone walked toward me. The light coming from their body glowed a royal blue. Something about their light brought mine to life, except mine was a glowing white, and the closer they got, the brighter I became, and so did they. I didn't know what this meant, but my heart began to beat a rhythm again, something unfamiliar but beautiful and wholesome.

Within inches, I could see the body form more clearly, and Mavryk's eyes met mine. I could sense his soul, as if it were mine. We belonged together. The powerful force of our energies was ready to collide and become one. I held my arm upward, and he extended the opposite arm in the same way. We started with our fingertips touching and finished with our elbows connecting. We leaned our foreheads together and then pressed the rest of our bodies as close as possible. Our souls intertwined for an everlasting love with an eternal destiny for greatness.

My eyes shot open. The smell of breakfast food filled the air. It reminded me of the times I stayed with my grandparents on my mother's side. The smell of coffee reminded me of my other grandparents on my father's side. I haven't seen any of them since my mother ran away. While the smell brought comfort and evoked good memories, it also brought an ache that I miss them all dearly.

I sat up and kept the blanket wrapped around me. Sasha seemed to be finishing the last bit of things and getting everything set at the table. Somehow, she had made the table almost twice its size, and what was once a window had now transformed into sliding glass doors. This allowed a lot of natural light to come in.

"How did you change this?" I asked, making a circular motion in the direction of the table and the glass doors.

She smiled and let out an amused laugh. "Magic, honey. That's how we're able to keep hidden from society. There's a shield that goes around the place that only certain people can see. It's called a protective shield." She paused, and realization came over her. "I have to wonder how you were able to see it." She looked at me. "Then again, if destiny calls you for it, nothing will get in the way of that. Except yourself, of course."

"So you're able to create magic?" I had read many books on it and heard things, but I never knew if any of it was ever true.

"Don't you think the glow is formed by magic?" she asked.

I thought for a minute before responding. "I do. It was nothing else I had experienced before. I have so many questions, but I don't know how to ask them. I feel like I don't know anything about what's actually going on with the world. That my life has been sheltered from the truth but exposed to—" I didn't know how to finish that last part.

Sasha put the last bit of food on the table and sat in a chair. "So much trauma. That's because it has. Your reality has been manipulated in a lot of ways. I can only imagine the confusion you're feeling right now."

Confusion isn't the only word I'd use, but that didn't matter. I needed information. "Could you possibly help me understand? About the magical stuff, I mean."

"Everything started with fairies," she began, causing my eyes to widen a bit. My expressions never hid what I felt very well. She showed an amused smile and continued explaining. "Before healers, drainers, and telepaths, there were fairies. Before that, there was the Sacred."

I shot my head up from fiddling with my fingers. "What's a Sacred?"

"The Sacred is the original one. He is the combination of a healer, drainer, telepath, and fairy. Five creations meant to live in separate parts. Didn't you ever wonder why there are five parts of the world?"

"Five? Don't you mean four?" I responded. She had mentioned something about Coastra yesterday, but I thought that might have been a building or an area, not another part of the world.

She looked at me, baffled. "You really have been sheltered." She sighed. "Okay, so this is going to be a lot of information. I'm going to explain what I can as best as I can. Do your best to follow and try not to ask anything until the end. It'll make more sense that way."

As difficult as that was going to be, I knew I needed to sit back and just take in the information she was going to give me. Before she started to talk again, both Mavryk and Steven walked in. Seeing Mavryk reminded me of the dream I had.

"Whew, baby! The food smells delicious!" Steven came up and kissed Sasha on the lips.

They smiled with a love in their eyes you don't see from most couples. It makes me happy to see that two good people found their way to each other.

"We went for a hike this morning." Mavryk spoke while looking at me. "I wanted to tell you, but I didn't want to wake you up."

"Had a pretty good chat about you too. I'll let him tell the details of that later."

Steven then did a finger-gun point with a funny facial expression and sat in the chairs next to Sasha and the empty one next to me. Sasha shook her head, while Mavryk gave him a look that said to shut up. I had to hold back a laugh because his mannerisms were so goofy, and a moment like this is comical.

Mavryk sat in the empty chair. "This looks amazing, Sasha. I don't doubt it'll be just as good as it looks."

She smiled. "You know how I am about my cooking." She got up and grabbed plates and silverware, handing each of us our own. "Please feast away!"

She made a gesture that showed she was really proud of her finished work. I couldn't blame her; it really did look that good. It smelled even better.

"Yes, thank you, Sasha. I appreciate you making all of this and feeding us. I need to work on offering to help out next time."

She waved a hand in my direction. "No need. I prefer no one being in my way."

I understand that. Being set on doing things yourself, in a particular way, can be more of a frustration than anything when someone wants to disrupt that, even if it is to help.

Everyone made their plates. Mavryk and Steven were scarfing down their food. Sasha had her plate made, but she wasn't eating. She seemed lost in thought. I took a couple of bites to not seem rude or to rush her, but I was eager to know more about everything I'd been withheld from.

I cleared my throat a few times. "Sasha, the food is seriously delightful. I must ask, though, could we possibly go back to the subject we were discussing before?"

She looked at me. Her eyes were filled with sadness. "I will."

I had the feeling she had seen something else, but it was clear how she didn't want to speak about it.

Mavryk stopped eating and looked between us. "What did we miss this morning?"

We both disregarded the question, and Sasha spoke. "The Sacred is the original ruler of the world. He had the powers of a drainer, a healer, a telepath, and a fairy." This caused Steven to stop eating and interrupt her.

"Babe, where's this coming from?"

She glared at him. "She doesn't know, and she needs to know. For me to tell her everything she needs to be caught up on, I need to be able to tell her what I know. I would appreciate it if everyone let me speak without interruption."

He sat back. "Of course, baby." He then grabbed her hand and kissed it multiple times in an apologetic manner. "Please proceed."

Her glare relaxed, and she squeezed his hand as a sign of forgiveness. A smile danced on her lips as she looked at their hands together.

"As I was saying, he was all of them in one. Along with them came the five parts of the world: Scarland, Egyptstra, Landomal, Outcastril, and Coastra. Each one was given to a specific magical entity for a specific reason."

She got up from the table and went to her bedroom. The anxiousness I felt grew more tense with every second she didn't come back to finish explaining. What felt like forever was only a few minutes, though. She moved her plate out of the way toward Steven and rolled out a map.

The map had been clearly drawn out. Not that it was bad in the slightest, but you could tell the difference between a map made in print in comparison to the ink. Whoever had made this had put a lot more detail into it than any map I had ever seen. It even included Coastra.

On it, the usual four you would see were displayed. It wasn't a particular shape, since the edges of the land weren't straight or curved in one direction. All but Coastra were clumped together with a river of water to separate where they ended on their territory. Scarland started on the top left side with Outcastril on its right. Below Scarland stood Egyptstra, with Landomal next to it, which made Landomal below Outcastril. In the top right corner, closest to Outcastril but not as close as the others, a little circle had Coastra written in it with an arrow pointing upward.

I pointed to Coastra and looked at Sasha. "Does this mean it's further than expected?" I felt it was dumb to ask, but I wanted to be clear on what I was looking at.

"It's an estimation. Mavryk is the one who drew this," Sasha replied.

I looked at Mavryk. "I'm an escaper." He spoke before I asked. "I've not been there myself, but I've seen the island a few times from a good distance while on a boat. We can only go so close before Coastra drains us."

"We?" I asked.

"Drainers," he replied, then went into a bit more depth. "Only healers can walk on the island. Something about its magic is specific to protect healers from drainers. Even going too close to it will start sucking life from us. Give it a day, maybe two, on the island, and you'll be dead."

"Isn't that enough time for anyone to go there and start killing them off?" I asked.

He looked at me. "They tried that years ago. A drainer who kills a healer dies themselves, that's to say if they're even capable by that point."

"They don't teach about Coastra for this reason. The less everyone knows of its existence, the fewer healers protected. It makes it easier to hide the fact that it's real when it's not connected the way the rest of them are," Steven chimed in.

"This is also why it's easy to convince everyone that healers are meant to be placed in Outcastril if they do not abide by the rules," Mavryk said.

My face must've given away how that comment confused me, so Sasha spoke. "To get back to what I was saying, each part of the world is meant for each of us. Fairies are designed for Landomal, telepaths are meant to be in Egyptstra, drainers are supposed to only rule over Scarland, and healers be kept safe on Coastra."

"Does that mean Outcastril was for the Sacred?" I asked.

"No one really knows the purpose of Outcastril. It became a place it wasn't meant for because one ruler decided it's fit to keep fear alive. There's less of a threat that a rebellious act happens from the rest of us who don't agree," Sasha replied.

We all sat there for a moment, then Mavryk spoke. "I think there's something else meant for it. Something we don't know about." Oddly enough, I had just been thinking the same thing.

"What else do you think is out there?" Steven asked.

"Not a clue," Mavryk replied, then looked up from staring at the ground to look out the glass door. "I don't believe someone as powerful as the Sacred, who possessed all forms of magic, would be fit for just one place. The Sacred hasn't been here for hundreds of years to rule over a place either. That's not mentioning how he's the only one who's ever possessed such powers. How is it there are multiple of the rest but only one of him?"

"The Sacred was meant to be the real ruler. We're meant to be where he placed us," I interjected. I didn't usually speak out about ideas I had, but even if I was wrong, I knew they'd consider what I said instead of making snarky remarks and making me feel foolish for thinking the way I did.

"It's just a thought, but what if Mavryk's right? What if there is something else out there waiting to be discovered? Maybe it's not even created yet because the world's not ready for what the other magic force has to offer. Maybe they aren't ready themselves." For some reason, that last part made it feel personal. Mavryk's face said he felt the same.

"Go back to the part about the Sacred." Sasha looked intrigued. "My grandmother used to say the same thing about him being the true ruler. What's making you say the same?"

I looked around for a minute, gathering my thoughts while moving my thumbs across my fingers. "As you and Mavryk stated, the Sacred possessed all the powers. That would mean he knew us the best. It's possible he created the world, and that's how he knew which place suits us best. While he's not here, we know of him and everything he's done, we have an idea of how capable he is. I can't imagine someone as powerful as him, who designed things the way he did, would do it for a bad reason. I imagine there's a really good one for it, and we are meant to follow along with that." I paused for a moment, then it dawned on me.

"This is probably why the world is as chaotic and broken as it is. Too many people are in the wrong part of the world, not living in their purpose and letting a few individuals decide what is best for the rest of us." I looked up at each of them. "The Sacred created us as we are for a reason and designed all of us for a certain purpose so the world can live in a peaceful place."

"More than likely, when the Sacred died, things started to change off course. The world's gotten worse as time's gone because the truth is forgotten and lied about. Therefore, leaving people not to live in their purpose." Mavryk's face looked as if he had discovered some kind of cheat code he couldn't piece together before.

"Well, shoot, you guys." Steven did a snort kind of laugh. "If that's true, that's wild, but what are the odds of any of that? I mean, drainer soldiers are always on the hunt to find new magic forces, and it's not like they don't keep track of everyone. They make sure there's nothing new getting by them."

"Explain to me how I so easily escaped the castle then." I understood where he was coming from. It was bizarre, to say the least, but with everything in me, I could feel I was not wrong—at least to some degree.

Steven's eyes got wide. "The ruler's castle. You escaped from there?" His voice sounded as shocked as his face expressed.

"A few times, yes, but this time was in a much different way." I paused, then added, "I was being made to marry the ruler."

The thought of that made me cringe. To be trapped with someone who made you feel so awful would have meant being miserable until death came.

"Sasha can catch you up on all of that later. My point is it's a miracle I am here. That I'm here with all of you, finding out so much I would have never known by anyone else I'd been around before." I took a deep breath in and ran my fingers through my hair to self-soothe in a way.

"The glow happened for a reason. It led me to Mavryk for a reason. I'm learning all of this for a reason. Why is it out of the question that the Sacred wouldn't hide another being until the time he knows they need to be exposed?"

"So what's the reasoning? What's the point behind creating all of this, all of us, if it just led to what it is now?" Steven asked.

I couldn't think of a response. Thankfully, Mavryk did. "I don't believe we're going to have all the answers all the time, if at all. Maybe we're supposed to listen within and know what feels right or wrong. Intuition is a very powerful and useful thing."

"You'll always have what you need in the time frame you need it." Sasha spoke. "I'm never shown a vision without its purpose. The reasoning always comes in time of why. Even if it's many years later, it pieces together eventually."

CHAPTER 11

The rest of breakfast we ate with small talks of hiking and how sleeping went. After we all finished eating, Sasha started putting the food away while Steven mentioned to put the dishes in the sink so he could wash them. Mavryk and I put the dishes in the sink and cleaned up the table.

I tried to engage in the conversation, but my mind kept wandering back to the conversation before about the Sacred, the five parts of the world, the fact that there was more than just healers and drainers among us.

Telepaths were something I understood enough, something Mavryk explained pretty well. I haven't developed much understanding of fairies and what they consisted of or what they were capable of.

"What is it that fairies do?" Everyone stopped what they were doing and looked at me and then at one another. They went back to what they were doing. I stood there waiting for a reply.

"They create the main source of magic. The protective shields and openings. Anything to make a change or create something. That sort of magic exists because of fairies," Sasha finally responded.

"Is an opening the glow, like the one I experienced?" I asked.

"No. An opening is something they can use to travel with, but it's also what breaks a protective shield. Fairies cannot create glows, and the difference between them is their color." Sasha took a moment before speaking. "It's been told that the glow is already planned for a certain reason, for a certain timeframe. It's an extremely rare entity created by the Sacred, he is the only one who can create them."

Sasha looked at me and stopped what she was doing. "My grandmother used to say he knew the way the world would go and placed the glows where they are so the world had a chance to survive. The people who experience the glow are the change the world needs, and so are the ones whose paths they come across."

"Looks like you'll be saving the world, and ol' Mavryk gets dragged into it." Steven had a smirk on his face as he spoke, while they both snickered after he said it.

I had a hard time believing I was destined to save the world when I could hardly handle myself. I hadn't worked on my powers in a long time either. I felt drained and exhausted all the time because my mind didn't stop racing. It was always worse when I went so many days without writing.

The emotions and negativity built up until I couldn't take it anymore, which usually left me lashing out in some way or breaking down when I was around certain people. Someone as broken and as lost as I was had no real chance of saving one person, let alone multiple. The world is out of the question. It's not possible.

"I'm going to step outside. Get some fresh air," I said out loud, then walked out.

The sun shined brightly again. It felt amazing to be able to do something I used to have to beg to do. A sharp ping shot across my chest—not in a physical way but like the empty ache you feel when the world crumbles around you. The thought of ever having to go back to being trapped like I had when I was finally tasting freedom again seemed unbearable. I couldn't go back there. I wouldn't survive it again.

I looked around. The earth felt still, and the air was warm. The way the trees surrounded the area, with fresh fruits and vegetation, seemed like the perfect way to live. What a simple and blissful life they had. I didn't envy them for having what they deserved, but I couldn't help but wish my life to be as peaceful as theirs.

I went to sit at the edge of where their land ended and where the forest began. I couldn't see anything besides trees. I had a feeling I would be traveling again but actually hiking in it this time. I usually saw myself by myself, but I couldn't get the thought of Mavryk by my side out of my head.

"Mind if I sit with you?" Mavryk's voice made me turn my head toward him as I jumped. He let out a chuckle. "Sorry, didn't mean to scare you."

I turned my head back toward the forest. "I'm usually more on guard and recognize when someone's coming up on me. I seem to be lost in a lot of thought."

He lay on his side next to me, his eyes still on me as he spoke. "I'm sure there's a lot of reason for it. You know what I like to do when I'm spiraling in my head?"

I slightly turned my head toward him without my eyes leaving the forest. "I like to think of music. I tend to sing too," he said.

A small smile escaped my lips. "There are record players out there, but I always thought it would be neat if we made something to carry around easier so we could listen to music anywhere we wanted." I looked at him, and my smile grew wider.

His expression showed an amused look on his face. "Maybe we can find someone to invent that." His eyes met mine. "You've probably been told this more than a handful of times, but you're quite the catch. Any man would be lucky to have you."

I quickly pulled my gaze from his and stared at the ground while my eyes began to tear up. The genuine tone in his voice made it more difficult to hold them back from falling.

"You hardly know me." I spoke softly. I didn't know how anyone could when I didn't know who I was.

His head turned away from me and toward the forest. "I believe I was wrong. Not too many have told you what you're worth. I doubt they've treated you any better." I looked at him and saw the sadness written all over his face.

"It hurts to know you've been through so much, that you think so little of yourself. I think within time, as you find yourself, you'll come to realize just how valuable you really are. Being around people who aren't trying to dim your light will help tremendously with that."

"I think no matter how much people build me up, I'm going to have to still learn my worth for myself. When you don't, you cling to others in a way you shouldn't."

I looked toward the forest. This made me think back to when I first discovered my emotional codependency with my mother. She was also the only woman I'd let myself look up to. You combine those together, and you really don't have a clue what to do with yourself once they're gone. You have no clue how to be you, and you realize you were never meant to clone another's identity.

"My mother loved me more than anything. She truly did her best, and with what she knew, that says a lot. I looked up to her. She wasn't like anyone else, she was so incredible, but she never saw it for herself. If she had, I can only imagine what more she could have done for herself. I even believe she could have helped save the world a little, but she never reached her potential. She never knew her whole value."

I adjusted myself to hold my legs, resting my head on my knees. "Watching her not be loved properly, not loving herself properly, and accepting far less than she deserved taught me to do the same. And when she died, I became lost and felt I wasn't worthy of that love again. She gave me all the love she had but never showed me how to truly love myself and that I shouldn't sacrifice my well-being for those I love. She told me that I need to love myself, that I deserve to be happy. She tried to show me how, but she never truly learned how herself."

Mavryk grabbed my hand closest to him and gave it a light squeeze. "She would be very proud of you."

"I should have realized it wasn't on her for me to know who I am, but I think I expected that from her. I expected her to do more than she could."

The tears left my eyes and traveled down my face. "The last thing she said to me before she died was how proud of me she was. She said I was the strongest and most beautiful person she knew. I wish I would have told her that back. It's not like she didn't try her best, she did. I shouldn't have been so hard on her that night."

I couldn't control the tears or how heavy everything felt. Mavryk scooted to wrap his arms around me, holding me close. I was not sure how comfortable I felt being vulnerable like this, but I couldn't hold it in anymore. I could only hope I was being held by him with the intent to be leaned on without any reason except that he cared to let me release what had been eating me alive.

After a while, the crying stopped. I usually felt numb afterward, but for once, I actually felt some of the pain release. I felt lighter. The world didn't seem to be spinning fast or caved in. There was a bit of peace right here where I was.

"Ann. I want to suggest something." I looked up to see his chin and realized my head had sunk into his chest. "Try to realize that you had your reasons for feeling like you did and that you were valid to feel what you did. It's okay to say you loved and admired someone for their beauty while saying their mistakes caused you harm."

The words hit me like a force as he took a pause before speaking again. "I also want to help you so you can finally start living. I want to take you away so you never have to worry about being somewhere you don't want to be."

"I'd rather die than to ever go back to any of that, but he'll search until he finds me," I said sharply, and then my voice changed to a sad tone. "I don't know how I'm supposed to hide forever. I don't want to have to either."

He put his hand on my hair and started stroking it. "I know, love. Let me help you get to Coastra."

"Don't play with me right now."

"I'm very serious, Ann. I'm an escaper. I take healers to Coastra so they can be free. You're in more need than anyone to get there. I've never failed at the job either. I can take you."

"You've never helped someone who's escaped from the castle either. They're going to have so many looking for me it'll be impossible to keep hidden until we make it there. Most of the guards have handled me at least a handful of times too. They won't second-guess on spotting me."

"Not unless something about your appearance changes." He helped me to stand up. "Come on. We're going to go see if Sasha can help us dye your hair."

I took his hand and stood up, moving my hand from his to wipe the grass off. When I looked up at him, he was smiling. I smiled awkwardly back. "What color are you thinking?" I asked.

"I think you'd be beautiful bald, but it's not what I think that matters. You should go with what makes you feel better about yourself." He turned toward the cottage and started walking. I followed behind him.

I thought back to the dream I had years ago where I had dark-blue hair. I loved it, but that would stand out in a world where no one had unnatural hair colors, not sure how that could possibly be made. I supposed a fairy could do it.

We walked through the door. Steven and Sasha were sitting at the table, looking like they had been in a deep discussion.

"Sasha, how do you feel about dyeing some hair?" Mavryk had a smirk with a bit of spunk to it.

Her eyebrows raised a bit, and she made a face that said she was interested. "Well, I only have black, but I'm not sure it'd be fitting for you."

He laughed. "I'd shave my head before I'd dye my hair." He threw his arm back with his thumb pointing at me. "We're going to dye her hair."

I could feel myself make a face that said this would look terrible. "Black won't suit me. I'm fairly pale for that."

Sasha waved her hand at me. "Nonsense. You have too pretty of a face to look awful in anything." She then looked intrigued and walked up to me. "Let me see your eyes."

I felt my face blush a little. Eye contact wasn't my strong suit; as a matter of fact, it made me uncomfortable, but I trusted her to have a reason. I lifted my eyes to look at hers.

"You have gorgeous eyes," she said kindly, with a kind smile to match.

"The sea could drown in the beauty they hold." Mavryk spoke. I looked at him, and he had been staring at me with eyes that danced with something I'd never seen before.

"Yeah, no offense, but I'm not going to give you a compliment like these weirdos." We all laughed at Steven's comment.

"No one asked you, anyways." Sasha looked at him with a playful smile and went to sit in the spot she was in before. "Your eyes will stick out more with darker hair, but it's your choice."

76

I looked around the room, pondering. There was no going back once I did this. Then again, what was there to really lose? If I looked worse, then that meant fewer people would pay attention to me, which meant I was less likely to be recognized. If I looked better, I might possibly feel better about myself.

I took a deep breath in and then spoke. "Let's do it."

Sasha shot up. "Oh my gosh, yes!" She clapped her fingers together a few times and had the biggest smile on her face. "I'm assuming your hair is virgin hair, which will make the process so much easier!"

She zoomed into the bathroom and came out with a couple of bottles, a small and thin brush I'd never seen before, and a plastic bowl that had a handle to it. She had a towel and a hair cap as well. She set them all on the table.

"So listen," Sasha started, "I forgot about the dark chestnut brown I made a while ago. I really feel like this will fit you, but it is your choice if you prefer to go with the black."

She held up both bottles that had a small circle painted on them of the colors she made, and I knew looking at them that chestnut would be the better pick. I nodded with a light smile and told her I agreed that the chestnut was a great idea.

Her enthusiasm made me excited with her. At least she would enjoy the process. It wasn't a bad thing to be more excited about what could turn out well than to be nervous that it turns out disastrous. I had already weighed out the worst outcome. My looks were the least of my problems right now, but the nice thing was, she had options, and one of them seemed like a decent idea.

She moved the chair out from the table and motioned for me to come sit in it. Once I sat in it, she wrapped the towel around my neck. "This is to make sure there's no chance of the dye getting on your clothes."

I nodded my head and awkwardly smiled. I couldn't see what she was doing, but I could hear her messing with the stuff she had set on the table.

"So once I have this mixed together, I'll start the process of putting the dye on your hair." She stopped what she was doing and put her hand through my hair. "You have beautiful hair. The texture is one of the healthiest and softest I've ever felt!"

She began the process of dyeing, and when she finished, she put the cap over my hair. "We'll let this sit on your head for thirty minutes, then—"

She suddenly stopped speaking. I looked up at Mavryk; he looked focused. Steven's expression showed the same. Steven glanced at me and then back at Sasha. He threw up his hand in a shush motion and pointed at his eyes.

I slowly turned around to look at Sasha. Her being frozen didn't worry me as much as her facial expression did. She looked upset. Her eyes began to fill with tears as she blinked. "They're searching for you." She then looked at me. "You have to leave once we finish the process."

Before I could bring anything up, Mavryk mentioned taking me to Coastra. Sasha began to protest, and then she stopped. "Yes." She crossed her arms as if she were trying to comfort herself. "Ann must go. It is part of the process."

I wanted to ask what that meant, but she went back to cleaning up and seemed lost in thought. Then she stopped.

"Excuse me, I need a moment." Sasha hurried to her room and shut the door. Steven took a deep breath and then got up and joined her.

I looked at Mavryk, and he looked back at me. "She had another vision."

"I caught that much, but of what? What could she have seen?" I asked.

"Sometimes it's best not to know what the future holds. That can cause more problems because we end up making worse decisions than what we must do." His eyes conveyed a story, one he experienced with tremendous pain.

The rest of the wait was in silence. When she came out of the room, she looked as if she had been crying; Steven appeared sad himself. I wanted to know what she saw, but I had already been warned it was better not to know.

Sasha didn't say much except what was necessary, so I knew what steps to follow next. We walked to the bathroom. After she washed my hair from the tub, she handed me a different towel, and I wrapped my head in it.

"You can brush through it anytime you'd like and come out when you're ready. We'll give you time to process the change. It's weird at first, but I believe you'll grow to love it," she said with a smile and then walked out and shut the door.

Looking at myself in the mirror, I noticed the tiny bit sticking out at the top of my head. I grew anxious to see but decided to brush through it before looking. I turned around, unwrapped the towel, hung it on the rack, grabbed the brush, and started brushing.

Turning back to the mirror, I couldn't believe what I was seeing. I felt as if I was staring at a whole new person, one I had never met before. Sasha was right—the darker shade did make my eyes stand out more. I decided on one more change: I'd always parted my hair to favor one side significantly, but now I tried parting it down the middle.

I was not sure how I liked it on myself yet, but I knew this change was needed a while ago. Some of the old me changed so the new could come through, embracing the next part of the journey I was on, not just with life but within myself.

CHAPTER 12

Before we left, Sasha gave me a satchel. It wasn't heavy, but you could tell she put a couple of different things in there. I wanted to see what was inside, but she insisted we not waste any time heading out. Mavryk was given a backpack with food and two water bottles. According to Steven, you can put the dirtiest water in them, and it will clean the water to make it drinkable. You can even put ocean water in them, and it will become drinkable.

"How is it Sasha and Steven seem to have all these magical things but can't produce them themselves?" Mavryk must've been lost in thought, too, because he jerked his head up a little by my question.

"What do you mean?" he asked.

"They have a protective shield around their place, they have the water bottles that turn any water drinkable. That's only two things from what I've noticed, but still, I thought fairies are the only ones who can produce magic."

He stopped and looked at me. "That's a good eye for detail," he said with a smile, then continued walking. "It's not my place to give away their secrets, but I know it'll bother you not to know." He paused for a moment before speaking again. "A fairy came to her in a time of need when she was close to death. The fairy put a shield around her until she arrived at Steven's. As he put it, he immediately fell in love. Sasha was hesitant at first but warmed up to him, telling him the truth about everything. He said he couldn't bear the thought of losing her or letting her suffer any more, so he offered to build a life with her where they couldn't be found, where she would be protected. This was when the fairy exposed themselves to Steven and agreed where they built their life together. The fairy then would put a protective shield around the land, along with making sure the vegetation and fruit trees would never go ill."

"What almost killed Sasha?" The stories I read about fairies, ones I thought were made up, only appeared to those with a great purpose and came in desperate times to help, much like a glow leading you to your destiny.

"Sasha was held captive. They were testing on her and others. Their excuse was to understand telepaths better, to make sure they aren't a threat to society because of their rarity in existence." He shook his head in disgust. "Sasha doesn't talk about the horrors they put her, through, but anyone who's been tested on isn't ever for a good reason. If you ask me, they wanted to use her. Steven himself couldn't tell what they had done, but I could tell by his reaction that it made him sick to his stomach to even think about it."

"That's awful." I didn't know what else to say. I couldn't feel the pain of what she had gone through, but I knew what it was like to feel trapped and used. I knew what it felt like to wonder how it's possible to escape. I could relate in a different way and knew from my experience how hard that was. I wondered if that was why she broke down so hard. She knew, in a way, what the torture was like.

From a distance, I could hear music. At first, I thought it was playing in my head, but as we continued walking, the music got louder and very familiar. I just couldn't figure out why. I looked over at Mavryk and noticed he had a genuinely happy, excited smile dancing on his lips. Ahead of us, you could see the end of the forest growing closer.

"You ever been to a highland game?" he asked playfully. The way he looked suggested it put him in a playful mood too.

The word highland brought me back. "I knew I recognized the music. My grandparents on my mother's side used to go to it every year. Usually, multiple times if they could. I would get to go once a year myself before the runaway."

"It must've been really hard to leave everyone behind." Mavryk gave a bit of sympathy as he spoke.

"I was very angry at first with my mother, especially since there was no warning, but as time went on, I did understand why and even became grateful. I missed everyone greatly, and we struggled in ways no one should have to, but any path she would have taken would have been very difficult. She was never given an easy life, and she did her best with what she had and with what she knew. Besides, it wasn't all bad. There were some amazing moments that I had with her that I never could have with anyone else. I'll cherish those forever." Her smile always played in my head when I talked about her. It lit up a room when the room had no light.

Before he got a chance to say anything, we approached the end of the forest, and there displayed the festival. We stopped to observe it. The music played lively with drums, bagpipes, fiddles, guitars, and wonderful voices. Tents of all different shapes, sizes, and decorations spread throughout the land that sold different objects such as jewelry, swords, clothing, along with so many other things. You could smell the tasty aroma of the food as well.

"The festival seems huge." It went on for a while. You didn't see any forest on the opposite side of us, but there was a steep hill that had rocks and what looked like moss.

"It's the biggest festival of the year. Aside from the annual gathering at the castle, you won't see this many people in one area or this much excitement going on," Mavryk responded.

"I promise you the festival is a lot livelier than the annual gathering," I said dryly.

We looked at each other. "It must've been a nightmare for you when you weren't given a choice." He spoke softly.

I looked down at the ground. "One I thought I'd never wake up from." I tried to keep the same dry tone, but it came out more depressing than I intended.

Mavryk took his hand and placed it on my cheek on the side that had less hair.

I turned my head away from him and toward the festival. Eye contact would be too much vulnerability for me to handle right now, risking another kiss and losing focus on what needed to be done. There was always the possibility that a kiss would jump us further like the other two did, but I wanted to explore this. If this would be my last festival, I wanted to soak it in and remember the good that I grew up with. I wanted to make one last memory count.

"We should keep moving." I sounded emotionless.

His hand slowly moved from my face and onto his side. I started walking forward, and then he grabbed my wrist, causing rage to build up pretty quickly. When I turned to look at him, I saw sadness fill his eyes. My rage turned into guilt. Had I hurt him by rejecting the affection he was hoping to receive? I knew too well how harshly that stung.

"I'm sorry if I'm hurting you. That's not my intention." I wish he knew how hard it was to resist him and how much I felt the need to keep some of what I felt contained at the same time.

"I know what it's like to protect yourself from more disappointment and heartache. That's not what bothers me." I felt my eyebrows furrow together. He pulled me in until his arms were around me and his lips nearly touched my forehead. What he whispered next took me by surprise.

"It hurts me that you've been through so much, yet you inspire me because you see the beauty when your mind doesn't let you see yours. You keep hope alive even when you feel like dying. I've never met a stronger soul." He then gently kissed my forehead.

I didn't have words. I leaned into his chest and rested my head. For a while, we stood like that. His breathing and heartbeat drowned out everything else. That was until I heard something undeniably familiar, something that tugged at my heart.

I lifted my head away from his chest and moved my body away from his. I then looked at him, and he looked back at me. "I have to go to it."

Before he could say anything else, I took off. I did my best not to push anyone or run like a maniac, but I knew that song better than any other. There wasn't any singing, but the instruments played a tune I had known since I was little. The melody had given me one of the greatest memories I had tucked so far away in my mind that I had forgotten it existed. One that made my heartbeat quicken as I raced to try and catch whoever was playing the song at the moment. Sometimes all we have are moments that keep us feeling alive again.

As I reached the spot where they were playing, other people had already surrounded them. I squeezed around everyone until I got to the front. The song was about halfway over, but I at least could embrace the rest of it. The dark wooded deck had a huge bush behind it, and while there wasn't much decoration, the scene seemed to fit it perfectly. Almost perfectly.

Every movement from the violin gave me chills. The song never failed to bring me comfort I couldn't have with any other song, and yet it brought extreme sadness, a reminder that I had been blessed not only to have had such a beautiful memory but such an amazing individual to share it with.

You never stop missing the person you create those memories with; that's what makes it sad. That's what makes your heart hurt and what causes you to cling onto anything that gives you a moment back in time. To keep the memory of them alive because a goodbye is that impossible to swallow.

As the ending of the song came, I felt tears roll down my eyes. I began to walk out from the crowd when a hand grabbed mine. I looked up to see Mavryk, and as our eyes met, he began to walk out of the crowd while still holding my hand. Once we got to a distance from everyone and in an area a bit less secluded, he stopped us.

"That song has meaning to me too. I want to share mine with you." His hands intertwined with mine, and I could feel the vibration of something deep sync us together. "Years ago, I contemplated killing myself. I was at another festival, much smaller than this, but something about it came to life when that song started playing. Something bigger than I could comprehend at the time."

He looked away as if the memory was playing out in his head. His eyes swelled with tears. "I couldn't tell you why, but that song saved my life that night. I was in the darkest battle with myself, and yet that song spoke to me in a way I never knew why. Not until now."

He looked back at me and placed his hand on my cheek. I saw his eyes dancing with so many emotions; I could have sworn what danced the most was a passion for something not of this world. How intense the emotions must be when your eyes can't hold back what is felt. Still, I wondered where his mind wandered to.

He slid his hand from my cheek to behind my neck and pulled my face in until our lips touched, while his other hand ended up on the other side of my head, tangled in my hair. I slid my hands across his arms, feeling the warmth of his skin. Then he slid his hands to my upper back, while one moved to my lower back and pulled me in closer. I melted into his body, and every single thing that troubled me no longer became a problem. I hadn't a clue what was going on around me except magic filled the air, followed by an electric feeling that traveled to the most precious parts of my heart that this was where I belonged.

As we pulled away, I felt the urge to pull him back in for more, but we both knew we couldn't lose our focus too much. I'd be lying if I said I hadn't forgotten for the moment we were in a place filled with people, possibly looking for me. I pulled apart from him and decided I'd share the meaning behind the song. It wasn't typical of me to share, but it was a good change of direction that we needed to get back to focusing. Regardless of what we felt, time would have us be apart as I stepped onto Coastra. If I even made it there.

"I've never been the type to dance, but my mom had always loved it. When I was thirteen, we met this group of what she considered musical geniuses that ran away like us. Mom decided it'd be fitting for us to travel with them for a short time. One day, they decided to play that song and called it 'Glycerine.' I'll never forget how Mom's face lit up as she told me that this is our song because it was the first one I had danced with her. I wish I could remember that moment, but seeing her talk about it gave me just as much joy. I should have danced with her every time she asked. Looking back, I'm not sure what held me back, or why I still hesitate from dancing. I guess it's the reason I act on other impulses more freely than I used to."

"How old were you when you first danced?" he asked.

"I was six, from what she said." It surprised me I couldn't remember that, but I could other things at a younger age. Then again, trauma has a funny way of affecting your memory like that.

"There's a tent I need to stop at before we continue forward." He took a step and then stopped. "Anytime you want to talk about anything, I'll gladly listen. I don't say much back because I would rather listen to what you have to say than to ask what you might not want to speak about."

He continued forward, and as I followed him, I couldn't help but really appreciate his character. I had a lot of respect for someone as thoughtful as that. The little things are the much bigger things that are usually missed.

After walking for a bit, we came to this white tent. Most tents were a lot more open than this one, and this one seemed bigger in comparison to most.

"Are you getting something?" As I asked him, he stopped midway in the entrance and turned to look at me with a grin on his face.

"No, actually. I am getting you something though, so stay here. It'll be a surprise." Before I could protest, he turned and went in.

I thought about going in, anyway, but I decided against it. I put my hand to my side and realized I never went through the satchel Sasha gave me earlier. Across from me sat a bench. I walked over and took a seat. The satchel had a design I knew wasn't common on other bags, but I knew I'd seen the symbol somewhere.

I decided I wouldn't ponder and opened it. An instant smile spread across my face. A notebook, along with a handful of pencils and a pencil sharpener, were inside. I picked up the small bag that had been tied up and shook it. The noise sounded like coins. I untied it, and sure enough, there were coins. Not copper or silver but gold. Gold has the most value, and it got harder for people to get their hands on some.

If she were here, I'd hug her. More so for the notebook and pencil. I could get by with little money, more so than I could without writing. I tied the bag of coins back up and put it in the satchel. I grabbed the notebook and opened it. Sasha had written in it.

Ann,

Never stop writing. The next time I see you, I expect to have lots to read! Let it be your journey, your thoughts or that destined romance with Mavryk. Write every day like you're writing to me if you must.

Much love,
Sasha

P.S. Be mindful of everything. Mavryk will do his best to protect you, but the real power of protection relies within yourself.

CHAPTER 13

Sasha,

I'm not sure where to begin. I more than appreciate you giving me the satchel and what's in it. I can't promise I'll get to write daily, but I'll do my best. Anything to show my gratitude for everything you've done.

We made it to the annual festival. It's a breath of fresh air here. The music is lively, and the people seem to be too. I haven't tasted the food, but I'll get to now, thanks to you.

I'm sure it doesn't compare to your food, though. Speaking of music, a song played earlier that Mavryk and I both found meaningful. A song that changed our lives forever. It gave us memories to cling to for better days because we know moments of hope exist. Now it's meaningful in a way that we bonded more so than before. Music is very close to magic if there's enough feeling to go with it.

The sun is starting to set. The colors are different shades of pretty. Light and peaceful-looking. I can't remember the last time I felt calm like this, for the most part, that is. Even though I'm on the run to a place I have no idea if it'll be where I'm meant to stay, I'm grateful to not be where I was. I just wish I could feel relief that I'm truly free.

GLYCERINE

I'd continue writing, but Mavryk's out of the tent now, and we'll need to continue onward.

Much love,
Ann

I closed the notebook and slid it into the satchel along with the pencil. When I went to look up, I noticed a man by the tent entrance staring at me with a serious expression. When I looked at Mavryk, he had the same serious expression with a hint of worry.

As Mavryk approached me, he spoke softly. "We need to head out. There are undercover guards looking for you."

"Here?" I pointed at the ground. He nodded. "Are they the guards from the castle?"

"I believe so, but who knows? From my understanding, you are a top priority to find, so anyone could be looking. There's a nice reward for your return too."

"Sounds like it'd be easier for you to take me back," I said a bit too sharply. His expression showed he was bothered by that statement.

"Your value does not hold a price. Anyone who doesn't realize that is a fool," he said as quickly as the last words left my mouth.

He then combined his hands with mine and spoke in a soft, deep, soothing tone. "And anyone who did see your worth and still thought to mistreat you is an even bigger fool." He lifted my hands to his mouth and kissed them ever so sweetly. Even after he put them down, I could feel the shape of his lips on my hand.

I knew he meant what he said, but my head screamed no. If he knew some of the things I had done, who I had been, the thoughts I struggled with not to go back to who I was when bitterness filled my heart, he'd look at me differently.

On the other hand, deep down I meant well, even when my actions didn't express that. I wished the best for everyone. I just didn't want to be hurt anymore. I wanted people to stop misusing and mistreating my kindness as if it were some kind of weakness that they saw to take advantage of. I never wanted the misery to define me.

"Ann?" My eyes shot up to his, then looked around. "Are you okay?"

How could I explain that I was stuck between no but yes? "We should head out. I do need to pee before we continue, though."

"There's a bathroom building not far from here. I'll show you the way." I noticed the look of what seemed like him being upset cover his face. He began walking, and I followed next to him.

"What's troubling you?" I had a feeling it had something to do with me, but I wasn't sure where to pinpoint the exact problem.

To my surprise, he pulled a ring from his pocket. "I want to give this to you, but it might be hard for you to accept. I had to engrave it pretty quickly, so don't mind that it's not the prettiest." He handed me the ring.

It was a silver band with words engraved on it that said, "The sun rises knowing it is loved another day."

I didn't know what to say. I was truly taken aback for words. I had no clue he had a way with words or could carve anything, especially something so small in such a little time frame. He did a lot better than he realized because it looked like a professional did it. I put it on my middle finger, and it didn't fit. I then tried my ring finger, and it fit perfectly.

"What made you do this?" I asked. "This is so beautiful and unique."

"It fits you then." He spoke, then continued after a pause. "You are the sun. There is a light inside of you waiting to shine, but the days have been cloudy because of what's gone on in your world. I believe once you rest enough around the right people, you'll come to shine again."

"How do I even respond to that?" I whispered while tears filled my eyes.

He gently slid his hand into mine. "By letting me love you," he whispered back.

We came up to a small brick building. Opposite sides had an opening with signs above them that said male and female. I looked at him; he stared at the festival going on around us. I followed the direction of his eyes. Two older couples were sitting on a bench under a tree, staring deeply into each other's eyes. We couldn't hear the conversation, but it didn't matter. You could tell that they only existed to each other right now.

I looked back at Mavryk, and our eyes met. "Love can be a beautiful thing when you decide to take a chance." His voice was lower and deeper than usual. The way he spoke played in my heart like a harp.

I went into the bathroom. There were three stalls and two sinks with mirrors well past their prime. You could hardly see your reflection, let alone the details of yourself. The toilets weren't in the greatest of shape either. Not that I was surprised. Anyone who was not connected to the kings or Venon didn't have the nicest of things. It always made me sad. Why did we deserve anything less than them? Why were we treated as less?

As I came back out, instant panic hit me. Mavryk stood there talking to one of the guards that not only lived in the castle but regularly handled me, Rohn. Every time I tried to escape, he was the one to throw me back in my room. Seeing him took me to a state of being paralyzed. Wait, did Mavryk set me up? Had he told them who I am?

The terror that crawled through me felt beyond sickening, but before I could think to hide back into the bathroom, Rohn spotted me. I immediately looked down at the ground. My heart was trying to pound out of my chest. I couldn't go back—there was no way, especially not back to Venon. I couldn't go back to being stuck in that room, drowning in the agonizing place that I was trapped in, being manipulated and shamed and made to feel that I was out of my mind.

"Shelly, you wouldn't know anything about a missing bride, would you?" Mavryk's voice was more perked up than before. I looked at him, and his eyes told me to play along. I gave a sly smile.

"No. Not at all." Relief came over me, but so did a bit of guilt. I couldn't let my mind go in that direction right now, though. I needed to focus.

As I approached them, I could feel the tension oozing out of them, which made it intensify with me even more. I looked up at

Rohn and then quickly away. He had to know what my features looked like and my body size.

Mavryk cleared his throat and then spoke with the same perkiness he had before. "As you can see, no bride here, so we'll be on our way."

"Hold on." Rohn's voice was harsh and stern. "You look familiar."

He stepped in front of me, and instantly I felt the frustration build up. I wanted to bolt, but that wouldn't do anything except be a dead giveaway. I needed to get clever and convince him of being someone different.

I shot my head up and gave the fakest, friendliest smile I was able to manage, with my voice a lot more perked up. I almost sounded flirty. "I come here every year! I wouldn't doubt you've seen me before! I just love the festival, don't you?!"

His overbearing seriousness didn't budge. His face was smug. His lips pressed tightly together, and his eyes showed so much hatred for the world. Anything else he could have possibly felt burned a long time ago.

So many misunderstand that emotions never die; they think they can be buried and magically vanish, but that's when the weight becomes too heavy to hold. Then anger and misery consume you, leaving you cold-hearted and hopeless. You're practically a walking corpse waiting to die. They willingly hurt anyone they can just to feel less alone in their agony. They can't be happy for someone else when they lost a part of themselves. People like that can't stand you when you cling to hope like an innocent child.

"I can't waste my time attending events," he said, his gaze shifting between both of us before settling on me, studying every part of my body. "I'm looking for a girl your height, your weight. She looks identical to you in every way except your hair. Yours is dark." With each sentence, he took a step closer to me. The feeling was beyond uncomfortable; I felt as small as a helpless child facing an aggressive adult. Before I could think of a response, he spoke with a tone that oozed disgust, amusement hissing from his tongue. His gaze lingered on Mavryk until the last sentence. "The ruler doesn't want what's his to be away much longer. After all he's done for her, I can't begin to comprehend what it is she thinks is out here for her, anyway. A simple idiot, really."

I wanted to scream. I wanted to hurt him the way his words burned my ears. I wanted to cut his tongue out and watch the blood pour out, so he'd never speak those words again. I wanted to smash his brain in so he couldn't have a thought like that again. More than anything, I wanted to hurt Venon so badly, in a much harsher way than anyone had ever been tortured.

Suddenly, Rohn dropped to his knees, holding his head where the temples are, making a painful groaning noise. Then he stopped and looked at me with what seemed like shock and a bit of terror. His breathing was slightly panting. "My mistake to believe you could be her. She's a healer, you're clearly a drainer. A powerful one at that." His statement threw me off, and the anger vanished.

He looked at the ground and lowered his head as he said that and got up. "I'll keep this between us. The ruler would have your head for what you did, but it's urgent I find the bride."

Mavryk spoke in a monotone, but I knew he had to have been as shocked as I am. "We'll keep an eye out. What's her name? You said her looks are similar?" His eyes and body language showed readiness to fight.

"Identical. It's uncanny. The hair is what's different, and the fact that the bride's a healer while she's a drainer," he said, motioning toward me but not daring to look at me. "Her name's Ann. The reward is close to resembling what a king possesses. Let any one of us know if you hear or see anything."

He marched off before either of us could say anything. We both stood there in silence, unable to comprehend what had just happened, likely both of us unable to even come up with a thought as to what the possibilities could be. I've never been more confused.

"I suppose we should see about a blanket. It can get chilly at night," he said, his tone different from usual, doing everything he could to keep his composure steady.

"Sasha left gold coins in the satchel. A decent amount. We can buy two and a bag to carry them with us," I mentioned.

He pulled out the same bag as the one that held the coins from Sasha. "Steven gave me some as well. Except he gave me copper and silver." He chuckled to himself a little and put the bag back in his pocket. "They know me too well to trust that I won't make the gold last. I have a bad habit of spending carelessly."

He looked at me, his eyes calm, but his mind clearly elsewhere. "Draining him saved you."

"He handled me a lot back at the castle, unfortunately."

"Handled you?" he asked.

I kept my eyes forward, looking around the festival, taking in that this might be the last time I get to hear music so lively. "More often than not, when I would try to escape, he would be the one to lock me back up in the room." He looked disturbed. "I don't have an answer as to why I drained. I'd never done that before. I can imagine that concerns you."

He looked away in an almost disguised manner. "I'm shocked, sure. I've never heard of a healer being able to drain, but I knew when I laid my eyes on you that you're different. I knew you had a lot more about you than you have a clue about yourself. It's easier to swallow the fact that you're capable of something unique."

He paused, and his tone changed as he spoke the next part. "What I can't stomach is how poorly you've been treated. Regardless of your status in life, you don't go treating people in a way that makes them second-guess their worth. Especially someone like you."

"You don't know everything I've done."

Part of me didn't want him to know, but the other part wanted to tell him everything—from the trauma that nearly ruined me to the fact that I was still trying to understand who I really was and to never become the ugliest version of me again. The war I was facing within myself was to shed everything bad in me.

He took a deep breath in, then exhaled. He looked at me in a way that seemed dreamy but heavy with sadness. "I don't need to know every wrong move made in life, Ann." His hands slid to my cheeks, and our eyes met past our looks. "You have always and will always be worthy of the most incredible things life has to offer you."

I didn't get a chance to take in the power behind his statement. He pressed his lips against mine, and without a second thought, my mind left this world, and all that existed in the moment were two bodies that have always longed for each other's souls to be together again. A kiss that makes the stars shine forever in the night sky and the moon light up a darkened world.

CHAPTER 14

As I pulled away, I could feel my heart trying to beat out of my chest. This time, my body ached for so much more than the kissing we shared. I looked down and noticed his pulse on his neck beating faster than usual, his breathing slightly heavier. He touched his forehead to mine. I didn't realize we had been against the brick building until he placed his arms above my head and let the weight of his body be supported by that.

He slowly backed away, giving me more room, and as I looked at him, he looked at me. Then he looked toward the festival and smirked. "It always gets wild at night here."

I looked around. From a distance, you could see a bonfire. The music had gotten louder, and almost everyone had a drink or two in their hand. I didn't see any children.

"Indeed, the wild ones get to really live. At least in the way they know how to," I said.

He looked over at me with his eyebrows slightly furrowed together, but his lips asked with curiosity, "What's your idea of a wild night if not this?"

"Don't get me wrong, drinking with live music is a ton of fun, but nothing about it is truly fulfilling." I paused to gather my words. He crossed his arms, waiting for my response.

"I love the woods, and I love writing. I'd love to get lost in the forest and be content never being found as I write adventures that play out in my head. To get so lost in another world that I forget this one exists. At least until I look up and remember I'm living this life. It wouldn't be so hard living if that were my reality, though. Such a simple yet peaceful paradise that I wouldn't need an escape from."

I looked at him and then looked down, a bit embarrassed. "Sorry. I'm sure that sounds silly to you."

"No, it doesn't. It sounds amazing. Whoever made you feel like it's silly is—"

"There's not a chance your hair got that dark on its own." Our heads swung forward toward the men's side of the building.

Narcson. What were the chances of running into an old fling while with someone I was supposedly destined for? Of all people, this was almost as bad as running into Venon at this point. Talk about having a horrible taste in love affairs.

His grin exposed he was up to something. That wasn't out of the usual for him. Whatever to gain what he wanted from people. "It surprisingly makes you look better than before. What are the chances that darker is hotter on a healer?"

He walked toward me, and his side leaned against the building close to me. Mavryk took a step closer to me. I swear his eyes were trying to burn Narcson alive. Narcson didn't even glance his way. "I hear you're being looked for again. I'm surprised you attempted to escape after the last time. Fairly impressed, really." He looked me down and back up slowly. "You found a way out. Again."

"What is it you want, Narcson?" I crossed my arms tightly together, trying to contain myself from having an outburst.

You don't realize how much you hold against someone even after so much time has passed until you see them again. "Want to take me back? Just like last time, there's a nice reward involved." I could hear the anger as I spoke.

"You put up too much of a fight for me to want to do that again. Besides"—his grin faded and his expression showed regret—"I should have never done that to you. Believe it or not, there are a few things I'm not proud of."

"What is it you want then? Clearly, you want something, or you wouldn't have bothered saying anything." Mavryk's tone sounded harsher than mine. Narcson turned his head toward Mavryk, and the stare between the two of them looked as if they were about to fight to the death.

"I want to help her." Narcson finally spoke, his eyes shifting back onto me. "I promise you I won't betray you again. You have my word on that."

"Your words are only useful on someone you can manipulate. I'm no longer the dumb girl you once knew," I stated.

I started to walk away; I could tell Mavryk was following behind me. What Narcson said next stopped me in my tracks. "Venon is going to force a binding marriage on you when you're captured."

Mavryk moved so quickly that Narcson didn't have time to react, and neither did I. By the time I turned around, Mavryk had Narcson's neck held by the blade of a knife with one hand, and with his other hand, he held both of Narcson's wrists. "If you think for one second you're going to play your pathetic mind games on her while I'm around, I will not hesitate to kill you." He snarled the words through his teeth.

I stepped toward them both. They both stared at me, waiting to say something, but what could I say? It's one thing to be forced to marry, but a binding marriage meant misery in a way I could never escape. Then again, Narcson had lied to me many times before. "I know you don't want to believe me, and I don't blame you, but"—Mavryk pressed the knife tighter on his throat, and a trickle of blood slid down his neck—"I'm telling you the truth." You could hear fear in his voice and a rasp from the pressure placed on his neck.

I thought for a minute about whether I wanted to hear him speak any longer, but if he wasn't lying, then I needed to know everything he knew. I stepped inches away from him and glared into his eyes. I spoke in a low but very serious tone. "If you're lying, I will let him kill you." I moved my head away from his and looked at Mavryk, making sure to relax my look some. "Release him."

I saw the hesitation and struggle Mavryk battled within his mind to let him go, but when he finally did, Narcson dropped to his knees, rubbing his wrists. Then he lightly rubbed his neck. When he touched the cut, he looked at his hand and stared at the blood.

"You've come a long way from the girl I once knew." He looked at me somewhat amused, but fear still stirred in his eyes. "I won't dare cross you again."

He stood up, then looked at Mavryk. "I've met many people in my life who are capable of some crazy things, but none of them can stand a chance against you." He held out his hand. "I'll make sure to never cross you either."

Mavryk put his knife back on his belt, not giving any bit of attention to Narcson's hand. "What's a binding marriage?" Mavryk asked.

Narcson put his hand down and spoke. "As we all know, a marriage is a vow to be together through it all and make it work for the sake of whatever it is you marry for. It's also something you can get out of. Divorce isn't easy, especially if the other fights it, but still possible. Even for someone marrying a king. You can't divorce the ruler unless he permits it, but you can still have a chance at running away."

He paused and stared at me for a moment as he said it and then continued talking, his eyes traveling back toward Mavryk. "But a binding is much more than vows of forever. It requires magic, and that type of magic cannot be broken. It also requires each other's blood, which is what will bind them together, forever in this life form. He cannot leave, and neither can she. Not without the death of the person who leaves."

"It's not an easy death either," I remembered Venon threatening me all those years ago, explaining the consequences if I kept trying to leave. "It's a very excruciating death from my understanding."

"Very," Narcson said dryly.

"We're not going to let that happen. I will make sure of that." Mavryk looked lost in thought as he said it, thoughts that seemed to make him angrier.

"I have a place you can crash for the night. A safe place," Narcson said, looking at me and then at Mavryk. "Feel free to come stay."

Mavryk glared at Narcson but didn't say anything.

"He's the reason I've made it this far." I didn't want to divulge our plan to make it to Coastra to Narcson, but Mavryk deserved to be acknowledged for his assistance.

"I have no doubts about that. Did he help you escape from the castle?" I'd seen that look. Narcson was trying to extract the details from me.

I glanced at Mavryk, then back at Narcson. "That's not your concern. You mentioned you have shelter?"

"Yes, over the hill by the river."

"What's to say I can trust you this time?" I queried.

"I'd like to live, for one," he said, his gaze flicking to Mavryk, then back to me. "Venon shorted me on my earnings big-time. I'd like to return the favor."

"Karma came back around, eh?" Mavryk said, a slight grin on his face, which then faded as he continued, "We need to head out either way. It's your decision, Ann. We can go with him, or we can go our own way."

I looked between them. They almost had the same expression as each other. As much as it was too risky trusting Narcson again, I had a feeling this time would be different. Out of all the reasons to not do it again, he wasn't one who would take being shorted on his earnings lightly. His coins mattered more to him than anything, including his life.

I looked at Narcson. "Take us there."

Narcson's expression showed being surprised but having some gratitude. "Just follow me and keep up. We'll need to be quick."

We weaved through the crowds of people. The music had gotten wild as did the people. The smell of different alcohols filled the air, and so did weed. It took a lot in me to not snag up some alcohol myself. I didn't struggle with smoking as I did drinking. I started at a young age, and it became a problem not long after that. Not long ago, I struggled drinking nearly every day. I tried many times drowning my sorrows with it and hoping I wouldn't wake up.

The hill was steep going up but not as badly going down. There were areas that had a stepping path, but there was also an opening of grass that was pretty smooth. I finally decided to not fight against what I felt like doing and run downward on the smooth area.

I hadn't run in so long it felt almost like flying.

I always imagined a bird being the closest thing to freedom. To be able to be admired from high views but nothing able to touch you, to be able to soar around the mountains and embrace views that go on for miles. Eagles especially are such elegant creatures that I almost envied and wished I could be. Hawks are an incredible creature too.

When I got to the bottom, I turned around to see the other two had been watching me—both smiling in a different way. Mavryk's seemed genuine, but Narcson's said something else that exposed some sort of sadness. Usually something like that would have me in my head and taken away my smile, but it didn't this time.

I felt alive in that moment more than I had in years. Even with the possibility of everything that could go wrong and what could happen to me, I couldn't shake the feeling that things were falling apart to eventually fall together. As Mavryk took the last few steps from the hill, I spoke.

"I no longer want to feel defeated and despaired. I'm tired of being another mindless body existing to please others. I need to live before my soul decides to die before I do."

To my surprise, Mavryk spoke back. "All of us are souls waiting to no longer be held in the bodies we're in. If we're blessed in this life, we'll find another one who understands and reminds us we are not alone as much as we think we are."

I looked at him and realized he had been staring at me.

"The sun shall rise again," he whispered.

"Anyways, we'll be sleeping in the barn." Narcson budged between us. The look he had on his face showed annoyance.

Mavryk stared him down until he whispered to me, "You two must've had a romantic history for him to be that jealous of us." He then looked at me with a smirk and winked.

He began walking to follow Narcson and I did the same except I caught up to Narcson. "Whose place is this?"

"Someone who keeps it civil toward the ruler but helps escapers when he can." He looked at me from the side. "Someone you'll want to smooth talk if you want a place to stay and their help to get across the river." He whispered the next part so low I barely heard him. "Keep your boy toy in check around him."

I didn't know why he said it the way he did, but he must know something I don't. My stomach started to twist and turn. Why did I have this feeling it was someone I knew?

"Whose place are we going to?" I asked him a bit nervously.

"Your ex, Alek. When I talked to him about you, he mentioned how the two of you dated and how you left him. He made it known he didn't want to talk about it." He paused and then said the next line in a matter-of-fact tone. "Whatever you did, you hurt him badly."

Of all people, it had to be the one guy for whom I was completely at fault. There was no way he'd help me. Not after how I left things between us and with what I had done. If anything, this seemed more like a setup to take me back. I slowed down until Mavryk caught up to me.

I hadn't seen Alek in years. We dated back when my mom was alive, I believe I was around sixteen. I didn't mean to hurt him the way I had, but there was no doubt I did. I remember the look on his face as clear as day. It still hurts knowing I hurt someone as good as him.

I was not sure if he knew I never meant to, but it couldn't take back what I had done either way. Unfortunately, we end up doing wrong to good people even when we try to be good ourselves. When we don't heal from our past wounds, hurt people will hurt people.

CHAPTER 15

In front of us sat a beige two-story house with gray shutters, white trimming, and a newly finished porch. The place looked like it had been freshly painted and well maintained. The red barn sat in a well-kept condition as well. Not as newly done but in better condition than most you see nowadays. From a short distance, close to the barn, you could see and hear the river running.

Narcson and Mavryk stood by the door, waiting for him to come through. I stood on the step farthest from the door, hoping Alek would notice me last. Wishful thinking led me to not wanting to be seen at all. Would he even recognize me after all this time? Not because of the hair or anything to do with looks but because of who I've become. Can we still claim to know each other after all this time?

People tend to change when they grow into themselves, and having a deep connection doesn't mean you know who they became, but I do believe you can know someone to their core. You can see the best in them way before they become it. In one sense, you're relearning them; in the other, you knew this to be them all along.

The door creaked open, and there he stood. He must've grown in height; he had gained a little more muscle than he used to have too. His face was still kept smooth. He hadn't seemed to age much in looks, which worked in his favor very well. He looked nearly the same as when I knew him. That caught me off guard more than I wanted it to.

He looked at each of us in a manner different from the others. None of it gave off anger, but there were certainly strong feelings toward seeing any of us.

"Narcson, I've told you before I won't help you with any of your schemes." His tone was more confused than anything else.

"Hear me out. This is more important than whatever you might have going on, and this isn't what you think it is." Narcson attempted to use his charm voice, but Alek's face grew irritated at the moment. Depending on what Narcson had done, which I didn't know, that comment would make me want to throw him in the river. Then again, Alek wasn't the angry type, and it took a lot for him to reach that point.

"Before you say anything else ignorant, let me speak," Mavryk interrupted Narcson. Narcson looked like he wanted to object and then nodded in agreement.

Mavryk stepped in front of him. "I'm Mavryk. I don't have time to explain everything, but I've heard you can help us. I'm not one to ask for help, but we're in desperate need."

Alek looked at me and then at Mavryk. "I don't like to get mixed into any kind of trouble, but I am curious what it is you think I can help with?" He was a lot calmer than I expected him to be.

"I've been informed that you could give us a place to sleep for the night and a way to get across the river," Mavryk responded. "I'm trying to help her get to Coastra."

Alek looked at me and then back at Mavryk. "How do you know her?"

"You might not believe me if I told you," he responded.

Mavryk then detailed the day I appeared in front of him and everything that happened afterward. As Mavryk spoke, Alek's eyebrows furrowed tighter, and his eyes expressed more disbelief as the story continued. When Mavryk mentioned that I drained Rohn, his expression halted Mavryk. I'd never seen Alek look more shocked or confused.

"You drained someone?" He looked at me as he spoke, his voice filled with disbelief. He slowly turned toward me and spoke more seriously than I'd ever heard him. "Did you really drain someone?"

I took in a deep breath before I nearly croaked out the word *yes*. If I hadn't been the one who drained, I was not sure I could believe it either. I had healed my whole life up until that point. Alek, having been healed by me, knew very well I wasn't a drainer.

"Can you still heal?"

"I don't know. I haven't had a chance to try and heal," I responded.

"I see," Alek quietly responded.

Suddenly, Narcson swiftly grabbed the knife from Mavryk's waist belt and sliced Alek's hand open. Blood gushed out. Instinctively, I jumped to cover Alek's hand with both of mine. Before panic could fully take hold, his hand had healed, but my hands were covered in blood. As I stared at the blood, I felt myself start to dissociate, my emotions numbing away.

Mavryk yanked the knife from Narcson. "If that were me, I'd knock you out. Don't grab my knife like that again." Mavryk spoke sternly as he wiped his knife clean with a cloth from his pocket.

Alek tried to contain his emotions better as he spoke, but he appeared conflicted. "How often has this happened?" He didn't seem to care that Narcson had just sliced his hand.

"That was my first time. It was toward Rohn. He was onto me. I don't know how I did it, but I knew if I went back, I couldn't survive another day locked up," I explained, my eyes beginning to water. "I know you can't possibly want to see me again, let alone help, but please find it in yourself to help us. To help me."

I sounded desperate, but I didn't care. I'd do anything to avoid going back there. While I rarely pleaded for anything or asked for help, I felt I had no choice. Alek's eyes softened. He had always been a kind and compassionate gentleman, and in that moment, his eyes glimmered with care, reminding me of the times we shared in the past.

"We'll talk as we get your hands cleaned up," he said, glancing between Mavryk and Narcson with a particularly stern look for Narcson. "No one is welcome to stay in my house, but I will allow all of you to sleep in the barn. I'll provide blankets and pillows, but I'll need you all gone by sunrise. I have a small boat that can get you across the river. There's nothing else I can help with, but I do wish you the best of luck."

Narcson thanked him and wished him the same, which Alek ignored. Mavryk nodded his thanks, his expression conveying unspoken words. Both turned to walk toward the barn, but Mavryk paused after a few steps. "I hope to one day repay you for your generosity."

Alek approached him and extended his hand. "I hope you can get her to where she needs to go." The handshake evolved into a hug, accompanied by pats on the shoulder blades and a nod. Mavryk then continued toward the barn, while Alek turned back to me.

He opened the door, holding it open. "We should get you cleaned up."

"Thank you," I whispered, barely audible, as I walked inside with him following.

Entering the kitchen, the scent of new wood filled the air. I washed my hands at the sink until the blood was gone. Turning around, I jumped slightly and then nervously laughed. Alek stood behind me, holding up a towel.

"For someone who has been through absolute madness, you jump much too easily at something as minor as a towel," he said, a slight smile quickly fading from his face.

I dried my hands and hung the towel over the sink. He sat at the table, sipping tea. "You're welcome to have some tea if you'd like."

"I'll just have water. I'm not a fan of tea. I appreciate it, nonetheless." He got up, filled a cup from a jug that sat on the counter, and handed it to me. I thanked him and drank from the cup until we sat at the table. We set our drinks down simultaneously.

Neither of us spoke for a minute, and then I broke the silence. "I'm not sure where to begin. I left things on a terrible note with you, and I'm terrible at saying I'm sorry, but..." I took a deep breath in and then exhaled as I spoke the rest. "I am truly and deeply sorry, Alek. I'm not saying any of this for your help either. I mean it. You didn't deserve anything I put you through."

He took a moment before responding. "I forgave you a while ago. We were young, there's no need to dwell on what was when there is so much of what is." Before I could respond, his eyes looked up from his cup and leaned in a bit toward me. "I hope you've learned to forgive yourself."

"I've tried. I don't know how," I whispered with a rasp. I adjusted myself in the seat and cleared my throat to speak clearer. "I'm not sure I can. Forgiving isn't a strong suit of mine."

"You don't want to risk throwing out your healing powers, so you will want to find it deep within yourself to forgive. Forgive others as well." I looked at him with my eyebrows furrowed together. He took another sip before explaining.

"I stumbled upon a book that someone wrote. They had different thoughts I had never heard anyone come up with before. They wrote about a perspective where drainers and healers could become the opposite of themselves. They put it into terms that when a healer starts to become bitter, the healer then starts a transformation of becoming a drainer. They brought up that it's a lot more common than a drainer transforming into a healer."

"I've never heard of that, but it does make sense and one heck of a way to think." I looked around, then down at my cup, and spoke again. "I can't help but feel that's not what's happening, though. Not exactly, anyways. I would have turned by now if that were the case."

"I haven't read of anything else that explains it. Have you heard of something else? Did you have a vision perhaps?"

"No, I haven't heard of anything else." I hesitated to speak about my dream but decided he could possibly help piece together what it means, at least give advice worth listening to. Even Mavryk trusted him enough to tell him everything that had happened, and Mavryk didn't seem to trust many.

"I had a dream, though. Last night." He looked at me curiously and took a sip of his tea. I told him the dream and every detail I could remember from it. "I felt whole as we came together. Like a part of me that had been missing wasn't anymore and unbelievably powerful."

"Does he make you feel that way?" he asked calmly.

I took a drink from my cup before answering, gulping louder than usual. "Yes, in a sense, but I don't feel anyone can truly complete you in another. I'm not sure how to explain that, but everything's confusing right now, and I'm still trying to process not being trapped in the castle anymore."

"He mentioned you entering through a glow when you met him," he said, his tone more curious than usual.

"Yes. From what I understand, it's a rare thing."

He stood up and walked to the pitcher of tea to refill his cup. "It hasn't happened in hundreds of years from what I've read." He turned around and walked back to the table, sitting down in the same spot. "Some say it is part of a mythical story, like a fairy's existence. Bedtime stories told to children to help their imagination."

"Is that what you believe?" He didn't say anything. "Do you think I'm making this up?" I asked a bit defensively, making a mental note to check myself since he wasn't the one I needed to be so guarded against.

"No," he responded calmly. "I can see it written all over your face how confused and exhausted you are. It's like you hardly believe it yourself." His gaze shifted to me. "I'm only trying to understand what this means. I can only imagine how you're feeling about it."

A bit of embarrassment washed over me. "I'm sorry," I said sheepishly. "I am not trying to take anything out on you."

"No need to apologize. I do wish you'd trust me more, but you've always had trouble in that area." He took a sip of his tea and then looked at me and gave a light smile. "I meant to tell you, that color really suits you. It brings out your eyes."

The smile quickly faded, and sadness crossed his face again. He calmly inhaled through his nostrils and then spoke as he exhaled. "Can I ask you something?"

"Of course," I said, offering a slight smile.

"What's made you finally stay away from men who hurt you?" His gaze avoided mine as he posed the question.

I understood he wasn't only just referring to Venon but also to the individual who had come between us, along with any other detrimental relationships I had endured.

I took a few moments to gather my thoughts before responding, "I guess I'm finally ready for something better." It felt like I didn't have much choice in the matter either way.

Observing him, I noticed a hint of relief in his reaction to my statement. "You deserve better," he affirmed and then looked outside, suggesting, "You might want to get some rest before you have to head out again."

He went into another room and returned with two large blankets—one thinner—and a few pillows, which he handed to me. "Thank you, Alek. Your help means the world to me," I expressed, wanting to convey more but recognizing that nothing else needed to be said. He offered a slight smile and nodded a few times in acknowledgment.

As he walked me to the door and I stepped out onto the porch, right before my foot hit the first step down, he called out my name. I paused and turned to face him as he let the screen door close, standing in front of me.

"We weren't meant to work out as I once hoped, but I know what we had was real. I'll always be grateful for our time together. Wherever your destiny takes you, I truly hope it leads you to the peace you need," he conveyed.

Tears formed in my eyes, and I set down the blankets and pillows to embrace him tightly. His arms wrapped around me, transforming the hurtful tension from our past into a wholesome forgiveness that nudged me closer to a brighter future.

I stepped back, wiping away the tears, and shared, "You gave me a real love that I will always cherish. I didn't know how to accept it back then, and to some extent, I still don't, but I hope one day you find the kind of love you give." A genuine smile spread across his face, mirrored by my own.

"Farewell, Ann," he said softly.

"Farewell, Alek," I replied, picking up the blankets and pillows. Glancing back at him one last time, I then turned and walked toward the barn, smiling up at the moonlit sky. The universe, in its vastness, seemed to offer signs and a sense of calm.

Many people pass through our lives temporarily but not all for negative reasons. Some demonstrate that not everyone is out to intentionally harm us, aiding us on our journey to living our truest selves. They may be there to help us in some way, teaching us valuable lessons about ourselves.

You grow to appreciate that through heartbreak, you learn things you might not have learned in the same way through someone else. You're even more grateful for those who understood you were coming from a place of darkness unrelated to them and who graciously offered you forgiveness.

CHAPTER 16

"So you think she's your destiny?" I overheard Narcson asking Mavryk, pausing at the edge of the barn door before entering.

"There's no other explanation," Mavryk replied, undeterred by Narcson's snicker. "What's the history between you two, anyway?" he inquired, brushing aside Narcson's attempt at mockery.

"I've been waiting for you to ask," Narcson said, likely with a smirk. "We were serious for about six months. She might tell you I never cared about her, but I did."

"And how did you screw up?" Mavryk's voice carried a grim tone.

Letting out a deep breath, Narcson admitted, "I helped her escape the castle, and for a while, we lived together, secluded from everyone, in the opposite direction from here. One night at a nearby pub, I overheard talk of a reward for her return. The offer seemed worth more at the time than staying with her. They didn't know what she looked like, and she was none the wiser, especially after drinking heavily that night. So I took advantage of her inebriated state to hand her over. By morning, I left with the payment, and they had her back."

His tone started off in mockery, but as he continued speaking, I detected a shift to a more serious demeanor. The last sentence, especially, conveyed a hint of depression.

"Karma didn't serve you justice." Mavryk's tone was calm yet imbued with seriousness.

"I owe it to help her," Narcson replied quickly. "You don't meet someone like that again. I live with the regret of losing her every day. I'd give anything to go back and make it right."

I stepped into the barn opening and looked at him. "That still doesn't make you trustworthy. Words are pointless if the meaning behind them does not match the actions to prove their value."

Their heads jerked toward me. Narcson appeared startled, but Mavryk's expression was a mixture of emotions. I walked toward them and handed each a large blanket along with a pillow, keeping the smaller blanket for myself.

"Like you said earlier, Venon screwed you over. The help you're providing is for revenge, nothing more." I believed he wanted to help me this time and not go back on his word but not for the reason he claimed.

"Believe what you want, like it or not, I am here to help you." Narcson's voice was quieter than I had heard him speak before. Mavryk started setting up a sleeping area, and Narcson began to do the same.

As much as I wanted to continue the argument to get my point across, I knew he would dismiss it and argue until I was completely exhausted. Either way, my feelings wouldn't be validated, and with how badly I'd shut down after being made to feel invalidated, I knew I couldn't afford to go down that route tonight, if at all anymore. I needed to save my energy for what really mattered if I was to make it through this journey to Coastra.

Then again, I had wronged Alek, and he forgave me, still willing to give me a chance not to make the same mistake as last time. I might not have committed an action as harmful as Narcson's, but Alek could have been just as hurt as I was. Maybe I needed to learn from Alek's example and forgive. I was not who I used to be, and maybe Narcson wasn't either, at least to some extent.

"You can't expect me to be okay with you having the lighter blanket and no pillow." I turned my head to see Mavryk looking at me. He smiled and shook his head. "Let's trade." He extended his hand toward me and motioned with his fingers while he glanced at the blanket and then back at me.

I smiled politely. "No, that's okay. I'll be fine."

He lowered his hand and then sighed and crossed his arms. "Will you at least lay next to me so I know you'll be warm? At least more than you would be using that." His eyes conveyed genuine concern.

Narcson snickered before speaking. "You think that will get you lucky? Ha! You aren't that smooth."

Mavryk turned his head toward him, his eyes flashing with anger. "I have a lot more respect for her than that. Not all of us are trying to take advantage of someone's vulnerability." He glanced at me and then quickly looked away, not saying anything as he stormed out of the barn.

After watching Mavryk leave, I turned toward Narcson. "You know, not everyone is like you. Some people do things out of kindness and want nothing in return."

"Alek was one of those for you, wasn't he?" Narcson asked.

"Yes, and I regret taking advantage of him."

"How did you stop regretting what you did?"

"When he told me he had forgiven me." I paused, a realization dawning on me. "I'm forgiving you today too."

Without waiting for his response, I left the barn. I noticed Mavryk lying by the river. I walked over and sat next to him. He was gazing at the stars, lost in thought yet seemingly searching for peace.

"It's amazing how much more you can see out here." I spoke softly.

"What is?"

"The stars. There are millions out here." I took out my notebook and pencil.

"Does it inspire you?" Mavryk asked in a gentle voice.

"Yes. As do you." I glanced over at him from the corner of my eye and noticed a hint of a smile on his lips.

I opened the notebook and began to write.

I should feel lost; in a sense, I am, but on the other hand, I can feel myself becoming found. Then again, maybe I was never truly lost. I had become something I wasn't meant to be because of the cruelty of people who convinced me I was much less than I am and felt the need to dim my light due to their inability to handle how brightly I shined. They told me I should aim to blend in with the rest of the world and think the way they do, that there is something fundamentally wrong with who I am and that I shouldn't want to be unique. They implied I couldn't be destined for greatness unless I was great myself.

Yet, there's another part of me that disagrees. I know the things I've done, the people I've hurt. I'm aware of the many wrong turns I've made and how I could have saved myself from more pain if I had listened to the intuition signaling that this couldn't be trusted. I acknowledge there have been those who saw my worth, but I pushed away, mistaking what is familiar for what is good.

Does any of it really define us if we decide to become better? Isn't the point of mistakes to learn so we can grow into better versions of ourselves? Shouldn't we give ourselves a bit of grace when we give everyone else multiple chances, especially when those we've hurt have forgiven us?

We don't have to stay stuck, believing we're not worthy of wonderful things when perfection isn't possible. We don't have to be labeled as a bad person if we decide we're going to do better than we were.

We usually don't notice when we're surviving rather than living. Sometimes, you get so used to survival mode that when you're no longer needing to survive but you're able to live, your brain hasn't comprehended that, and you end up making the same decisions that saved you at one point but now cause damage.

No one talks about the process of rewiring everything you had no choice in learning. You aren't taught what needs to be done to break bad habits and that it feels like you're being ripped to shreds, with pieces exposing the years of agony and misery that you carried.

You clung onto it because you figured this is as good as it can possibly get, that you deserve nothing better. It's not mentioned how uncomfortable you'll have to be for a while and how honest you have to be with yourself about yourself to make the change.

The problem is, growth can feel unbearable when you're not used to it. So much so that people fear it, so they stay stuck forever rather than temporarily going through the process of becoming better. I've never seen someone become better if they do not heal their inner wounds; it always turns them bitter. Much like a broken bone, if it's not set back into place correctly, it doesn't heal properly and damages so much more than what was harmed before.

We don't get to decide certain things for ourselves while we're young and in someone else's care. No matter how unfair things were, how poor your treatment was, we have all the chance to make better choices in life once we're responsible for ourselves. It's one of the simplest yet most complex decisions in life to make: to become better or to turn bitter.

Neither is easy because life will never be easy. You have to decide which one is worth living through, and when it's put that way, I have to wonder why I didn't decide to make the steps sooner. I held myself back from my calling, and no matter who did what, I still could have chosen better for myself sooner. At times, I could have been better toward others too.

Then again, I wouldn't have been ready. I wouldn't have understood what I do now without every single thing that's happened. I wholeheartedly believe everything happens for a reason, even if we never get to the point of understanding why, or how, or from what.

If we look past how deep our pain feels, we can realize that having all the answers to our questions still wouldn't take away what we feel. For all we know, it

*could add more confusion with twice as many questions
and greater pain. We can't control the things that have
happened to us, but what we can do is accept, even as
soul-crushing as it is, and make the most out of the life
we currently have.*

I looked up at the sky and over at Mavryk. He was already staring at me. "You write with passion," he remarked. It was challenging to focus on responding when his gaze was so soft and comforting. "You haven't read what I wrote," I countered. "I don't need to. I can see it while you write," he replied, looking up at the sky. "However, from what I have read, you are gifted."

It was hard to believe that when it was me writing. I wrote what I felt, and sometimes I felt I sounded dumb, but I also realized I had been very insecure. That insecurity stemmed from what others had fed me, especially those I loved. I had loved everyone else so much more than I had ever loved myself, being more lenient with their mistakes but expecting myself to be something no one could ever be no matter how hard they tried.

"I expected perfection from myself all these years without realizing it, and then when I finally cracked, I ended up shattering. I've been judged so harshly because I didn't always react in the best manner."

His expression didn't change, but I saw compassion and softness in his eyes. "Instead of taking accountability for being wrong in the first place, they used your reaction to their abuse against you. Manipulating the situation with guilt and confusion. They knew you'd feel bad because it's not in your character to act like that."

"It took me a long time to realize abuse was much more than physical. I'm still learning just how damaging the mental abuse has been on me. I've suffered it my whole life," I responded. It hurt to realize that even the person I loved deeply and admired the most had been part of that trauma. The difference was, they didn't mean to; others had. It's easier to forgive someone knowing they did their best, even if it wasn't healthy. They did what they knew and meant well in their heart. They didn't always know what to do given the circumstances.

I believe that's the biggest difference in what separates a person from being genuinely good or bad. They hurt you without meaning to, or they hurt you knowing it will but doing so, anyway. I don't believe any of us are truly born bad, regardless of who we become.

"Will you sleep next to me tonight?" Mavryk's voice was filled with sweet softness. I looked at him, and his eyes mirrored the gesture of his voice. I couldn't say no, even if I wanted to.

"Yes," I whispered in response.

I put the notebook and pencil in the satchel. As I went to lay my head on his chest, he moved his arm out of the way. My body relaxed into him. Every touch felt like I had finally found a home I had been unknowingly searching for most of my life. The longing for somewhere I belonged had been with a person and not a place. Magic exists in the moments I had with him by a single touch.

"I know you're used to men wanting more, but I really do just want to hold you," he assured me. His words were as genuine as his character. I had never trusted a man, not even a good one, to say that and mean it. I didn't know how, but I knew he meant everything he said in that specific tone. The way he spoke wasn't another deceiving attempt to win me over for some type of gain but something authentic and mesmerizing that my soul understood I could finally rest, knowing there was no lying. It was as beautiful as instruments that collided perfectly together, as real as the air we breathe. You can't see the nature behind it, but you can feel the way it brings something real to you that a lot of the world forgot about.

CHAPTER 17

I woke up to being locked up in a place with concrete walls. The blanket, thin as a sheet of paper, covered my body; there was no pillow, let alone head support of any kind. I wasn't lying on a bed but a cot. In front of me, a rusty metal bucket sat in a corner. I sat up and let my back sink into the wall. It didn't matter how cold it felt as I pressed against it because I had already been cold nonstop for days.

The clothes I wore were worn out and almost as thin as the blanket. The shirt had long sleeves and was buttoned down the middle. The pants didn't cover my ankles, made of a beige fabric that I wanted to rip off but couldn't because I had nothing else to wear and nothing worn underneath. I hadn't been able to wash myself at all either. At this point, I'd shave my head to get rid of the awful greasy feeling that crawled all over my scalp.

I'd been locked up before but not like this. If I hadn't been stunned in place by crippling exhaustion, I might have bashed my head against the wall by now, but I couldn't move. I felt paralyzed in place by manic depression.

Hopelessness had really won this time. I'd wait until my body dissolved into nothingness and let my existence disappear. Being drained couldn't describe what I felt. I had become lifeless and saw nothing left for me except a long-awaited greeting by death. For so long, the thought danced in my mind, but now it stayed. I'm ready to die.

My heart raced with panic. My eyes shot open, and my body jolted off Mavryk as I sat upright. I wrapped my arms around my legs and began moving in a motion. If I sat still, everything about my body would burst into pieces and fly everywhere, and the world would then explode from such an overwhelming anxiety. This is how I felt, anyway.

"Ann, are you alright?" Mavryk stared at me with concern, but the sound of care left his voice as he asked the question. I looked around and noticed it was still dark without a hint that morning would be here soon.

"Bad dream," I whispered.

"Do you have nightmares often?" The term nightmare bothered me. A reminder that my mind wouldn't let me rest even when I was supposed to.

"They come and go in stages."

He sat up and breathed in deeply before speaking. "We should go in the barn and sleep the rest of the night under a blanket. It's a bit chilly. I'm sure adding some warmth will help soothe your nerves."

He wasn't wrong. I feel more secure under a blanket. The heavier the better, and after the dream I had, it'd be really nice to be wrapped in one.

He stood up and held out his hands. Some stubborn part of me wanted to wave his hands away because I was used to picking myself up and feeling safe relying on myself for any support, but between the exhaustion and overwhelming feeling still stirring in me, I knew it'd be easier to take the help than to resist.

I grabbed his hands, and he pulled me up. I had barely used any of my strength to hang on, but he seemed to show no strain of struggle. I let go of his hands, and before I could reach down to grab the satchel, he grabbed it then handed it to me. He gave a gentle smile before turning to walk toward the barn.

When we stepped inside the barn, it was dark, but the moon peeked in with a hint of its light, which helped guide us to the spot Mavryk had made earlier. Narcson had made a spot on the opposite side of the barn and was passed out.

"Would it be alright if I held you again? I'll try better to keep the nightmares away." His eyes were sleepy but playful as he whispered. They also seemed to beg for me to say yes.

I grabbed his hand and wrapped our fingers together. He looked at our hands and then at me, and our eyes locked. We didn't exchange words, but I could see in them that he felt something as deeply as I did. It was something deeper than love that came with admiration for the other.

We walked the rest of the way to the spot and crawled underneath the blanket. Mavryk rested his head on the pillow while I laid mine on his chest. I was not sure when I drifted back to sleep, but when I did, I felt a calmness I'd never felt after waking up in a horrible state. I'd never been able to fall back asleep until hours later, if at all.

When I woke up, the sun shined brightly. I was a bit shocked to feel as rested as I was and relieved that I didn't experience another bad dream. I didn't recall dreaming at all, thinking about it.

I held my head up and looked around. Mavryk and Narcson weren't there. Narcson's spot where he slept didn't have the blanket or pillow either. I sat up, then got up, and walked out of the barn. I stood by the entrance and looked toward the house, then I looked over by the river. From a bit of a distance, you could see all three of them standing there talking by a dock that had a small boat.

Halfway to them, Mavryk stopped talking as he looked at me. The other two looked at me as well. I felt awkward walking the rest of the way, especially when I reached them, and no one went back to talking.

"What's the plan?" I asked in a bit of a hoarse voice. I cleared my throat and felt my face heat up with embarrassment.

"A couple of guards came to me earlier this morning, asking if I had seen you." Alek's voice was more serious than usual. "They almost decided to look around to see if you were hiding."

I didn't know what to say. I was trying to not only still wake up but also calm my nerves from seeing them all together talking to not talking as I walked toward them. Now I was hearing that within a very short distance, I could have been sent back. Was my dream a warning of what was to come?

"In other words, we're leaving now." Mavryk spoke in a quick and harsh manner, looking at Alek and then toward me with a less sharp tone. "Narcson will be returning the boat to Alek, so there's no suspicion of either of them being involved. Are you ready?"

I looked to my side to make sure I had the satchel on. I looked up and noticed something bothering him. I nodded my head in response to his question, but I wanted to ask what was bothering him. By his tone, I knew it was something he needed to calm down from first, and I decided I would ask while on the boat. Alek went inside while Mavryk got the boat in the water. Narcson stood there, staring at me.

"Mind filling me in?" I asked Narcson.

He didn't seem certain that he wanted to, but he spoke, anyway. "The ruler is really set on bringing you back. Though I'm not sure why. He plans on marrying Princess Rezna now. I think he wants to keep you so no one else can have you."

Not that I was surprised, but I could feel the numbness beginning to set in to protect the hurt that came from how I really feel.

"How do you know this?" I asked in a monotone.

"Alek. He filled us in. He doesn't work for them, but he keeps it civil, so he gets the insider of what's going on depending on who it is. I have to say I'm not sure why Alek would risk his life after what you did to him."

Mavryk came up behind Narcson and grabbed him by the back of his neck. In that moment, Narcson's eyes showed terror, and his hands grabbed ahold of Mavryk's hand. Mavryk looked at him with a rage that worried me. Narcson tried loosening Mavryk's grip, but it didn't budge.

"I've already warned you to watch how you speak to her." Mavryk's voice was a snarl. "If you show an ounce of disrespect toward her again, I will snap your neck."

Mavryk's eyes flickered toward me, and then he let Narcson go, and he backed away from Mavryk while rubbing his neck and catching his breath. Narcson didn't look at him. I went up to Mavryk and looked at him. He wouldn't look at me.

His mind raced somewhere else, much darker than he wanted to admit. I slowly reached for his face, and my fingers gently touched the bottom of his cheek. My fingers slid upward until my hand covered every part of his face that my hand could fit. In that moment, his head leaned on my hand, and tears began to fill his eyes. He looked at me, and I saw so much pain.

"Mavryk," I whispered. "You don't have to hurt anyone to prove anything to me. I know you care for me."

A tear rolled down his cheek, and then he grabbed my hand. He took it off his face and kissed it and then pulled me in to kiss my forehead. I pulled back after his lips left my head, and our eyes met. In some unexplainable way, I could understand what he battled with. He was someone who understood how difficult it was to change.

I know I had been through some horrible things that caused so much trauma and agonizing torture that repeatedly played in my thoughts, but I never realized how much his had haunted him too.

I was not the only one battling who I used to be and who I was becoming, letting go of what was and accepting what was new. We were traveling the same path with different obstacles in the way—the obstacles that had stumbled us from being able to fully grow just yet. We so badly wanted to break free from our minds and our old ways but didn't know how to.

I couldn't help but feel we weren't the only ones either. How many others were at war with themselves and desperate to break free? How do you send a message to the rest who currently feel broken, confused, and uncertain that you're not alone and worthy of real love? That in time it came together, and those who were for you would be there to defend who you really are and were always meant to be. They see the real you, and while they hold you accountable, they don't condemn you for making mistakes. They embrace every part of you with where you currently are without making you feel terrible for trying to figure it out along the way.

"This isn't much, but there's some food to get you both by until you figure something else out. Here's a canteen as well." Alek's arm extended out toward us. I leaned away from Mavryk and grabbed it from Alek.

"Thank you." I spoke. I was going to leave it at that, but something came over me to speak the next part. "You've done a lot to help us, and that really speaks volumes about you. When you told me you forgave me last night, it helped me break free of some of the unforgiveness I hold toward myself. You put your livelihood at risk to help others, and that makes you a very noble and admirable man. If I ever get the chance to repay you, I promise I will."

He smiled. "I appreciate you saying that. Take care of yourself and have a safe travel." He looked at the other two and nodded and then walked back to the house.

"We should get going," Narcson said sourly.

I almost began walking to the boat but decided to speak my mind first. "I'm not going to claim I'm perfect and that I haven't hurt people who didn't deserve it, but that doesn't mean I deserve to have it held over my head. Especially not by someone who's done worse to me than I've done to someone else. I've been forgiven, which taught me how to forgive you last night. Not so you can freely pass judgment or have the chance to hurt me again. It's freeing myself from the pain of what you did. It's so I can hold less against myself and learn how to be wiser next time. If you learned how to focus on yourself, you'd realize just how much you need to set yourself free too. It's easy to condemn others but to reflect on our wrongs is a lot more of a challenge. Not a lot do it, and it's because they choose to stay stuck instead of growing into a better individual."

I walked to the boat and sat on it. I wasn't sure what took over me, where that all even came from, but I felt relief. Something inside of me sparked with fire, and I felt for the first time in such a long time that I had found a hint of my true voice. I found a piece I thought was long gone, but it was merely just tucked away in hiding, waiting on me to find the courage again to speak up instead of catering to another's feelings in fear that they would lash out and try to convince me that I was delusional in some form of manipulative way.

Even with the truth represented in front of their face, I'd time and time again be made to feel that somehow what I had seen wasn't really what I had seen or what I had felt wasn't to be true either, but deep down I knew. I had quit fighting them out of exhaustion; at times, I didn't put up a fight at all. I would knowingly go along with the lies because I craved the good they did give until I had enough of settling. Then when I would finally speak up, that's where the accusing me of being crazy came from. I suppose they figured I would play along forever.

Manipulation and gaslighting at its finest, not just by someone else but from myself as well.

CHAPTER 18

Mavryk sat in the middle row rowing the boat while I sat in the front looking toward the direction we were going, and Narcson sat in the back. It was nice none of us had to share a spot; the boat was small enough as is. Any more people added on would have made for a tight fit. Thankfully, it didn't take long to get across to the other side. Going to Egyptstra or Outcastril would have been a different story.

As the boat drew closer, Narcson grabbed the pole that sat on the side in the middle of the dock, holding us in place. "Go ahead and get off. I'll hold it still so you two can get out."

Mavryk stepped out first and then turned around to help me out. It was a good thing, too, because I nearly stumbled into the water by my foot slipping. His hand caught my arm, and I fell into him. I flipped my head back and sighed.

"And I'm supposed to make it to Coastra," I let out a sarcastic laugh and pulled my body away. His hand didn't let go and instead glided until it entwined with mine.

"I'll gladly be here to catch you every time you fall, love."

Hysterical laughing came from Narcson. "I'm glad I don't get seasick because that's the cringiest thing I've heard!" He pushed away the boat from the dock and began rowing as he still mockingly laughed.

I noticed the expression on Mavryk's face go from soft to annoyed. He glared toward Narcson's direction and spoke loud enough for Narcson to hear his comment.

"You're not in a sea, genius. That's a river."

Narcson made one last haughty comment and shouted, "Touché." Mavryk shook his head.

His eyes went back on me, and his expression relaxed.

"I think I'd like to not meet another ex of yours. If they're worse than him, I'm not sure how I'll act." His voice, though not stern, was serious.

"Speaking of which, what had you so upset with Alek a bit ago?"

He looked away into the distance and took a minute to respond. "He's not my issue exactly. I'm naturally jealous anyone had you before I did, so feeling a bit off with any ex of yours is going to happen. Venon, however, enrages me on another level because he doesn't want you for any reason that's good." He then looked back into my eyes with a look that could have made me stay entranced forever.

His free hand lifted to my chin and then gently held it there. "I don't believe you've ever been loved the way you deserve, and if that's what makes you so hesitant with us, then I understand, but time will prove that I am not them. In time, I hope you come to understand that I was made to love you with my entire heart and protect you for the rest of my life."

I didn't get a chance to say anything in return. I'm not sure I could have said anything to match how that made me feel. His kiss was a lot more intense than it had been and filled me with a passion that only real love can exist from. Once again, I was in a moment where nothing else existed except what was now.

His smell, his touch, it wasn't just electricity shocking my nerves but awakening another part of my soul that had never seen the light of day until now. So much of me wanted to stay forever locked in with him, but another part of me wanted to run so far away that I'd never be found.

My soul knew him, but my mind couldn't bear the thought of my heart dying if anything were to ever happen between us. I pushed myself off him and out of his arms that were wrapped around me. He looked disordered, deeply offended. He lifted his hands and ran them through his hair. He closed his eyes as his free hand clenched into a fist.

He inhaled deeply and then exhaled loudly. "I wish you'd stop resisting us," he whispered with aggravation.

He opened his eyes and let his arms drop in defeat. "I want to be mad, but I can't because the moment I look at you, I want to fall to my knees. I'm willing to die for you so you can finally be free, and you deserve that, but can't you at least let me have these moments with you to hold onto?" His eyes had watered enough that if he blinked, the tears would run down his face.

He took a slow step toward me and placed his hands onto my arms; they slid down to hold my hands. I watched as our hands cupped together and then looked up. A few tears had fallen out of his eyes and glided down his face. One dropped from his jawline and landed on the ground.

"I don't mean to do this. I don't understand it myself." I could feel myself tear up.

I held onto his hand as I lifted mine to wipe his tears away. He closed his eyes as I did. I'd never seen someone more beautiful than him, but I couldn't speak it. I spent my life looking away from the faces of so many other men, but his I felt drawn to. He opened his eyes.

"Your eye color is different." I spoke. His brows furrowed together, looking intrigued. "It's not a bad thing. It's actually really neat. I've just never seen someone have the same color as yours." It was possible I never noticed since I struggled with eye contact so much, but I didn't tend to miss the details either.

He made a slight smile. "Steven mentioned that they used to be a sky blue, but this last time he saw me, they were a greenish gray color. You must have something to do with it."

"They were a green, gray color when I met you, but they've become an almost all-gray color. There's almost no hint of green anymore," I responded.

His smile faded, and his eyes went soft again. "Your eyes are always a deep blue with gray. The brighter the sun, the brighter they shine. I swim in bliss every time I get a chance to get lost in them." That better explained the looks he gave me when I caught him staring.

"So you're not sad when you look at me?"

"Sad?" He smirked while his eyebrows lifted. "No, usually not." His smirk dropped. "When I see you're hurting, yes, but otherwise, I'm just falling deeper for you. When you first appeared to me, it wasn't because you came out of the glow that stunned me in place. It was that you shined in a way no one else has, looking like the most beautiful angel I've ever laid my eyes on. You woke up something inside of me that I had no idea was never even born. You took a hardened heart and have been mending it back into a whole piece."

I think he didn't plan to say more but added the next part. "What I'm trying to say to you is, I love you but not in the way most consider love. I love you with a love that won't perish. It has no conditions."

Tears escaped and fell to the ground. I knew he wasn't lying, so why did my body want to run? What was terrifying me so badly? Could I not accept such a love that he had to offer? Would my mind always tell me no one could truly love me for me?

A gust of wind blew in the direction of Landomal. As I looked in its direction, I saw a little stream that went straightforward from where we stood, with an open field. From each side, at a distance, you could see the same river that we had come from on each side, with some miles' worth of distance.

Mavryk had let go of me and sat down, while his feet dangled from the dock, with the map spread out on his side. I sat on the other side of the map and looked at it with him. It would be a lot less traveling in the ocean to get to Coastra by going through Outcastril than it would be to go through Landomal. It seemed it would save more time as well.

"Why didn't we just go through Outcastril?" I asked.

"You can't go through Outcastril." He looked up away from the map and at me. His face expressed a lot of sorrow. "There's a metal wall that goes around all of Outcastril. I'm not entirely sure what all goes on there, but I know it's horrible."

"So what do you know?" I asked.

I was not sure if I truly wanted to know, but I knew I needed to know. He looked away from me and toward the river. He seemed like he was trying to be careful with what he said next, as if to not disturb me.

"There's a lot of the world you don't know about. Things you've been kept from being told, as has most of the world." He adjusted himself and inhaled and then exhaled. "I don't doubt you've suffered through a lifetime of pain, but you've also been kept confined from everything outside of where you came from. Brace yourself for what I'm about to tell you."

He began telling me what it was before. "Outcastril was beautiful, much like Scarland but with more mountains. Ones you could climb and get lost in the clouds. A terrible fire broke out, and the whole land went into flames. They say the fire wasn't red like the usual color it is but a blue so breathtaking that if you stared too long, it made everything else seem dull."

In that instant, I remembered my dream where Mavryk and I came together as souls, and all you could see was the same type of blue, but there was no way they could be tied together. How would that be possible?

"They say it lasted for seven days, and then it instantly stopped. Nothing was left. Not even the tallest mountains. Just ashes that fell for forty days and forty nights. Then when those stopped, they suddenly dissolved into the ground. Nothing grew back no matter what was done, so for a long while, it was left alone. That is until people were discovered hiding there to escape from society's rules. Especially those that aren't drainers."

"This is where they built the wall?" I asked.

"Not quite. They came up with a course of action on what to make of it first." He seemed troubled about what came next but continued talking. "The ruler at the time, Venon's grandfather, decided the name fit best for the outcast. If you weren't willing to follow the rules, then you belonged stuck there too."

"Stuck?" I cringed at the sound of that.

"Once you agreed to go there, then you couldn't leave, which made living impossible since nothing grew for food. Besides the river, there wasn't any other source of water, but that wasn't possible to drink once the wall was up. As you can imagine, no one willingly agreed to go. They found other ways of hiding. Escapers began help-ing healers move to Coastra, so when Venon's grandfather died and his father took over, he decided more action needed to take place."

He paused and looked around. "We should continue moving. The last thing we need is for you to get caught." He put away the map, put on his backpack, and then stood up. He reached out toward me. I took his hand and let him lift me up. "I won't argue that, but while we're walking, could you continue telling me about Outcastril?"

He looked at me. I watched his eyes study the surroundings of my head. "I never complimented you on how well the hair color suits you. You look amazing." Then he laughed. "I didn't mean to change the subject. If you don't speak, your face certainly will." He held out his hand as a gesture to hold mine. "Come now, love, I'll tell you everything you want to know." I smiled, shook my head, and then grabbed his hand. I'd never met another soul like him.

Those are the kinds of people who leave marks on our hearts far beyond the lifespan of living. There's some truth behind the afterlife, that we only live one time in our flesh, but the souls are never-end-ing. That's why you can conclude that home is never about finding a place. It's about what kind of life you built with the ones who you'll know after the body can no longer carry you. Even if it's short-lived, you can build memories that carry on forever. As Mother Dear once said, it's not a goodbye but a "see you later."

"This is where things get ugly." He took a moment and then continued where he left off. "Venon's father, with the help of guides and the kings, came up with Outcastril being its own society. Only this came with a lot less. You can't grow your own food of choice. They decide that for you. You're fed once a day what they decide with your daily water intake. You sleep where you're assigned, with who-ever they decide. You labor every day except one day, and that's spent locked up in your assigned place. The clothing you have is what you were allowed to take with you when you're sent there. You cannot make your own, and there's no shops to buy anything, so new cloth-ing doesn't typically happen until one dies. Then guards give out to whoever is on the list for what's needed, and that's if they're approved to receive new. Same goes with blankets and pillows."

"What did you mean by 'being sent there'?" There was no way anyone would agree to live like that willingly.

"Those people who break the rules, who go against what the ruler says in any way he finds unforgivable, where did you think they sent them?"

I didn't respond. I had seen Venon cast out a man trying to feed his family by growing food without permission. My heart suddenly sank, thinking about the family and what they had dealt with that day. How they could possibly be getting by now. After that, I couldn't bear being sober when a sentence would happen. Even though I didn't know where he had been sent, I knew it wasn't good. The truth behind it stings even more.

"When you're sent to Outcastril, before they assign you anywhere, they mark you on both of your inner arms."

I stopped and looked at him. "Mark them?"

He didn't look at me. "They brand them with a hot iron that is a certain symbol."

I felt repulsed. My eyes began to water, and I realized why they did that. "If they escape, they'll know."

"We need to keep going, Ann." His voice said he has a hard time stomaching it himself. "I know it's a lot to process, but this cannot be what stops you from receiving freedom. You can't save the world, even if you'd like to think there is a possibility to do so."

I stood for a moment longer and then realized he was right. It didn't do any good to sink into myself. I just couldn't help but feel terribly guilty. I wanted to save them all from such a place. I didn't get that horrible of treatment, but I knew about being controlled and locked away, so I couldn't even imagine what they had to be feeling.

I stood by for years, watching people who didn't deserve such treatment be stripped away from their loved ones. I couldn't have done anything even if I had tried, but that made it feel worse. That made me feel helpless and practically worthless in my existence. What could our purpose be if we can't help those most in need? I didn't have it in me to believe that we're meant to suffer for the rest of our days until death greets us. There has to be more to life than this.

CHAPTER 19

Landomal had more of an open atmosphere, with not a tree in sight. The grass, shaped, colored, and textured differently than in Scarland, with a perfect mixture of yellow and beige, reaching halfway up my legs from my knees to my feet. Patches of grass were missing, making it manageable to navigate as I stepped from one open area to the next. The childlike part of me hopped around, making it a game not to touch the grass.

The little stream of water seemed to have a lot of dirt, which made sense given how dry and chalklike the dirt around the grass appeared to be. The dirt had a red and brown mixture that reminded me of a painting I had seen before called *African Clay*. Of course, this was just the narrow part of Landomal. I had no idea what to expect once we got to the open area that I had seen on the map.

I knew this wouldn't be our path forever, but after a few days, some shade would be a treat. I missed the trees and how the land looked covered in them. If I knew I wouldn't be found, I could have stayed surrounded by them for the rest of my days. I could only hope Coastra offered something as appealing. Still, to travel and see something different really was an awesome experience.

"You seem to be having a lot of fun for someone who's been baking in the sun." Mavryk's voice had amusement behind it. We hadn't talked much, so there were moments I forgot he existed and got lost in my own world.

"My mind likes to wander wherever it decides to go. It never stays in one place for long. I don't do well with small talk for that reason."

"I'd rather be in silence than have a pointless conversation. Who wants boring conversations, anyway?" he responded. That made me smile.

"I can keep my focus if it catches my interest. I just can't seem to pay attention unless it does, or unless I have to for safety. If I'm too panicked or trying to process the last bit of information, I'll have a hard time comprehending what's been said or what I read. It also depends on my comfortability. If I'm in a room with a bunch of people I know I can't be myself around, I tend to shut down and have to fight off not spacing out, which makes focusing nearly impossible. I always felt dumb and out of place for it." As I said it, I realized just how unusual that sounded, yet I had never been able to explain myself as well until today.

"You are the furthest from dumb, love. People have misunderstood you and mistaken it for ignorance when it was them who never cared enough to understand. Do you know how many people lack understanding of themselves? Yet you can explain yourself in an in-depth way. That takes a lot of reflecting on yourself, and it's remarkable you have. Not only that, but you also have no desire to be like anyone else. You don't hide who you've been or the mistakes you've made. The only real problem I see is you lack the confidence to realize how incredible you are for how far you've come."

Once again, he caught me off guard and left me speechless. I wish I knew how to take a compliment better so I could respond properly, but I don't even know how to accept him, or anyone, saying something so nice toward me.

"Do you hear that?" he asked. I looked at Mavryk, and he seemed thrown off. His eyes wandered around, and his brows furrowed. "It sounds like water falling."

"There is a river on both sides of us." I can't hear anything else we had already been listening to.

"No. This resembles a waterfall. Much different than running water."

As dry as everything looked, I couldn't imagine anything else besides the little stream next to us, but who knows. I tended to drown out a lot of background noise when I went into my own world. Sometimes I got so lost in it that I forgot that where I really was is the reality of life. I'd never seen a waterfall either, at least not a good-sized one.

"Have you seen a waterfall before?" I asked.

"A few but not here. I typically travel through Egyptstra and Scarland to find people, then meet with others around those places and send them off to whoever is taking them to the next person to reach Coastra."

"I forgot you had mentioned being an escaper. How many are there?"

"More than you'd think."

"I can't imagine most of them being drainers."

He took a moment before responding. "No. There's only a few of us."

"What made you decide to become one? How did you learn about them?"

"I used to be a capturer. An escaper saved my life, ironically while I was hunting for him. I went out to a pub that night, and another capturer tried killing me, accusing me of stealing his position. The man I was sent out to kill jumped in and protected me. Liam saved my life."

Sadness was expressed through his voice. "He took me out to his hiding spot that night and fed me. He said he could sense I didn't belong with them and asked me to join him and the others like him."

The tone in his voice changed to regret. "He taught me many things, but the most valuable lesson was what a dad should be. I never got to thank him for it."

I felt myself choke up. Not only did I relate to his pain on unspoken last words to a close loved one, but to know he knew the depth of how heavily that weight burdened him hurt me. No one decent deserves to feel that, and he was more than decent.

"If he didn't know how you felt, he does now," I said softly.

He dropped his head toward the ground as if shame came over him. The pain on his face said that didn't matter to him because he still wished to have said it while Liam was here. I grabbed his hand and turned to him. He turned to me.

"You are amazing, Mavryk. Anything you had done is in the past. It only matters what you do now and who you are today. The man I see in front of me is a man worthy of forgiving himself for not knowing what he knows now. A man who learned and grew into someone to be proud of."

He closed his eyes, trying not to let tears fall out. He leaned into me, and I held him. We never realized that at any moment the last things we say could be our last words spoken to them. We never realized we might not get another chance to express our love and gratitude toward those that meant something to us. You don't realize how short of a time you can have with someone until one day you don't get another day. I had forgotten that valuable lesson myself until this moment here with him.

We continued walking for a bit longer, and as we did, I heard the noise he talked about. Before we knew it, the little stream grew a lot wider and the noise a lot louder.

"I can hear it now." I looked up at Mavryk, and he smirked.

"Look in front of you," he said, staring ahead.

I had been watching my feet and where I stepped the whole time that I didn't realize we had made it to the waterfall. There was not only a waterfall but a massive pond too.

I had no idea how the water became so clear, but you could see every bit of what the water held. The water didn't fall directly into the pond until after it went through layers of rocks that weren't leveled. The rocks were rugged but stunningly collided together. Any climber would want to test them out to see if they could withstand the challenge of making it to the top without slipping. The rock formation on each side of the waterfall made it tempting to climb.

"How did you hear that from back there?" I didn't take my eyes off the surroundings, but I could tell he looked at me as he spoke.

"You learn to become alert with your senses when you're constantly needing to."

Maybe I needed to do the same. Then again, my imagination had always saved me from total despair. I couldn't face reality as much without partly living in my world. It became a need to escape to keep my sanity intact. Out here, where I am, I needed different survival skills. Or maybe I needed to find a better balance.

I shifted my focus from the waterfall and pond and realized both sides of the waterfall were different. My right side consisted of a gorgeous jungle. I couldn't see a hint of anything else that might show differently. On the left side are a bunch of different-sized mossy rocks that seemed to fade into them not being mossy within a close distance. The sun seemed to shine even brighter on that side.

"I never realized how much beauty the world held. How different it is from Scarland." I spoke.

I looked at Mavryk. He had been facing me. I wasn't sure what that look might have meant, but by what he had expressed, he seemed to truly show how real those feelings were. If love danced in anyone's eyes, his did for me.

Then again, maybe my imagination started to play tricks on me. After all, being a deep-down hopeless romantic, one can dream of such admiration, to be loved so passionately and effortlessly. It's making sure to remember what's real and what we create, separated from the other.

"Neither did I." He spoke softly.

"You've traveled, though. You've seen different parts of the world."

"I didn't stop to appreciate it." He took the canteen out of his bag and pushed it into the water to let it fill. "Until I saw you absorbing everything like a sponge, I didn't realize how breathtaking nature is." He lifted the canteen out of the water and drank from it. When he was done, he continued speaking. "You made me realize how ungrateful I've been about life."

He handed the canteen to me, and I finished it off. "I was thirstier than I thought." I smiled sheepishly.

He made a slight smirk. "We've not had a lot to drink since our travel started. Drink up. The water tastes pure. Who knows when we'll run into that again." He grabbed the canteen from me, filled it again, and gave it back.

I took another gulp. The water definitely tasted amazing. "Come to think of it, I prefer this. It's fresh and not messed with. I wouldn't doubt if it were a lot healthier for you."

He made a quiet chuckle. "There's no telling what they do to our means for survival, but you were in the castle. If anyone got close to the safest water, it would have been anyone living there."

"The cost of freedom comes with it. I'll take poisoned water over them corrupting my mind." I stopped myself from saying more. "I said that harsher than I meant to. I'm sorry."

"Don't apologize to me for that. I can't blame you for feeling the way you do. Matter of fact, you've done a lot better than you give yourself credit for."

"What do you mean?" I felt my brows furrow together as I asked that.

He sat down next to me and looked me in my eyes. "You're a lot tougher than you think. Somehow you push yourself even when you feel like giving up. Too many underestimate the power that comes with that."

CHAPTER 20

I had longed for freedom for so long that I didn't stop to think what that came with. Freedom meant living, but I don't know how to live. My mind still cages me. I need to shift my mind from survival mode to where I am now.

I realize that involves healing, but where do I start? How do you heal a lifetime of suffering? How do you rewire all the twisted knots that come with trauma? How do you convince yourself that the past doesn't dictate your future? That you no longer need to fight the same way you always have. You need to fight in a way that proves what you have gone through cannot define you.

The hardest part about healing is knowing your worth. There's no room for sinking into yourself and believing the self-esteem issues planted by others who more than likely never really knew you to begin with or who didn't want you to see for yourself. Some of them went out of their way to attack out of nowhere. While you were sticking to yourself and kind to those you did bother with, others came at you for no real good reason.

My theory is that they see your light and, before you get a chance to realize it yourself, they want to dim it as much as possible. Jealousy is a much uglier trait than people want to admit. Most won't dare admit that that's their issue either.

The problem is the negativity is planted and grows within my mind because I never dug it out, so its roots developed. I rooted how others valued me without recognizing it until it became too late to easily remove it. That's my biggest issue. I can piece together what's wrong and what needs to be fixed, but the root of where it needs to be dug up is where I fumble. My mind tends to blank out when I dig to a certain point or jump to another memory that throws me way off. It's a defense mechanism, I believe, and I'm not sure how to break from that.

Habits are a funny thing because we develop them out of an interest or a way to help us through something. That can lead to a problem when it's used in a way to help cope. Drinking became a habit for me, as it has for so many for so long. Drinking to cope is damaging, no matter how much you want to convince yourself it's not. However, it's still easier to recognize it as a problem than to piece together damaging thoughts.

The ones triggered by someone's actions, which remind them of past manipulations, often develop the worst trust issues. Even though you aren't dealing with the abuser anymore, and there are those who don't intend to hurt you, your mind sends a signal that you can't take the chance of being betrayed again.

You've built unbreakable walls, coated in layers of an untouchable entrance. There's no way you'll let another climb over to the other side to prove they aren't the same.

There's a misunderstanding between the two of you, but you're not used to that. You're used to people degrading you, lying to you, and deceiving you. So, the first impulse sends a wavelength to the brain to react as poorly as you have in the past. A need to react before letting your nerves calm down because you won't feel validated if you don't get to speak, and you're not used to being listened to.

Lash out, curse out, and be the loudest. Get worse if they interrupt or yell back. Throw something if you must. You just can't lose another fight; you can't handle another fight where you don't feel heard. You can't feel disrespected anymore. You won't tolerate being treated so poorly anymore. You've had enough. It's even worse when you know for certain they're trying to manipulate you and fool you, as if you're new to something like gaslighting.

Regardless if it's because of a misunderstanding or because they are trying to fool you, your reaction makes you feel terrible. Terrible for taking it out on them when they didn't deserve it or for giving them the power of a reaction they didn't deserve. Either way, you stepped out of your authentic character. You showed a part of yourself that's not really you—an unhealed mask placed there by someone, or multiple people, who purposely tried to break you into who they wanted you to be. A mask that helped you cope. It's that part of you that wasn't there in the beginning because it was never meant for you to hold.

Hurt people hurt people, and this is why it's so important to break those cycles of toxic behaviors. It has to stop with someone. Someone has to shed off the layers of abuse that have been going on for generations. Someone has to unlearn what's been shown and relearn what is healthy. Someone has to stand and fight for future children to have a better outcome. Someone who's willing to leave it all behind to gain the freedom and peace that no one could before.

I know this is random to write out, but reflecting tends to make me go down the rabbit hole of things I've come to learn through the traumas and experiences that I've gone through or things I've done. I don't like *to sit and dwell on the past, but I find myself constantly learning and understanding more. Sometimes it's a bit much to handle, especially if I should be enjoying a moment, but I suppose this is why I reflect so much. I want to understand so I can figure out a way to change.*

I'm wanting to heal sooner rather than later, but you can't rush this sort of thing, can you? Healing takes time. Healing involves not picking at a scab, so the scars don't bleed again. There's not much you can do when you have picked a scab enough that the scar continues to bleed, but you can always decide not to pick at it anymore.

The outcome will be the same as soon as you remove the scab. You'll bleed and feel the sharp sting that comes with ripping off what needs to stay. It's all a matter of when you're ready to sit with the uncomfortable feeling of it for a while.

When you truly want real healing, you have to sit with the uncomfortable feeling of wanting to remove the scab in order to let it heal properly. It may not heal as fast as you want, you might have to sit with it longer than you expected, but in the long run, this is how a wound really heals. The irony is, you end up healing quicker when you let it naturally heal than if you keep delaying sitting with the temporary discomfort.

A big splash startled me. My head jerked up to look in its direction. Mavryk came up from under the water and wiped his face. He smiled at me. He had taken off his shirt, shoes, and socks but kept his shorts on.

"You should join! It might help relax your mind." He went back under the water, and when he came up, he was closer to me. "Come, love. Come join me."

I made a slight smile and looked at the waterfall. "Which side did you jump from?"

"On your right," he responded.

He turned and pointed at a certain rock ledge that stuck out more than the rest, right before the water made a drop into the pond.

"You see the one that's got more of a flat surface than the rest? That's your opportunity to jump in," he said with a bit of enthusiasm.

He turned around and had such a happy smile that froze me in place. "Sometimes jumping into the unknown makes the moment a memorable one. It can make the difference that is needed for you to realize happiness is right in front of you."

"Always so clever with your words," I responded with a slight smile.

"Yet you're never impressed." His smile faded, but he still seemed content and unbothered. He leaned backward to let himself float in the water while slowly moving his arms to swim around.

"I'm left speechless, actually," I said, low enough for him not to hear. "A swim would be nice, but I'm not a fan of sitting in wet clothes," I said louder than I had with my last sentence.

"The sun will dry them," he responded quickly.

"I need to write a little bit more, then I'll think about joining you."

He lifted his head and looked at me. "The only way to come in is by jumping." His lips danced with a playful smile.

I smiled back at him, looked around one more time to soak in everything, then went back to writing. I decided I'd leave where I left off as its own thing with a space in between and start writing differently.

I wish I knew how to talk the way I write. It's easy for me to write what I want, how I feel, but I stumble so badly on how to verbalize what it is I mean. My mind races at a thousand speeds and moves onto the next thing while barely leaving me any time to comprehend where the thoughts originally started or what was thought before.

I struggle greatly to place them into a few sentences when details of what I'm wanting to say mean everything if I'm going to get the bigger picture across. I can write the biggest book imaginable on the random thoughts and emotions that cross me daily.

There are times I can't process what I'm feeling or how something led to what I'm feeling. Oftentimes I find myself triggered by something and I'm never totally sure if it's harmless or not on their end. What's small to most can have a big effect on how I feel that takes so much out of me and usually leaves me drained. I have to work harder to communicate with most people. I have to work even harder to keep myself from panicking if I'm triggered. I have to try and keep myself collected until I'm in a safer space where I can gather my thoughts and emotions.

Not to mention if there's some type of sound that's too loud or incredibly irritating in some form, some type of touch that I can't shake from making me uncomfortable (what I wear makes all the difference), or if there's a brightness that's too bright for my eyes, then that takes away the majority of my focus, if not all, on where it needs to be. I'm still not sure how to help soothe some of those sensory issues I have once they've become an issue either.

I prefer being alone. My mind is collected and calm, especially when I'm surrounded by nature. Being around people can be exhausting for many reasons. Those people holding what they think is secret animosity toward me is something I especially cannot handle, nor do I understand it. I sometimes wonder if people take offense to how content I am with myself when most people aren't.

Maybe they are so uncomfortable with themselves that me being comfortable with who I am in my own presence makes their comfortability with themselves worse.

CHAPTER 21

I reread what I wrote, as I always do. I wish I had better handwriting; then again, I already had a hard enough time keeping up with my thoughts even when I scribbled the words fast. Writing came a lot easier than talking, but it could still be a struggle. I could hardly keep up when my mind was racing. There had been a few times I couldn't, mainly when I had no idea what was going on with me because of how overwhelmed I felt.

I put my notebook and pencil in the satchel and decided to leave it there along with my shoes. I usually wore socks, but socks weren't an option with feet like mine when they couldn't be washed every day.

I looked at the cliff and then at the rest of the surroundings while listening to the birds chirp melodies and felt a small smile form. The amount of beauty this spot held tempted me to stay and live in such a paradise. The peace that overcame me had been something I was not sure I'd ever felt. I could only imagine how freeing I'd feel if I constantly lived in this state of mind.

I looked at Mavryk and noticed him staring at me. He did that a lot.

"Tell me something," Mavryk said playfully.

"What do you want me to tell?" I asked with an even bigger smile.

"If the situation were different, could you live here with me for the rest of your days?" The tone in his voice said he wished we could.

"If only," I responded with a hint of sadness.

"Let's pretend you can for the rest of the day. Give me something to hold onto forever."

I really adored him. His imagination danced around like mine, and ours played well together, but his was a lot happier and more fairy tale–like, while he didn't struggle to keep track of reality. My world sucked me in so intensely that it made most of the time hard for me to focus on the reality that was going on.

When reality sank in, it became easy to fade into the darkest parts of my mind, trapped in an overwhelming feeling that it couldn't possibly get better, which is why I didn't understand how hope had stayed alive like it had, almost as if something supernatural had been keeping it alive, a strength outside of my own but somehow living within. As soon as I was ready to give up, something came over me to do what was needed. To stay for another day when I was ready to give up. It got very exhausting.

Recently, I'd been given some of the best days I'd had in years— today especially. Even if I had been captured and sent back, I could at least come back to these moments, cling onto them until death took me. It wouldn't be the same, but it's better than nothing.

I walked over to the waterfall and looked up. It seemed like the perfect combination of fun and challenging on an easy level. I began climbing up. With every step I took, I felt more confidence to take the next step. Any tension I had melted off and was replaced with an intense rush that zoomed through me. My mind focused on each step, which kept it from racing all over the place. I could enjoy the moment without a care in the world about what had come before or what would come.

As I made it to the top, I looked over everything. Truly spectacular to see it from this point of view. I looked over toward the side that held the jungle and could tell it only went so far before it led to an open field of what seemed to be a lot of dry and grassless land. The farther I tried to look, the fuzzier everything became, so I didn't spend much time observing far away. I focused on what was closer, like Mavryk in the pond.

"I'm waiting!" he shouted excitedly, his hands cupped around his mouth.

As I got ready to run and jump in, I suddenly started hearing whispers. Of what, I had no clue, but I knew I heard them.

"Did you hear that?" I asked but didn't look down. I looked around me and everywhere else to see if people were heading this way.

"Hear what?" I didn't have to look at him to know he struck being concerned when his tone expressed a good amount of it. "I don't hear anything."

I find that odd given how well his hearing was, but maybe it had been in my head. I couldn't hear anything now.

I shrugged while I made a face. He shook his head and laughed. "Stop goofing around and jump already!"

I sprang forward, and as I jumped off into the water, I heard the whispers again, only slightly louder. As I swam up for air, I looked around with a bit of panic taking over. I knew I was not imagining this, but there was no one else around. Had something in my brain finally snapped?

"Ann, what's wrong?" I looked at Mavryk. The whispers stopped.

"I keep hearing something," I said.

"What is it you're hearing?"

I heard every word of what he said, but I was too shocked to respond. I didn't know how to explain it without sounding maddening.

"I'm hearing whispering, but I can't make out what's being said. There are multiple voices." I inhaled deeply before speaking the next part. "There's this other sound, but I have no way of explaining it. It's not wind chimes, but it resembles that. It sounds magical in a sense."

"What about the whispers? How do they sound?" I couldn't tell what he was possibly thinking, but his brows were furrowed together intensely. "I'm not sure. It's not a cry for help but almost like they're communicating something." I looked around and still couldn't see anything. "It's going to sound strange, but I feel like they're trying to lead me somewhere." Then again, it couldn't be any stranger than me hearing voices someone else wasn't.

We both waited a bit longer, but I didn't hear anything more. I swam closer to the opposite side of the waterfall, so my feet touched the ground. The ground made a perfect slope to walk to the shore about halfway from the waterfall. I came to a stop before my chest left the water and looked toward the jungle area.

Mavryk came up behind me and slowly moved his hands up my arms. His arms ended up wrapping around me. I leaned into his chest while he gently placed his chin on my shoulder. His head slightly turned toward mine. "One day, you won't feel so anxious, my love. I'll make sure you get to Coastra one way or another." He spoke with such a gentleness that he could have told me something rude about myself, and I would have still found his voice soothing.

"I'd love to believe that, but something tells me it'll be a while before I can rest in peace." I realized how that sounded and further explained myself. "I didn't mean in death. I meant with life getting easier, where I can sit back and truly relax from time to time."

"Maybe, but you can still search for peace until then. At the very least, try to be content that you're not where you were."

"I wish I knew how," I whispered.

"I know, love. I'm sorry." He reached his head around to kiss my cheek.

Suddenly, I heard the voices again. They were so clear, but I still couldn't make out what they were saying. There were too many talking at once.

"I need one voice at a time! I can't make out what you're telling me!" I said in aggravation.

I pulled away from Mavryk. He started to ask something, but I shushed him. Suddenly, the voices stopped, and so did the noise.

Follow me.

This voice spoke clear as daylight with no other noise or voice. It sounded like no one I'd heard and not in the way I had ever heard someone speak. Something much more powerful than I knew how to describe. The voice came from within but somehow pulled me in the direction that sat on the opposite side of the jungle. I looked over toward it.

There weren't many trees covering the boulders besides when you first step onto them, but after that, the direct sunlight beamed on them. The boulders varied in size. Most were good for stepping on them one by one. They seemed to get bigger the farther out you looked.

I looked at Mavryk. His face expressed worry and confusion. "I need to go that way." I pointed toward the direction needed.

"There's nothing except rocks and eventually a river. Over that river is Outcastril, even if you can get in, you wouldn't want to."

Follow my voice. You know where I am calling you to be. I will never misguide you.

I had no idea who or possibly what spoke to me, but I knew I needed to listen. With no real clue what I would be getting into or where I would be going, I knew I had to go. I started walking. Mavryk stopped me by grabbing my hand. "Ann, did you hear me? That is toward Outcastril. Do you remember what I told you about that place?" His worry increased in his voice, and he had said every word slower than usual.

I slowly turned toward him while our eyes locked in each other's. I placed my free hand on his cheek and gently squeezed the hand he held. "This is where I need to go, Mavryk." I kissed him, and quickly after our lips pressed together, a jolt to run took over me. I pushed him hard enough for him to fall into the water and started running. I had no idea what took over me or why I bothered to push him so hard, but I knew I needed to go, and with how worrisome he was, something told me he would try to stop me. I couldn't have that.

I had never heard voices like that before. There were times my own voice yelled a lot harsher toward myself and others. I'd even thought I heard someone I was around call my name faintly or say something in their voice I couldn't make out when they never said anything, but I had never heard this voice before. Nothing like that. There was a distinct difference between anything I'd experienced, and this voice resembled an intuition, almost.

After a bit of running, I slowed down. I kept looking around at a distance, waiting to see something that stuck out. I could faintly see the river that separated Outcastril and Landomal. I stopped and slowly looked around. There wasn't anything except boulders for miles.

Go toward your left. That is where you will enter.

"Enter? Enter what?" I said out loud. Suddenly, I could hear the sound from earlier. Hearing it this close reminded me of the glow.

"Ann!" Mavryk panted as he shouted. As he caught up to me, he nearly collapsed, using his knees to support his weight with his hands resting on them. He caught his breath a bit more, straightened his posture, and then spoke. "You are way too fast for my liking and strong. What are you doing? Who are you talking to? Ann, what the heck is going on?!" Frustration left his voice at the last sentence.

I stared at him with no response. I didn't know what to say. I almost couldn't believe what was happening or what was being said myself, but I knew it was real. I knew I needed to do what it said. Or *he* said. I was not sure yet, but it felt like it could be a male's voice. It definitely resembled one, just in an unusual way.

I turned and walked in the left direction. I expected Mavryk to try and stop me again, but he didn't. He followed. I felt halfway insane doing this, following some voice I couldn't explain, not knowing where it was taking me or if I had finally lost it and imagined everything. I needed to find out either way. Part of me hoped to prove that my sanity wasn't all gone; the other part hoped I had lost my mind because it seemed more logical than to hear such a distinct voice.

I had been watching my feet again and spaced off into why I had begun doing this in the first place until Mavryk spoke. "Do you see that?" I looked up. From a short distance, there was a dark opening between boulders in the ground. Within a few steps of entering, we approached the black hole. I couldn't see anything in it. This gave me an eerie feeling. This couldn't be what the voice had guided me to.

This is where I want you. You are safe.

That didn't seem likely, but it had led me here for a reason. I looked at Mavryk. "This is it." I felt like he had been staring at me as if I had lost it. "Trust me. I know what this seems like, but there's something guiding me. I can feel it. It's clear right now with what it's saying." That seemed to be the only real reassurance to me. The voice was too clear for me to disregard it.

He looked away from me and stared at the dark opening. "This is extremely bizarre, but I do believe you. Something has been telling me to follow you when you lead. As it has told me to help you when you need it. I can't hear a voice, but that feeling is very real." He then looked at me with a more relaxed look but still firmly serious. "Whatever is guiding us is much bigger than any of us can imagine. I'll follow you wherever it takes you and help you when you need it."

CHAPTER 22

I thought I would have fallen onto a ground of some sort, but somehow, I ended up with my feet planted on the ground. Above my head, the sun beamed through an opening. As I looked up, I saw Mavryk looking in. It was clear as day on this side, but on the other side, you couldn't see into this at all. It was not bright in here, but it was certainly not pitch black. It reminded me of an underground cave that had been abandoned. Other than from where I stood, I was not sure why it was not pitch black in here. There was no other source of light being used, and there was no other hole above that I could see. The cave seemed to have a natural glow to it. Come to think of it, when I entered through the opening, it reminded me of that feeling when I crawled into the glow, but it had its own twist of a feeling to it.

"Mavryk! Can you hear me? It's safe down here!" I had begun turning around and then jumped. He stood right behind me and started laughing.

"As clear as can be." He finished his laughing by saying that with a cheesy grin.

"How long have you stood there for? Never mind, have you ever seen something like this?" I went back to looking throughout the cave.

"No. I've never seen something like this."

I looked at him. He couldn't hide his fascination with this even if he wanted to. "I've been in a lot of caves, seen so many hidden places, but I've never experienced something like this. I mean, this is beyond incredible." He looked at me and then asked a question. "Did you manage to do this?"

I could feel my face form into confusion and then relax some. It made sense that he would assume that. "I don't believe so. I can feel when I heal, I've felt what it's like to drain, so I can't imagine doing this without knowing in some way."

He walked over to a tall formation of rock in front of us and touched it. As he did, the light grew brighter around his hand. "Remarkable." The look of joy on his face made me smile. "It feels like there's healer magic to this. Come feel."

I hesitated for a second and then took every step slowly toward him. I came to a stop as I reached the other side of the rock. "Something's about to happen once you touch this," he said.

I looked at him, wondering if he knew what I had been thinking, and responded. "I can't help but feel the same way either."

I looked at the rock and studied it. The glow had intensified. "I can feel the magic already," I whispered as I lifted my hand up and pressed it against the rock.

A cool sensation started in my palm and traveled into my fingers and then my arms. Before I knew it, the cool sensation filled my body. Not only did the rock glow brighter, but the brightness traveled throughout the cave. Instead of the golden brown color, it became white.

"Ann. Look at me."

His tone gave off a shock that nearly left him speechless, and his facial expression showed him being stunned. I couldn't believe what I was seeing. The reflection from his eyes showed me glowing in white as well. When I looked at my arms, my mouth nearly dropped open. My skin had become this beautiful pigment of white like snow, just as bright and as elegant with a pearl touch to it.

"I don't even know how to describe you right now, but I want to feel what you feel like. Would that be okay?"

I nodded my head yes in response. He lifted his hand and inched toward my face. Suddenly, the first dream I had with him came to mind. I jerked away before he touched my cheek. He pulled his hand back and looked frustrated.

"I thought you were okay with me touching you?" he asked with confusion.

I stood up and took a few steps away from the rock. The cave still glowed a white light. I knew enough of what could come next.

"Stand up," I instructed in a calm but confident voice. "Stand in front of me. As I hold my hand up, I need you to do the same."

I can't tell what ran through his mind, but he knew I knew something, so he stood up and made steps until he stood in front of me. "Lead the way, my love."

I had to compose myself from a smile forming. Something about the way he said "my love," with the smoothness to it, made me a bit giddy all over inside. An emotion that wanted to burst at the seams. I took a deep breath in with my eyes closed to regain my focus.

I lifted my left hand up and felt him doing the same. As I inched my hand into his, I felt his doing the same. Significance no longer had hold over our bodies because our souls gravitated toward each other. As our hands touched and our fingers entwined, I felt a charge of powerful electricity I had never experienced, not even when we kissed.

When I opened my eyes, I gasped. His skin tone had turned into a calming dark blue. As I studied him, I noticed the light started fading into less of a dark blue the closer it got to our hands. Our hands that pressed against each other had turned into a very light crystallized blue as a blaze of fire. It glowed so brightly I had to squint my eyes a bit to tone down the intensity of it.

As I looked between him and me, his dark blue and my white light started to turn into the same color of blue our hands were. We stood there, looking like we're on fire, but we contained the power of light.

I looked up and around. The same vibrant color that took over us had become the color of the cave. The brightness didn't touch the surface of the energy that flowed from us or within this cave. This wasn't something to feed curiosity or to lead you to a discovery. This was the discovery. This was something the world hadn't imagined being possible—an awakening to something new, something compelling, shaking, and captivating all into one word to possibly describe a moment like this.

GLYCERINE

I had no words to match how amazed I felt by everything. Waves of different emotions passed through me, and for the first time, I felt nothing bad could come from an experience. A new sense of hope struck me like lightning, waking up what had been sleeping. There had been so much screaming at me to wake up from this deep slumber, and all along, this was what I had needed to awaken me.

"By yourself, you're white. Now you're this..." He paused and took a deep breath in while his eyes looked around at every part of me. "Breathtaking blue. I've never, in my wildest days, heard of something like this."

"We. Not just I." I spoke softly. His brows furrowed together, and then he looked at himself, and his jaw dropped open. "Let go of my hand, Mavryk."

I pulled my palm away and then my fingers and watched as he did the same. His hand fell to his side, and instead of letting mine fall with his, I held up my other hand next to it. I shaped my hands into a ball without them touching. It didn't take long for a ball of light to form. It started off small and grew until it became the size that fit between my hands.

As I held it in place, it held sparkles that twinkled everywhere like the glow. The twinkles created it to be a pearl color rather than staying white. I didn't have a clue what I had created, but I knew it couldn't be wasted. I knew this was meant for such a significant difference in how the future played out, as if it meant life versus death. Something extremely personal and of the greatest value, I could hold within my hands.

"Whatever that is, you do not want to waste that." A female's voice spoke.

The ball of light in my hands disappeared as I dropped my hands to the side. Mavryk's head whipped around the same time my eyes looked past him. The blue blaze of fire that Mavryk and I were went away, and so did the blue coloring of the cave. It went back to the golden brown tint it had been before.

I had to blink a few times and rub my eyes a bit to make sure I saw her correctly. She stood shorter, I would guess nothing above five feet tall. Her build was curvy yet still petite. Her hair sat in a perfectly

153

neat bun, and her eyes reminded me of the color of honey. Her skin had a beautiful light-brown color that glittered, while the tops of her ears were pointed. But what really fascinated me were the wings on her back. They're traced in black, with mostly yellow, followed by a neat pattern, comparable to a butterfly. The difference that separated them was how thin in width her wings were.

"I can't believe what I just saw with you two!" She had a perk to her voice that I couldn't imagine being anything other than cheery, and her smile lit beautifully. Her teeth were full and gorgeous.

She fluttered over to us and took turns looking at us as she spoke. "Magic comes from fairies, and neither of you are that, so what are you?" She referenced both of us and continued talking. "One of you must've heard the whispers to find this place. It's truly incredible what the two of you have. The magic you two possess comes from something much greater, and I have to say, that is way more than I have ever seen. Oh gosh! Where are my manners? I'm Naomi. I'm a fairy!" She threw up her hands and fluttered a spin as a playful giggle escaped.

Mavryk stared at her, dumbfounded as if he couldn't believe what he saw. I cleared my throat a bit to make sure I wouldn't talk with some type of croak. "Hi. I'm Ann. This is Mavryk." I made an awkward wave, with probably an even more awkward smile. "I've never seen a fairy before."

"That's because most of you don't know we exist." She used a lot of body movements and hand gestures when she talked and looked incredibly happy. "We've been hiding for such a long time, way before my time. I'm also a very young fairy, I bet that explains the babbling I always do." She giggled.

"Well, you look only about sixteen, but yes, you definitely have some spunk to you." It was adorable, really. She reminded me of a child in a sense. Innocence still shielded her from the chaos of the world, while things like depression and anxiety hadn't touched her yet. I hoped it never did.

"I'm sixty-four, dear," she said it proudly. I felt my eyes widen. "Oh, and our age group lasts much longer than the rest of the beings' groups. See, fairies can live for hundreds of years. Our elders are nearly six hundred years old, but they don't look a day over three hundred, so they're doing pretty amazing."

We both let out a laugh. "That's very interesting," I responded.

"Uh. Okay, so forgive me for not having humor in any of this, but I'm lost. What did you mean by being groups? And how is it possible to live that long?" Mavryk's tone matched his face with the many mixed emotions he had to be feeling.

She rolled her eyes and waved her hand in a playful manner. "Yes, yes, leave it to the guy to be so serious. Anyways, beings are the groups that everyone is. No one is without some type of power, or that would make them human, and thank goodness for that, right? They were the creations before us. Washed away once the Sacred decided how terrible of an idea that had been! That's one of the stories told, anyways."

She shook her head a bit. "Forgive me, I'm terrible about staying on track. There's healers, drainers, telepaths, and fairies. So which are you?" She looked between us, waiting for a response.

"He's a drainer, and I'm a healer. Supposed to be, anyways." I could tell that threw her off. "I've drained recently. It was only once."

"Very powerful, nonetheless," Mavryk added.

Naomi's jaw dropped open as she cupped her hands over her mouth and then moved them to her cheeks. "It's you. You're finally here." She threw up her hands and grabbed my arm. "I must take you to the elders! There's no time to waste!"

She began to pull, but I hesitated. She stopped and looked back at me, making a gesture on her face to come with her. "What are you doing? You realize every second wasted is one less soul saved? This isn't something to be hesitant about!"

Mavryk spoke before I did. "I think she's as lost as I am now. What is it you mean that she's the one you've been waiting for?"

She let go of my arm and crossed hers together and then made a dramatic sigh. "Look, I don't know all the details, but I know enough. We've all been taught about a chosen one that would come along. One who had the ability to drain and heal. The one who not only heard the whispers but the Sacred's voice." She looked at me with a curious look. "That's who guided you here, isn't it?"

I looked between them and then around the cave. "I'm not sure who it was, but it wasn't like anything else. A soft yet confident and powerful voice, but it wasn't a voice you'd think of hearing. I felt what I believe to be a *he* who said it. I have no idea how else to explain it."

She smiled, and her eyes lit up. "We've waited for you. So now it's up to you. Come with me to the next part of your destiny or turn around and go back where you came. The choice is always yours. Only one will lead you rightly."

Choice. I had a choice to ignore what was being called or to go into the unknown without all the answers, with others I'd never met and knew nothing about. To somehow trust that I would be taken where I was meant to, and it would turn out okay. That somehow everything I had suffered through would make sense, and that it was all a part of this divine plan for something so good. That my future had something so wonderful in store that nothing in my past could have ever stolen or destroyed this purpose set in place for me. It seemed unlikely, but that feeling stood stronger than anything else ever had.

She held out her hand, waiting patiently for me to decide. I was not sure how I knew I could trust her, but I did. Even with all of my trust issues and uncertainty with many things in life and with the amount of betrayal by people, I somehow knew.

Something in me knew this to be right, with no hesitation to continue going forward. I suppose this is how you know for sure you're on the right path. When many are out to be against you and your mind becomes your worst enemy in a way it hasn't before, but there are a few of them helping you along the way by playing a part in giving you what you need. Along with unexplainable things that haven't happened before that are now happening, that's a sign you're onto something greater than you can imagine.

CHAPTER 23

Never in my life did I imagine something so enchanting and mesmerizing to exist. Anything you think of that described a place for a fairy fit the description. Huge mushrooms of different coloring, plants of all kinds with different colors of green, every flower you could think of. Butterflies fluttered everywhere while birds sang their melody and flew around, landing in different spots. There wasn't an inch of here that didn't have something beautifully stricken with the most vibrant colors. Everything had a glitter or glow about it.

The trees stood miles high, so full of life, with vines wrapping around them. There were different styles of homes. Some reminded me of birdhouses that hung from thick tree branches. Others were a part of the tree, like a carved-in tree house. The biggest mushrooms had been made into homes, and certain spots that had a hill on the ground were made into a hobbit hole for them to live in. Anyone's eyes that had been or would be blessed enough to get a chance of a glance to view all across this beauty would know of a fairy's existence simply because this is where a magical fairytale truly begins.

"This is the most astonishing place I have ever laid my eyes on. I'm truly speechless. I'm not even sure I could have imagined something that would touch the surface of how spectacular this is," I said with as much sincerity as my voice would let out.

"This place feels like it's covered in layers of magic." Mavryk's stunned expression gave me amusement. If any facial expression could speak for itself, his surely did.

"How else could we have created it? We had to make a safe place to escape to in order to survive." She spoke with less spunk than she had before.

That quickly changed as she changed the subject. "Now let's go forward! There's plenty more to see, but more importantly, we need you to speak to the elders. I shall warn you it is a long way to get there on foot."

"We've traveled far, a little more walking won't hurt. How big is this place?" I asked.

From the top, light beamed with sunlight, but only in certain areas did they touch the ground since the trees shaded some of it. Was it possible they created their own sun, or did a layer of magic somehow take the light from the sun and hold its place here? Magic is such an amazing mystery.

"Big enough to feel like we have a part of the world to roam." She paused and then continued talking. "We once were a part of the world like everyone else, but the worldly ruler and others in his position felt we were a threat. They thought the same with telepaths. Healers aren't as threatening to them because of their overly giving and submissive nature."

Thinking about it, I was not entirely sure how we went from the cave to what seemed like another magical world. I grabbed her hand, and we had somehow appeared here. That was more than likely the only way to appear here. She did say fairies needed a safe place to hide. I couldn't blame them one bit. I was surprised they let anyone in at all.

Crap. I needed to focus. I hadn't been able to write the way I needed to, nor had I been able to let it truly wander in all the places it liked to. My attention span became harder to hold, especially when it needed to focus on a task at hand.

"How many of you are there left?" I asked.

"Not as many healers and drainers but more than there are telepaths. They're nearly extinct." She looked at me. "Something tells me you know of one."

"Yes. Sasha. She's wonderful," I said excitedly. Images of her crying came to mind, and sadness quickly washed over me. "When she had the visions of my past, she saw everything. She told me things I didn't know about." The feeling of anger started to poke through as I remembered her telling me what my father had done.

"Sasha heard the whispers, that's how she knows of us, and I'm not surprised she was able to tell you so much about your past. She has a lot of power and is very gifted. As are you. The Sacred has such an amazing way of lining everything up the way he does to work things out so perfectly. The best part about that is the mystery behind it. How he is so capable of giving us what we need to go where we are needed while letting so much be unknown until the right time. It's marvelous." She lit up as she talked about the Sacred.

"This guy, the Sacred, who is he? How do you know so much about him? Have you met him?" I stopped myself from asking more.

"The Sacred is our true ruler. Everything you see is because of him. The sounds, the colors, the sky with its sun and clouds, the night with the stars and the moon, all the world's natural settings. Anything living, he created. All of us, the beings that we are, he made us like this. Each of us is special for a specific purpose. Not one of us is made incorrectly, nor did he plan wrongly."

"But my parents made me, and your parents made you. Parents are the ones who make us. So how could he have made any of us when we came from them?" I tried to follow, but it didn't add up to me.

"Yes, they had a part in it, but how do you think any of us started? We didn't appear out of nowhere. Out of nothing. Nothing does not become more than nothing because it is nothing," she said, the last sentence slower than the others. "There is always something that makes it into a beginning." I wanted to ask more, but she continued before I could gather more questions. "You see, there were two of each kind created—two fairies, two telepaths, two drainers, and two healers. The Sacred made the world first, then those first pairs, and each set of beings had a part of the world designed for them. To strive and—"

"Except there are five parts of the world and only four kinds of beings."

Naomi's head whipped at Mavryk. She didn't glare, but I noticed the annoyance written all over her face.

"Sorry for interrupting. We've discussed this before and noticed that. It doesn't exactly add up." He apologized and explained himself sheepishly.

She inhaled deeply but then softly exhaled. "I understand how this sounds, but this is why I need you to listen without so many questions or interruptions. After all, silence can be the reason answers are found."

Her face relaxed back to the calming look and continued where she left off. "The Sacred saw it fit for each being to go to those specific parts of the world. The part that wasn't assigned, Outcastril, he made clear he would watch over it until he left. He warned that once he left, Outcastril would burn into a blue blaze of fire and the ones who claim to be in charge would make it into something terrible."

She looked at me in such a serious manner and then spoke. "When the time comes, one would be born as a healer that had the power to drain. The one born as such would not only hear our whispers but his voice as well. This would be the chosen one."

She looked forward with less seriousness, but the total calm in her voice didn't return. "I know it is a lot to take in, but you are destined for this. The Sacred chose you." Excitement left her tone. "I watched how you and Mavryk beamed with light. He had a part in it, but it originated from you. The light within you is like nothing I have ever seen before."

I didn't have it in me to believe that. "I don't mean to sound so down and depressing, but it's not possible I'm some chosen one. I don't even really know what a chosen one is. I'm not sure how to explain everything that's happened, but there's no way I'm anything special, especially to that level. I might be different, but it's not in the way that makes me spec—"

Naomi cut me off before I could finish and stopped us from walking farther as she stood in front of me. "I cannot believe you are talking about yourself this way! Like, I am not going to listen to this blasphemy!"

Her hands had waved in the air, and then she took a deep breath and crossed her arms together. "My dear, different is the exact reason why you are so special, but more important than that, it is the purpose behind your life. There is so much more involved than just you. You have been called for something so miraculous that helps save others, but because you see yourself so little, you deny the incredible journey ahead of you. You believe you are not capable of pursuing it, but you would not have been called for this if the Sacred had not chosen you."

She grabbed my hands and held them with a distance between us, making sure I could focus on her seriousness as she spoke. "You are not who they thought you are or what they said. You are not your pain. You are not your mistakes. You are not the bad person you believe you are. You are who the Sacred designed you as, and that is wonderfully and uniquely made." The magnitude behind her words forced tears to form. "He only makes good, the corruption behind the mess others plant in your head has never been what he intended for you to believe."

She straightened her posture and relaxed her shoulders. "So are you going to stay stuck believing things that were never meant for you, or are you going to accept the significance you make and stop holding yourself back from living the life only you are destined for?"

The lump in my throat had burst, and the tears fell like a water-fall. Crying had become something I only did in isolation because one too many times, my feelings were invalidated. Today, however, I stood bawling my eyes out in front of others I'd known for a very short time. One of them I met today.

I had become so accustomed to people belittling me, pushing me to the side, and treating me so poorly that it had shaped the way I see myself: overlooked and undervalued, unappreciated not only for everything I had done but for who I'd been. Invisible until something was needed. When I finally set boundaries, it was seen as disrespect, but the real disrespect was how much had been expected of me when they didn't make any sacrifices themselves or sacrifices that didn't compare. I made so many at one point that being drained, mixed with an exhausting numbness, had become a part of my daily dose of reality. I even shaped myself into someone else to fit the script they wanted me to read. I pretended and acted like someone else in hopes of finally winning their approval.

No one noticed that I was one push away from crossing a line that I wouldn't have recovered from. No one knew how ready I really was to never be seen again. No one knew, behind the smile I faked, that screams of desperation to be set free got so loud in my mind that I had silenced my voice. Everything else around me sounded like muffles and echoes that came from a distance. I was surrounded by multiple people at my loneliest and most misunderstood times.

"Thank you."

My voice would have cracked if I hadn't mouthed the words. I wanted to say so much more, but I didn't know how to express the magnitude of my gratitude. I didn't know how to take someone being so uplifting and kind toward me.

She graciously smiled. "Let us continue walking, shall we?" She let go of my hands, turned forward, and then looked back at me before walking. "No more self-negative talk. Even if you do not believe it, speak only good toward yourself. The words you release circle around you and create their own type of strength or weakness, depending on what you say. Your own words have the most control over how you view everything in your life."

As she continued walking, I followed behind her. Mavryk came up beside me and took my hand. He held it to his lips and gently kissed it for a good moment—the perfect touch to finish calming my nerves down. When he moved our hands to the side of us, he spoke low enough to be almost considered a whisper. "I didn't know how I felt about her at first, but I really appreciate her. She sees what I see in you. Do you remember our conversation with Sasha and Steven?"

I thought for a moment. "There was a lot we spoke about. What specifically are you talking about?"

I spoke in a low tone but didn't bother to speak as low as he did. I had forgotten all about any of the conversations until now. If I had remembered any of it, I possibly wouldn't have doubted Naomi so much. Then again, she went on about me being a chosen one. I was still not sure how much I could believe her on that.

"About the Sacred. I brought up him creating another kind with a power not discovered yet. What if Naomi is right? What if we aren't out of touch to believe that something else is made because the discovery couldn't have happened yet. You weren't born. Until recently, you didn't know you were capable of both, and she said the chosen would do both. You can't tell me there hasn't been other signs directing you to be something greater." The whispering tone got louder and filled with what seemed like passion.

"You believe her then?" I asked him.

"I believe in you. I've known how valuable you are the moment I laid my eyes on you. You crawling through a glow didn't throw me off. It was your light that stunned me in place."

He paused for a moment and then continued talking. "I believe the Sacred gave us all a purpose and that some are higher than others. I also believe that means facing greater hardships. You've been through it, love. You've suffered through so much it's unreal how strong you are. I know how tired you are and how little you believe in yourself, which is why I think the Sacred has led you to me and others. He knew you'd need what you can't give yourself."

"What's that?" Whatever he was about to say, I knew it would hit me a bit.

"Love. You have no idea how to love yourself. You have no idea how to stop second-guessing yourself. You have no idea how to accept how amazing you truly are. We're all our harshest critics, but you are as brutal to yourself as those that hurt you, possibly worse, but, Ann, look at me. Please."

My eyes had watered so much that one blink would have a few tears escape out of each eye. If I spoke, I wouldn't get anything out. I'd break down again. I braced myself for it as I looked at him, knowing whatever he had to say would be something nearly impossible for me to know how to take.

"You really are a phenomenal woman. Your soul isn't like anything else, your heart contains a love that is genuine, and that's such a beautiful rarity." He looked away as the tears slid down my cheeks, his face exposing the sadness he felt seeing my pain. "Those that hurt you in a way that ripped your self-esteem apart are idiots. They were threatened in some way because even though you don't truly see yourself, they did. I can imagine it's blinding for weaker individuals. They can't control you, so they did what they could to control how you saw yourself." He squeezed my hand a couple of times. "Nonetheless, let yourself be found. Stop holding back on who you are and own every bit that is begging to burst through. Take your power back and let it soar like an eagle. You can't please everyone, and even if you could, you'd be so miserable trying to, which you already know about, so don't hold back anymore."

He paused and then added the last part with a kiss on the hand. "Find her, Ann. She's in there. You only need to search within."

CHAPTER 24

We walked for less than a mile when we reached what fit the description of a village. There were still a lot of enchanting parts in place, but huts had been built, and a ton more homes hung from the trees. They weren't built in the trees like the other ones before. The trees still kept it pretty shaded in comparison to the outside of the cave, but the sunlight definitely exposed itself brighter in this area. Different colors of fairies with different patterns and colored wings fluttered and walked in all types of directions doing different things. Not a single fairy had the same color of wings, but they had the pointed ears. For the most part, the patterns weren't the same either; theirs seemed to be a few closely resembled. The majority of the sizes of their height seemed to match the shorter side like Naomi, but the weight was different in sizes.

"Are we deep in the cave, or did we travel somewhere else?" I looked at Naomi and watched her smile.

"It makes me wonder where your mind travels to and how far it decides to explore. I can relate to the random, unfocused thoughts." A giggle escaped, and then she clapped her hands together and held them cupped to each other. "To answer your question, yes." She made a face to gesture that she was thinking through what to say next. "We are in the cave that is in another place. Through fairies, you can come here, but without us, you will only discover the cave. The beauty of magic." Her hands parted and waved them in the shape of a rainbow.

I could get used to her spunky, cheerful self. Her hand gestures always seemed to mimic something not common. I didn't envy her for being such a delight, but I couldn't help wishing I had some of the same characteristic traits that she had. The thing is, I used to be

165

a carefree, goofy individual. Once upon a time, my mind didn't try to convince me I was better off not being here. The weight of my trauma beat me down, and so did most of the ones I loved. I was so beat down at one point that I still didn't know how I got back up at all. I supposed that's how you know your most divine purpose isn't served yet. What would have kept many down pushed you to get back up and fight harder. Even while it felt like it killed you to keep going.

I looked around and realized fairies had started circling around us. Everyone was talking, which made it very difficult to concentrate on anything being said. Nearly impossible when I had to shift my mind to a focus I didn't prepare myself for. "I take it you guys don't get outsiders often," I said to Naomi.

"There hasn't been another being in a while. From what I know, no one's ever heard the Sacred's voice. Don't be surprised by everyone's reaction when they find out you have." She had a bit of a nervous look as she said the last sentence.

Before I knew it, all the fairies had gathered around. A male fairy with jet-black hair and fair skin that stood taller than Mavryk stepped out of the crowd. He towered over all the other fairies. He had slanted eyes that showed he was constantly alert and focused and always serious. His built was toned and lean.

Everyone quieted down. His expression, along with his posture, seemed tense and serious. "Which of you heard the whispers?" He looked between Mavryk and me.

"I did," I responded.

"She heard the Sacred's voice too," Mavryk chimed in.

A bunch of gasps and more speaking came from the crowd. The male fairy didn't seem to be impressed. He didn't show any change of emotion.

"No one outside of a fairy has heard the Sacred's voice. I highly doubt some girl can compare to an elder."

"She's not just some girl. If she were, then she wouldn't have been able to drain while being a healer," Mavryk snapped in defensive mode and stepped to the side of me. The crowd gasped even louder, and the male fairy moved his eyes to Mavryk.

GLYCERINE

"You've seen her heal and drain with your own eyes?"

"Yes. I've seen her do both. She was labeled as a healer growing up, and I could tell when she drained that she was more than confused. It completely threw her off."

He wasn't wrong. Any part of me that thought I had myself figured out no longer existed. I felt like a broken child all over again, trying to understand who I was becoming and what the meaning of myself could possibly be. The level of power I really held. The teenager who didn't have a clue who she was came back to the surface, making reality much more difficult to handle. The guilt of feeling like I should have myself figured out by now and where I was supposed to be weighed heavily.

In the same sense, I could feel myself shifting into an alignment of all the good and bad that made me, me. Embracing the good as it is and not expecting perfection. All while I tried to accept the bad, make realistic improvements, but also accept that I couldn't be good in every way. It was a growth that had been fighting to push through.

Something in me was so close to gaining confidence that I never knew but more than ever feeling totally lost and unsure, knowing I was where I should be because there was a particular path set in place that had a reason for going this way. How do you make sense of two opposite sides of yourself going back and forth?

The male fairy didn't respond back, but he looked back at me as he spoke. "Can you drain again?"

I looked around and then at him. His contact intimidated me to the point of causing me to look away. I wanted to respond without stumbling on my words.

"I'm not sure. I had never drained until that moment."

His mouth opened as if to respond, but another male voice spoke. This voice had a deep and wise tone to it. "I will ask the questions from here, Kent." Out of the crowd of fairies, a path had cleared.

An older male and an older female fairy appeared. His hair was a light-gray color, and so was his beard. It was the longest beard I'd ever seen on someone. He reminded me of a wizard I had once seen in a series of books I read when I was younger.

The female fairy's hair went down to her waist and had a soft black color to it. The condition of its health was like no other. Both of them stood confidently, but his seemed more relaxed while hers had a strong posture. Their wings matched in color and in pattern. Their colors were gray and black. Strangely enough, the colors matched their hair and had one of the most unique patterns I'd noticed out of everyone. Their eyes slanted like Kent's.

"You'll have to forgive him. He's harder than most on newcomers, but that is what makes him the best guard. Forgive me too. I'm a bit slow when it comes to moving around these days." The male fairy made a slight chuckle.

"You'll want to forgive him on introductions as well." The female fairy spoke with such a force to be reckoned with in her tone, but kindness and compassion filled her eyes as it did her smile. "My name is Anadella, and his name is Arnerius."

"Call me Arny. Arnerius is too serious and reminds me of my age." He made the same chuckle as before. I couldn't help but smile a bit. He had a young but tired spirit.

Anadella continued talking. "We are what is known as the elders."

"What are the elders?" I asked.

"The elders are the oldest beings left alive. So in other words, Anadella and I are the oldest fairies. We are the fourth generation of the originals." Before he kept talking, Anadella gave him a look. If I had to guess, it would be a reminder to stay on track. "But never mind all of that right now. You are here for a reason." Arny looked at Anadella and gave a slight smile.

"A big purpose, from the sounds of it." Anadella took over the conversation. "I overheard you heard the Sacred's voice. What makes you believe you heard him?"

"I'm not sure what I heard, and I'm not sure what to believe, but I know it was a distinct voice. One that didn't compare to anyone else's."

I hesitated to speak the next part, but I felt a tug within to say something. "It's more like a feeling, but somehow, I knew what they were saying. Somehow, I can feel the power behind their voice. I know how that sounds—believe me, I do—but it was very real."

It seemed more real than most of the things that had come to my mind. I looked around and realized how heavy the stares were. If I had the option to disappear at that moment, I would have jumped for it.

The elders looked at each other. "It is time." Arny shook his head in agreement with Anadella.

"She resembles the girl from your dream," Arny said, still looking at her.

"The girl from your dream?" I asked.

Anadella looked at me and then spoke. "I had a dream many years ago about a little girl. She had features like you did but with short, light-brown hair. Her eyes were blue with streaks of gray just like yours. She had freckles across her nose and fair skin." She paused and came up to me. As she grabbed my hands, she examined them and continued talking.

"A tall man who glowed a golden light as bright as the sun walked up to me with her by his side, holding hands." She looked at me while placing my palms upward. "One of these hands held his." She let go of mine and folded her hands together in front of her. "He didn't say anything, but when she came forth, she glowed white and formed a ball of light in a sparkling white color."

"She did that exact thing in the cave!" Naomi exclaimed.

The little girl she described fit the description of what I used to look like and still displayed some of those features. I didn't have the freckles I had, neither was my hair short or its natural color anymore. Thinking about it, this was the longest my hair had been since I chopped it to my shoulders. That was not long after they found me and began locking me in my room at the castle.

This just didn't seem real, though. How could one be powerful enough to place things so perfectly? How could one plan all of this or see how everything would play out the way it did? I needed to know more about the Sacred to understand before I grew more frustrated trying to comprehend anymore.

"If he glowed as bright as the sun, how could you bear to look at him? Wouldn't it have been too bright to look their way?" Mavryk asked.

"I asked the same thing!" Arny had a smile on his face as he shot out his hand to make some sort of gesture and then made more hand motions with intriguing facial expressions as he spoke the rest.

"The wonderful mysteries that aren't made clear yet define the Sacred so precisely. He is such a remarkable experience. Such a divine and marvelous being. One can only hope to come to not only know of him but to know him."

"It is an experience like no other. I'm not sure how I was able to look at him, but I could see him as clearly as I am seeing you right now." The corners of her lips curled up but not enough to define it as a smile. "Arnerius makes a very sensible point about the Sacred. Having a relationship with him is far greater than trying to under-stand everything about him."

"How can you build a relationship with someone not here any-more?" Mavryk didn't look at anyone.

A few whispers left the crowd, and a bunch of fairies with facial expressions that seemed offended he would ask such a thing. He stared at the ground, looking more confused than I had ever seen him, but I understood how he felt. That, along with so many other questions, was something I wanted to know too.

"There's much to learn about the Sacred, and we want to answer more questions, but I think it would be wise to continue our conver-sation further in the Oaklen den."

Even if Anadella didn't express it in her voice, you could read by her face that there was a good reason for this. From the vibe of the crowd, I hoped he wouldn't argue with her. When Mavryk looked up and around and then at me, I made a face that hopefully said to agree to going.

He looked at Anadella when he finally responded. "Yes, that would probably be wise. I'm sorry for my unkind hospitality. That's not my intention. Ann and I have had a long journey getting here."

Anadella didn't say anything, but you could tell she appreciated the change of tone he had and that she seemed to understand where he came from.

"There is no real knowledge without enough curiosity to ask and to even go out and discover the questions our minds think of. To be young and without knowing again." Arny chuckled. "Naomi, I have a feeling you will need to be a part of this, so why don't you come with us?"

She tried to hold the excitement back, but you could see it all over her face and body language that she was not only proud but overjoyed. She shook her head in response. The elders turned toward the big oak tree at the same time and walked toward it. Naomi, Mavryk, and I followed behind.

CHAPTER 25

Arny waved his hand, and an opening to go inside the oak tree appeared. The opening revealed the inside of the tree with a sort of shiny yet clear-coated pearl entrance. The separation from the tree and the opening held a thin white sparkling line. The white reminded me of the ball of light I held back when Mavryk and I were in the cave.

Arny turned his head and looked at each of us with a serious expression. "Never enter in pairs through a fairy opening. Always enter one at a time." His voice had a warning about it, to not test out what would happen if anyone did.

He turned his head forward and stepped inside. I looked at Mavryk; he kept his head forward, but his brows furrowed together like mine. Knowing him, he wanted to know as badly as I did, especially since Arny didn't seem to be the type to ever be serious. Then again, I had just met him.

The inside of the tree resembled an old but well-kept cabin, with carvings of beautiful designs that filled the top, bottom, and sides. Like Sasha and Steven's place, there weren't windows on the outside, but on the inside, there were windows you could look out of and see everything, with enough natural light coming in to brighten the place.

"The carvings are beautiful." I meant to whisper that to Mavryk, but it came out louder than expected.

"Every fairy that is born has a unique design on some area of their wings. That certain design appears on the wall or ceiling." Arny chuckled. "I would have to say that the designs will start forming on the floor before long." His expression went back to the carefree, relaxed look he naturally carried.

I made a slight smile in response and then looked at the carvings as I tried to think through how to bring up the fairy opening without it being too direct of a question. "When you mentioned the fairy opening, I noticed you seemed pretty serious about only one entering through it at once." That sounded smoother in my head.

Arny didn't say anything, so Anadella answered, "It can kill you or the person entering. Unless the two of you are truly each other's half, one of you will die."

I wanted to ask more, but I could see the pain on Arny's face as the memory of something tragic taunted him.

"I'm sorry I brought it up," I said in a low voice.

I decided I would change the subject and start basic with a more perked voice. "I'm terrible about introductions. My name is Ann." I looked at Mavryk to signal for him to introduce himself.

"I'm Mavryk." He leaned against the wall as he continued to study the carvings.

Arny relaxed in posture and let out a sigh of relief. "I appreciate the change in subject." He looked at me, and then for the rest of the time, he looked between Mavryk and me.

"Right now, knowing the two of you is what is most important. I'm not sure how much you two know, so I'm going to fill you both in as best as an old man can, but first, everyone needs to go against the wall."

Naomi and I were the only ones close to the middle, but instead of asking why, we glanced at each other and then stepped to the side. I stood next to Mavryk while Naomi stood next to me.

Anadella waved her hands around and then put her hands back to the lower part of her stomach, holding her hands together graciously. At first, nothing happened, and then without warning, a wide rectangle table with six matching chairs appeared, and so did a bunch of different foods with a glass of water at each spot.

I didn't stop to realize how hungry I had been, but at that moment, my stomach hurt, and my mouth watered as much as it was possibly capable of. Anadella went to one end of the table farthest away from where the opening happened, while Arny went to sit next to her. They looked at us, and Naomi went to sit next to Arny, which was on the opposite side of where we're standing. Mavryk and I sat next to each other while I sat by Anadella.

"I can imagine the journey has been a long one and will continue to be that way for a while. Who knows when your next nice meal will come from or how long. Please eat as much as you desire." Anadella seemed proud to be feeding us.

Mavryk practically pounced on the food and started filling his plate with all the options laid out. I filled my plate, and then the rest of them did too. As he scarfed some of it down, he thanked Anadella and Arny multiple times while hardly looking away from his plate.

"Yes, this is appreciated much more than I know how to express. Is this how all meals are prepared?" I asked as I took another bite of the chicken leg.

"We like to all rotate who prepares the food, who does the cleaning, who takes care of things that are needed. Some fairies have the same specific positions if they fit that one very well. It depends on the fairy. Their feelings are always considered in the matter. We do our best to make sure everyone feels included and feels that they are at home." Anadella spoke proudly again.

"Things seem to run much better here than in the rest of the world. We could use guidance like yours over at the castle." Every time I mentioned the castle, a pang of nausea poked the inside of me.

I wish I could forget about its existence and everything that came with it. "I can't blame you for hiding out the way you all do. Protection is needed more than ever it seems."

Arny wiped his mouth with a cloth and finished chewing. "That's all going to change soon. You'll be a huge part in that."

"I'm having a hard time wrapping my head around all of this. I went from being nobody to suddenly being someone who's going to change the world. You don't think there's any possibility that there's some kind of mix-up?" My voice sounded more negative than I intended it to be, but I meant what I said.

Anadella took a deep breath in. "This is much bigger than you or I. This involves the world. The change Arnerius and I have waited so long for and the change the world desperately needs. This is no time to let doubt fill your head with such thoughts."

I was not sure how that was meant to sound, but it hit a nerve, and I'd had enough of people talking to me in a disrespectful manner. "You want me to believe I'm meant to save the world? I couldn't even save my mom, and I'm somehow expected to believe that I'm chosen for some type of evolution. Take this to someone else because there is no possible way I can do any of this!" I slammed my fist down on the table with the fork still in my hand, and then I let it fall from my hand and onto the table.

Regret started to surface, but so did frustration. She didn't understand where I came from, so it wasn't fair I snapped at her, but how dare she tell me that doubt shouldn't fill my head.

It'd been pounded into my head since I was young how little I meant to those I loved dearly, by actions and by words. From a young age, I'd been implanted with this doubt that anything I did wouldn't be enough. That's not to say all had given me this treatment, but for the ones I tried to receive the most approval from so desperately, they made me believe I wasn't anything worth putting real effort into. I couldn't even begin to let myself think through everything I suffered inside the castle. The treatment was cruel and internally damaging, to say the least.

"Ann, I don't think she meant it the way you took it." Mavryk had gently grabbed my hand while he spoke softly.

As I looked up, everyone was looking in different directions. My eyes began to water, and shame overcame me.

"I'd like to know about your journey here." Arny spoke in the tone he usually had, like I hadn't just snapped at his beloved. "Would you be open to sharing it with us? Maybe we could have a better understanding of your feelings in this."

Shock washed over me. People typically snapped back or would have interrupted me from finishing what I had said earlier. Anadella had even shaken her head in agreement.

I didn't know how to respond; I kept looking between the two. Anadella didn't look at me, but Arny did. His eyes had understanding in them, and I could see Anadella did, too, but also a little bit of hurt.

"I'm really sorry for snapping, Anadella. You didn't deserve that. I don't want to give you excuses for why I did either. I'm sensitive and need to work on that."

"No," Anadella said sharply but respectfully. "Don't ever apologize for how something made you feel. Working on your approach to communicate how and why something upsets you would be wise, but I understand that I can come off harsh."

She paused and then spoke again. "I know what is at stake, but that does not mean I should disregard how much pressure you are already under. Please forgive me as well."

I had more respect for Anadella in that moment than I thought I could have for anyone else in the world. I smiled at her and wiped my eyes.

I took a deep breath in and then breathed out. "I suppose I should start with the glow appearing in front of me and how it led me to Mavryk."

From there, I explained the magic I felt when I entered and the experience of meeting Mavryk. The kiss we shared and where it led us. Realizing who Steven was and meeting my first telepath, Sasha. That became my discovery of telepaths and of fairies. Then the discussion on the Sacred that we had, and the long hike to the festival and how I still didn't understand how I drained but I did, gaining the help of a few exes and how we came to the waterfall.

"That's when I heard the whispers, and the whispers turned into a voice when I spoke out loud that there were too many talking. His voice led me to the cave. Once Mavryk and I entered the cave, we had this experience like no other. Naomi was there to witness it."

As I looked at her, she took over with disbelief she still saw it happen. "It really was like no other experience. I can only imagine the magic they felt. The cave glowed this beautiful blue, and so did their hands as they touched. Mavryk, however, glowed this dark blue, and Ann glowed the same white we possess. Ann did something I've never seen anyone do before. This ball of the same color she glowed grew in her hands, and she was able to hold it there. That's when I told her not to waste it, and after she told me about the voice, I knew I had to bring her here."

Their faces sat as speechless as it had felt to experience everything. Talking about it still seemed unreal, but I knew it all happened.

"You've experienced a glow you said?" Arny asked me.

"Yes. It's a golden color that's a circular shape, right? There's a type of magic to it that isn't like anything else in this world."

He sat back and stared at me in awe. "The glow will only ever appear to a chosen one that the Sacred chose to fulfill a life-changing purpose. The Sacred shows himself to send messages to those that will relay a message to the chosen ones."

"I can imagine from a young age people have been threatened by you and the power that you hold." Anadella spoke. "The chosen ones always go through the hardest trials in life, it makes sense why you would believe so little in yourself. They tried to dim your light because fear overtook them."

She leaned forward toward me, and chills went up my back as the power behind her next set of words brought so much truth. "When you decide to no longer let the fear of what others think of you hold you back, you will fully embrace who the Sacred created you to be. It is the day you gain wisdom on how important it is to never hold back on how great you have always been." In that moment of her smile forming, realization hit me so hard that she knew from a personal level what that was like.

Before anyone had a chance to say anything else, a very small golden light appeared in front of the entrance that Arny made earlier. It grew until it became my height. Instead of a circular shape, it stood as an oval. Through it, you could see crystal-clear water that the sun was beaming on.

I second-guessed and doubted a lot of things in life, but this was something I had experienced before and deep down knew it to be for me. This was another glow waiting for me to step through toward the next chapter into my destiny—my calling to so much more.

CHAPTER 26

Everyone's faces showed disbelief as they stared at the glow.

"That looks beautiful." I didn't mean to speak that out loud.

"What is it you see?" Arny asked with intrigue.

I looked at him with confusion. "You don't see water with land?"

"I see a glow, and through its coloring, I see the tree we're in right now. It's like I'm looking through golden lenses." Mavryk spoke.

"That is what I see too," Anadella said, and Naomi shook her head in agreement, still in shock at seeing it appear in front of her.

I sat back, puzzled. "Why am I the only one seeing it?"

"Because it is only meant for you," Anadella said.

Arny smiled as he shook his head in agreement. I didn't know how to take that, but I figured not to waste time. Who knows how long it would stay there for.

I hesitated before I slowly stood up from the table and started to take steps toward it. As I did, a hand grabbed my wrist. I recognized that touch anywhere. I turned around toward him, and something in my heart pinged with a bit of dread.

"Ann." Mavryk's tone was laden with sadness, which made it come off more gentle than usual. "I know you have to go but wait." He stood up and stared at me.

Tears formed in his eyes as he entwined both of our hands together. "I need to say something before you go." He took a couple of deep breaths before speaking.

"I know you don't believe in yourself, and you think you aren't important to the world, but from the little bit of time we've had together, I cannot express enough how much of an impact you've had on me. Outside of the bizarre, magical moments we've experienced together, there's something about who you are that sparked inspiration inside of me. After everything you've been through, how much people have beat you down and hurt you, you still manage to keep going and give people a chance when you have every reason not to. You seem to hold onto hope as if the next step will finally lead to something greater." He paused, took a deep breath, and then continued talking after he exhaled.

"I don't need to know everything you've gone through because when I look into your eyes, I can see how cruel it's been for you. I see the hurt and the pain that tries to consume you, but you still manage to hang onto the belief that everything that's happened has been divine signs for something greater, and I don't think you're doing any of this for yourself. You think so poorly of yourself that you think this doesn't have anything to do with you, and while Anadella is right it's not just about you, it cannot be done without you taking every step that you have. I believe them when they say you are a chosen one. I believe you know you have to do this in order to help others, or you wouldn't have traveled so far simply because you don't believe others should suffer anymore. I believe your heart is deeply rooted to care for everyone, even when you don't want to."

He looked at every part of my face, and that soft look of love that danced in his eyes seemed even deeper than before. "You are far more incredible than you can possibly imagine, and you're going to do something that is going to shake people back to life."

He wiped the tears that had left my eyes as he held onto my hands still. "I'm not sure if I'll get the chance to see you again, so in case this is our last time together, you need to know I love you. I have loved you since I laid my eyes on you. You're so beautiful beyond comparison, and one day, I hope you see that. You don't deserve to see yourself any less than that."

He took his hands from mine, grabbed my face, and kissed me with such a burning passion I felt like fireworks were going off around us, accompanied by music that belonged in the most cringy love stories. I forced myself to pull away, and more tears fell from my eyes.

In this moment, realization hit on how fulfilling the purpose called on someone's life comes with some of the most difficult decisions. We feel torn because of what we feel, even when we know what is right to do. The importance of not letting your feelings get in the way of your calling can make the difference between a right or wrong turn in life. This must be why most never make it to their final destination of what they're supposed to do. It's no wonder so many people feel lifeless and unfulfilled, with little to no true meaning. Hardly anyone is making the harder decisions or surviving the toughest battles for a life others can prosper from.

Naomi stood up, fluttered over the table, and hugged me. "I hope to be loved like that someday," she whispered in my ear.

As she pulled back, she said the next part in her normal tone of voice. "Whatever it is you do, please take care of yourself and don't forget about us. Including me." She framed her face with hands underneath her chin and gave a cheesy smile, something to hold onto forever.

I looked at Anadella and Arny. "Thank you for believing in me."

I looked between everyone, trying to hang onto the last moment of seeing them. "I could never forget any of you." As I said *you*, my eyes shifted to Mavryk.

He, especially, will stay locked in my memories as an unforgettable one forever.

"I love you," I whispered.

"Before you go," Arny said as he slowly stood up and walked toward me.

He reached out his hand. I held out mine, and he placed a necklace in my hand—a dark-green arrowhead that glowed as I held it up. "Just as I thought," he said, smiling.

"I've been told once upon a time that arrowheads are a guide toward the right direction." I spoke, admiring what he had given me.

Arny looked at me and gave a smile that was followed by a chuckle. "In the moments you feel the most uncertain, it will be a good guide to help you. If nothing else, a reminder."

I didn't know the importance behind it, but I knew it meant a lot to him, and he had waited a long time for this moment to give it away. I'll never let it go.

I put it around my neck. "It's a great reminder that there's good left in this world."

His eyes glossed over. Anadella stood up and walked over to me. "I do not have anything to give, but I do wish you the very best and to be careful." She held out her arms, and we hugged.

The warmth of her soft skin took me back to my mother's hugs. There was no comparison to my mother's hug, but there was no doubt hers brought comfort you couldn't find in many people. She stood strong and proud, but when the time came, she had nothing but love to give. Beneath that tough exterior was an individual willing to make many sacrifices for a greater cause, I believe, especially for those she cared for.

I pulled back and wiped more tears from my face. I took a deep breath in and let it out. One more look to cling to. I stared at Mavryk last. He stepped toward me.

"Don't lose your mind while trying to find your soul, my love." The tears he had held back escaped. I wiped them away, and he grabbed my hand and held it to his cheek.

"I'm not ready to say goodbye, Ann," he whispered with desperation not to have to face this.

"My mother once said it's not a goodbye, it's a 'see you later.'"

He opened his eyes to look at me, and a small smirk appeared on his lips. "I want to hold your hand as you walk through."

I managed a smile and turned toward the glow, with his hand still in mine. He stepped to my side, and we walked toward the glow. Standing in front of it with one step left to take before I entered the next part of my journey, I took a deep breath in, feeling Mavryk squeeze my hand.

"I love you, Ann." The pain in his voice was evident.

"I love you, Mavryk."

I stepped into the glow and felt his hand release from mine.

I'd never experienced the sun beam down on me like this. I had to squint my eyes almost shut to bear the brightness. The warmth, at least, felt incredible. In front of me, all I could see was water—an ocean that started off as clear blue and faded into a deep, dark blue. I could see why people compare my eyes to the deeper parts of the ocean. On a cloudy day, of course—I don't want to exclude the gray in my eyes.

I had forgotten how different the texture underneath my feet was. I recall being very young, with my mother and my grandparents, and being on a beach somewhere. I didn't focus on the details of the sand as I did now. It was fascinating how there were so many different colors of grain pieces that made the sand, which from a distance seemed as if it was one color. I crouched down, buried my hand, and watched the grains fall as I lifted it up, like a waterfall of different textures.

I looked at the ocean and realized my eyes had adjusted better to the sun's brightness. I didn't know why I had been led here, but I knew better than to pass up a moment to do something I might never get the chance to do again. I sat down, kicked off my shoes with the opposite foot of the other, stood up, and inched toward the shoreline. I rolled up my sweats a bit past my knees and made sure they wouldn't slide down my legs.

My feet slightly sank into the sand as they went into the water. The feeling was cool and soft. I kept walking and got knee-deep before I stopped to look around. I'd never seen water so clear before. Corals of different colors, shapes, and sizes and different types of fish swam around. I didn't know what the other plant life in the ocean was called, but so much else sat in it, swaying in a relaxing motion.

As much as I enjoyed reading to let my imagination take over and loved looking at paintings that others had created based on what they had seen, none of it compared to the experiences life offers. When you see, feel, and even smell it all for yourself, it's a moment to remind you why being alive is such a precious thing.

I read about so much and had seen so many kinds of pictures, but I hadn't stopped to really take in all that I'd seen since I left the castle. All that I had imagined didn't compare. For once, life took me by surprise in such a beautiful way.

I stood there until the sun started to show hints of getting ready to set. That made me realize the water had gotten cooler. I turned around to walk back to the sand. A gasp escaped my mouth and left me breathless. I didn't stop walking to the shoreline, but I walked slowly and gazed in amazement at what looked like paradise.

Mountains, miles high and miles long, stood completely covered in green. The only flatland I could see in front of me was a small open area. Farther down, I could see some structured homes and others roaming around. I couldn't make out the details of anything from how far back I was, but it was a start to finding a new place to settle in.

Before heading to the community, I decided to sit in the sand next to my shoes. It had been such a long time since I sat and watched the sunset that I forgot how mesmerizing and serene it was. To watch it set surrounded by water, with the coloring of the sky, was enough to make anyone forget that any sort of problem existed. It was only this moment right now, reminding you that beauty is all around us. If only we stopped to embrace it more often.

CHAPTER 27

"Hey, you!" a young boy shouted while running toward me.

Once he reached me, I figured he would be somewhat out of breath, but he didn't even show a trickle of sweat going down his head.

"I've never met you before. Are you a newbie?" His dark-blue eyes, almost identical to mine, showed excitement and so much curiosity.

I couldn't help but laugh a little bit as I answered, "What's a newbie?"

"How do you not know what a newbie is? Uh, okay." He gave an exaggerated sigh as he continued talking. "So those people who show up from wherever? That's a newbie. New. Be. The name gives itself away if you think about it."

It was hard not to laugh at the silliness behind his facial expressions and how he pronounced most words. He was trying to be serious, but I couldn't help but find his quirkiness adorable.

From a distance, another male was walking up. The young boy must've noticed me looking away because he turned his head to look back.

"Oh great. My brother is coming," I looked down at him as he turned his head back around.

"What's your name, anyways?" he asked me. "My name is Samuel, but I really like Sam. Never call me Sammy." He crossed his arms together and had that facial expression that was meant to be serious but came off as silly. "There's a girl who goes by that, so it's a girl's name, and I am not no girl."

"I'm Ann. It's nice to meet you, Sam," I said, smiling at him.

He smiled back. "Nice. Short like mine."

Sam's brother walked up next to him and put his hand on Sam's shoulder. "I hope my little brother here isn't giving you much trouble. He's always being such a rascal." He held a proud, playful smile as he ruffled Sam's hair.

Sam shoved his hand off his head while giving his brother a look. "You think you're so cool." Sam looked at me and had an annoyed look on his face.

He threw up his hand and pointed with his thumb toward his brother. "This is my very annoying big brother, Joshua. All the chicks want him until they realize he picks his nose and eats his boogers."

Joshua playfully nudged Sam's shoulder with his elbow. "Very funny, turd. Go get Gran and let her know a new arrival showed up."

"I thought we were called newbies?" I asked in a playful manner.

It's easy to lighten up and joke around with people when you feel that these are people you can be yourself around. Something about kids, especially, brought it out. Sam smirked before he started running back to the village.

"I'd introduce myself, but my brother decided to do that for me," Joshua said, his teeth white as snow and with a smile that made you feel welcomed.

His eyes were almost as black as his pupils. His skin tone was much darker than Sam's, but Sam's still wasn't as pale as mine. Joshua's hair had brown dreads in it and went down to his pecks. Nothing like Sam's messy blond hair.

I had never seen someone with dreads before and had heard people speak poorly of them, but I found them intriguing. They definitely suited him. His build reminded me of Mavryk's but with broader shoulders. Joshua's torso was almost as lean as Mavryk's. A sense of dread came over me as I realized he could never come here.

"I'm Ann," I finally responded, realizing my mind had started to wander. It didn't need to go down that road right now.

"It's nice to meet you, Ann. We haven't had a newcomer in a while, so it's good to know escapers are still saving who they can. I didn't see a boat drop you off. Were you dropped off in another area?"

My brows furrowed together in confusion as I shook my head no.

"I didn't think so. They never drop anyone off anywhere else. How did you end up in Coastra, anyway? Have they finally figured out another way for others to get here safely?"

"I went through a glow," I said slowly, still trying to properly process what he had said without my mind growing sad from the thought of Mavryk.

He wasn't saying anything wrong or asking difficult questions. My mind was trying to shut down and numb out since I hadn't allowed myself to process the negative emotion I felt trying to come through. I couldn't make myself explain that without becoming overwhelmed either. That was when another side of me came out that I preferred to keep managed.

"A glow?" he asked, confused. "No one's come here on anything other than a boat. Is the glow a newly made boat or something else?"

"No." I took a couple of slow, deep breaths. "The glow is—" My brows furrowed together. *How do I describe it right now to someone who has no clue what it is?*

"Gran, this is the lady I told you about." Sam's voice spoke.

I looked up, and beside Joshua stood an older lady. Her hair had highlights of different tones of white; it was put up, but you could tell it was long. Her eyes matched Joshua's. She had a ton of wrinkles, but some of them looked more like cuts. Her skin tone was a shade of tan between Sam's and Joshua's, at least from what I could see. The boys dressed appropriately for the warmer weather here, but she was dressed in long sleeves. Nothing except her feet, neck, and face were showing.

Each of them had a different nose structure than the other. Their eye shapes had the same slant look yet were differed in size. Joshua's were the biggest, Sam's the smallest, while their gran's somehow had a size in between theirs. There were a lot of differences in the structures of their faces and the features that went with them, but you could still notice the relation between them. Genetics always fascinated me for it.

"Welcome," she said without a hint of a smile.

186

Her eyes said she was guarded. It's a look I could understand. She knew a kind of pain that was too painful to talk about and one she wished she could forget.

"It's lovely to meet you. I'm Ann."

I held out my hand for her to shake, but she instead responded by closing her eyes and bowing her head forward with her hands clamped together in front of her. I put my hand down to my side and bowed back, keeping my eyes open to observe her. When she lifted her head back up, I followed.

"You are welcome to stay within our community and do your part, or you can fend for yourself in another area of Coastra," she said, not waiting for me to respond before turning around and walking back.

After she walked a bit away, I looked at Joshua and Sam. "She's tough to get to know, but she means well," Joshua said.

"In other words, don't expect much talking. She's grumpy most days," Sam said with a facial expression that made it hard not to smile.

Joshua smacked him on the back of the head. "Show her more respect than that."

Sam looked at him upset while rubbing the back of his head. "Whatever." Then he ran off to catch up to her.

Joshua looked upset. "He always says something dumb." He shook his head as he said it.

"Maybe he didn't mean harm by it. He could've been joking in a weird sense of humor," I said, hoping to give him the perspective I have with the way Sam talked.

"You think that until you see him misbehaving. He's very rebellious. He doesn't realize how lucky he has it here." He watched his brother, and something filled his eyes. I couldn't tell exactly what, but it seemed like regret in some way.

He shook his head again and then went back to the welcoming smile he had before. I wondered how much of it he faked. "I'll show you around. There's not much of the community to see, so it won't take long."

"I'd appreciate that. What's your gran's name, by the way?" I asked.

"None of us knows. She's always gone by Gran and never introduced herself as anyone else."

That struck me as odd, but people have their reasons for doing things like that. As we walked back, we talked about others who made it here, how many had tried but never did.

"There used to be a lot more escapers helping healers, but there have become more capturers outnumbering them. The last escaper told me that there are only a handful of them left and that he isn't sure if he'll be able to save anymore healers. We started to think no one else would come."

"How long has it been?" I asked quietly.

"Close to two years." His tone had a hint of monotone to it, trying to hide the sadness.

"How steady did healers use to come in?" I looked at him as I asked the question.

"Four to five a month when I was little. It gradually decreased over time."

"You haven't heard from anyone since?"

"No. No one has come to the island since then. Not until you." He smiled without showing his teeth. "It's nice to have someone around my age show up."

I smiled back. I wanted to be as nice as he was about it. I should be, but something about being here didn't feel quite like home, more like a vacation. Maybe because of everything I'd been through, but I needed to give it more time to settle in.

As we walked up to the community, most were outside staring, some talking to each other. Most were friendly enough to wave. A few came up and introduced themselves. I introduced myself back.

The huts were all the same, lined up in a structured form, built like a square and made from bamboo. It was simple living, which was kind of nice to see. Farther from the huts, there was a huge garden full of food to eat. The rest of what I could see was just mountains of green, a few going up to the clouds.

We walked in a U shape and stopped at one of the huts, three huts away from being the closest to the water on the left side when you faced the ocean.

"It's not much, but it's where we sleep," Joshua said.

"It's freedom. It's more than enough," I responded, hoping what looked like a smile that showed gratitude.

We stepped inside, and the setup was simple enough. There was one bed on one side of the hut and a bunk on the other side, a three-layer shelf made of bamboo with folded clothes on each one. The top of it had different-sized towels folded. On the bed, Gran lay with her eyes closed.

I went to take a step forward and jumped, startled by her voice. "Shoes must be off your feet before stepping on my rug."

I looked down and realized there was a rug filling the rest of the floor, not under the beds and shelf. I also realized I never put my shoes back on.

"Is there a way for me to clean my feet off? I walked in the water earlier and—"

She got up and interrupted in a sharp tone, "Joshua, go fetch her a bucket of water. Do not fill it with too much water."

"Yes, ma'am," he responded and then left.

From the shelf, she grabbed one of the small folded towels. As she flung her arm out to give me the towel, her sleeve went up with it. I noticed a red design on the inner part of her arm. It looked like it had been burnt into her skin, and the anger that started to form quickly vanished as I realized that must have been what Mavryk was talking about.

She noticed me staring at the mark and quickly pulled her sleeve to cover her arm again. "If you are going to stay here for the night, you will need to scrub them good. I will not have anything on my rug."

She made an irritated face and shook the towel. I took it from her hand but couldn't help staring at her. I wondered what she had gone through to get here herself.

"Thank you," I said quietly. "Not just for the towel, for welcoming me into your home too." She nodded her head in response and then lay back down.

I wanted to ask her so badly about the design on her arm, but I knew she hid it for a reason. She was not the type to show and tell. I couldn't make out what exactly it looked like or how I could describe it, but from what I could see, it wasn't anything I had seen before.

As I stepped outside, Joshua walked up next to me and set down the bucket. He walked beside the hut and grabbed a chair made of bamboo and set it behind me and then stepped to stand in front of me.

"Thank you," I said with a slight smile. "Everything seems to be made of bamboo here."

"It's the best material here that lasts the longest." As I reached for the bowl, Joshua kneeled next to me. "You've had a long journey to get here. Why not sit back and enjoy a foot rub?"

He smiled, presumably a charm for most. I was sure most would have taken the offer, too, but all I could think about was Mavryk and wishing he could be here.

"I'll make sure they feel better," he added.

"That's kind of you, but no, I'm okay. I can do it myself."

His smile faded, and he seemed a bit surprised. "Are you sure? I really don't mind."

As I started cleaning my foot, I said, "I'm sure there's enough on your plate." I quickly changed the subject to ensure he didn't persist. "It's beautiful here. Everyone seems friendly too. It's certainly calming." I began to clean my other foot.

"Yes, it's the safest place to be. By the way"—I looked up at him as he spoke in a tone different from before—"you told me how you got here but you never told me where you came from. Or is that something you prefer not to talk about?"

"We'll share stories another time," I responded, putting the rag down. "I'm a bit exhausted and kind of just want to watch the sun finish setting, you know?"

GLYCERINE

I didn't want to sound offensive, but he nodded, showing he understood and even agreed. "Yeah, that sounds nice. Care if I sit and join you?"

I had gotten used to being alone all those years in the castle, and at times, I preferred it, but I didn't want to be rude, so I shook my head in agreement. Not that he was horrible company either. He sat on the ground, next to me, and we watched in silence as the sun disappeared into the ocean.

CHAPTER 28

It's the silent cry for help as you drown, slowly sinking to the bottom of the ocean, even though you've learned to swim. You wonder why, after making it somewhere safely, you still cannot call it home. Why can't you find what you came for? Why am I still unsettled in this place I was convinced would be my forever rest? After surviving and fighting through fire, I made it out alive. I'm in a place of prosperity but not at true peace. I feel there is much more for me than to stay here.

There's this undeniable sense that there's much more to accomplish. This is not my final destination. Something else, much more meaningful, awaits to impact not only me but others. A voice, not mine, urges me to go, to leave. I cannot ignore this any longer. I feel like I'm going mad because this is what most dream of, but my feet never belonged on the ground. I have wings waiting to take off.

I've always been the type to soar above the clouds, where the sun's rays bring me back to life and twinkle in the night. I've always hoped another dimmed light finds their way to where they were always meant to go. That they look up and realize they belong up here too.

I never wanted to stay anywhere that didn't challenge my mind or be around others that didn't suit my purpose. I need so much more than mediocrity. I can't shake the feeling that I'm not alone in this desire to reach higher.

I need to awaken those who believe they can't survive another day, to start healing. I want them to realize living is possible because nothing is ever impossible when you decide to breathe again. That when you build this trust in something that seems nonexistent, that is when living really begins.

Nothing can truly stop you when you decide you're going to search until you discover what you're meant to do. You find the best parts of yourself along the way. You inspire others by your ability to never stay down. You create hope when you learn to fly with damaged wings.

I want to help save those who are just like me: curious, confused, unwilling to settle, broken into pieces, and waiting for a miracle to happen to break free from this prison. Others tried so hard to convince us that we are not miracles ourselves, didn't they?

I want to bring hope to the hopeless. I want the hearts of stone to beat back to life and the souls that withered away to spark fire again. I want the people just like me to come together and make one enormous flame, so the others who are hiding, almost dead, find their way to their family. I need to help save others from this vicious cycle of a generational curse that's been long overdue to be broken.

There's more than just me knowing there's so much more than this. Maybe all it takes is one person to remind others that they aren't delusional as they've been programmed to think, and that they are capable of so much more when they start to believe in themselves. They're capable of fulfilling their calling when they start to trust that voice within.

I closed the notebook and stared at the ceiling. It had been two weeks since I arrived here, and everything in me felt relief to write that. I didn't want to come off as rude or ungrateful for being here, so I kept it to myself and didn't bother writing because nothing else would fulfill my need to write except what I just finished. For whatever reason, I thought I could push this away better if I did my best to completely ignore it in all aspects.

Every time I stared at the mountains, I felt something pulling me to walk toward them. Resisting this had become almost painful. I hoped the feeling would go away, so I kept busy, telling myself it was something I needed to give time to get used to. Instead of it going away, I became more restless and irritable. Nothing soothed or calmed it down. I felt a need to go in that direction.

It wasn't like me to wake up before the sun, but for the last few days, I had. I hadn't been sleeping for more than a few hours at a time, which was common for me if something wasn't settling right, and staying here unsettled something deep within my soul. I'd had this feeling one too many times before to know rest wouldn't come until I answered.

I couldn't ignore this any longer without risking an outburst. I'd already isolated myself as much as possible, so I didn't risk any lash-outs. I had to go out and see what else was there. It was always possible there wasn't anything, and curiosity could be getting the best of me, or that I missed hiking in the woods so much, or there really was something ready for me to discover. Whatever this was, I had to know for certain, or I would become miserable ignoring whatever this is that was tugging at me.

The person who would understand better than anyone was Meera. She lived in a hut a little farther from the other huts. Not heading toward the mountains but to the right of the huts, about a mile out, you'd find her living there. Hers was bigger than the rest, but from my understanding, she built it herself and made it known she would make room for extra food to store. No one argued with her.

She never trusted anyone to work with her from the time she came here, from what Joshua mentioned. She told me herself how selective she was. Who she allowed to be close to her wasn't something she took lightly. I understood that better than she probably knew. Then again, she had a skill set like nothing I'd ever witnessed in reading people. She somehow knew where I came from and seemed to even know the struggles of my childhood.

Come to think of it, the only other person who knew that in-depth about my childhood and who could know so much about someone without being told anything was Sasha. Meera couldn't be a telepath, though. Only healers could come to Coastra, or so I'd been told. The thought had crossed my mind that maybe there's more to the world we don't understand like we think we do.

Before I reached her hut, she came outside of the entrance and yelled, "It's your day off, missy! Go be normal and enjoy it!"

I laughed and yelled back, "I missed you already!"

I could see her shaking her head but smiling. She went back inside, and as I reached her hut, I went in with her. She was scrubbing the dirt off potatoes on the counter.

The setup was simple. It was a rectangle shape and wider than the huts the rest of us lived in and taller too. In the middle of the floor was a six-layer shelf that held food on both sides. At the end, her bed sat with a back door available. The front, where I entered through, was where the big, bulky counter sat. On the side away from the wall, a few barstools sat.

The counter table had two shelves underneath filled with different sets of tools. On the wall, three shelves were built into the hut with rags, towels, herbs in jars, bowls to eat out of, plates, and utensils to eat with, among a few other things.

Behind the counter sat a lot of different things that she created to give to others when they needed something. They were tools no one knew how she found. Funny enough, she got on me for not enjoying my time off from work, but she was worse at keeping busy than I was. If I didn't know any better, I'd believe she worked in her sleep.

"What is it you plan to do with your time today, Ms. Ann?"

I pulled my notebook from the satchel and dropped it on the counter. "I haven't written since I've been here."

Her eyebrows rose, but she didn't look at me, continuing to clean the potato in her hand. "Do you plan on it today?"

"Yes, I did before the sun came up. I want you to read it."

I started chewing the inside of my cheek as I grew nervous. I didn't want to share my writing, but I had no idea how I was supposed to explain what was going on with me. I trusted her over anyone to not judge my deeper thoughts and the emotional parts of me that I hid.

"I hope my writing can explain it better than I can."

She stopped cleaning the potato and looked at me curiously but didn't say anything for what felt like forever. I kept looking around and then back at her, waiting for something to happen.

She let out a little giggle. "Ms. Ann, you are a character. You never told me you liked to write." She picked up the notebook and began reading on the page I left it open.

"I love to write. It's silly, really, but I feel like it's a part of who I am." The part of me where speaking often failed but words written did not.

My leg began to shake as I moved my hips and lower body from side to side, anxiously waiting for her to say something. I couldn't tell by her face what she could possibly be thinking, and that made the anxiety worse. She lifted her head away from the notebook, looked like she was rereading something, and then set the notebook down. She looked outside with something I hadn't seen in her eyes before.

"I've been waiting for someone like you for a long time, Ms. Ann." I looked at her, confused. She looked at me. "I need you to soak in everything I'm about to tell you." She raised her pointed finger. "One, you've got some damage to you that requires you to forgive if you want the best part of peace. Let that hurt go. Two"—she raised two fingers—"you never need validation from others. Always go with what you feel is right because more than likely you are, and they always call the chosen ones crazy, but they end up being the most unique. Three, and I'm only going to tell you this once"—she held up three fingers—"I believe in you, and I think you need to adventure out because nothing here suits you, and I mean that in the best way possible." She then smiled and went back to cleaning her potatoes.

"You could come with me. You're special, too, you know." There was a bit of desperation in my voice as I said it.

"No, Ms. Ann. They need me here, this is where I need to be. I reckon you let Joshua and Little Sam know what you're doing, or they'll worry sick about you. Ol' Sam boy will be real hurt if you don't say nothing to him."

She wasn't wrong. I had grown a strong bond with Sam. "I'll be sure to let them know." I began to walk out of the hut but stopped at the entryway to look at her. "Thank you, Meera. You've been a real friend to me."

She stopped cleaning and got up from the stool, standing next to me with her hand on my shoulder. "I knew from the moment I saw you there was something very special inside of you. It is only a matter of time before you recognize it yourself." She then pulled me in for a hug, and my eyes filled with tears.

"It doesn't ever get any easier saying goodbye to those we love, Ms. Ann, but it is always necessary to go where we are called." She spoke it so comforting and meaningfully that I could have sworn she spoke to me in the manner my mother always had when I needed it most.

She pulled back and looked at me, wiping my tears as she spoke. "There she is. The girl who loves with her heart. Don't be afraid to show your vulnerable side. That is something more of us need to see."

I smiled, knowing if I had spoken anything, I'd choke on those words. I grabbed her hand and squeezed, hoping she understood it as me saying "I love you" back. Her eyes filled with tears, and as hard as she tried to contain them, one escaped. I wiped it away and smiled one last time at her before letting go of her hand and turning to walk away.

As I walked to the village, I spotted Sam and waved him down. He excitedly waved back and ran up to me. "Ann! Are you ready for today?"

"What's today?" I asked, confused.

"Our day off, what else could be more exciting than that?" He made his usual goofy serious expression.

"Oh. Right. About that." I rubbed my arm, trying to figure out how to explain this to him.

"What? Aren't you off?" He looked a bit bummed out.

I took a deep breath in and then exhaled slowly. "I'm off, Sam, but I'm going to be gone for a couple of days."

"Gone? Where are you going?" His voice revealed how upset this was making him feel.

"I'm not sure, but I know I have to go explore the mountains."

"Okay, but I am going with you then. It's not safe to go alone, and I want to protect you."

My heart dropped. "Sam, I can't—"

He interrupted, with panic starting to get the best of him. "No! I want to go with you. You can't leave me." Desperation cracked in his voice. "Mom never came back when she left. I can't lose you too!"

I could feel my eyes begin to water, and the pain of understanding stung. I knew the fear he felt and what losing another loved one would do to an already fragile heart.

I kneeled down and looked him in the eyes. "I know this isn't easy to understand, but I have to go." An idea came to mind. I pulled out my notebook and extended it to him.

He grabbed it from me and looked at it. "What's this?"

"It's a part of me that I want you to hold onto until I come back."

He looked at me. "You promise you'll come back?"

I held out my pinky. "Back where I come from, these mean an unbreakable promise. Hold yours up and loop it into mine."

He hesitated and then looped his into mine, and I squeezed his tight. "I promise to come back to you," I whispered. "When you feel like you need me the most, just pick something to read so you know I'm with you. Always."

Tears had fallen from his eyes, and mine did the same. I pulled him in for a hug and choked up. Whatever the amount of weight that came from hurt he had been carrying, he let fall into me, and I knew that trust had truly built between us.

I pulled back with my hands on his shoulders. "It's not a goodbye. It's a 'see you later.'"

He wiped his eyes and mustered a smile. "I'll make sure to keep this safe. I'll guard it with my life!"

I smiled while tears swelled in my eyes again. "I know you will, Sam."

I took one last look before I stood up and realized Joshua had been standing there.

Neither of us said anything. Hurt had filled his face.

"Sam," Joshua tried to sound more stern than usual, "do me a favor and go check on Gran."

He'd usually argue, but he didn't. We looked at each other, and he waved. I waved back and then put my hand on my chest and pointed where my heart was. He put a fist to his heart and then turned his head away.

"Can I walk with you?" Joshua asked.

"Of course," I said quietly.

We began to walk, and neither of us said anything, so I broke the silence. "I know you're probably upset with me, but this is something I have to do."

"I don't understand, not one bit, but I know something isn't sitting right with you. You don't have to say much when your face gives it away." He paused before adding the second part.

"And here I thought I was hiding it well." He didn't respond, and I realized I needed to be more validating that this was hard on him too. "Joshua, this isn't anything anyone has done wrong. You all have done wonderfully in making me feel welcomed. There is something deep within me being called to go further explore, and I don't know what it is, I don't know why either, but there is something I need to do, and if I don't, then this feeling will never stop. I can't push it to the side anymore."

He didn't say anything for a minute and then spoke. "That means you need to go."

I looked at him, and he smiled at me. "I'm not you, so I can't say what you're feeling is wrong. It makes me sad to see you go, and I wish I understood, but I don't, and maybe in time I will, maybe I won't. A true friend is here to support another friend no matter what."

I stopped and practically jumped to hug him. He squeezed me, and I squeezed back. A wave of overwhelming emotions came over me, and tears swelled in my eyes again.

We pulled away and let go of each other. "Hey, like you said, it's a 'see you later,' not a goodbye, right?"

"Right," I said as I wiped my tears.

He smiled one last time before telling me he needed to head back and wanted to check on Sam and then started walking back. I watched him leave, sitting in appreciation for such amazing people. I turned back toward the mountains and walked forward, destiny relieved for answering its calling once again.

CHAPTER 29

I'd been traveling for a couple of days now. Thankfully, berries on bushes had been keeping me fed. I'd stayed close enough to this little stream of water that seemed to have appeared out of nowhere to keep myself hydrated and as clean as possible.

Everything I'd needed had always been provided in some way, even in my most desperate times of not knowing how. There came a way with what I needed, sometimes by a complete miracle, and when all my hope had disappeared.

As I looked in front of me after scanning the rest of the area, I saw something fluttering toward me. I gasped excitedly as I noticed it was a butterfly. It came up to me and then stopped, flapping in place. The top part of its wings was half black, and the bottom was half blue. The color change went as a slant with a slight fade to the change.

"Hi there. You're the first butterfly I've seen on Coastra. Are you alone?"

I expected it to flutter away, but instead, it landed on a leaf plant in front of me and then turned to my right. I looked over, and at first, I didn't notice anything unusual.

I looked back at the butterfly and slowly squatted down, sitting right next to it. It turned toward me and walked onto me. My eyes widened, and my mouth hung slightly open. I'd never been touched by a butterfly before, and since I was little, I wanted to hold one so badly.

A thought came to my mind. I lifted my hand from my side and very carefully slid it under the butterfly; without hesitation, it stepped onto my hand. It started to move around until I twisted my hand for it to rest on my palm. I studied it for a moment and took in this experience.

"It's silly to grow up and stop wishing for the little moments like this. I forgot how much I used to imagine what holding a butterfly would be like." I paused and then whispered the next part. "You're not a typical butterfly, are you?"

I held it down farther from my face. It went back to staring at my right side. "If you want to show me something, I'll gladly follow you."

It started flapping its wings and going in the direction it had looked toward. I walked behind it. I'd talked to many butterflies and had gotten little responses before, but nothing like this. However, its presence threw me off way more than its responses ever could have. I felt spiritually connected to it. Even its coloring seemed to speak to me. A soft black always brought me comfort to the loneliness I faced a lot throughout life. The blue was the same color as the blue that Mavryk's hand and my hand turned when we touched in the cave.

He crossed my mind multiple times a day. I wondered if he went back to helping other healers, if he stayed with the fairies, or if he decided on something else entirely. I wondered where his thoughts were, if he missed me like I miss him. Did he have moments where he craved our touch?

More than any of that, I wondered about his safety. He risked everything by helping me, and that sometimes caused panic, thinking about what they would do to him if Venon found out. The truth always has a way of coming to light. That kind of reality sickened me. As important as it is to be present in what's going on, this is the main reason I loved living in another world. It was my greatest escape and the most pleasant way of coping. It still baffled me I ever tried living without my imagination.

Then again, it didn't surprise me. I tried fitting in with people for their approval because I couldn't stand myself, and I couldn't stand not being accepted. I thought I needed to prove my worth to them; I didn't realize I had any bit of worth within me.

Looking back, I was not so sure they ever liked themselves, let alone loved who they were. If I was going to be honest with myself, I was not so sure how much of my life really mattered, but I did know I shouldn't have made myself miserable trying to be someone I could never be or try to belong somewhere I was never meant to stay.

I came to a stop as I noticed the butterfly landing on an enormous rock wall. We had been following along beside it for a while. I thought maybe it wanted me to look outward to see something, so I scanned for a little bit. Nothing except the same scenery that had been out here was here.

I went to look back at the butterfly, but it didn't stay put. Instead, it had been slowly walking up the wall. It then turned and looked down toward me. I couldn't help but smile a bit. A silly thought crossed my mind that it wanted me to climb up with it.

"We're not made the same. I have no way of climbing up." Its antennae started to wiggle. "Well, you're the one with the wings. Why is it you don't fly up?"

Its antennae stopped wiggling, and it started flying upward and then came back down and circled me. For whatever reason, the thought of spinning came to mind, so I did. I followed where it went while still circling around.

I slowed down after a bit and let my vision catch up until my vision went back into place. The butterfly landed in front of me and looked at me. I managed to step farther away from the wall to see more of it better.

At first, I didn't notice; my eyes were fixated on the way the vines sprawled out and somehow hugged tightly to the wall without much support to hang onto. That was when an indent caught my eye behind a part of the vine. I squinted to see better and then remembered I could walk up and get a better look. The butterfly fluttered with what seemed like excitement and landed right next to the vine I had been observing.

I grabbed the vines and pulled them back. There were indented stepping stones. My eyes followed them upward, and as my head lifted toward the sky, I noticed a dark spot. That must be an entrance.

I looked back down toward the butterfly. "You've been trying to lead me up there, haven't you?" It fluttered up until it went through the dark entrance.

I looked back down to my eye level and decided to rip off as much of the vine as I could. The stepping stones went in a zigzag formation, one foot in front of the other. I grabbed one of the holes above my head and pulled myself up while putting my foot in a different hole. I couldn't help but smile at the fact that my feet fit so perfectly, almost as if they were meant for me.

The climb up felt exalting. With every step, I felt more capable of going into whatever it was I was supposed to discover. I really had no idea what I was getting myself into, but that irritable feeling that kept pulling at me to go out and do more started to die out. How much time had I wasted holding myself back from doing what I knew to be right? How many people did I let control my life and stop me from fulfilling all of this sooner?

I grabbed the edge of the dark entrance and paused. It was a cave. I pulled my arms over the edge, holding my weight while each foot sat in a stepping stone. The sun's light filled most of the darkness, making it manageable to see inside. However, it made me a bit nervous not knowing how deep the cave goes. The dark had always scared me because I never really knew what was in it, but I couldn't go back. I needed to face everything that lay ahead.

I pulled myself up from the edge until my feet were planted on the ground. I turned around, looked down, and became a bit overwhelmed and semi-shocked at how much I had climbed. I scanned over Coastra and really took in how much paradise this part of the world holds. I could see the ocean coming in waves but not the shoreline or the village.

I turned back around toward the cave. Staring into the darkness began to mess with my mind a bit. The butterfly must've sensed my nervousness because it fluttered out of the darkness and came up to me. I smiled and, as silly as it is, I felt relief.

"I have a hard time being in the dark. At night, I used to make sure there was some form of light to sleep in. My mind likes to play tricks on me that something is there. Thanks for coming to help me through this."

I could have sworn the butterfly nodded its head, but before I had time to react to that, it turned toward the darkness and fluttered into the unknown. I inhaled and exhaled deeply as I followed the butterfly. I didn't walk my usual fast pace, not only to keep myself from tripping but so I could be more cautious of my surroundings. The darkness really crept in, and as it did, I realized the blue part of the butterfly glowed. It wasn't super bright, but it was extremely neat to see.

My eyes started to adjust at this point, and I noticed up ahead was another entrance. It wasn't as open as the one I entered through; something seemed to dangle in the way, but I knew it was an opening because of the light streaks from the sun that popped through.

I reached the entrance and realized it was covered in layers of vines. I would have possibly continued to walk through the cave out of curiosity, but it came to a stop here, giving me no choice but to either turn around or go through the entrance covered in vines.

I noticed the butterfly had rested on the vines. "If you're that tired, you can rest on my shoulder as we walk through this together."

I held up my hand in front of its feet, and it slowly walked onto my hand. It began to climb up my arm, and I moved my hair out of its way, so it would have full access to my shoulder. Once it reached my shoulder, it faced forward and waited.

"I suppose there's nothing left to do except pull these back and see what's on the other side."

As a response, the butterfly moved its wings a couple of times. I meant to only glance, but I began to stare and realized that this butterfly and I had bonded in a way that wasn't usual. For that, it deserved a name.

"I'm not sure how to tell genders on a butterfly, so I'm going to give you a name that I think will fit regardless."

I thought for a minute and decided, "Midlight. The black reminds me of the dark during the midnight hours, but you hold a lot of light to you that makes you more special than any other butterfly I've ever seen."

It fluttered its wings, which I took as an agreement. I smiled as I looked away from the butterfly and at the vines. There were too many to see through to get any hint of what could be on the other side. Only light gave a hint of anything being there at all. I put my hands on the vines and pulled them out of our way.

CHAPTER 30

I thought the fairy forest blew me away, but this was on a whole different level of enchantment. The sunlight didn't just add brightness; it added a sparkling glow to the place. The perfect amount of light that didn't blind you but shined so beautifully that even the darkest soul would feel compelled to change or not to bother with it and flee away.

Every type of flower you could imagine blossomed everywhere in all types of colors. Bushes and plants were scattered throughout the place. All the trees held fruit, and some had differently colored leaves. Some of these I had never seen before, not even in paintings.

The number of different living things that existed fascinated me—butterflies, birds, lizards, dragonflies, other creatures I didn't know of until now. The insects that flew around didn't seem to have stingers and didn't seem to be aggressive. All types of different insects flew around, and to my surprise, the noise level wasn't overly noisy and overwhelming to deal with.

The sense of safety I felt here was unlike anything I had experienced before—a calming I hadn't experienced. This wasn't just the most breathtaking place I could have stumbled upon, but something much more magical than that. Something beyond the comprehension of life and its meaning.

Taking all this in made me realize I had been standing there, staring over the edge of a cliff. Looking down, I noticed there were stone stairs with no ledge to hang onto. They went downward in a wave motion, reminiscent of a slide I used to go down as a child—one that was super tall and one you went down fast on.

I walked down slowly to look around and really take in everything. Not a single soul was in sight, not a hint of anything negative. This place had a power beyond anything or anyone contains, and everything glowed in a way that reminded me of the glow. The Sacred crossed my mind at that moment.

"I can't help but wonder if you, the Sacred, lived here at some point. I experienced the glow, and people have told me only the most powerful being to ever exist creates those. I've been told you lived in Outcastril, but if someone had all the power to be a creator, wouldn't you have traveled everywhere? I mean, how can I even be sure you exist? With everything that's happened, why would you just let all the bad stuff happen like it has? You have the power to stop it, why don't you do it? That's what makes it so hard to believe. Someone who is almighty just sits back and does nothing? It's beyond me."

I didn't expect anything to happen, and I knew the rambling might have confused Midlight, but I couldn't help myself from wondering all these things. Everyone had told me bits and pieces about him. I'd heard his voice, from what they said, walked through only what a chosen one is called for. I was still not certain what a chosen one is either.

I'd never been someone capable of much of anything; I'd been betrayed in ways that would make anyone want to never care for another again, and I'd been through a lifetime worth of suffering. All of that had caused me to believe it was impossible to trust that anyone could find me worthy of really loving and made me feel incredibly lonely. Easily disposable and far from wanted. Pushed to the side by multiple people, and I'd been pathetic enough to try and be anything, anyone, besides myself all in the hopes of being accepted enough to be noticed for more than someone's punching bag or for someone to use as a personal gain.

This also unfortunately had caused me to push away the few who tried to love me, and I did mean really love me. It was so foreign to me that at the time, it looked like a setup or an absolute lie. My reality of right and wrong became so twisted and sick that I even let someone convince me that the few who had my back didn't. It was the ones who'd throw me in a fire for a night's worth of warmth that would burn the world down just to watch me go with it.

By the time I realized the truth behind the good individuals, I kept away in hopes they could heal from my mess that they didn't deserve. How do you explain how sorry you are when you know you don't have it in you to truly change that toxicity just yet? You never wanted to hurt anyone; you just don't understand how to stop sabotaging the good in your life.

It crashes down on you hard when you come to terms with the fact being I had become toxic at one point in my life because of the toxicity that came into my life and from people I tried being accepted by. The bizarre thing is, you love those that you hurt, too, and you don't love them any less, but because of their love being unfamiliar, you do not know how to accept it, making it seem like you never had any love for them.

I still loved those that hurt me, too, because no matter what had been done to me, I could not seem to unlove someone once I loved them. It took me a while to understand that it wasn't them that I hated; it was what they had done to me that broke me a bit more than the last. My heart would never be capable of anything except love, and that is why the sting of betrayal burned a lot longer for me. It got harder to deal with each time when healing never happened in the first place.

This is why I found it impossible to believe that I was able and destined for some divine purpose that was bigger than my grasping. I was supposed to believe I could make such a worldly difference. That I could somehow wake up the part of light that died and bring it back to life in others. It's not that I wouldn't love to inspire others, but to believe someone as messed up as me could was just beyond my belief.

See through my eyes the worth of one's soul, and you will not find yourself of such little worth.

I stopped and looked around. It was that voice again. It had become dark within the time frame that the words were spoken. At first, my heart sank because of how dark it was, but fireflies lit everywhere. I looked up at the sky twinkling with millions of stars and at the fullness of the moon. Suddenly and unexpectedly, a bright light that resembled a meteor lit up in the sky. As quickly as it appeared, it vanished. A thought came to mind.

"Was that you?" The words escaped my mouth in an almost whisper.

Yes.

The sky came back to daylight, and I stood stunned. I wanted to believe that I had imagined all of that, including the voice, but I knew I couldn't deny it even if I wanted to. Truthfully, part of me wanted to because it seemed easier to accept that I had lost my mind than to accept that these bizarre things were happening.

"Okay, Sacred. I believe there's no doubt you're real, but I have so many questions." I decided to continue walking.

Before I could start asking and talking through everything, the word soon came to mind. This left me confused, how could he answer everything I wanted to know when I felt the need to know so much?

Hang onto your faith.

Trust. He wanted me to trust after everything I had been through. Everything and everyone had been such a letdown in one way or another, including myself. I'd been through so much suffering, and he had let it all happen. Granted I'd possibly been led to the most beautiful place that existed and I made it to Coastra, which was freedom, but by the help of good people. They helped me, not him.

I placed those people in your life. They are my creations, as are you. I placed them in such a time as this, knowing they would help. My heart weeps in everyone's pain, but those that decide to walk in their calling will be restored with so much of what has been lost.

Tears swelled in my eyes, and anger surged in me. He couldn't possibly understand how much I had really lost. "Let's get this correct. My innocence was taken from me at an age barely old enough to remember, and when the truth was revealed, almost everyone turned their back on me. That was a lot of betrayal and suffering, don't you think? My father scolded me for being alive, so that took away ever feeling loved by the first man who was supposed to teach me how to be loved. My mother was dead, the only one who came close to never making me feel unloved. But even then, there was so much trauma caused by her because of her sufferings and hardships. Still, that was my only true security and the bit of safety I felt in this cruel world." Tears were rolling down my face, and the agony showed in my tone.

"Only a year later, after losing her, my first child died within me, and two more had died after that, with only about a year apart from each other. So many people made me feel less of a woman because of something I can't control and acted as if I had been a disappointment to them. That took away any hope of ever being a mother. Let's not even talk about falling heavily into a trauma bond that has killed off any self-esteem that I had left."

My voice grew more aggressive as I said the rest. "The effect of all the rest of the horrible things I've dealt with, the betrayal from fake friends and so-called family members, has caused me to shatter and lose all parts of me that I cannot ever gain back. Unless you can take it all back from happening, I will never believe anyone when they say more is to come. That better is finally to come."

I had been heavily crying, and the feeling of so much torture started to put me in a chokehold. I fell to my knees as the weight of my emotions beat me down, and my thoughts spun me dizzy. The other part of my body fell to the ground, so I wrapped my stomach in hopes to hold myself together, but I had unleashed something I had been holding onto inside for so long that it didn't just escape, it burst out. Going back to containing it after releasing it in that way wasn't possible.

I had to sit with all of this and let myself be tormented as I remembered my younger self—the teenager me, the child me. She was so naive in believing that good exists in everything and became corrupted in many ways before she had time to process life itself. She created these beautiful worlds for herself to keep passion and hope alive but was made to feel dumb and intolerable for being so different.

She begged to be loved in the same way she had been loving all the wrong ones. She became desperate and settled with nothing more than wanting acceptance, so she pretended to be everything she wasn't, and she still was made to feel it wasn't enough. She went all her life truly believing she was nothing more than a burden, someone who shouldn't have been born.

The tears had dried up, and I lay there numb at this point. As the memories died down and I noticed more of the surroundings, I realized I was a few steps away from leaving the stairs. Midlight sat on the step above me.

"I'm sorry you had to see that," I whispered. "Anyone else would have left through that, and you didn't. Thanks."

I have always been with you. I will never leave. I will always give you strength when you have none left. I am with you. Do not give up.

My eyes widened. I lifted my head and then sat up with my arms wrapped around my legs while my body sat on one step. I stared at Midlight and watched as it fluttered on my knee. I felt too heavy in that moment to do anything except rest in the present moment and hope that one day I'd be set free from all the pain. That one day I'd let go and just live.

CHAPTER 31

After a while, I stood up, looked around, walked from the last few steps, and stepped onto the grass. It would have been more comforting to lie on the grass than to sit on the steps during that moment, but I didn't usually think of things like that. My mind went into a frantic state, which ended up throwing me off more than it probably should. What I processed easily and what I didn't process at all seemed to be different from the average person.

Once my mind caught up with moving forward, I followed Midlight. I thought it knew to wait for me because it kept fluttering in circles and began going forward once I started walking. Then again, that was the Sacred's doing, from what I understood now. The Sacred was somehow using Midlight to guide me.

The response I had a moment ago proved that he was able to do more than I thought and would use anything to help me. The way Midlight had been this whole time was as bizarre and intriguing as it could get when it came to any life form that was not a person—or maybe this was just the beginning of really seeing what the Sacred was capable of.

The place went from an entrancing garden to an open field of grass full of life, but not far from us stood a forest that looked dark and gloomy within. I was not sure "depressing" fit the description, but it was definitely not sunshine and roses like the garden was. If it weren't for Midlight, I was certain I'd turn around and never take a chance to go into it. I walked into the field and toward the forest of uncertainty.

I stepped into it and immediately felt the coolness of a morning that had lived through a night of pouring rain. It wasn't dark, but "gloomy" fit the description. There weren't many colors except green and the little bit of gray bark that peeked through the vines and moss covering all the trees. Not far from us was an interesting pathway.

Stone statues of people separated four choices to enter through, but past the stone statues were bushes that stood at least eight feet tall to continue separating the paths. Each stone had a female and male side by side, except the statue on the left end side. There, a man stood alone, much different-looking than the rest. Each couple, assuming that they were a couple, stood in different stances.

It was uncanny how he reminded me of a painting that was named Mystical Middle Eastern Man. I never understood the name, but the story behind the painting of his face was because it was a man who visited the painter in their dream. They said the power this man held was exceptional and like nothing they had felt.

The pair next to the alone male statue held each other intimately while looking forward with friendly smiles. They had wings on their backs and stood shorter in height with a petite build. The wings were definitely like those of fairies, but theirs were much bigger and fuller than any fairies I had ever seen. The female, much like Anadella, had long straight hair that went to her hips; she stood on the left side. The male had hair that went to the shoulder with a goatee a couple of inches long. They fit a hippie description perfectly.

The next pair featured the male standing on the right side, with his arm wrapped behind her back as his hand rested on her waist. The other arm hung to his side, while his posture stood straight with his legs spread a bit, as if he was holding his stance firmer. The female had her arm wrapped behind his back, while her other hand rested on his chest as her body relaxed into his, but her face held alert, as if to say, "I know he'll protect me, but I'm willing to fight by his side." It was uncanny how much their looks reminded me of Sasha.

The next pair stood upright and forward, the male behind the female, with an expression that was serious, and gave off a look that said they were ready to fight. Their fists clenched tightly. The male's hair was cut very short, and hers was in a braid, while the hair that was not sitting on her scalp rested on her shoulder. Both were fit in an athletic way, but neither of them looked like they overdid their workouts. They didn't look familiar to me, and I was a bit grateful for that. Their looks alone could intimidate anyone with a hint of insecurity in their own appearance.

The pair next to them stood side by side with their hands held in front of them. They weren't touching each other's hands, but they cupped their own hands together, as if ready to give something. Her hair was slicked back in a low bun, while his hair was an inch or two long with short facial hair. Their build seemed about average in height and weight. They were still a highly attractive couple as well. All of them seemed to be in their own ways.

My eyes widened as I studied the last pair. If I weren't looking at them, I wouldn't believe it myself. In front of me stood a statue of Mavryk and me, facing each other as our hands touched without folding. The statues showed us staring into each other with a love that went deeper than the ocean and farther than the galaxy.

"There's no possible way," I said in an almost breathless manner.

I had no idea who these statues were, but I knew they meant something important. I just couldn't wrap my head around why Mavryk and I were a part of this. Was it possible they weren't us, and my mind was tricking me because of the resemblances? Maybe in time, I'd receive more answers than my mind would ponder questions. After staring for a little longer, I looked between all of them and decided to continue moving forward.

"That one is the only one that has stepping stones. I guess I'll start with going that way," I pointed toward the path to the farthest left, in between the fairy statues and the male.

It threw me off that the stones weren't covered in moss or green of anything like the rest of the place, almost as if they'd been scrubbed clean a short time ago.

Midlight fluttered to my shoulder and sat there instead of leading the way. I started to wonder why, at this point, but that didn't really matter. I needed to stay focused on my surroundings. I wanted to do my best to not get lost, though I had little faith in that. I didn't usually have the best sense of direction.

As I began walking on the path, the stones disappeared into the grass. It didn't take me long to realize I had entered a maze. The farther I went, the more the bushes started to turn from green to red, like the ones at the castle in the garden. After walking straight for a bit, I came to a stop. I had to decide to go left or right, but I couldn't go straight any farther. I looked both ways, and to my right, I noticed from a short distance the bushes had changed to an orange. To my left, they didn't change from the red, so I went right. After all, taking a different path requires change that isn't familiar.

Every time I came to a stop, the bushes offered an option of going left or right. Only one way would show the leaves changing color, so I kept choosing the one that changed. After orange came yellow, then brown, then pink, then purple. It switched between left and right every time I picked which way to go. Each one got longer to walk through, but when I finally came to a stop, blue immediately showed which way to turn.

At first, I didn't see anything except a long and narrow way straight, but as I kept walking, I noticed a small building made of stone and covered by vines. When I finally approached it, I realized the door had no handle and a word carved in cursive. I moved the vines out of the way and took a step back to look at it better.

"Selah." I felt my brows furrow together and looked at the butterfly. "I wonder what that means."

I went back to looking at it and ripped the vines off the door. I had the sudden urge to trace each letter, so I did. As my fingertip left the H, the words began to light up in a bright white that resembled the ball of light that I made in the cave.

Suddenly, the door started to slide to the side as bits of dirt fell from the top of it. There weren't any windows, but the size of the building lit by the sunlight, and right in the center of it was a book. The book didn't sit on anything; it floated in the air with a ring of shimmering golden tint somehow holding it in place. It dawned on me that this was a very similar thing to what I walked through those times that led me to each destination that came with a different purpose. This was a glow of protection.

The book wasn't thick or big at all, and there were not a lot of pages. It was a hardback, and the color of it was a royal blue, much like Mavryk when he had flames lighting him. The make and design of the fabric showed how old it was but somehow preserved to be in new condition, like it had been written once and then never touched again.

Something kept pulling at me to touch it, but logic told me I needed to leave it alone, that I didn't know what would happen once I did. I didn't care enough at this point because, for whatever reason, everything had led me to this book for something beyond my comprehension of using logic. If I was not meant for this, then why did everything lead me here?

I didn't believe any of this to be a coincidence. There had been so much uncertainty in my mind, but if I let fear take over now, I'd be walking away with too many what-ifs. Knowing myself, I could never find the peace my soul desired. I could never live as free as I was, for my mind would continue keeping me caged if I turned around.

I lifted my hand and slowly moved it toward the book. I could feel myself begin to shake, and my heart rate increased rapidly. As my fingertips touched the glow, I felt its magic surge into me, and the glow grew brighter. The book began to glow as well, and as my hand grabbed the book, a power like nothing I had experienced shocked my hand but not in a way that hurt. It made me feel more alive than I had ever felt. That feeling traveled through my entire body.

As I held the book in both hands, not only did the book glow, but I glowed, too, and the protective shield disappeared. I stood stunned, trying to process how powerful all of this was, but before I could, I realized the book had a title to it, carved in the same cursive as the word "Selah."

"The Book of Sacred," I whispered and gasped as my eyes grew big and my mouth dropped.

There had not been one recording of any sort of book written on the Sacred that I had known about. From what I knew, no one did. The Sacred had hardly been talked about at all. This didn't add up to me, though.

How was it that no one had ever stumbled upon this? Did the Sacred purposely keep this hidden until this moment? If the purpose was to hide it until someone found it, what was going to happen now that it was found? Why, out of everyone out there, did I end up finding it?

I called you. Now read my word. You shall understand. Selah.

I stood there, staring at the book a bit longer. I kept trying to take in every time I heard that voice, but it seemed so impossible and unreal that something from beyond a physical standpoint could truly be speaking to me. And why did he use that word just now?

I decided I needed to sit down, so I turned toward the opening, and as I sat, I rested my back against the wall and stared outside. I knew I had to read this, but some part of me wanted to walk away.

Whatever came from reading this was going to change every-thing. I had been so anxious to get to a place of purpose that I didn't stop to think how heavy it would be to really process what role that would lead me to, and to some point, I was still not sure what this meant. All I knew was, it was going to require a lot from me that I was not sure I was prepared to do. I took some deep breaths in, then out, and looked down at the book. I flipped open to the first page and began reading.

CHAPTER 32

In the beginning, He created all that you see and everything that you cannot. Everything is formed by His goodness. Who He creates is formed with purity, cleansed. The evil you see is not what He caused.

He then formed me in the garden of Leah, setting me apart, made by a golden light. I am sent here to teach His ways, to help guide all in their purpose. I am not created as one being; I am all of them combined. It is said I would be the only one to ever be created in this way. I am the Sacred. He is our Creator.

He formed four beings from the ground: the first beings as fairies, one man with one woman. The next day, He formed the first telepaths, one man with one woman. The day after, He formed the first drainers, one man with one woman. The final day of forming, He formed healers, one man with one woman. Each was given a day before the other to be taught what their powers are.

I told them of our Creator, the one we are to consider our only true ruler. This led to the discussion of who I am. We discussed the world. There are five parts, each designed differently from the others. He assigned the firsts to these parts.

Fairies shall be placed in Landomal. Telepaths shall be placed in Egyptstra. Drainers shall be placed in Scarland. Healers shall be placed in Coastra. They will discover why this part of the world is designed best for them. They will strive in it the greatest way. They will come to know He made them for a specific place as that specific being for a specific reason.

Certain beings will not belong to these parts if their purpose is suited for another being. Every being has a being made for them to enrich their calling. This being will be the only one to awaken something within you that will help you grow in your purpose. There is a specific time aligned with when you meet them.

Let it not be forgotten that it is our Creator that keeps us whole. You must seek Him even with your forever being. Without our Creator, the two of you together will not complete everything that has been called. It is possible it can leave the two of you stranded from the other. Above everyone, our Creator must be served first, even above your children.

I shall stay in Outcastril as long as I live. When our Creator calls me back home, Outcastril will burn in a blue blaze while its ashes rain down for forty days. I shall leave nothing there. Our Creator warned me that there will come a day when misguided generations will make it a place of torture, injustice to those that never caused real harm. I have placed a protection shield around the Island of Coastra from the ones who share the same power of the false ruler.

By the seventh false ruler's birth, a female of a new being will be born, as will a male. They will be called Pariah. One Pariah will be born of a Healer; the other will be born of a Drainer. They will grow more within their power to discover who they are called to be. They will come to notice they possess the power of both. No other born on their day will be born of the same being.

Our Creator calls all of us to grow into our most powerful self, to help each being grow into their most powerful self. Stand together. Do not live in envy toward another. Do not live with jealousy of what another can do. Envy carries bitterness; jealousy carries hatred. You will turn against the other instead of being for each other. What you carry inside influences what you do.

You are made from His love. The Creator calls all of us to love one another. He carries a love that is not of this world. His love gives us our free will of choices. Love is never done out of control. For those of you who do not live by this will carry the weight of hate's cost. For those that cause harm with ill intentions will not escape the consequences that came with that.

The protection from our Creator will not come for those that face the final judgement of death if they live out this way, deciding to never change, to never ask for forgiveness. It is asking to be separate from our Creator. Amend from your ways to live in His ways.

The wicked-hearted shall suffer without our Creator's mercy. They will forever live the life they caused onto others. A place without our Creator is made in complete evil. This is where the wicked shall end up when they do not amend.

Forgive those that have wronged you so the heaviness that weighs in your heart can set you free. Justice will be dealt by Him. Forgive yourself. Make right with your wrongs. The Creator, I, the angels above the sky—all of us celebrate when a life decides to turn around, following righteously.

Once it is known to you that our Creator is the truth, believe He is the truth. Do not doom yourself. Do not turn away from Him. This will separate you from Him in the eternal life. There are no more chances to connect when your last breath has left.

You must become reborn again, within. Die to what you know. Die to who you became in the midst of learning. Let your mind empty out. Let the Creator pour in. There is a wisdom He has that no one else can come to imagine. No longer shall your heart guide you when it is His spirit that is meant to lead, for your heart can deceive you.

A purpose is placed on each life. Some are called to go higher. None are of less importance. Seek the Creator. Answers of who you truly are will be shown, as will what you are meant to do. Trying without Him will lead to misguidance. You shall find in time that the purest desires of your heart have been what our Creator called you to have, to do to begin with. You will not always know what the desires of your heart truly are until the connection has set within.

This is why I say the purest of your desires, not the deepest. The difference of those can be opposite of the other. When the mind has been corrupted, when the heart has been deceived, you become filled with hurt, led by what you are taught. It is not the way He planned your life to be. He did not plan for you to be this way.

Giving you your deepest desires that do not align with the Creator's plan for you will continue the cycle of destruction He calls you to stray away from. For a heart of purity will want to follow His plan. He wants to guide you away from further suffering. He wants to guide you to never sabotage yourself again.

GLYCERINE

*Be careful of a heart that only knows deceptive behavior, for it
wants nothing to do with Him. This can influence you further away.
Even if most beings are living a certain way, this does not mean it is the
correct way. Correction can only be led by truth. Our Creator is the truth.*

*There needs to be some sort of clarity when we are seeking answers
from our Creator. Understand that our Creator does not call for anything
when there is only confusion with no answer given in time. This is not to
say that we will know more than is needed at that time. Do not let your
mind overtake what your spirit speaks. You will be left with no clarity.*

*There will be times when time is needed as our timeframe is never
our Creator's. A thousand days to us is comparable to one day for Him.
Our perception of time is not the reality of His, for the soul will live
forever while the body meets death. The time will come when our frame
of time will align with His. Until then, we cannot comprehend all that
He does. He sees what we cannot, knows the outcome of everything. A
wait can be a preparation for change, so seek Him. Be still in the midst
of waiting. His timing is the best.*

*When He speaks, His voice will sound unfamiliar until you become
accustomed to recognizing that His voice was there all along. You must
accept He is the truth first. He waits for you to listen. It will be an unset-
tling feeling within until you grow accustomed to Him. We must see with
our spirit, not live by our flesh. This will connect you to our Creator.*

*As you build this relationship with Him, it will become easier to
know which thoughts are His. The visions that are planted by Him. Do
not confuse thoughts that come from fear made by corruption or abuse.
Being scared because you must be brave is not the same as something that
causes fear. There will be other times He guides by using His creations. As
you grow in Him, you will find it easier to recognize His signs.*

*Stay rooted in Him. Stay rooted in these words. You are less likely to
make a wrong decision. Mistakes will be made along the way. Perfection
does not exist in any of us, for we can only have a piece of Him within us.
We are not the Creator Himself. The Creator is perfection, while we are
far from it. Yet, we can be perfected through Him. The longer we seek,
the time we spend, we learn to grow back to who it is He called us to be,
originally. It is a matter of keeping close to Him in all ways, always.*

Do not spend your time overthinking. Do not waste thoughts on being unkind to yourself for fault. You are made by His love. He will forgive those that ask of it. Changed behavior brings the true mending that our Creator waits. What good is saying you are sorry without the action to prove it? Do you not feel wrong for harming another, even by mistake? Do you not grow weary harming yourself? Is the wicked within worth clinging onto?

Never let the corrupted beings lead you wrong. Learn discernment through our Creator on who to be influenced by. Some will purposely abuse their will to do wrong. They will only look out for themselves. They will do what they see fit to get what they want. They will take what is not theirs. They will be cruel to anyone they find to be in their way. They will be unkind. Selfish. Their hearts will not know how to love. They will claim it with no remorse that they lied to possess your love.

Do not grow in bitterness toward those that do evil works. Those that are lost. They do not know the wrath that comes with the evil they do. What they do cannot prosper a win. He will give back in a much greater way what you lose. What they take is when He takes away more. Anything you lose comes with something greater.

Rejection is His protection. When you plan things without His guidance, without His approval, it is not His plan. He will let your plans fall apart. This way, you are directed to do His will. You think you know what is best when it can be the very thing to cause your spiritual death.

Even with good intentions, this can cause you to be used by those that do the works of evil. Only help those that your spirit leads you to do. You are not to be mishandled. You are not made to be taken advantage of. You are made with love. His love. Called to be loved.

He did not create you out of mistake. He did not call you wrongly. You shall hear from Him greater as you seek within. There will be times of discomfort where you will need to wait on the Creator. This will build trust. Trust is needed to hold a strong bond. What is having faith in Him without trust? He knows the outcome that will take place. He sees all that we cannot. Trust that He knows when the time is right. The action He calls us to make is right. His understanding is greater than ours.

Trust in Him as He trusts you to come to know Him. He knows all of whom that will come to know Him. He knows what is needed to be done to reach you. He waits patiently. To truly love is to have patience for the other. For He knows the good that is still alive within you.

Finding who you are in who He created you to be will require seeking Him constantly. You will find some part of you always falling back into corruption if you do not stay focused on Him. A life without Him keeps a void within that will keep you stuck feeling unsatisfied, unfulfilled. This will lead you to wrongfully use things to mask the rooted issue. Continuing the cycle of destruction. Taking the misguidance from others who live in corruption.

A spirit is placed inside of you that He planted, one within your soul. It is a piece of Himself. This is why you remain incomplete. Disappointed when you refuse to connect with Him. You are rejecting the most divine part of yourself.

All are called. Only a few are chosen. Will you listen to His will for your life to be among the few? Will you lay down your life as He has given you one to live? Will you make the sacrifices needed? Will you love for the sake of others seeing His love through you?

This particular life will require you to speak as if He is right next to you. You will have to know within that the feeling of knowing is His voice. You will have to grow much further than most. You must accept that hardships will come with more sacrificing. You will need to forget worrying on how the world perceives you. It does not matter what another thinks of you when our Creator knows you. The ones against Him will slander your name, as they will continue to slander His.

This life is filled with sorrow. There is no escape from that. That is why it is temporary. That is why it is short. As is the body's life span. After death comes a new life, one away from here, one that is our forever home to our soul.

You can have all the wealth, all the riches of this world. It will never be enough to contain peace. Anything temporary that is idolized will deceive you. Idolizing is anything put above our Creator.

Your destined partner cannot complete you. Your soul cannot be plenished by them. Though they enhance your calling, though they help you become better, though they will fill you with love that another cannot, your soul is yours alone.

Neither of you can ever possess the glory that only our Creator holds. Neither of you will do exactly as needed by the other without His correction. This is done by the spirit. Without the spirit alive in you, without His guidance, you will do wrongly many more times to your beloved. Seek Him to love each other properly. Seek Him to help each other fulfill the purpose upon the other's life.

His spirit is the heart of your soul. You must become one with His spirit, wholeheartedly connected in His spirit. Not doing so will leave you drained. You will always long for more worldly things, never being content where you are, longing for more than you have.

Very dark times will be placed when this book is revealed. It is only fit to bring into the world something to restore the brokenness, to wake up the sleeping spirits. Most will not be where they belong by the birthing of the first Pariahs. The first Pariahs will be born specifically to release those that are trapped. They all will be free. Outcastril will need to be made new again for there will be more Pariahs to come. Rise the rest of them to live once again in their place of belonging.

Selah. Be strong. Be courageous. For He is with you wherever you go.

CHAPTER 33

I sat back stunned. My mind couldn't do the usual "drive myself crazy with endless questions" until it was all fuzzed away into a numbness that froze me in place. This wasn't the typical frozen in place I'd felt because I didn't feel overwhelmed or stuck.

I felt something that resembled clarity but in a way that was much more powerful, somehow freeing. Pieces of a puzzle that were so difficult to find finally found. So much of the unknown came to light, amazed by the power that these words held.

The book says the Creator will communicate to us, so it was not Sacred's voice I'd been hearing like it was believed. It had been the Creator's this whole time. I couldn't explain why I believed this wholeheartedly, but I did, without a single doubt.

That was the weirdest part to me. It was not typical; I didn't question what was written or said. It was not typical that I instantly felt something so eye-opening that life dawned on the unanswered questions I'd been begging to know. Nothing had come close to this. This went beyond my level of comprehension. It wasn't what I read that blew me away or confused me; it was the belief I had in every word written.

However, it said the Creator was the truth, and it had been said the truth shall set you free. Subconsciously, I knew that all along without realizing it. I believed once something clicks in our minds, it's because we know this information has been missing. When you're searching for the truth with no opinion that it has to be a certain way, the truth becomes revealed.

I couldn't help but wonder, though, why did the memory of Sacred stay alive but the Creator become forgotten? Was it possible

He was never known? No, because the firsts were told, so what happened to the Creator being mentioned? Why was there so few with little information on the Sacred in general? A sinking feeling came over me that the answer was much darker than I knew.

Hold on. Selah. I saw that word on the door, I traced each letter, and it glowed my color, and then the door opened. I looked down at the book and reread the last part. Why did this feel so personal reading it like that?

I gave you a name before your mother. Selah.

My eyes widened, and my mind stood stuck on that. *Selah*—it felt so fitting somehow, as if another part of me came to the surface. Like digging up an old, hollow, worn-out tree, then planting an unknown seed that was promised to give you a newness to living, one that would bring you to life in a whole other way. One that fulfills your soul and is whole.

You have to wait on the roots to develop first. It seems like nothing will happen. Within the waiting period, the questions about whether you made the right decision or not drive you nearly to an insanity that has no way of returning.

Suddenly, during a moment you need it the most, you notice a tiny stem of green out of the blue. You didn't know what you were waiting for exactly, and you still don't know the details of what comes next or how to even keep this alive, but you know more than anything that trying to put back a now dead tree would leave you without any oxygen at all. The new roots give you strength you didn't know before. The other tree would have never flourished like this one will.

I reread the part explaining a Pariah, and it dawned on me—I was the female Pariah. I drained Rohn when I'd been a healer my whole life. I was also the only healer who was born on my birthday.

The feeling of never feeling like I belonged made a lot of sense now. I could never think of myself as special enough to be made into someone with such a world-changing purpose or as unique, but everything was making more sense than it ever had. All the signs weren't a coincidence.

Wait. The book mentions two Pariahs, one a male and one a female. The statues appeared in my mind, and I sat remembering that the last two looked like Mavryk and me. Not looking like us—they were us. Tears swelled in my eyes as I tried to gather the wave of emotions from this.

All these years, I've created this out-of-the-world, life-changing, shaken-to-the-core love that you only read about, but in my mind, it was very real and always with the same two characters I imagined. One I believed to only be in fairy tales.

This wasn't a fairy tale; we were clearly designed for each other, and I knew from the moment I saw him I felt something I knew I'd never find again. He couldn't make me whole, as the Sacred explained, but looking back, he saw me—the me that had been buried—and all he wanted to do was help bring the true me to the surface. He wanted to help lift me higher, and even though it hurt him to let me go to live out part of my purpose, he believed in me and loved me when I hadn't been able to do the same for myself.

I kept rereading everything to let it sink in further. Since I was one of the first Pariahs, I was somehow supposed to restore broken-ness and free everyone. How in the world did I go about this? Where did I even start? I hadn't even gotten myself figured out; I still felt broken inside, so how could anything be accomplished?

He had to have picked wrong, mistaken this somehow. I mean, maybe there was a twin in my mother's belly destined for this, and somehow, I survived instead.

I called you. Selah. You are chosen for this. Seek me in every step you take, and you will succeed.

I guess doubt can really suck us into a lie of being less important than we are. This whole time, I'd placed value on the opinions that others thought of me. Snarky belittling comments were joked when I knew deep down they weren't a joke. I'd been letting the negative that had been said wrap me completely in this bubble of delusion that I'd never be anything that mattered and that I hadn't gotten any sense within me to be considered anywhere near intelligent.

Except I'd always mattered, and it was only a matter of time before I realized how much of a difference I make by being alive and making it through another day. Each day was a day closer to serving my purpose. The Creator wouldn't have let anything prosper to destroy me; the book says that. The choice of what I do does matter enough, though it's never been about what another has done to me but what I had done to get through it.

It's not that I was ignorant in any sense; it's the fact that they never took the time to notice who I really was, and out of fear of rejection, I hardly ever showed that side of me. Some see different as dumb when it's usually the unique ones who have the most brilliant ideas. They see things on a much different surface level that has made others lack comprehension, and it led them not to take a moment to see it from this perspective. They decide to stay stuck in their mindset and disregard something that is insightful and could have helped them grow mentally.

Sometimes, to get through everything, I broke down and survived many days while begging for death. I found myself grateful that wish didn't come true. I never thought I'd find myself thinking that. I believe the only reason we wish to die in the first place is to stop feeling so terrible; if we felt okay enough, I don't believe anyone would want that. If we realize our value and love ourselves, we could find an understanding that proves the difference we make in this life.

Knowing there's a purpose for each of us was enough to make me want to push forward, not just for myself either. I truly wanted others to know they matter just as much as anyone else. That no one is greater and we're all equal but on different paths. That being different from each other is something to embrace.

I could only imagine a world where we were all gathered together, embracing each difference that holds our greatest strengths and becoming a nation of wholeness. One where no one envied, no one belittled, no one caused harm. We all came together in acceptance and loved each of us for who we were. In all reality, wasn't that what we craved the most?

I sat back on the cool stone wall, staring ahead at the maze. *This isn't my destination to stay, so where do I go from here? What is it I do?* I knew I had to share this with whoever I could, but how? I felt my mind start to slip into endless questions that caused me to feel overwhelmed until a thought came to mind.

"You want me to go back to the village and read the book to them."

I didn't need a response to know that the thought crossed my mind for a reason. This must've been what the book meant. Things like this will answer our question in a very random way that will be a knowing of this is what needs done. Almost like intuition telling us what's right or wrong. Except, maybe, what's considered intuition is another word to replace the fact that it is communication from our Creator.

As I got up to walk out, I stopped. The feeling of anxiousness started to take over as I realized what this meant. I'd have to talk to people and not in a casual manner. Not that I was a fan of that, but it had got to be a whole lot easier than what I was going to have to do. Visions of me in front of the villagers speaking flashed through my mind, and I started to sink into myself.

"Why on earth would you pick me of all people to talk about something as serious as this? Why would you create me to do something I've struggled with my entire life?"

What seems impossible becomes possible when I am involved.

"I understand that, but it is me we are talking about. We're not talking about someone great, we are—"

The opinion of others still corrupts your mind and deceives your heart. Does what I know matter less than what they think? Everything I ask of you is within you because I made you. You are made from my love, and that does not come with faults. The fault is within the corruption. Everyone is made in a genuine way, but only a few will stay as such. You are one of the few left with a heart of purity. It is because of this I have chosen you.

All are called, but few are chosen—this is what he meant. Everyone is made in his image, which consists of love. The ones chosen and destined for higher callings are the ones who are willing to help anyone he calls you to help with the gift he created you with. Love is willing to help in the way our Creator would.

This doesn't mean you're meant to be taken advantage of, though, and not everyone is set out to do that. Not everyone is like those that hurt you. There are others listening in on that voice on how to be loving and genuinely hearted.

What if I pointed all of this out? What if people became curious enough to spiritually dig deep enough because I brought it to their attention? How could they believe it, though?

This world is wicked and cruel, and so are some of the people who walk in it. The existence or reality of the Sacred and Creator are not known by most either, so their truth must first be brought to everyone's attention. Then maybe they'll start searching out of hope for something greater to happen in their life. Maybe that love that died inside of them comes back to life.

"What if they don't believe me, though? What if this book isn't proof enough?"

Those that will believe were waiting for a time such as this, those that turn an eye were never going to accept me.

It dawned on me right then. All this time, I'd feared rejection to go where I was called and be told I was wrong, but it was He who was really being denied. If I decided not to pursue at this point, He would still make a way for my life, but how many souls would be left behind with the feeling I once had?

A feeling of knowing there's something so much more, that we don't exist to live in such a broken and unfulfilled world, permeated my thoughts. That no matter what is done to us, in the end, there's a plan, and all the Creator asks of us is to believe that what He says is the truth—to go a step further than that and live with His presence actively inside of us.

It's as if we are His children, and His best interest at heart is to give us the best life possible—to be the father some of us never had. To be loved in a way we cried many times for. To walk with trust and in faith that He's guiding us on a much better path than we could have done for ourselves, even as the harshest storm is happening around us. To especially lean into Him as we fight the greatest war we'll ever face, which is inside of us.

Personally, I tried many times doing it my way and always found myself back in the same circumstances: confused, torn, lonely, lost, without something that was needed, and an emptiness that I thankfully no longer felt. That was the best part about this—not feeling like I was going the wrong way anymore. For the first time in my life, I knew I was doing what was right.

Maybe that's why I always went back to what I knew, even though I knew it wasn't good for me. It all had the same feeling in the end, and I at least knew the outcome from what was familiar. I also knew myself well enough to know I couldn't have handled worse. There weren't signs that it would get better, but this has had the signs I needed right when I needed them the most, reminding me that uncertainty is scary, but it would kill the best parts of who I was if I stay put where I didn't belong.

I looked at my shoulder and realized sometime or another Midlight had left. I looked around and couldn't see Midlight anywhere. Sadness started to take over until I noticed another butterfly. This one had the same color of blue as the bushes, with no black besides the lines running throughout its wings, like a monarch.

A couple more appeared out of the bushes of the same color and pattern. Then a few more, and before I knew it, there were hardly any of the blue leaves on the bushes, and blue butterflies were flying everywhere. I took a step out of the building and watched in amazement. Through the branches of the bushes, I could see purple butterflies start to flutter around.

I began walking and followed the butterflies that flew from the bushes. Every butterfly had a solid color of whatever color the leaves were, and all of them resembled a monarch pattern. They didn't seem to be different sizes; they were all fully grown and shined with sparkles of gold. Even the leaves on the bushes that came from the other end of the maze formed butterflies.

As I made it back to the entrance, I looked back, and all that appeared were butterflies of their color and an open field with the sun setting in the background. The bushes had completely disappeared. My breath had been taken by such a sight. I'd never in my life seen so many with such vibrancy.

As I turned to look forward, the statues still stood in their places, but there only stood an open field; the gloomy mossy green scenery had disappeared as well. From a short distance, I saw the garden welcoming me back, and what you would think would be filled with darkness didn't fill the air. Thousands of lightning bugs lit the way to see everything.

Before heading toward the garden, I took one more look at the statues. I thanked the one I knew now as Sacred and walked slowly to observe the others. When I got to the one of Mavryk and me, I stopped, and a small smile formed. I reached to touch Mavryk's statue and closed my eyes.

I didn't know how I knew, but I could feel that he felt heartache. He was okay in another sense, though, and that brought comfort, knowing he was not harmed. Still, I didn't like how he felt such an intense emotion that caused dread in everything you do.

Does he miss me like I missed him? I didn't quite believe I could mean that much to him, but if two people are destined for each other, then surely, he must feel some kind of way not being around me.

I lifted my hand away as my head lifted to look one last time, and then I headed toward the garden. As I entered it, surrounded by all the amazing nature it contained, I felt such peace come over me that somehow numbed my mind from everything except the sight of what I was seeing. The moment of feeling now came more alive with every breath I took.

I decided that instead of heading back tonight, I would sleep right here and forget the problems I'd face tomorrow. I didn't know what to expect or how difficult it would get, but I knew that it could wait until the morning. All that truly mattered in this moment was that beauty existed in every single way in everything my eyes saw. All I felt was something I never thought I'd feel, and somehow, I knew that this gave me an idea of how the Creator's presence has to feel.

As wonderful as this was, it couldn't possibly touch how mesmerizing the Creator is. I was not sure my own imagination could find a way to picture such an exceptional being. Then again, He made all of this—there's a touch of His magic in everything natural we experience.

CHAPTER 34

I woke up to the sound of birds tweeting their melody of morning delight and sunlight welcoming the day. Thankfully, the sun's rays weren't on me but around me, giving my eyes time to adjust.

I sat up with my legs stretched out. As I began to stretch my arms toward my toes, a blue butterfly fluttered toward me. It didn't sparkle like the others, and its pattern resembled only one butterfly I'd encountered. I smiled, and excitement spread within.

"Midlight! You got all your blue color!" My posture shot up as I nearly yelled it.

It fluttered around my body faster than its normal pace and did loops above my legs and then landed on my foot as it stared at me.

"We have a big day ahead of us. Are you ready for it?"

Midlight fluttered her wings a few times slowly up and down, which I assumed to be a resounding yes.

"Of course you are. We both know I'm the one who might never feel ready for this." I wiggled my toes that Midlight sat on. "I'll need you to move in order to get up."

Midlight didn't budge, and a strong feeling of needing to wait a moment longer settled in me, so I stayed sitting in place. I didn't know what to expect, but when I looked up, a rainbow started to form. No, not one but two, and as they began to grow, the sun shined brighter, making everything come to life more than it already was. Specks of gold sparkled in the rainbow and on everything around me. I had read about a rainbow being a significant sign of something but never knew of what, let alone the meaning of two.

After all that you will face. After all that you have faced. This is my promise to give back more than is expected. I will give back more than

you have lost. Do not be afraid. Do not be dismayed. For I am with you.
Selah.

A chill traveled throughout my whole body. Tears began to form in my eyes as I marveled at the stunning view. After all the doubt and negative thoughts, I finally felt hope that I thought had been lost. Grace captured my soul as my heart mended back into a wholeness that filled with purity that only wants to love.

I stood up and held out my arms with my head toward the sky and my eyes shut. In that moment, I felt the sun's light beam on me like it had never done before. Usually, warmth wrapped me in reassurance that better was to come, but this filled me with heat. Not in the way that makes you hot, it's in the way that lights your soul on fire and brings you to life in a way that transforms you into something stronger. When I opened my eyes and looked at my hands and arms, I lit into the white light as before when Mavryk and I came together.

I slowly lowered my arms but not fully to my sides. My head lowered to look at them, and I knew I needed to focus on creating what I had before. That ball of light meant so much more. It was a power within greater than the original powers we'd been gifted with.

We aren't created to only possess healing or draining, to see others' stories beyond what we tell or to see parts of others they try to keep hidden from everyone; we aren't only here to bring magic into the world. We have a light inside of us that can do more than anything we have ever imagined. It's the part of our Creator that lives within. It's more powerful than the soul and lives within the spirit. It's the part of us that most of us never bring to life.

Suddenly, white light filled both of my hands. As I kept focusing, the light on each side grew bigger. I brought my hands together, and as the lights came together, it formed bigger than expected. Sparkles of gold formed around the light, and a powerful sensation I'd felt once before electrified my body.

In front of me, a golden glow began to form, with nothing showing in the glow, but the thought of putting my light into it came to mind. I took the steps needed to be inches from the glow and moved my hands toward it until the light started to dissolve into the glow.

Once it fully dissolved, the glow stayed as a golden light with silver sparkles dancing. It began to lift to the sky and filled one of the rainbows with sparkles of gold and silver while the colors remained. It then turned into a ball of light with all the colors a rainbow has, still containing the sparkles, and moved to the other one. It did the same as the first rainbow the glow touched, but this time, it started moving toward the sun. As it collided with the sun, it created a masterpiece I had never seen before.

The sun had a light tint of the rainbow colors in it, but the sun's light still stood bright and sparkled with something beyond the golden glow magic. I had never been able to look at the sun and its details because of its brightness, but somehow, I could stare at this without it blinding me. The feeling of its intensity froze me in place, and I couldn't help but know I was looking at the power of the Creator. Tears fell from my face as I embraced such a beautiful sight.

The world will know of my promise as they look to the sky. They will see that I am with them.

I looked forward and stood in place, staring at the stairs. There was nothing left to do here now. I must go, speak on what I found and what I'd experienced. Even if no one believed me, the truth had to be told. I didn't come all this way to not move forward. I had to do this even if my voice shook, my hands sweat, and my heart felt like it would beat out of my chest. I could only imagine that was the least of what would happen.

I started walking up the steps, and that was when my mind began to race the way it did. The what-ifs of what would happen, how it would happen, and how many people—it was hard to picture. It was harder to believe anyone believing me. I was only so certain myself because the signs had been clear.

Even then, my mind wanted to tell me I didn't see what I knew I saw. I couldn't expect anyone to believe it. Then again, I could. Why would the highest form of a being that exists lead me all this way just to fail? I couldn't believe in myself, but I could believe in the Creator to know that they aren't guiding me pointlessly. There was something major to come out of this. Not even doubt could shake the feeling of knowing that this was right to do.

I got to the top of the steps and felt the need to wait. Sparkles started to appear, and shortly afterward, a glow began to grow. Looking into it, I saw the village from a little distance, the ocean's shoreline, and a blue sky with no clouds in the background. I saw some of the villagers out and about, one of them being Samuel. A smile spread on my face. Once the glow stopped growing, I stepped in.

"Sam!" I shouted.

He whipped around fast, and the look on his face brought joy to my heart.

He ran, and I held out my arms. I squeezed him tightly as his arms wrapped around me.

"You came back," he whispered.

"I'll never break a promise to you, Sam."

"Never?"

"Never ever."

He pulled back, and we looked at each other. Then I spoke. "You won't believe what I discovered."

I finished the rest of the way, pulling apart, and pulled out the Book of Sacred from the satchel. Sam's face looked curious and confused.

"You found a book?" he said in a laughable way.

"Not just any book but *the* book." He looked at me as if I had lost my mind in some way. "Do you know about the Sacred or the Creator?" I asked, disregarding his facial expression.

"No? What are those?"

"Not what but who," I responded.

I opened the first page and began reading. I never looked up to see his face or what he might be thinking; I only read and hoped reading to him would bring some of the same clarity I had. When I was done, I looked at him and explained the butterfly appearing to me, guiding me up the rock wall, and discovering the garden.

"Then I stumbled upon an open field, and on the other side stood another forest, but this one had statues of the Sacred and all the firsts, including Mavryk and me. This maze stood behind the statues, so I went into it and, as I was walking, I had a choice to go the same color or choose the different color. Well, the different colors led me to a stoned building that shielded this book by a glow, the same glows I'd been walking through. I read the book and knew I had to come back, so I did."

I then went on to explain the leaves turning into butterflies, then coming back to the garden, and everything that had happened there. I turned my head before I spoke the next part, and he turned his.

"That's why you see the sun as it is right now. I created a light, and it formed with a glow, and that's when it formed with two rainbows, which became one with the sun."

I looked back at him and studied his face. Shocked couldn't begin to describe his expression, but I didn't expect such a smile of excitement to come with it.

He looked at me with bewilderment in his eyes. "I told everyone you went looking for something and that this happened because of you. As soon as I saw the light fall into the sun, I freaking knew! We all saw it happen, and I knew it had something to do with you."

"So you believe that this book holds the truth?" I asked.

He looked around, thinking about how to respond, and then responded, "I believe you believe it, which makes me believe it is true." He looked at me, and as he did, I heard nothing but authenticity.

"I knew when you showed up you stood out, not because you're pretty, even though you are. I knew there was more to you. I get treated like I'm stupid because I'm seen as a clueless child, but I see so much more than the adults do. I hope I never become an adult who forgets how to see everything the way a kid does. Like you. You don't treat me differently than anyone else. You kind of make me feel special."

Tears formed in my eyes. "The wonderful thing is that our Creator sees us when we feel like no one else does, and then there are people that remind us we are not as alone as we think we are. You're far more incredible than you could ever know, Sam, and you are beyond special. Never let the opinions of others make you forget who you really are inside. When the thoughts get too bad to fight off, though, talk to the Creator. He'll remind you every time."

"How do you talk to someone who's not there in front of you?" I could hear the curiosity and confusion in his tone.

It was my turn to think for a moment about how to respond. Maybe see if the Creator could speak through me in some superficial way. A thought came to mind in that moment as I remembered what I had read.

"It says it. There's a piece of him in us, and that's the most divine part of who we are, so everywhere we go, anywhere we end up, he's there. At any moment, for any reason. You can talk out loud or think the thought, he'll know. When we are at a loss for words, he can feel the pain we feel in our heart, giving us the answers, knowing in the way we need it. We just have to reach out in the way we're capable of doing, and it's nothing to him to be there. When all is said and done, that's all he truly wants."

"So he wants us to talk to him and nothing else?" He used a rolling hand motion, and I couldn't help but laugh a little.

"I think there's more to it, but it's the best way to start."

Sam scratched his face and had that serious but funny expression on his face. "Well, I'll try talking to him, but I don't know if I'm ever going to understand any of this."

I burst out laughing, which made him laugh too.

After a little bit more time of talking, we ended up looking through the village to find Joshua and then Meera. Gran ended up joining, which made me a bit nervous, but I knew I needed to get used to being uncomfortable to pursue my calling.

Instead of beginning with Midlight, I showed them the book and read it to them and then explained the glow from the very beginning and things along the way that had happened—Midlight guiding me, the garden, the statues, the maze, back to the garden, then me putting a light into the glow and what happened to the rainbows.

"I walked up the stairs, and another glow appeared in front of me that led me back here—but not to just be back here. It took me to Sam first, and now I'm coming to you guys because I believe if anyone's to believe, it might be with you guys next." I swallowed nervously and breathed in, then continued talking. "I know how this sounds. It's insane, and if someone came to me about this, I'm not sure if I'd believe them. But if you look to the sun, you can at least see with your eyes that I'm telling the truth."

I held the book in both hands and stared away while I talked. "When I read this, I felt something I had never felt before. All my life I've questioned the meaning of my existence and why I'm here. What is my purpose, do I even matter enough to exist? Those questions melted away once reality set in that we really do have a higher being in ultimate control and how we aren't created for nothing. The voice I had been hearing, with thoughts that I thought were random, are his guidance. And the wild thing is, it's always been him, but I never knew. Not until now."

I looked at all of them, and as I suspected, they had a look of shock and disbelief written all over their face. Grans was the only one who remained unmoved. Before I decided to say anything else, Gran stood up, and to my surprise, a tiny hint of a smile formed.

"I have waited a very long time for this." She slowly stepped close to me, pulled her arm out of her sleeve, and showed me the design I had seen before on her. "This is the symbol they brand us with when you are forced to Outcastril." She pulled her sleeve back down and showed the other arm with the same branding. "They brand you on both sides of your arm." She put that sleeve down and held her arms within her sleeves below her chest. "I never told anyone how I came here or where I come from. I was out working further from the others, and in the corner of my eye, this golden light appeared out of nowhere. I heard a voice speak to me. It told me to walk through it if I wanted the chance to see the day that freedom comes. I had nothing to lose, so I grabbed as many as I could then walked through it, right before it disappeared. That voice never made any bit of sense, but I knew it was not something to ignore. If I can help in any way, I'm willing to die to see that day."

Disbelief and huge relief came over me because of all people, I thought she couldn't stand me. I definitely didn't think she'd believe me. This whole time she lived with this war inside that brought no bit of peace to her, and yet someone in her stance, with the things she'd experienced, was ready to face the real war for the sake of others one day not having to suffer as she did. I couldn't think of anything more admirable than that.

"Suga." I wiped my eyes before any tears fell and looked at Meera. "I am very proud of you. Your momma would be too. I think it is safe to say you need to tell the others about this." More tears formed.

"The villagers? She needs to tell the world of this! I mean, this changes everything!" Joshua had the biggest smile on his face.

I looked at each of their faces and felt nothing but so much love for each of them.

"So why are we standing here?" Sam's voice perked up. "Let's get everyone to the front of the beach and have Ann give one heck of a speech!"

Joshua and Sam at that point raced out, and you could hear them yelling door to door and person to person to meet in the same spot. Meera shook her head, but we all had a laugh. Gran even had a smile on her face.

"Well, I'm gonna head over and get me front row. I'll see you in a few, kid." Meera went to pat my shoulder, but I grabbed her hand and stopped her. She looked a bit thrown off but stopped to look at me.

"Thank you for believing in me and encouraging me to seek this out. Your support means so much more than you can imagine."

She faced me, took a breath in, held it, and then spoke. "Dear, you have no idea what you're capable of, but I'll tell you right now, it is even more than what you have already done. I am the lucky one to experience you."

We hugged and held each other for a moment. She then pulled back, took another look at my face, and walked out. I watched her as she left and had this feeling this would be our last time for a while before I got to have a moment like that again.

I looked at Gran, who went back to lying down, but her eyes were open, staring at the ceiling. I went to leave and then felt the need to say something.

"I misjudged you, and I'm sorry for that. It's never easy to share the painful parts of our past, but you showed me what kind of strength it takes to hold onto hope when everything seems hopeless. Thank you for trusting me with something so personal. Maybe one day we can swap stories, and I can relate to being as heroic as you."

Her eyes closed as she spoke, but nonetheless, a smile sat on the ends of her lips. "The day will come when we see each other again, and that is when we will smile at the difference we make in living for another day."

CHAPTER 35

Every single person from the village had gathered around. Everyone talked while many faces said they didn't understand what the fuss was about. This roughly consisted of two hundred people. I could hear my breathing becoming heavier. I looked down to make sure the pounding of my heart didn't show through my chest. My hands began to sweat, and heat filled my face, though I was certain I looked more washed out.

"Ann!" Sam's voice made me jump, but I mustered up a smile, probably an awkward one. "I got everyone together. Well, okay, Joshua helped, but the point is, everyone is waiting. If you're ready?" He threw his hands toward me while his arms bent at the elbow and made a face that said he was a bit nervous for me.

"I wish I could be ready for this, but I'm not sure I'll ever be."

"Well, I can tell them you got sick and try again tomorrow."

I laughed and shook my head. "I so appreciate the support, but no, Sam. This needed to be done now. The world needs to know."

He tried not smiling, but the curve on his lips showed excitement. "Cool. I think you're going to kick butt in this. Just be you, you know, and they'll believe you. At least most of them will. Remember, you told me you can't please everyone, so don't focus on that. Focus on the story you need to tell, and I believe more people will believe than those that won't."

I stared at him in amazement as he talked and felt so honored to know him. He really had no idea how amazing he was and the difference he made in my life. As much as he admired me and looked up to me, I knew he had no real clue the difference he had made in my heart and the magnitude behind who he was to simply exist.

I wondered if this was how the Creator sees all of us when we are being our authentic self in moments of genuine kindness and compassion. Maybe he stared in awe at the fact that after everything, we still had it in us to talk life into a loved one. We'd still support another even if we constantly doubt ourselves. Maybe our biggest purpose in life has nothing to do with us but what we can do for each other. Maybe, just maybe, love is the answer to the problems we have.

I held out my arms to hug him, and in that moment, he gave me the strength and courage to do what I needed to. I pulled back and looked at him.

"Thanks, kiddo. You just gave me the nudge I needed to go out there and speak. You don't know it, but you really do make life better."

I must have caught him off guard because he looked down as his eyes glossed, and when he blinked, tears fell from his eyes. He held his hand to his eyes as he squeezed them and then backed up.

"I'll be waiting in the front to hear you." Then he turned around and ran to be with the villagers.

I began to walk toward everyone, so I fixed my posture by taking deeper breaths to help relax my shoulders. As I approached, everyone began to look at me. I looked away toward the ocean, then up to the sun, and that moment of what happened flashed in my mind. Even if they didn't believe me, I knew what happened. This wasn't for those that didn't believe; this was for those that did.

I could hear the murmurs of others talking as I stood staring at the ocean. I looked down at the book and then slowly turned around to face everyone. I placed my hand on it, remembering what I felt when I first read this. I looked up at everyone and figured I was too nervous not to stumble on my words, but I had to try.

"This is strange for me too." Everyone grew quiet in that moment as I said those words.

"I appreciate everyone coming together. I can only imagine what you all are thinking. To be honest, I'm still trying to process everything that's happened. I went from being locked away in the castle to being set free by something I had no clue existed. I don't expect anyone to believe. I almost can't believe it myself, but what I'm going to tell you is completely true. So if you can bear with me to hear me out, hopefully by the time I'm done speaking, enough of it will make sense, and you'll feel it in your heart that I didn't have you all come together to waste your time."

I looked back down at the book and spoke again. "I found this book in a garden, hidden by a cave on the other side of here." I looked up and scanned the villagers. "I'm not sure if any of you know where the world started from or if you know about the Sacred, but if you do, then you'll know he walked this world and had been known as the one who started everything. He came as proof that everything is made purposely and with a purpose, and he did possess all the powers—he could do far more than anyone else ever would be able to do. He wasn't the one who made us, though. No, in this book, I discovered that there was a higher being than him, one that was so hard to comprehend but was very much alive in a way we didn't think could be possible. I could feel what only a divine being could have you feel, and hopefully, by the time I'm done reading this, you'll come to believe that this holds the truth."

I took a couple of slow, deep breaths as I opened the book and then began reading. The words flowed from my mouth more smoothly than how I had just spoken. I could feel the passion leave my mouth with every word I spoke, but I knew better than to look up. I'd surely stumble and lose my momentum if I decided to take my focus off what truly mattered.

Nothing anyone else thinks comes close to mattering like doing what you know you're supposed to do. Even if everyone laughed and mocked me and said this to be the most ridiculous thing, it didn't matter. What matters is exposing the truth for what it is and hoping you do have someone else to believe you.

I finished the last sentence and then looked up. Most of the faces said they were dumbfounded. My heart sank for a minute, and then I realized I was not done talking yet. I pointed to the sun, explaining what had happened for it to become like it was and how as I walked up the steps to come back to them a golden glow appeared.

"Then I walked through it and appeared in front of Sam. I've been led back here to tell every single one of you about our Creator and how he created all of us with a purpose. Some of you, maybe all of you, belong here, but not everyone else is where they're supposed to be. They aren't even being who they're meant to. I'm just now learning how to be my truest self, and I'm still comprehending all of whom that consist of. I've without a doubt been very doubtful walking my purpose. However, I also know our Creator will continue to guide me until I've finally got it figured out. I believe the same for all of you. I believe there's so much more in store for everyone in this messed-up world. If the world came together willingly, ready to stand together like you all did today, then I believe, within time, we are more than capable of making the world a better place. A place it's always been meant to be."

Before my mind could touch the surface of embarrassment, clapping came from Meera. It didn't take long for everyone else to start clapping too. Cheers and whistling began to happen. Suddenly, people began walking forward to me and hugging me or patting my back. I almost couldn't believe that this was happening.

I'd been criticized and belittled all my life by so many more people, while only a few seemed to have really seen something in me. I'd been scolded for speaking genuinely kind things, and I'd been rudely interrupted because I wanted more detail on how they thought. I'd been talked at while they wouldn't let me speak without being yelled at on why I was wrong. I'd been made to feel that anything I said was ignorant and wasn't worth listening to.

My eyes began to water. The gratitude I felt majorly outweighed any doubt I had suffered from. These people, who had barely known me, made me feel safer and trusted more than most of the people I had gotten the closest with or known for a long time, if not most of my life. For the first time, I felt like I had truly made a positive impact on life.

As everyone was talking and I was taking turns talking to others, I heard someone gasp and then a few more. I looked toward a middle-aged lady whose eyes said she couldn't believe what she was looking at. I turned around in hopes that I would see what she did, and sure enough, I did. A glow the size of an apple appeared there and grew until it fit the size I was. I smiled, knowing that was a forest you couldn't forget even if you had tried.

I looked back toward everyone and stepped back some. "I've been told that if you can see within the glow where its destination is, then you're to walk through it. Does anyone else see what's on the other side?" I asked as I scanned the crowds. No one came forward or said anything.

"I see the forest of fairies. It's been said they went extinct a long time ago, but I've seen them. There's a hidden cave that leads you to them, and to get to the forest, they must use their magic to take you. It is quite the sight, as is the garden. Go out and explore it for yourself."

I took a minute to catch my breath and process that not only would I be speaking again, but I was leaving people I loved again. "I hope to one day see all of you again. There are a few of you I've gotten very close to and have really touched my heart in ways no one else has. I want everyone to know that if I don't see you again, your trust and kindness will never be forgotten and means so much more to me than I know how to explain. Thank you. Don't forget what I've taught you today and begin to connect with the Creator. With our Creator. The best you is still yet to happen."

I turned around and saw the glow had become brighter than I'd ever seen it. I didn't really know why, but I had a feeling that this was confirmation that I'd never been more on the right path for my life than I had today. A breakthrough, not just with my path but within myself. It was the toughest journey to travel, and today a new part of me came unlocked—a boldness I never knew I had, a more empowering feeling than any magic I've produced.

As I stepped through the glow, I appeared in front of dozens of other fairies. They all looked at me, stunned, and were talking to each other about how I appeared. As they began to gather around me, Naomi burst through the crowd.

"Oh my gosh, Ann, you're back!" She flung her arms up in the air and nearly tripped over her feet to give me a hug. It felt so good to see her again and to know she felt the same way. "I can't believe you're back! I keep overhearing that you appeared from a glow! Is that true?" Her voice held onto the excitement.

"You won't believe everything else that has happened." I stepped back a step and pulled the book from my satchel. "This is the Book of Sacred."

She stared at the book with bewildered eyes. "You mean to tell me you found a book about the Sacred?!"

"Not just that, but the book he wrote in, and there's something else, something more powerful than him that created everything." I looked up and realized everyone was trying to listen in, so I began speaking louder. "He is called Creator. I'm sure by now everyone's heard about how the Sacred has spoken to me, and I believed he had until I read this book. It turns out there is a much higher being than him who can do the unthinkable. He's more than what can be imagined, more than what you see."

Naomi spoke with less excitement but with more eagerness to know what had happened. "Wait, so where did you find this book?"

I responded with, "Coastra."

"And you're certain it was he who wrote this?"

I wanted to say yes and get on with reading the book, but I knew I needed to explain things for her and everyone to better understand. "Coastra is a beautiful and peaceful place, but not a day went by that this feeling of not being at home kept pulling at me. The more I tried to resist that feeling, the more I tried to give it more time, the easier I became frustrated. I couldn't take it anymore, so I wrote what had been heavy on my heart and shared it with a good friend. She encouraged me to adventure out, so I did. The moment I was ready to turn around, a butterfly fluttered to me out of nowhere. I'd never seen a butterfly in Coastra before, so I knew it meant something. Well, it led me to climb a wall that led to a cave, and that's where I discovered the Garden of Leah."

"The Garden of Leah is said to be where all of the firsts were created." I shot my head toward the direction of Anadella; Arny stood next to her. I could feel the excitement fill my face.

"Yes! It is! This book talks about that and more. I just want to read it already, so you'll understand better."

"Oh, we know." Arny's heartwarming chuckle rang like a melody in my ears. His smile grew bigger as he looked at my neck to see the straps still in place from when he gave me the arrowhead necklace.

"I also saw statues of them, the Sacred and Mavryk, and I—" I stopped and looked around as I realized he was not here. "Where is he? Where is Mavryk?"

Naomi went ahead and spoke in a saddened tone. "He left. I tried to get him to stay, but he insisted on leaving, so I transferred him back to the cave. He walked out and didn't say where he was going."

My heart sank, and I could feel that depressed, numbing feeling trying to overcome me. A hand gently grabbed my shoulder. As I turned to look, it was Arny's. His eyes said he understood my pain, but I needed to continue. I took a shuddering deep breath, closed my eyes, and when I opened them, a tear in each eye fell out. I wiped them away and began reading from the book.

It didn't take more than the first sentence for me to get back into focus. I could feel the words coming alive and passion filling my lungs, on fire to speak as if life depended on it. Reading it out loud this time went smoother than at Coastra.

I closed the book and looked up toward the trees. The sun shined brightly on me, and a warm embrace filled my soul with peace that I'd realized only existed in one way.

"And now you see why we saw so much more in you." Anadella's voice sounded as sweet as her smile. "Selah is a wonderful fit for you."

"I entered through a stone door that had the word Selah written on it. When I traced the letters, it opened, and that's when I found the book. It stood protected inside a glow."

Suddenly, the light from the sun quickly shone so brightly down on everything that all of us had to look away. When the brightness dimmed, we all looked around. Toward the forest area, where I had first come in from, a glow appeared. A painful dread filled my entire body with the worst possible feeling and nearly brought me to my knees as I noticed where it would be taking me next.

"Hey, what is wrong? What do you see?" Naomi's voice said my reaction scared her. What she didn't know is how terrified I felt.

I almost can't get myself to speak without wanting to vomit, but I managed the words anyway. "It's the castle. I have to go back."

Many gasps escaped the fairies' mouths, and the forest began to be filled with talking. "Silence." Anadella's voice went stern, but she did not shout. As everyone went quiet, she spoke again. "There must be a mistake with what you are seeing. Are you sure?"

My eyes shot at her, and my head slowly turned with them. My mouth slightly hung open to breathe easier. "I wish I could forget what it looked like, what it felt like to be imprisoned there, but nothing will ever make me forget. Nothing."

Tears rolled down my cheeks, and I felt it on my face as it went to my chest the beginning of a breakdown, but I didn't have time for it, so instead, I shifted my thinking to what makes me angry. It's probably not considered healthy, but I can't fall right now. I have to do this no matter how desperately I want to run away.

I began to walk toward it. I could feel everyone else behind me, following me, as if they had to face the same terror that lay ahead. Maybe it's their way of comforting and wanting to be with me as long as they can, but at this moment, I envied them so badly. They didn't have to relive a waking nightmare.

"Ann!" Naomi had desperation in her voice. "Do not go. You don't have to. You are given that choice." I turned to look at her. She had been crying.

Seeing her like this weighed on my heart and reminded me of the compassion I felt for those that I loved, and I didn't know how to love any other way except deeply.

"Naomi, you've been an amazing friend. I can only imagine what childhood would have been like if we grew up together." She broke into a cry and covered her mouth as she shut her eyes. "The choice to stay would make me selfish, and while many would say that it is fair to be selfish at this moment, we both know I couldn't live with myself if I gave up now. Sometimes we have to go back to the place that nearly killed us, so others do not die."

At that moment, I realized how selfless you have to be to prove real love makes the most sacrifices. You can do so much for so many, and at the end of the day, you will never lose what needs to stay. He will make sure it is restored one way or another. The choice to follow the Creator with what He says, no matter what it is that is ahead or how something seems, is walking in belief that He is doing what is best, anyway.

She flung herself at me and squeezed me tight. I didn't have the strength to squeeze back, so I sank into her, soaking in that this might be the last time I ever get a moment like this again. I looked up at everyone and looked between Arny and Anadella before pulling away from Naomi. She walked back with the crowd, and Anadella held her in her arms as Naomi still cried.

"Love is the most powerful force, isn't it? Continue to love one another because you never know when it will be your last day to love. Or to be loved."

I didn't hesitate a second longer and stepped inside the glow.

CHAPTER 36

I couldn't believe I was here again. Staring at the place that had kept me bound for years and had me locked away from reality was such a gruesome feeling. Having to face what you never could before left me clueless on how I would get through this.

More importantly, I would need to convince them that their way of life wasn't correct. Convincing anyone with a luxurious lifestyle that what they knew is highly corrupted feels like an impossible task. All I could do was what I'd been doing and then hope that at least one believes me. I'd like for more, but it felt nearly impossible.

All around me were carriages of sorts, which confused me at first until I realized that there was only one reason for this—the annual gathering. Every year during this time, all the wealthy from around the world come together in celebration of what they see as accomplishments. Of course, you can't forget the gossiping about each other while everyone pretends that no one is talking about the other.

I'd always been a hot topic when I'd been made to attend, so it would be fitting to crash the party. At least this time, I'd give them something to really talk about, and maybe they'd think through something that involved being more open-minded.

I began to weave through the carriages when I noticed Rohn unloading one of them. He then looked up, and as his eyes met mine, they widened, and a tad bit of color left his body. He shot straight up and tensed like I had never seen him do.

"Rohn, I need you to take me to Venon," I said in a calm voice.

"I knew it was you, but how? How is that possible?" He tried to keep his voice from sounding breathless.

"I didn't know I was capable until I did what I did to you. I was as shocked as you still are, but to save some time on explaining things, this book has the answer to it. I'm a pariah. I'm one of the first. The guy you saw me with is the other pariah."

Rohn looked as he asked, "Where is he?" Then back at me with even more confusion and some frustration. "Never mind that, what is a pariah? How do you know this?"

I pulled out the book and held it outwardly so he could see it. He went to grab it, but I quickly pulled it away. "That's not an invitation to grab it. I'm the only one who's touched it. I'm only showing you, so you know that the answers are in this book."

He put his hands behind his back, as if to not tempt himself from trying to reach for it again, but studied it closely. "Where did you find this?"

"I found it in Coastra."

His head and eyes shot up to look at me as if he couldn't believe what he had just heard. "Coastra?"

"Yes. That place is very real."

"How did you manage to get there? No one understands how you escaped here, but to make it to Coastra and to make it back here in this little amount of time isn't possible."

"It's possible when a higher being is involved. Have you heard of the Sacred?" I asked, wondering how much they'd kept from teaching even their own kind.

"I've heard of him. A lunatic kind of man who believed he created the world and swore that fairies and telepaths existed." Something must have clicked in his head as he spoke because then his voice changed, and he seemed to catch on to what I was trying to get at. "The Sacred is real. Is that what you are telling me?"

A sad smile formed. "Yes, and those fairies and telepaths still exist, but he didn't create the world. Our Creator did. All of nature and all of us, as we are, were created by the highest and most divine being that will ever be."

"So where did this Creator come from? If everything is made from something, what made such a divine being?"

I felt taken aback a bit because the question was a very good one, and the harder questions like this hadn't been asked until now. "I don't believe anything does. I think that is what makes Him the Creator, because nothing exists unless He wills it. I believe there's a tiny piece of Him in everything He makes, as there is with us. Without our Creator, none of this would exist. It only exists because He does."

We sat for a moment, letting that thought fill the air. It seemed beyond bizarre and not the slightest bit possible when you think of Him as anything close to human. A divine being, on the other hand, with no trace of being in human form left endless options open that the impossible had always been possible through this divine source that was beyond our capabilities.

"The Sacred contained all of the powers, and the things he could do seemed impossible, yet he proved to do them, and he walked in a human form as we do. The Sacred came to prove that the idea of limits is limitless when you are connected to the highest being. He will do as He sees fit. He came as an example that no matter the power you possess, you are not above the Creator, and to trust the Creator more than yourself. He sees everything that we cannot."

A gust of wind came through the air, and Rohn looked at me, baffled. "How is it you know these things?"

I didn't say anything for a moment, then looked at him. "Take me to Venon. Stay to listen, and you'll understand."

He seemed hesitant at first, but he slightly nodded his head yes. As we walked, I followed behind him. He spoke one more time before entering. "You must know what he might do to you. Are you prepared?"

"No. Not one bit, but I never feel prepared for anything. I'm trying to learn how to trust the Creator's process."

No matter how many scenarios I played in my head, it never ended up being like I thought. It only added unnecessary stress. What used to help me survive no longer served me without damaging the good moments I did have, so I made a commitment to myself to focus on the now. I had to unlearn unhealthy coping skills in order to gain the skills that would let me live without a constant feeling that I was always going to suffer.

We got to the main entrance, and a couple of other guards stared me down with intense eyes. This would have intimidated me not long ago, but I stared ahead of me while I held my head up and kept my shoulders from tensing.

"I need to take her to the ruler," Rohn said in his strict voice.

"Who is she? She looks familiar." The one on the right spoke.

"You dingus, that's Ann. She ran off, colored her hair obviously, and, like an idiot, thought she could escape this time." The left guard spoke with arrogance that frustrated me.

"You have no idea where—"

The guard on the left stepped toward me and threw his hand in the air.

"Shut it, or I'll teach you a lesson! The ruler won't save you this time either. You have no idea what's to come, princess, but I know he's got—"

Suddenly, he stopped midsentence and held his chest. The guard on the right asked what was going on with him, and the guard on the left could barely get the words out. "I'm being drained." As he dropped to the ground, color began to leave his body.

I stepped toward him and got on his level so he could look at me. As he did, I nearly hissed in a voice I didn't recognize, "I have no idea how I'm doing this, but I do know how good it feels, and I don't want to stop. I see why drainers suck the life out of people."

Rohn then scooped me up and threw me over his shoulders. "I'll take her to the ruler to be dealt with accordingly."

He rushed through the doors and ran to the closest room that didn't have anyone in it. He nearly threw me onto a chair, but I didn't feel any sort of pain. All I could think about was finishing that guard off.

"Are you out of your mind?! Do you real—"

He stopped talking and stepped away from me. I looked at him and realized he looked petrified.

"What?" I asked. Concern started to fill me. The revengeful rage vanished, and I looked around. "What was that?"

"I've never seen you look like that. Did you get possessed by a demon?"

I looked at him, offended, but I realized he meant the question seriously. "No. Not that I'm aware of. Ever since that day that I drained you, I haven't been able to do it again. I haven't tried either. It scared me, to be honest, because of what I feel when I do it. I don't feel myself, but this is the way I'm created, so it doesn't make sense."

"How is it possible you can heal and drain?" Rohn asked with frustration in his tone, but I could feel worry start to take over his senses.

"That is what a pariah is. A mix between a drainer and a healer. The book explains it." What it doesn't explain is how to deal with the change. What if I lose myself worse than before and never find her again? What then?

Rohn didn't respond to my question. "He will not believe you, and most of them won't either, but I believe what my own eyes have seen. It will not do any good to tell them. Are you still sure about this?"

I thought for a second about turning around, but that feeling within to do what is right wouldn't let me live in peace. This wasn't about what I wanted or what was easier. It was hard no matter what I chose.

I am with you. Selah.

There it was. That voice.

"Yes," I responded to Rohn. I stood up and waited for him to take me.

He sighed big and then spoke. "I give it to you, kid. You are a lot tougher than most."

This wasn't about strength, I wanted to say, but anything else that needed to be said had to wait because this was going to be one of the toughest things I was going to have to do. I didn't know what to expect, but I knew something dreadful would happen.

We walked in silence until we reached the ballroom. He turned to me and whispered, "I'm sorry for treating you so poorly in the past. Whatever happens, know that I stand beside you."

"Thank you," I whispered back. I swallowed the lump that tried forming in my throat.

We walked up the stairs until we came to the floor that held the ballroom, which had the same setup every year. Chandeliers hung from the ceiling, and fine dining tables were set up, but most people stood with some alcoholic beverage in their hand. Everyone dressed their best, and here I was without any sort of bathing since I adventured off from the villagers. I wouldn't mention how worn out my clothes were.

It didn't take long for others to notice either. The looks I was getting were of disgust, as if I was a pest. I might as well be in their eyes. There were the few I never minded that told me they were worried for my safety. Safety wasn't what needed to be worried about, though; it was my sanity.

We approached Venon's chair, the one meant for the rulers. On the right side, the king of Egyptstra sat, and his daughter, the princess, sat—David and Rezna. She noticed me before Venon did, and the glare she gave me said she wanted to burn me alive. Venon and the king were talking away.

"Ruler," Rohn said after he cleared his throat. Venon's head turned, and so did the king's, as Rohn continued talking. "She came to me asking to see you. It turns out that I had been wrong about the girl I had seen. She is the same one who drained me."

His eyes never left me as he spoke to Rohn. "Her cousin, as you said, correct?"

"That is what she had told me, and because I knew she had healed, I didn't believe at that time that it could really be her."

Venon slowly looked me up and down. I felt tension begin to creep up, and I had to look away to contain my posture. "You can't tell me the hair color fooled you."

"No, ruler. I don't know how to explain it, but she drained me. She drained one of the other guards by the doors a moment ago."

People began to talk and then went silent as Venon stood up. He very slowly stepped toward me until inches away. My heart began to pound, and my mind started to shut down. I started to regret coming here.

"So you can drain now?" he asked me in a low voice.

"Yes," I barely whispered.

"And you still heal?" he asked in the same tone.

I barely shook my head. I know him well enough to know that he was going to find some way to belittle me in this and that he wasn't believing it, which meant Rohn would be in trouble and accused of lying for me.

"There's a book I need to read. To everyone," I managed to whisper.

He laughed and blurted out, "Did you hear that? She wants to read us a story!" Laughter from others echoed, and I felt my face burn up.

He walked back up to his chair and sat down. I looked at him, and that grin he had out of mean amusement lit his face. "It's good to know the reason why you left. I was beginning to think you really weren't coming back this time. Now we don't have time for a long story, but a short story I'd love to hear. Would you like a drink while you tell us this story? I know how it eases you."

That comment sparked anger in me. "Actually, I've been doing pretty well being sober. I've traveled to every part of the world except Egyptstra without a drop of it. I've even been to Coastra, which is where I found this book."

Gasps escaped mouths, and whispers were circling around after I mentioned Coastra. They began to quiet down as they noticed Venon's annoyed look on his face. His eyes didn't leave me, and Rezna kept looking between him and me with irritation, especially directed at me.

I disregarded her hatred for me a while ago when I realized jealousy didn't discriminate, no matter how much something wasn't your fault. I grabbed the book out of my satchel and didn't hesitate to read it.

CHAPTER 37

I looked up after I finished reading. I hadn't convinced all, but some of their faces said they felt something from what I read. I found it most surprising that Venon didn't seem to have anything to say, so I went ahead and continued talking.

"I know all of you are taught about the Sacred. The rich have the privilege of an education, but you're taught falsely about him. You're taught that he was this madman who made up a lot of things. Now you've been told the truth. You can deny it all you want, but I've seen enough to know how real this is. I can see it on some of your faces that you feel something. That is the Creator pulling at you, and He'll do that for as long as you live until you come into acceptance that He is real."

"I think you have had enough fun for one day." Venon's tone went sharp.

"This isn't fun for me. This isn't what I wanted to do. All I wanted was to be free, but I wouldn't have even been free if it weren't for the Creator. Did you not wonder how I escaped?" I could feel some part of me grow bolder instead of shutting down like I always had.

"Enlighten me." He took the last swig from his drink.

"After you went inside, a glow appeared to me." Gasps and murmurs filled the room.

The king stood up. He stared at me with some kind of expression I couldn't figure out how to describe, but he seemed to have felt something that made him curious enough to possibly believe that I was telling the truth.

"This is the golden light that transfers you to other places?" he asked in a tone that matched his facial expression.

"Yes. I've gone through a few of them. I walked through one to get to Coastra and another to be back here. I even went through one leaving the Garden of Leah to make it back to the villagers. That all happened in Coastra as well."

A younger lady with blond hair that had perfect curls, red lips, and the look of a princess that I used to read about in fairy-tale books and who had to have just turned sixteen bashfully stepped to the front as she spoke quietly to me. "What is Coastra like? I have been taught it is not real, but I have seen an original map that showed it exists. We are not allowed to question things like that, but I would love to hear from someone who has seen it."

Something about the innocence in her tone lightened my irritation a bit. "It's beautiful there. You live freely with others who are as kind as you."

I wish I could have mentioned the escapers, but I asked the Creator to send her one someway, somehow, sooner rather than later to come free her. She was the furthest from a drainer and completely a healer who had been born into one of the wealthier drainer families.

You might not be booted to the streets, but the treatment you go through is cruel and damaging to the soul. Not just from the family but from the whole community of entitled rich drainers. I want her saved before she loses hope that better is out there, before she lets the goodness in her die.

"That is enough." Venon's anger began to spill through his words as he talked. "You fill their heads with ridiculous ideas of a false figure and places that don't exist, and you begin to turn people against who is the real leader." He then looked around. "Who is it that can give you the things of this world? Do you not have enough? And by a show of hands, have any of you experienced this so-called Creator? Anyone else walked through a light?" He spoke with arrogance.

"They are only done for chosen people, and you aren't here just to have things. Every single one of you has a purpose to do good. Everyone is—"

Venon began to laugh. "And you truly believe you have done good in your life? What is it that you have done that is special? Besides write this book." A few laughed at that, Rezna laughing the loudest.

Seeing her look down at me gave me an idea. "Rezna, I'd like to ask you something."

She looked at me with furrowed brows and spoke with an attitude. "Okay?"

"If you could do anything, what would it be?" I asked.

She now seemed confused. "What do you mean?" She asked with less attitude.

"I mean, if you were given the choice to do what you truly found yourself drawn to and not what you're told to do, something you're naturally gifted at, what is it you would do?"

It was written all over her face that she didn't expect the question and she didn't know how to answer. I went ahead and continued talking.

"You've never been given the choice to figure it out." I looked away from her and scanned the room as I spoke. "Most of you aren't. You're made to feel from a young age that this is what you need to do, and if you don't, you'll be left alone. What do people do when they don't know how to be comfortable in their own company? They codepend on the ones closest to them. What is the point of any of this if you're going to be so miserable that you wait for death to come? Don't you want to live out a purpose? Don't you want to discover the truth of your existence?"

"I've had enough of this." Venon came up and snatched the book from my hand.

I went to grab it back, but Rohn stopped me, and his look pleaded for me to not do anything further. I stepped back, but my anxiety began to bounce around inside of me.

Venon opened the book and scanned it. "Ah! This is the part I wanted to get to. You pretty much made yourself overly special in comparison to everyone else, so everyone has a purpose, but not like yours. Why do I say that? Because what you wrote says here that you are the first Pariah. Wait a second, there is a male pariah involved too. I'm guessing you met someone and believe him to be this fantasy lover?"

"I appeared to him when I first went through the glow, and no, I don't believe this is some fantasy. Sacred wrote the book, and we have a Creator."

He mocked me as he said, "Yes, I know you say you did not write this, but what's the question you asked Rezna? Come now, what was it? The question about what would you do if you had a choice to do anything?"

He was trying to humiliate me by making me seem full of myself and that I was completely delusional. That I'd lost my mind.

"I would write," I responded, anyway.

Whispering came from the crowd. "And there you have it. As always, her head is in the clouds, daydreaming about nonsense. She cannot begin to accept what world she lives in." He shut the book with one hand and tossed it onto his chair.

He then slowly stepped to me and eerily spoke near my ear. "I will give you one more chance. Confess that this is foolish and that I am the rightful ruler, and I will let this all go." Then he got even closer to my ear and whispered so only I could hear. "As for tonight, you can make up for this chaos you caused."

Rage filled me with burning hatred, as did fear, remembering what Narcson mentioned about the binding marriage. All I could think about was hurting him in the worst possible way. Instead of acting on the thought, I clenched my hands into balls of fists and screamed loudly, "No!"

Before I could finish my scream, he shoved me so hard I went flying back, my back landing on the ground, and I slid a few inches. My back should be burning, but I felt nothing except the urge to destroy him. I stood up and began to walk toward him. I only got a few steps in before Rohn stepped in front of me. He didn't look at me, but I could see the plea on his face.

"You had the choice to be forgiven one last time. Now you will get exactly as you want. A pariah is an outcast after all. You can rot in Outcastril in a lone room for the rest of your life. Right where you belong." Venon snarled the last sentence.

I didn't understand why I couldn't drain him. My heart shattered all over again as the memories of all the other times he had embarrassed, belittled, and shamed me began to freeze me in despair. The suffering he caused all these years, all the ways he tortured my mind, began to overtake me. No matter how much I tried to fight back, I never won. I was always left defeated and exhausted to the point of wanting to die.

Something told me not to fight this, which made no sense because everything in me should fight. I shouldn't freely go to Outcastril, especially to a lone room, but anything would be better than staying a second longer around him, and who knows if another glow would appear. I had no idea what to expect at all or why I had to come here. Where was the Creator when I needed him the most?

"Go ahead and lock me up," I said cruelly, hoping he would feel the hate I felt toward him. "My body can rot there. You can keep me from the world, but you cannot destroy my soul."

I spoke through my teeth the rest of what was left to say as tears rolled out with an angry passion. "You will never have another chance to stomp all over my heart and make me believe I'm worthless. You will never have my love again, and I will never fall for your lies again. You think you've won, but there comes a day when everyone falls due to their evil ways. You will be the one to suffer the greatest, and when that day comes, no one will be there to save you."

I looked at Rohn and spoke. "Take me to Outcastril. I won't fight you."

Rohn turned to Venon. "Ruler, if you will it, I will see to it that she makes it there."

Venon stared for a moment and then spoke in an unusually calm voice. "See that she makes it, or your family will not see another day."

I had never seen Rohn show a hint of fear besides when I had drained him, but this was so much worse than that. His eyes showed something I had never seen before, and in that moment, he seemed as fragile as a small boy being abused, desperate for it to stop. No matter how tough a person is, they have at least one weakness that will bring them to their knees and cause them to do the very things they do not want to.

Rohn turned toward me and looked ahead. He grabbed my arm, and I grabbed his. He looked at me desperately.

"You do not have to force me. I will go," I said.

It took him a minute to let me go, but as soon as he did, I turned around and signaled to him to lead the way so I could follow him. We walked all the way down to the dungeon and through another door that led us to the outside that held carriages for other beings sent to Outcastril.

They had locks on the doors, and the only source of seeing the outside world was by a small barred window opening that was behind where the person sat to steer the horse.

He opened the door, and I stepped inside and sat down on the part they had you seated on. Before he finished closing the door, I stopped it with my hand and spoke.

"I could never risk your family's life for mine. Thank you for being the one to take me."

He looked at me with a mixture of sadness but gratitude. "I wish things could be different."

I looked forward and, instead of saying I do, too, I managed a slight smile and tried to sound convincing. "The impossible is possible when we have a Creator doing work we cannot see."

My brows furrowed together, and I looked at the floor, confused. Where did that come from? I hadn't even had the slightest bit of a thought like that just a second before I spoke it. I didn't even feel like myself when I said it. This felt like something greater that took over me, while I never actually felt out of control or out of place. This felt like nothing I had experienced before.

"I admire you, kid," he said in a low tone as he shut the door.

He got the horse, sat in his spot, and ushered the horse to begin moving. The doors, out of this metal cubicle, opened, and we began the journey to Outcastril.

CHAPTER 38

We stopped at the only buildings that went this way from the castle to Outcastril. The rest was a dry dirt road surrounded by the woods to and from the places, from what Rohn told me. There was more open field than he made it seem, especially by these buildings, at least from what I could tell.

It had become dark and a bit maddening to be stuck in such a confined place with nothing to look through except a small area that only revealed half of the sight due to Rohn's head being in the way. I supposed I should get used to being confined, since a lone room was probably a lot worse.

I couldn't tell where we parked, but we sat in front of some kind of metal building. Rohn got out of his seat. I got closer to see through the barred window and watched Rohn tie the horse to a pole. This place had a wooden porch. The door had a glass window that you couldn't see through. The design on it had the same symbol Gran's arms had, except hers was red.

The door to the carriage opened, and I whipped around to look at Rohn. "This is where I get branded, isn't it." I didn't mean to make it sound as a question but more of a statement.

He looked at me, shocked. "How do you know about that?"

I scooted out of the carriage, stretched my back and arms, and then responded, "I've been shown the symbol by an older lady who lives in Coastra. She escaped because a glow set her and others free."

"They killed the guard who said that happened. They didn't believe him when he brought it up and accused him of being one of the escapers."

I looked at him, and he stared at me with what seemed like regret.

"The truth will always come to light because the light is the truth." I spoke.

I looked away and around the town, if you can even call it that. Two other replica buildings, with the same design on the window, sat across on the opposite side of the road. The spacing of the buildings resembled a triangle. I also noticed on that side the designs were colored in blue, the other in red. The one I would be entering was black.

"Why are the designs different colors?" I asked.

"I'm commanded not to tell anyone, so keep this to yourself." I nodded my head in agreement to his comment. "Red is the symbolism for most people. They can be with the others, share rooms, and socialize. They can even share and trade with each other. Blue is for those who worked closely with either a king or the ruler himself but betrayed them in a way they saw fit to ban them. They are treated better and have nicer things regardless. If the guards allow them, which they do most of the time, they can even join them in the townhomes, which are much nicer than the rundown apartment buildings the reds stay in."

I expected him to continue, but he didn't say anything else. "And the black symbol? What's that mean exactly?"

He seemed hesitant to answer. "They are banished to a concrete cell that's partly underground. You can only step outside if you do the guards a favor, and even then, sometimes, they will get what they want and throw you back in there. It isn't common for them to put someone in a lone room."

I gulped. "Leave it to me to be so lucky."

"You'll be isolated with one meal a day and a cup of water if they decide to feed you. You'll wear the same clothes and will have to wash them when you shower. There's a bucket you'll go to the bathroom in that they will dump out whenever they feel like it. There's no sink. The bed is a cot with a very thin cover, usually a bed sheet that's been worn out. You will not be given anything else."

My heart sank, and numbness began to take over. He couldn't have me in the way he wanted, so he was determined I suffer in the worst possible way. He didn't kill me because he knew I'd rather be dead than suffer any longer. The worst part about this was, I wouldn't be able to write again, and I doubt I'd ever get a chance to sit in the sun again or walk surrounded by the woods.

I took off the satchel and threw it into the carriage. "Let's get this over with."

He walked me to the door and opened it. We stepped inside, and to my surprise, there was a bar with stools and all different kinds of alcohol. There were stairs that led to the upstairs, and on the opposite side of them, there was a chair with the back of it semipushed back and armrests on both sides.

"I'm assuming that's where the branding happens," I said, looking at the chair.

"Yes." He tried to come off monotone, but I could hear him dreading to do this.

Footsteps came from the stairs, and a man who looked about mid-thirties walked off the last few steps. From his shoulders to the top of his hands, he had the symbol repeatedly branded on him. He has a buzz-cut hair, bright blue eyes, and a widened jaw. He was built muscular with a slight tan to him and a facial cut kept nicely trimmed.

He smiled in an overly charming way. "It's not every day we get an attractive criminal. We never get anyone this attractive. I'm going to take a wild guess that you are the one who tried to get away." He spoke with a thicker accent I was not used to hearing.

"Cut it out, Xiaver. We're here for business," Rohn said sharply.

"Ah, come on now! Don't be such a stiff about this, my man!" he said in a playful tone.

His sort of arrogant attitude would usually irritate me, but at this point, I was seeing it as an opportunity to get what I wanted more than anything right now.

"It's okay, Rohn." He looked at me in a serious matter. "This is my last night of freedom. I'm not going to run off, so if he's down to drink, then so am I, especially something to numb me out before I'm branded."

I made myself smile at Xaiver and looked him up and down to make it seem like I was interested. The left side of his mouth lifted into a mischievous smirk, and one eyebrow popped up.

"Oh, I like her. Come on, Rohn, she said it. She isn't going anywhere she just wants one last night of good fun. No one's going to tell so you won't be in trouble. I won't be in trouble. She can't be in any more trouble. By morning, you both can leave, and we will act as if it was a traditional night of branding."

He moved his hands to point at himself and then at Rohn as he made a gesture while talking. As he spoke the last sentence, he threw his hands up while his elbows still bent so his hands never went over his head. After that, he held his hands behind his head while biting his bottom lip in anticipation for him to agree.

Rohn glared at him and then looked at me with the glare never leaving his face. "I will not risk my family for anyone. If you try to leave or do anything to get away, I will throw you in the carriage and travel the rest of the way tonight to make sure you get locked up."

I wanted to be angry at him for threatening me, but I understood where he came from. "I promise," I responded.

Subconsciously I lifted my pinky and remembered Sam. My heart dropped as I realized I'd never see him again. Instantly, the feeling of being a failure took over. He believed in me so much and look at where I ended up. Where I was going was much worse. He'd be disappointed once again by another adult and possibly lose hope forever. All because of me.

I crossed my arms together while my shoulders tensed and sped over to the bar. I hated warm alcohol, but I needed to numb myself before I decided to do something much worse to myself than drink.

"Hey there, bartender, you going to leave any for the rest of us?" Xaiver came behind the bar and grabbed a glass and poured himself a shot. "You know that cooler underneath the bar is filled with cold drinks. I can only fit so many because I have food in it, too, but you're welcome to drink whatever is in there."

I pulled back to look, and there was a long cooler with a glass door at my feet. "How does this keep it cold?"

He shrugged his shoulders and took another swig before answering. "Not sure. A while back, they delivered it to us and told us it would keep what we needed cold. They never mentioned how, and I didn't care enough to ask."

"I don't see how something like that is possible." I studied it, looking for some kind of hint on how it worked, but nothing stuck out.

The thought of fairies crossed my mind, and I had this horrible feeling some were being held captive. Who knew what they were being put through. Then this made me realize that in the book, which Venon now had, it mentioned further about fairies, which led me to wonder, would that make them search to find the rest in hiding?

Someone was bound to piece together that there was more, and knowing Venon and the others in power, they would stop at nothing until they discovered them and used them for their own advantage. They would use the fairy or fairies they had now to make them reveal where it was they hid. My heart dropped even further knowing I doomed them. They spent decades hiding, and I had ruined everything they had built.

"Let me know when you feel good enough. We still need to brand you." I looked at him and realized I had started spiraling in my thoughts, which slowed down getting drunk and kept me from numbing out.

"Listen, I don't want to, but if I don't, then I'm getting in big trouble, and no girl, no matter how hot she is, is worth me losing my position."

I wanted to roll my eyes, but something told me he ended up here because of a female and not in a good way. "Yeah, I got you. I'm getting there."

"You got to get out of your head if you want alcohol to do its job, so let us conversate. We'll stay away from the personal stuff. Here try this."

He handed me a drink he had mixed. In front of him, he had a couple of colored containers and a bottle of clear alcohol. I took a drink and realized it tasted smooth and delicious, so I chugged it down. He laughed.

"I used to bartend and learned a thing or two when it came to making something bad taste good." I watched him make this one this time.

I took another drink before talking. "I'll give you that. This is one of the best drinks I've ever had, and I've had a lot of drinks in my time."

As he made himself another drink, he spoke. "You don't seem old enough to have had that many drinks in your time. You are somewhere in your twenties, right?"

I giggled. I can feel the alcohol begin to take over. "I'm twenty-four, so I'm in the mids technically, but I started drinking at fourteen, and by fifteen, if I saw a chance to drink, I took it." I took the last swig out of the glass and followed with this next part. "I mean men love younger girls, and at that age, you think it's so cool, and if you're desperate for attention, you take it because why not?"

I threw my hands to the side with my elbows bent and then gestured for another drink. He glanced at me with a hint of concern but went ahead and made another drink.

There was a moment of silence sitting in the air, and then as he finished his drink, he set it down. "I'm thinking we can use some music. What do you say?"

I looked at him with excitement. "No freaking way. You actually have one?"

He grinned in his mischievous way, and I couldn't help but find him incredibly attractive at this moment.

"I will be right back," he said.

I watched him as he went upstairs, and before my mind could go where it wanted to, Rohn cleared his throat and then spoke. "You will regret doing it."

I took a drink and then asked, trying to play off that I didn't know what he meant, "Do what? I'm just trying to have a good time."

"It started that way, but if you keep going, it won't end that way."

I took the last gulp from my drink and began mixing the bottles together the way Xiaver did into the glass. "I tried making the right choices and look where it led me. I might as well do whatever at this point."

He didn't respond. Before I could say anything else, Xiaver came down the stairs carrying a record player with a couple of different covers that held disks. He sat it on the bar and laid the disks in front of me. He turned around, standing in front of me.

"Pick your choice. We will get the branding out of the way once it starts so we can go back to enjoying the rest of the night. Together." He then looked at my glass with amusement and then back at me. "You learn quick. I'm curious about how well you did."

"I guess I'll have to make you one so you can be the judge of that."

He stepped closer to me. "Or you could let me try yours."

His voice became smoother with every word he spoke. I handed him my glass and stepped around to look at the music choices. I had no clue what any of it played. There were no labels or anything written. Each had a different color of covering: one purple, one blue, and one yellow. I picked up the blue one. It reminded me of Mavryk and how he lit a similar dark-blue color. It resembled the book's color too. I turned around with it in my hands. Xiaver had finished the drink and stood even closer to me than before.

"Perfection," he said slowly and seductively. He then touched my hand and grabbed the disk, speaking low. "I believe you made that better than I had. If you do not mind making me one and you another, I'll put this in and get the difficult part over with."

I let go of the disk, stepping away from him, and grabbed the glasses. He began playing the music and walked over to set everything up for the branding. I went slower at making the drinks until Xiaver walked up to me, and then I finished them at a faster pace. I handed him his and held mine in my hand.

"I really do not want to do this to you. It's going to hurt badly."

I took a swig and spoke. "I'm used to pain."

He took a sip before we put our glasses down and walked over to the chair. He walked me through the process, trying to prepare me as he strapped me in to prevent cringing and messing up the symbol. Both arms were laid out, strapped as well. He put this clear coat of cream on both areas where the symbol would be placed and explained it would numb some of the pain.

"I'll have to let the mark sit for a second to cool down, then I will put more cream on it and wrap it up. Let me know when you are ready."

"I'm ready, as can be expected," I replied.

He put on his thick gloves and grabbed the iron bar. It had a handle, but from what he said, it still turned hot enough to burn without the gloves. I should've made myself look away, but I couldn't. He told me to take a deep breath in and then hold it until he pressed down, so I took a deep breath in. As he pressed down, my body went into shock, and a bloodcurdling scream left my mouth.

CHAPTER 39

I woke up the next day groggy, not remembering anything at first. I sat up and looked around. I was in a room, and across from me, Rohn sat in the bed. He didn't seem to have any emotion on his face. I went ahead and scooted my back to the wall, brought my knees close to my chin, and wrapped my arms around them.

"What's the last thing you remember?" Rohn asked.

I rubbed my neck, trying to recall last night. "I remember showing up and walking in. I don't recall much else." Blacking out most of the night wasn't uncommon, depending on how much I drank.

"Might be better that way. We need to rewrap your arms before leaving."

"My arms?" I looked down as I said it, and to my surprise, they were wrapped in bandages. "Oh." I touched them, and a sharp burning pain shot through my arm. I clenched my teeth, trying not to let out a yell.

"You'll be sore like that for a while," he said in response.

"What happened? Why—" Suddenly, the memory of being branded flashed, as did some of what happened before. "Did I do anything with Xiaver?"

Rohn seemed thrown off by the question. "No. Why do you question that?"

Relief came over me. "Good. Never let me drink again."

"You won't have that problem in Outcastril."

The memories of what happened with Venon came to mind and how I ended up here. Usually, feelings would follow, but the really nice thing about a night of overdrinking was the blocked-out emotions. The head pain sucked, but I'd rather deal with that right now than all of the emotions that came with everything that had recently happened.

I jumped in surprise as a knock at the door interrupted my thoughts, and Xiaver's head popped around the door. "I need to rewrap your arms whenever you are ready."

I saw no reason to stall anything, so I scooted to the edge of the bed and slowly stood up and then stretched and made some groaning noise to go with it.

Xiaver laughed. "I feel your pain," he said as he left the door open and went downstairs.

Rohn followed behind me. I cringed, looking at the chair. Xiaver stood over by the bar with the same cream he used last night and new wraps. I walked over and sat on a stool.

"How are you feeling today?" Xiaver asked.

"I'm all right. Hungover."

He snickered a bit. "I'm not surprised. You chugged down a couple of bottles' worth."

"How are you?" I asked.

"The same." He gently grabbed my arm and started unwrapping. "How much of last night do you remember?"

"I only remember up to the branding. After that, nothing."

"Want me to fill you in?" he asked.

"I only want to know if we did anything, and Rohn said we didn't. I don't see him lying or letting me leave his sight."

Xiaver rubbed the cream on the symbol as he spoke. "He is right. We didn't do anything," he said in a smug way.

I could tell something was on his mind to talk about. "What is it?" I asked. "What are you wanting to say?"

He finished wrapping my arm and moved onto the next one. "We had a conversation over many things that makes me think through a lot, but I am mostly envious of your lover."

"Wait, you mean Mavryk?" I asked, surprised.

"I've never been turned down before, and you are the first person since my ex that I had a connection with. He is a very lucky man to have you loyal to him. Many women in your situation would have caved in. Many women claim to love someone so much but turn around and cheat on them with a guy who only wanted a night of pleasure."

His comment made me realize this didn't have to do with me but whoever his ex was. "You must've really loved her."

I could hear the shame in his voice about what happened to him. "I tried to give her everything and be someone she wanted me to be. She ended up cheating and leaving me for him." Bitterness stilled the air as he said the last sentence.

"I hope you know that has nothing to do with your worth."

He finished wrapping my arm and then looked at me. "I swore off ever loving someone again, but if I ever get the chance to meet a woman like you, I will take the chance to risk another heartbreak."

I stood up and, as I did, I stretched out my arms to hug him. He looked me up and down, a bit surprised, and then hugged me back.

"Love is the one thing that keeps our hope alive for better days to come."

I pulled back and began to walk toward the door.

"How can you have any hope right now?" he said, stunned and confused.

I stopped. "I'm not sure I do." I slowly turned around to face him as I said the next part. "I don't have a clue what to expect except being locked up for the rest of my life, so hope isn't what I'm leaning on right now. I only know that there's a Creator who has a purpose for me that is doing something beyond my comprehension. I trust in the Creator, even if it looks like I shouldn't."

He looked blown away. He wanted to say so much but could only muster out one question. "How can you believe in something that allows so much chaos?"

I smiled at him with what I knew held sadness but truth. "I've seen enough proof to not doubt His existence anymore." Then I turned around and walked outside.

"I was hoping for the sun."

It was a cloudy day with drizzles of rain filling the air. I wanted to embrace the warmth one last time, but I knew better than to expect that.

Rohn opened the carriage door with no response. I stepped inside and sat on the seat. He locked the door, hopped onto his place of seating, and steered the horse to get on the road again that went toward Outcastril. I ended up falling asleep all the way there until we reached the destination.

I woke up to Rohn yelling to let the door down. I sat up, looking between the bars while closing one eye to see with more view, and saw the river that separated Scarland and Outcastril. From what I could see, Outcastril was wrapped around by a metal wall. It stood tall enough to be half the castle's height.

The door began to lower down and lapse on our side of the river and became a bridge. Rohn ushered the horse to move forward. As we got close to the entrance, I could see six grown men on each side, not letting go of the handle that connected to the wheels that controlled the chains that had control over the door. They didn't look up or around. They seemed beat down and exhausted.

We came to a stop as we entered Outcastril, and you could hear the men being yelled at to raise the bridge. A man in a type of uniform outfit I had never seen before came up, looked at me, and then looked at Rohn.

"What is the sentence?"

"Black," Rohn responded.

The man in the uniform seemed a bit thrown off but nodded his head once toward another set of guards who wore the same outfit. Rohn ushered the horse to walk behind the three of them. I wanted to see all the surroundings, but all I could see were brick buildings on both sides.

Doors stood a certain distance apart, while the windows seemed to line up with the doors, going upward. It was as if there were floors layered within. Some of the windows exposed faces peeking out to look at us.

After a while, we finally came up to a different setting. These must be the townhouses Rohn talked about earlier. They had spaces between each one with a decent bit of yard space. From a distance on my left side, I could see a few more rows; the right side had more backyard space before it met the wall.

Once we passed those, we came up to an area of dry dirt that matched the path we walked on. The only other thing I noticed was a long rectangular concrete building that stood a few feet tall. They had glass windows that matched the rectangular shape.

We came to a stop. Rohn turned and whispered to me, "We're here," and then hopped off the carriage. I sat back in the seat, and my heart began to beat harder. They unlocked the door and opened it.

"Time to get out," Rohn said.

I slowly stepped out. I went to turn around to grab my satchel, but a guard slammed it shut. "You have no right to bring anything with you except what you are wearing. Once you are in the lone room, you will change into what we give you."

On each side, a guard grabbed my arm. Both of them locked their hands firmly around my upper arm. I looked at Rohn. If you're not paying attention, you'd think he's just staring at the ground, but I saw the helplessness in his eyes. He never wanted to do any of this. It didn't start with me. He wasn't given a choice; he'd been forced into this, as had some of the others. These guards were much different about it, though. What I had suffered before wouldn't compare to what I would be suffering from here on out.

We began walking to the building as the guard ahead talked. "We will not tolerate anything you do. Expect the worst when you decide to pull something. There are no warnings, so I advise you to act right, or we will beat you senseless until you gain your senses. Am I clear?"

Anger began to rise in me. "No. Make it more clear for me."

Without a moment of hesitation, he swung the back of his hand and slapped me. I would have flown to my side and landed on the ground if the guards hadn't been holding me. I bit the inside of my lip and tasted blood. I spat out what I could and had to swallow the rest.

He glared at me and spoke in a sharp tone. "I will not put up with your crap like other men have. All a pretty face gets you here is a whole lot of attention you do not want, and I promise you, if you try anything else, by tonight you will be paid a visit by someone who will not show you any mercy. They will do as they please to you for as long as they want to. So I will ask this one more time. Do I make myself clear?"

I nodded my head yes.

"I can't hear a head rattling!" he shouted an inch from my face while some of his spit landed on my face.

I felt repulsed but flinched in fear as he yelled at me, and then I spoke in a shaky voice. "Yes, sir."

"I better not hear about anything else you pull," he said in a low tone but, nonetheless, just as threatening.

He whipped around, and I quickly wiped my face on my shoulder. As he walked forward, the others pulled me with them. I started to shut down, and my body began to feel heavy, but I used whatever energy I had left to walk. I did everything to numb out every thought to stop myself from crying. I couldn't imagine what they would do if they saw me break down.

In the middle of the building, two metal doors sat on the ground, each secured with a lock. The guard leading us unlocked them and opened the doors. A ladder led down into the darkness. Fear started to crawl all over me as I realized how dark it was.

One by one, we went in. Two guards before me, one after. I could barely see a step in front of me, but I supposed that didn't matter when I had two guards hauling me to my room. We made a turn to the right, and after a bit of walking, we came to a door. The doors were metal with a small slot that stood at a person's stomach area if they were about six feet tall. Above the door, the number 222 was carved.

As he was unlocking it, he spoke. "You are allowed an hour of outside time a day. It's a new rule they gave to prisoners in the lone rooms, but what you pulled earlier takes three of those days away. Behave, and maybe by the fourth day, someone will come and let you out."

He opened the door and stepped out of the way. The guards holding me stepped forward and threw me in. I made a painful grunting noise as my body hit the concrete floor. They all laughed mockingly. I pulled myself up to sit, even though the pressure from that made a tear escape from the pain that shot to my brandings.

"Someone will be back with a change of clothes," the guard said before shutting the door harshly.

I sat there staring for a minute and then looked around. Rohn described a lone room pretty well, but he left out that they gave a roll of toilet paper to wipe with. I realized a little bit of light source peeked in, so I looked up. Against the wall, opposite the door, there was a window. They were the ones I had seen earlier from outside.

I stood up and walked toward the cot. I grabbed the worn-out, thin sheet that they called a blanket and wrapped myself in it. I sat back against the wall. Before I could begin to fully shut down, I heard the slot open and watched a hand put a set of clothes on the little shelf underneath the slot.

I got up and walked over. I realized Rohn had given them to me. "You will need to place the clothes you undress from on the shelf."

I didn't say anything, not knowing if anyone else was on the other side. I grabbed the clothes and realized something sat in the middle of the pants and the shirt—my satchel. I took the blanket off me and wrapped my satchel in it and then placed it on the cot. I quickly took my necklace off and put it in my satchel. Then I changed my clothes and placed the ones I had changed out of onto the shelf. I wanted to say something to show my gratitude, but I knew saying anything would expose him.

Rohn grabbed the clothes as he looked through the slot. I cupped my hands together and mouthed the words "thank you." I could barely contain the tears. He slightly nodded his head once, as his eyes said he wished he could do more. He stood straight up and shut the slot.

I heard him confirm to a guard that I had changed out of everything. After a bit, silence filled the air, and I let my guard down a bit from keeping my emotions contained. I went to sit back on my cot and unraveled my satchel from the blanket. I looked inside of it, and everything was there. I even noticed a small container of cream that I hadn't had before, along with a few bandages. It looked the same as the stuff Xiaver used.

I stood up and rewrapped myself in the blanket. With nothing else to do but drive myself mad with thoughts, I decided to open my notebook and write. I wouldn't be able to write forever, but I could until there was not a bit of space left. I opened to the last place I had left off and realized someone else had written in it.

> Do not get caught with any of this. Keep it under your cot, against the wall, right in the middle. They won't check unless they see a hint of it. Do not give off any hints that it is there. Say as little as possible. Xiaver wanted me to make sure you had cream and a couple of wraps. He is very fond of you and wishes he could do more. He told me to add that. I wish to do the same.

> Best regards,
> Rohn

The tears I had held in broke out in the ugliest way. I wanted to feel grateful. I knew I should be, but everything in me felt hopeless. This added guilt and shame to the mix. All the negative emotions that someone could feel right now flooded me to the deepest part of my core and left me feeling far worse than broken or even shattered.

I felt worse than that helpless little girl again, trapped in a home filled with one yelling in resentment and another crying out in desperation. Now it was only me who sat here, only my thoughts and emotions suffocating me into wishing I had never existed.

CHAPTER 40

I'd made a tally mark for every day I'd sat here; today made day 40. As far as writing anything else was concerned, I'd been at a loss for words. My mind had completely numbed out. I'd been here before, where I was blocked out of writing anything because of my mind numbing out, but this felt worse knowing that I had had all this time and not one word had been written while my thoughts clashed and collided with each other. This did give me an idea of what I should write.

> *I don't know what to think because I know I followed what the Creator wanted. I know He led me where I had to go, but why am I here? What am I waiting for? I feel lost, but I'm trying to keep hold of my faith and trust that this can't be the end of it all. I only believe that because of the familiar feeling of knowing. I've seen enough proof to know that it's not been wrong.*
>
> *The other part of me never fails to say that I should give up, let myself starve, that there is nothing left for me to do. As despaired as I feel, I know I cannot give into these terrorizing thoughts. It seems unfair that I must sit here and wait on some kind of miracle to happen, but that is the importance of knowing what spiritual warfare consists of. Nothing is ever fair when it comes to bringing justice back from so much injustice.*
>
> *The feeling of what feels excruciating but knowing that it is still right, and I need to wait, makes my emotions more irritable to fight through. Hardly*

tolerable in a lot of ways. As much as I want to give up, I know I cannot without altering the process of what the Creator started. He will finish one way or another, but who am I to become a failure when I have already been shown mercy for the things I have failed? I must walk in my purpose so further delay does not take place.

I can no longer stay chained to what I have known to do in the past. As difficult as it is to trust with what I am not yet familiar with, I know that things are happening and that they will work out the way He needs them to. I must hang on and know that whatever happens and has happened is a part of His plan. I will not victimize myself any longer into believing that I am made to suffer forever.

After all, this life is temporary, as is any pain we feel. It is what we do and how we do it that will show our love for the most divine being. How can you bother to say you're willing to believe in their existence but do not prove in action that you trust in the one we've been created by?

That says nothing more than I want to manipulate others into thinking I believe but do not actually believe. Worse of all, you want to try to manipulate the one who cannot be manipulated. You only doom yourself, and it is what makes you the ultimate fool.

Still, as hard as I try to keep my mindset on what is the truth, my mind is set out to destroy any hope left in me. I see no possible way of being free, and I do believe I'm not deserving of it. As much as I want to keep positive in a realistic manner, my brain screams at me that I am a failure, and I am now going to suffer worse than I ever have before.

My pencil broke. I guess it at least let me finish my sentence. I had a bad habit of pressing down harder than I should, which left this bubble on my thumb that the other one didn't have. More people seemed to notice you being a left-handed person as you write than that small detail that gives it away. Such is life.

I stared down at what I wrote and decided this would be the last thing I wrote. I was not sure of the purpose it served except for myself, so what was the point? There was none. It was as meaningless as I was. I didn't even deserve to have any final thoughts. I deserved the spot I was in. I deserved to suffer greater than I was. Maybe that's why I was still here. I deserved more suffering before I rest in peace. If peace even awaits me, who knows what death leads to?

I wished my mind didn't jump to think like this so effortlessly. I rested against the wall and stared in front of me. Sparkles began to form. At first, I thought that this might have been the light shining through brighter from the window somehow, but the sparkles kept growing into a circle. I guess I had gone delusional and was that desperate for an escape. The sparkles turned into a glow, but I could not see through to the other side.

It sat in the golden color that it was and moved in the wave motion that it did. How cruel could your mind be to play such tricks on you that it dangled a false escape in front of you? Suddenly, a hand reached through on the other side, and before I knew it, a man crawled through. He stood tall, looking around, and then turned toward me.

"Ann!" Mavryk shouted.

I never saw him smile so big and look so relieved. He nearly jolted toward me as he grabbed me and squeezed me to his chest. Then he began kissing my forehead and all over my face. His touch felt so warm and comforting, but I knew this couldn't be real. Had he ever been real, or did my loneliness and pathetic needy nature get to me so badly that I had imagined him to begin with?

He pulled back to look at me with his hands holding my face. He kissed me a few more times before speaking. "Ann, you can't imagine how sorry I am. I should have never left the fairies, I should have waited there. I'm such an idiot! I should have—Ann?" He held my face up even more, being gentle as always, with worry in his voice. "Ann? Love, it's me. It's Mavryk. Can you hear me?"

He stared at me, but I couldn't make myself look him in the eyes or the face at all. I decided to finally respond. "You're not real. I know once I look at you, you'll disappear." Then again, just responding could very easily make this all go away.

"Ann. Look at me. Please," he said it so kindly and sweetly that tears began to form in my eyes. "I'm truly here. A glow appeared to me and led me to you. Do you remember how it led you to me first? You saved me that day, and now I'm coming to save you. I'm not sure how yet, but I'm going to get you out." He sounded sincerely determined to do so.

I didn't want to, knowing that would be the way he disappeared, but it was not like I deserved comfort. Not even a delusional one. I had never deserved to be loved at all, especially in the beautiful way that he had loved me. I blinked, and the tears fell from my face, and more formed. Still, I didn't want him to go. It'd be wholesome to have this fictional piece of bliss stay until my last breath.

After a few times of blinking tears, I numbed myself out enough to make the tears calm down—at least enough for them to not blur my vision. I slowly moved my eyes to his face. I marveled at all the gorgeous details that made him so remarkable to look at. Every bit of him I had fallen so deeply in love with. I could never love another in this way. Who knew loving someone like this existed?

When I finally looked into his eyes, they brought me back to the first moment we came across each other. This is what made me realize how real it all was and how real he was. He was truly here right now, in this moment. I grabbed his face and pulled him in to kiss with more passion than I had ever done before.

I had no idea how this was possible, but I felt as if I was being brought back to life and brought back into reality. My head had gotten so trapped inside the darkest parts of myself that I became my worst enemy. Not only was I giving up, but I was self-sabotaging in the most destructive way. I was trying to destroy my own heart and kill off my spirit for good.

I never left you. Selah. I have been here waiting for you to let me in again.

I pulled away from Mavryk quickly and threw my hands in the air, clenching my fists. My mouth dropped open, and for the first time in a while, a small smile escaped. My eyes watered so much that I didn't have to blink for tears to fall out.

Mavryk looked surprised but slightly smiled too. "What?! What is it?!"

"I heard His voice again." I then grabbed his arms and rubbed them up and down with my hands. "And you're here."

I used both hands to place them on his neck, with the fingertips going up his jaw and having to split my fingers so they could rest around his earlobe. "You're really here." My voice broke a bit as I spoke the last words.

His eyes began to water. He took my hands and wrapped them around him as he pulled me in to rest against his body. One of his hands held the back of my head while the other wrapped around my back and pressed in, squeezing me enough to feel safe but not too tight that I couldn't breathe properly.

I had no real clue what it was I was feeling, but the intensity of the emotions I felt pushed out a cry that I could not release until now. A cry of disbelief that this was real. A cry of something beyond gratitude. A cry that it was not over when I was completely convinced that it was, even though the Creator tried reassuring me otherwise. A cry because I missed Mavryk so much that it hurt deeply. A cry because I had thought the Creator had left me alone when it was I who shut Him out. I cried because I was losing all hope and willing to let myself die, and a miracle happened.

After I finally calmed down and settled into the moment, Mavryk reached into his side pocket that went between his hips and knees. As I pulled back to see what it was, he pulled out what looked like a book wrapped in cloth. He held it out to me.

"This belongs to you," he said.

I took it from him and noticed it to be the same size and weight as the book I last had. I looked at him in disbelief, wondering how this could be possible. I looked back down at the book and removed the cloth. There it was—the Book of Sacred.

I opened it, and every word was untouched, with nothing else added. I held it to my chest and thanked the Creator. I thought I had cried myself tearless but found a few more releasing. Mavryk gently wiped them away. I looked up at him and thanked the Creator for him too.

"How did you get this?" I asked.

"A younger girl named Charlotte, whom Venon was messing around with, managed to sneak off with it. She ran off once she had it in her possession and stumbled upon Naomi, who was traveling to the castle to get to you. She told Naomi what happened to you, and then that's when Naomi searched for me. She flew to Sasha's and Steven's place, hoping Sasha could help her find me, but I had already been there."

"Who is Charlotte? How does she know me?" I asked.

"From what Naomi said, Charlotte didn't know where she was going, but she knew she needed to go this way because of a voice that spoke to her. She said you read the book. She was in the ballroom while it happened."

"Did she say what she looked like?" I couldn't place who it was at first, then it dawned on me. It was the girl who asked about Coastra and reminded me of a princess. "She's a healer. We need to help her make it to Coastra."

"You know who it is?" he asked.

"I believe so, and if I'm right, they won't forgive her for this. They'll send her here." The thought pained me, knowing such a sweet person would suffer something like this.

"When we get a chance, we will help her, but for right now, we need to worry about getting us out of here. We can't help anyone without helping ourselves."

As helpless as that made me feel, he had a valid point. I had done enough being swallowed up by what I didn't get the chance to do. I could only do what I was able to at this moment. I shook my head in agreement.

"What do you suppose we do?" I asked him.

He looked around and then at me. "There are only two ways out of here, and neither of us can break through that window. How often do guards come in here?"

"Not often. The last time I saw anyone was a week and a half ago to let me shower. They come once a day to put food and water through the little opening and usually don't say anything. I'm surprised you can tolerate my smell, come to think about it. I probably reek right now."

"Your natural odor comforts me no matter how long you go without washing." He put his hand around my neck, kissed my forehead, and then placed his forehead on mine. "I love you and everything that involves you. You could never disgust me. What I'm disgusted by is the treatment you've had. They will pay for this, especially Venon."

His name rang with bitterness in the air, and the rage I had deep inside started to come to the surface. I pulled back and spoke with malice in my tone. "He will be tortured by my hands and plead to die. I will make him suffer for as many years as I can keep him alive. That is when he will finally understand and realize that he should have never done the things he did."

Mavryk pulled back, and I looked at him. He seemed concerned. "This isn't like you."

I felt confused and spoke with irritation. "After everything he has done to me, I am expected to still show him mercy?"

"No. That's not what I mean. I've just never heard you talk like that." His concern turned into worry.

I couldn't say why this bothered me even more, but I knew I began to feel that hateful feeling bubble to the core of me. "You have no real idea what I have been through. I—"

Before I could say anything more, I started to hear talking, voices, but I couldn't say from where. Suddenly, within a moment, a glow formed and grew twice the size I had ever seen. Mavryk and I stood up. On the other side was an empty room with sunlight shining through the window.

"Do you see it?" he asked.

"Yes," I whispered with disbelief in my voice.

Mavryk grabbed my hand. As he rubbed it, I looked at him. He had already been staring at me. Our eyes met, and my emotions came back to a calm reality. No matter what happens, love is the answer. Nothing else truly matters.

ABOUT THE AUTHOR

In simple terms, she is nothing more than a soul who had big dreams of becoming something others believed would be impossible.

Printed in the USA
CPSIA information can be obtained
at www.ICGtesting.com
LVHW091124021124
795328LV00001B/154